Finding Gene Kelly

A NOVEL

By Torie Jean

Creative

Sunset and Camden Creative

FINDING GENE KELLY

TORIE JEAN

www.toriejean.com

Cover Design: Torie Jean

Editing: Writers Untapped

For information on subsidiary rights, please contact the author at www.toriejean.com

Print Editions ISBN: 9780578380766

To the two Endo Warriors who changed my life:
Jo and Zoe
& Everyone else living with this disease.
You are loved.
You are worthy of your daydreams.
And you deserve to find your Gene Kelly, whatever that looks like to you.

And to my husband, procurer of heating pads, bringer of tea, and flare caretaker extraordinaire, I'm thankful every second of every day for you.
Thank you for always believing in me even when I don't.
I love you to the moon and back.

"With delicious chemistry, effortless humor, and visceral honesty about navigating life with a chronic illness, *Finding Gene Kelly* is the most heartfelt and addicting romance of the year. I felt every crackling moment between courageous Evie and charming Liam, even (okay, especially) as they resisted the inevitable: love conquers all."

   -Allison Ashley, author of *Would You Rather*

Author's Note and Content/Trigger Warnings:

Hi, there! Just a quick note to say—hey, thank you so much for picking up my book! That was so very kind of you.

But before you start reading, there are a few things in this book that might be too heavy or triggering for some, and if that's you, it's really okay if you use this book as a paperweight or a doorstop or put it on a shelf with its other friends and open it when you're good and ready—or never at all. Be kind to yourself first and foremost! Please and thank you.

And just an extra special note to those of you with endometriosis: Sometimes writing this book was like entering the third dimension of hell, especially when my endo was poking my side and Evie's simultaneously, and there was just too much endometriosis in my life. Please, please, please, be gentle. It's okay if you can't handle a book with endometriosis right now. Using books to escape is one of my favorite coping mechanisms. I'll understand, promise!

While this list may not cover every aspect of this book that could be heavy or triggering for some, here are some topics of note:

- Mentions of depression and anxiety

- A toxic mother/daughter dynamic

- Multiple instances of on-page vomiting (Sorry, Evie!)

- A concussion

- Mourning a loved one who passed many years ago

- Discussions of infertility

- Multiple pregnancy announcements

- Conversations about survivor guilt and how people with endometriosis were treated in the past

- And, of course, our beautiful soul sucker: endometriosis, chronic pain (and pain management with narcotics), and other daily aspects of living with the disease

Content Warnings: This book has many instances of adult language and an open-door intimate scene. With that said, the open-door scene is authentic to the endometriosis experience, so it may be more frustrating than relieving—if you're looking for good steam, I'd recommend finding another book. Intimacy with endo can get, *erm,* complicated.

Final note: The chronic illness rep in this book is . . . well . . . chronic. It will affect plot points, and it will be present in major scenes. Use that knowledge to proceed accordingly to your personal tastes.

1

La Vie en Donut

WHAT I WOULDN'T GIVE for a bite of that man's hulking French stick right now.

The decadent aroma of butter, salt, yeast, water, and flour—mixed, kneaded, and baked to perfection—wafts through the bleary Métro car shimmying along the Paris underground.

Stomach rumbling, I pin my stare on the elongated Adonis in the hands of the blond man standing in front of me. Saint Honoré, that'd pair nicely with the can of "depression cheese" I'm clutching.

He rips off another hunk, his head bopping along to whatever tune is blaring through his headphones.

Maybe I could snatch and run at the next stop.

No. No. Running wouldn't work.

Too gruesome.

A woman in a blue pleather seat nearby peeks up from her FNAC bargain bin buy of *L'étrange histoire de Benjamin Button* and narrows her gaze on the baguette, undoubtedly plagued with the same indecent thoughts.

She's most likely a new import from the US judging by her walking shoes and the nervous energy flicking through her left foot. A stereotypical lost soul studying abroad at the Sorbonne, but her heart belongs to a former generation of Americans in Paris: the wide-eyed individuals who were enamored with the simplicity, grace, and decadence of Parisian culture.

The City of Lights is more than Pinterest-perfect vibes to her; there's a replenishing energy to it that builds up and nourishes souls—*a moveable feast*. She'll disembark at Saint-Michel Notre-Dame, even though the photo opportunities in front of Our Lady are minimal. Maybe recite a line or two from Victor Hugo's *Notre-Dame de Paris* before losing any chill she has in front of the green and yellow facade of Shakespeare and Company, a famous bookstore sitting across the slow waters of the Seine from Notre Dame, as I once did.

She's one of three Americans in this car if my keen powers of observation are correct. Well, four, if you count me.

"I'm skipping my language class. I'm close to fluent anyway, and it's boring," one of the other Americans clad in a red beret declares, Face-Timing in the corner of the cabin. Her seemingly unfounded confidence garners a few snorts. She has all the makings of a quintessential Cyclops, and they're not exactly known for their linguistic capabilities.

A Cyclops experiences Paris behind their phone's camera lens, preferring to focus on the sepia-toned vibes of the place above all else and remains ignorant of the rich culture and history breathing out of every inch of this city. They use one eye for a quick snapshot rather than gathering through all the senses to create a masterpiece.

"I'm headed over to the Chomps Eelisses," Red Beret says, running her ivory fingers through the ends of her rich chocolate brown hair falling in loose waves under her atrocity of a chapeau. How is she even getting reception down here?

I've tried to load something, *anything*, for the last ten minutes to keep my brain from spiraling into terrible person mode and judging and nicknaming everyone. But it's too late now.

Keeping my features neutral while my ears bleed is a feat. Still, I manage, tightening my grip on the aluminum can of cheese and re-centering myself, finding solace in the fact that Red Beret should have changed lines two stops ago if her intended destination really is the Champs-Élysées.

"I saw this super cute café on Harmony in Paris's Instagram," she continues, butchering Harmony's handle with her American accent.

Harmony, the passive-aggressive queen, wouldn't stand for that massacre.

"*It's Pair—ee.*" She'd glower in her patented glimmering tone. "*If you say it right, it rhymes, silly.*"

"She was drinking water from a wine glass with a leafy salad that totally popped against the background. The aesthetic was everything."

Huh. I must have missed that.

I try my luck at the Instagram app, and to my genuine surprise, it actually loads. Like always, Harmony's picture sits on top of my timeline. *Daily reminder—you gotta nourish to flourish* captions a highly filtered photo of a salad with an ever-present, Roman-inspired limestone arch looming triumphantly against a blue sky.

Typical Harmony line.

"Saint-Michel Notre-Dame. Saint-Michel Notre-Dame," crackles over the speaker. The car jostles to a halt, and a man with Bunyanesque proportions and prominent sea legs wobbles precariously close to me at the sudden deceleration. The third and final American is an Aptly Named Tourist or ANT—a seeker of the Tour d'Eiffel (I'm certain that's the word's actual etymology). Off-balance, he stumbles into me, and I barrel toward an elderly gentleman in a scally cap. I bump into his back, and cigarettes, Roquefort cheese, and a hint of citrus overwhelm my nostrils.

"Pardon." I muffle a cough, righting my stance. My hand fumbles, and my traitorous thumb double taps the photo. The little heart underneath turns red.

Oh, son of a biscuit.

This slip of the thumb will cost me, both physically and mentally. In thirty minutes or less, Harmony will be sliding into my DMs asking for a lunch date, guaranteed. Which as a recovering people-pleaser, I will agree to, attend, and then smash my head into the hard surface of the table while she attempts to cure my chronic illness through the power of suggestion.

"Have you tried yoga?"

"If you cut out gluten and dairy, you could cure it naturally."

"Your state of mind is so powerful. It's how you choose to approach it. Think positive, and you'll feel positive."

Maybe if I preemptively hit my head, I could avoid the entire situation. Far less of a headache for me in the long run.

Sliding my phone back into my purse, I claim the Lost Soul's vacated seat while a sharp spasm grips my lower left abdominal. The crowd's thinned significantly, courtesy of Our Lady of Paris.

Unfortunately, my bread also departed.

Seeking an alternative distraction, my eyes fall on a guy reading a small, leather-bound book across the way. He's handsome, right on the edge of thirty, well-dressed, with a light brown complexion, sharp cheekbones, and a short haircut.

A nervous energy gently hums through me. My body doesn't bother with the internal fireworks anymore; it's far too much of a production for something that will never pan out. But men who read are a particular weakness of mine.

"Definitely going to grab some super cheap wine," Red Beret muses to her friend, "and pre-game at my apartment if you want to come over.

I'm thinking we go out at like ten or eleven and then stay out until the Métro opens again."

My chronic fatigue is tired for her.

M. Biblio-Hunk rolls his eyes behind his literary shield. I snort at his mutual annoyance, and this catches his attention as he picks his gaze up from his page to meet mine.

My mind pilots through my mother's guide for catching a man's eye. I've never successfully employed her lessons in my life, but there's a first time for everything, I suppose.

Use whatever you can to draw his attention to your lips.

A faint smile tugs the corners of his mouth as his eyes drop to the depression cheese resting in my right hand.

Ah. Perfect. I raise the nozzle for a hit and attempt to charm him with my feminine wiles.

This is how you flirt, right?

It's been so long since I've tried—maybe this is a bad idea. Maybe I should slowly dust the cobwebs off first.

But he's reading Proust.

What the heck. Shoot your shot. A semi-solid canary yellow cheese spirals out of the can with added pressure. Cobwebs be damned, I've got this.

Until I don't, and my finger—in an extreme act of desperation—presses down too firmly on the nozzle. My can of joy and wonder betrays me, and cheese suddenly explodes beyond the limits of my mouth.

With what little dignity I have left, I choke down a swallow—a particularly wasted skill of mine—and wipe, tucking an errant tendril of my strawberry-blonde hair behind my ear and feigning like some part was intended.

Apparently you can't shake the cobwebs off a flirting game that never existed.

"Oh my god," Red Beret shrieks across the cab.

"Luxembourg. Luxembourg."

Snapping his book closed, M. Biblio-Hunk clears his throat and stands. His eyes avoid my general area as the car slows to a halt.

I'm free Monday through Wednesday. Or you can catch me at The Quays on the weekend where I'm a pretty mediocre bartender.

Red Beret side-eyes me, lining up behind Monsieur Didn't-Take-the-Cheese. "Brittany, you'll never guess what just happened. Paris is so weird."

The doors slide open, and they both exit.

A soft, "No, she definitely wasn't flourishing," wafts its way back into the car, along with the pungent stench of urine.

Right. Well, to be fair, I judged her too.

Sighing, I bring the nozzle back to my mouth, drowning out the stifled screams vying for attention in my chaotic well of a mind and ignoring the apparent stares my can-do spirit attracted. Red Beret was right, among her ocean of so much wrong. I'm not flourishing.

And I'm probably weird.

I doubt Harmony envisioned me inhaling copious amounts of artificial cheese on public transportation when she wrote that stupid caption. But hey, for some people self-care means twisting yourself into a pretzel and planting an organic garden that you mainly subsist on, on your balcony, which is actually weird. And for others, it's traveling halfway across the city for processed cheese. Less weird.

Both are equally valid.

Except yoga is stupid. And dirt is messy. And processed cheese is neither.

A sudden halt on the track jolts my body forward. The lights flicker, and a collective groan undulates its way over the cabin. A good minute from our next stop, any type of stalling bodes poorly for us.

In a jumbled static, the conductor announces there's an issue on the track ahead, and it'll be ten to fifteen minutes before we travel forward.

Darn. I pull out my phone to text my friend Eli. I'm meeting him and my roommate, Maria, at American Press, a café with donuts on the edge of the Latin Quarter, a charming part of the city filled with medieval churches and narrow alleyways. Already cutting it close, I'll be a good twenty minutes late now.

ME: Train stalled. Get to you when I can.

ELI: K. We're almost there. I think.

ME: Who's we?

The dots dance and disappear before another message populates.

ELI: Just my coworker.

ELI: OMG. Why is a dude pissing in a red box on the street?

ME: It's a urinal. You'll get used to it.

Dots dance for far too long. Oh, hell.

ME: DO NOT ASK ME HOW TO USE THEM.

ELI: But I've been holding one since our meeting.

ME: I love you. But hard NOPE.

With an internal groan, I stretch my legs out in front of me, careful not to crunch too much in the seat. I should be excited that my best friend from high school is working here for the next month. And I am.

Mostly.

But I'm already barely functioning from exhaustion, and Eli will unintentionally create a lot of work for me.

He's your typical Tom Brady is god, fridge deep with Sam Adams, flannels for days, Boston bro who is highly uncomfortable with the unfamiliar. Not the recommended disposition for living abroad. Hopefully his coworker will adjust and help him out.

The train finally jerks forward again, and I send a quick, **be there soon**, tucking my phone away and standing for my stop.

"Port-Royal. Port-Royal." Metal on metal screech. The car slows to a halt, and the doors slide open. I rush out with the rest of the hoard, fighting against the incoming passengers, too impatient to wait for us to unload before boarding.

Social etiquette exists for a reason, people! I huff, climbing the concrete stairs and blinking in the fraction of light on the street. Today is still grey, much like my present mood.

Marshal Michel Nay's statue, sword drawn ready for battle, greets me crossing Avenue de l'Observatoire. An entry I penned dedicated to his story drove an uptick of traffic to my recipes and travel Blog—*L'Evie en Rosé*. People love those who fearlessly stare death square in the face. And damn did Marshal Nay slay that, refusing his blindfold during execution and giving the firing squad the freakin' command, ordering the soldiers to aim straight at his heart.

Turning up the street, my phone vibrates in a hey-you're-getting-a-call rhythm. **Incoming: Caleb Buttface O'Shea** flashes on the screen. I could mature and change my brother's entry, but little sister habits die hard.

"Hey, buttface, what's up?" I answer, scurrying past an old red brick building out of place among the Lutetian limestone. A long-leashed golden retriever I dub Midas cuts in front of me, and I halt and pivot, narrowly avoiding a cluster of café chairs scattered ahead.

The dance of the Parisian sidewalk.

"Hey. How you feeling, kiddo?"

A comical squish beneath my heel elicits a groan.

"Everything hurts, but I'm fine." I drag my foot, letting it scrape along the cement. Thanks for nothing, Midas.

"Oh. That's . . . good? I guess," Caleb says, wavering. I can almost hear him swallowing his kneejerk "Hope you feel better soon" response. He's a former fixer, but he's finally accepted that my chronic illness is, well . . . chronic.

Which is more than I can say about most people I interact with.

Cementing a fair amount of my organs and ligaments together, endometriosis has negatively impacted enormous swaths of my life. Incurable, treatments and management plans range from miserable to soul-crushing, and true relief is hard to come by.

Most of the time, people are too uncomfortable with negativity and pain for honest answers. Wanting to fix it, fix *me*, they offer positivity and solutions, which become toxic in their frequency. I'm an optimistic person in my own way, but there's a danger in forceful optimism and not recognizing reality.

I exist in a state of perpetual pain, and I've had to accept that to survive—it'd be nice if others acknowledged and were okay with it. Otherwise, the guilt and anxiety of being "a downer" are put on me too.

"It is what it is," I say, passing the intricate iron fences lining the Luxembourg Gardens. Tree branches dressed in a fresh spring coat of leaves drape over the golden spires, a promise of renewal after a long barren winter.

"Huh, yeah—hold on, I gotta turn on the blender." The muffled whir of blades crushing ice blares through my phone's speaker. Pulling the phone off my ear, I pause in front of a vacant storefront and allow myself a moment to imagine what never will be.

A gilded pâtisserie sign sits above sage green awnings with Evelina, Paris printed in gold across them.

Decadent gâteaux, macarons, and meringues fill the single window, drawing the attention of hungry eyes while a bell perched above the front door rings as customers come and go.

Inside, tall display cases burst with freshly baked treats ranging from traditional croissants and pain au chocolats to my creations: cupcake donuts and mini peach pie tartlets.

Rushing to greet an incoming customer, covered in flour, I freeze, catching sight of the one. Chris Evans (obviously), on break while shooting a remake of An American in Paris, sleeves rolled to his elbows, revealing toned forearms rivaling Gene Kelly's.

Tongue-tied, he fails to utter a single syllable as my large blue eyes hold him arrested. My mother always complained they were two sizes too big. "Try to be more demure, darling. You always look surprised." But he finds them just right.

Sugar and melted butter swirl around us in the pastry shop, and in a drunk-on love haze, he finally tells me he'd like to taste my buns. I blush. He groans and then points to a case of cinnamon rolls in the display case, thoroughly seduced by my soft and gooey buns, tarts, and biscuits.

Sighing, I snap back to the present. It's foolish to give in to hope, but from time to time, my former daydream believer escapes the cage my endometriosis-filled reality built, and I have the audacity to suppose a greater existence still awaits me. Chris Evans aside, at this point, it would benefit my sanity greatly if my past self accepted the truth.

This is most likely it.

On the precipice of twenty-seven.

Chronically ill.

A struggling blogger and part-time bartender, currently inhaling copious amounts of artificial dairy on a side street in Paris while devoting most of my mental energy to ignoring the barbed wire torturing my insides.

"Kiddo? Kiddo?" Caleb's voice vibrates through the speaker in my hand. Right. The conversation I'm having with a human.

"Is there a reason you're calling this early?" I shake myself out of my depressive spiral with a hit of cheese.

"Oh, yeah. I wanted to talk to you about the wedding."

Oh, dammit, of course he does.

Fat raindrops splash on my forehead, falling from the gray clouds looming above. No way I move past this block dry.

Plop. Another drop falls.

Plop. Plop. Come on with the rain.

Face tilted upward, I smile through the downpour, just like my dear Gene Kelly taught me to do.

It's becoming progressively harder to keep singing through the rain, and the sun has been noticeably absent from my heart for some time, but just like Gene pushed his way through his most iconic dance routine with a 103 fever and a smile plastered on his face, I keep pushing through too.

No one needs to know I'm sick of the rain.

"Holly still wants you to be a bridesmaid, but we haven't heard anything from you. You got your bridesmaid box, right?"

Yes, and I am suffering the consequences of it every day, dear brother. How could I forget the pink and gold box that came in the mail a month ago, filled with bridal puns and entirely too much confetti, the silent but deadly fart of the crafting and gift-wrapping world.

After the box came the Save the Date, a cute picture of Caleb and Holly standing backs to the camera wearing matching jerseys. Holly's said, "Save" with the number five, and Caleb's "the Date" with the number twenty.

I received them all, ignored responding, and placed them in my room to taunt me until a decision was made, because I suck, and I'm both a masochist and the ultimate procrastinator in any uncomfortable situation. Of course I want to go to my brother's wedding, and I wouldn't mind being a bridesmaid, either. Holly Bell is fantastic. The problem is more with where Caleb's wedding is.

Tallow, Massachusetts—*home*.

A place where my overbearing, high-society Southern belle of a mother, Caroline, reminds me what a constant disappointment I am for, well, everything.

Since any boundary I establish with Caroline crumbles faster than a day-old donut under the pressure of her patented guilt trip, we need the robust and unchanging confines of the Atlantic Ocean between us to survive.

I doubt I'd make it past baggage claim before she greeted me with a critical scan, her mouth twisted into her perpetual my-daughter-is-a-disappointment frown, and I apologized for my general existence.

"Oh, Evelina," she'd say with a sigh, *"what a shame that with your little situation (my endometriosis) you've wasted so much time on trivial things (pursuing my lifelong dream of becoming a pastry chef). I've always wanted what's best for you, sweetheart (marriage and children)—even if it'll take a miracle, bless your heart (I'm hopeless)."*

But dealing with my mother from hell-planet Georgia aside, Caleb should understand being in the same wedding party with the lifelong infliction that is Liam Kelly isn't the charming situation other women might think it would be.

After fifteen years of second-place finishes and unending torture at Liam's hands, my first trip home in six years to small-town purgatory as a shell of my former self might be one blow too far.

I'm barely surviving. I don't need to add smug men who pull childish pranks and use their dimples to their advantage into the equation.

"Yeah, I have everything. Sorry, I'm swamped with work. I want to come, obviously, and I'm super happy for you both. But a transatlantic plane ticket isn't cheap, and then there's the bridesmaid dress . . . and . . . three months was rather soon for me to scrounge that all up. Seriously, isn't this whole wedding happening fast?"

"I don't think so?" Caleb laughs. My stomach twists into a knot. That's his signature he's-omitting-part-of-the-truth laugh. "But don't worry about the money, we can purchase your plane ticket, and Mom wanted to buy your bridesmaid dress anyway."

"Of course she does, and it'll be two sizes too small, so I have to lose weight too." With the rain slowing to a trickle, I round the corner, nearing American Press.

An exasperated breath from my gentle giant of a brother echoes through the phone. "I'll talk to her, Evie. Just please come. I need you there."

"I'll need to get a few things in order before I buy tickets, but I'll let you know soon, okay? I love you, and I'm trying." A familiar streak of platinum blonde hair dances through the crowded sidewalk ahead—my roommate Maria. She catches sight of me and halts, huddled in an over-sized turquoise scarf and her favorite blush trench coat, providing me with the out I need here. "Maria's waiting for me, though; I have to go."

"Sounds good." He sighs. "You'll have to tell me how today goes too. Say hi to Eli for me."

"Wait, how do you—" Caleb hangs up before I can ask how he knew who I was headed to meet. Considering he gave up wishing me a "Happy Birthday" because "dates are hard," this sudden awareness of my social calendar is peculiar. But I shake it off, approaching the Swedish love of my life. She quirks an eyebrow, gaze narrowed at the can hanging by my side.

"Did you really have to go to the American goods store, dear?" She laughs. "You know there's perfectly good cheese in Paris. Cheaper too."

Yes. Yes, I did. My soul identifies with this cheese on a deeper level than any soft, pressed, or blue-veined cheese ever could. We have the same origins, body composition, and general lackluster appeal. This synthetic cheese and I are one.

"But if I didn't go there, how would I have gotten you this?" I tease, reaching into my pocket to grab the well-adored peanut butter cup nestled there. A box of Reese's and a waffle iron brought us together in a dorm room six years ago, and we've been in a platonic state of love ever since.

Clutching the chocolate to her chest, she squeals, "You're too good to me."

"Queens deserve to be spoiled," I say, leaning in for a bise.

Our cheeks press together, and an unsatiated rumble only donuts can satisfy growls in my stomach. Luckily, we're close. I just need to travel a few meters around this last corner, and then bam, Eli.

And a buttload of donuts.

Which I will promptly shove in my face.

Our steps slow, and we pass the corner flower market Maria frequents in her capacity as the best wedding planner in Paris. Colorful blooms bunch together in galvanized tins and wooden baskets, scattered at various heights. Fragrant hints of lavender and rose swirl around us, offering a brief respite from the city's less pleasant aromas.

Linking arms with me, Maria huddles into my soggy self. "Do you see him?" she asks. Her light blue eyes sparkle, roaming the rain-coated cobblestone, glistening in the emerging sun. They've never met in person, but Maria and Eli became fast friends over my regular FaceTimes with him.

Whenever we talk, he's quick to say "hi" to her, listening to Maria vent about working with the destination wedding brides who demand the *Devil Wears Prada* experience. Whatever that is.

I'm not as attentive. Conversations centered around marriage usually end in a bad case of mental hives for me, much to my mother's chagrin. How anyone is well-adjusted enough to shoulder someone else's life and burdens, or vice versa, is beyond me.

"Oh, there he is." Maria points ahead.

Scanning the area for Eli, I mindlessly sidestep tourists, pedestrians, and puddles. "I don't—*oof*, pardon." My shoulder digs into the side of a tall-statured businessman talking on his phone, and I stumble, detaching myself from Maria.

A strong hand grips my shoulder, righting my stance before I topple to the ground.

"Easy there, Peaches," a rough baritone voice says behind me.

A nostalgic shiver terrorizes my spine. Only one person calls me Peaches.

The person who beheaded my American Girl doll.

Cut my hair.

Spread rumors that left me dateless for dances.

Convinced our entire high school to call me "Toots" after an unfortunate period-induced bout of gas plagued me in AP chemistry. Even though *he* still referred to me by his own personal pet name.

Used the charm that oozed out of his every pore to his advantage and my constant detriment.

And took advantage of my traitorous body's attraction to him to break my heart on multiple occasions.

The bane of my existence.

Salt in the wound.

Liam Kelly.

"What—" I stammer, pivoting to face the lifelong building brick under my very bare feet. The gold flecks in Liam's eyes sparkle like they have a thousand times meeting mine, and any sense of coherent thought is arrested under his bewitching stare. Once out of self-preservation, I'd built up an immunity to it, but after years in its absence, I fear that judging by my increasing heart rate and tightened airways, I'm severely out of antibodies.

"Hey, there," he says cheerily, like we're long-lost pals and not bitter enemies. Although, it *would* be easier to overcome past transgressions as the instigator and not the injured party. A soft smile spreads across his face and dimples his cheeks, hidden under a neat layer of scruff shadowing his high cheekbones.

"Uhm. Hi." I blink. This isn't real. He's not in Paris. He's on the other side of the Atlantic Ocean where he belongs. I try to say more, but the rush of emotions spiraling inside has rendered my verbal capacities useless, so my mouth waffles between various intervals of open instead.

He raises one of his brows in a slow arch. "You okay?"

Old decrepit butterflies—who never minded their own freaking business—shake dust off their wings, waking from their six-year hibernation, and flutter around at a dizzying, alarming speed. There's a strong chance I could be wrecked by Liam if I stay any longer, willingly joining some odd cult where I bow to his every whim and listen to his demands to give up bread or something.

Can't risk that.

"Nope!" I declare emphatically, deciding this isn't a reality I want to acknowledge.

"Nope?" His smile falters. "You're not okay?"

"No. I'm fine, but this—" I shake a trembling finger at him. "Nope. Nu-uh. No way. This isn't happening. Whatever sneak attack you have planned, I'm not dealing with it. Not today, Satan. Not. To. Day." Words lodged in my throat minutes ago fall out of me at an embarrassing speed.

"I don't—" Liam's eyes narrow in confusion, pinning me in my spot. My pulse quickens under the heightened attention. But then he lifts his gaze over my shoulder. A dark cloud shrouds his features in a thunderous cover. "What the hell, Blythe? You said she wanted to see me, but you didn't tell her, did you?"

My head snaps around to catch the culprit. A guilty Eli Blythe waits next to Maria, mouthing sorry.

Coworker. My. Ass.

"Look, Evie, this isn't what it looks like." Liam reaches for me, his fingers brushing against my arm, jolts shooting up from the contact.

"Nope. I can't—" I toss my hands up in surrender. "I'll—I'll deal with you later. Excuse me."

I march toward Eli, but the pull to glance one last time at his betrayal is too great.

Liam's stare collides with mine. He rakes an agitated hand through his neatly coifed hair, and a spark flickers, reigniting embers long since smoldered in the far corners of my soul.

I can't believe Eli would do this to me. Seriously! A little warning would have been nice!

Day-old makeup adorns my face. My hair's disheveled, and there's no way this shift dress is hiding the Violet Beauregard level of bloat happening today.

A rush of adrenaline spirals through me. My pulse races as a cold, massive panic falls from the pit of my stomach, moving down toward the muscles in my legs, which wobble before stiffening into heavy, useless appendages. What the actual fuck?

Whatever you do, Evie, keep walking. Hide the panic. And Stop. Staring.

But I can't pull my focus off Liam. There are no other people, no other sounds.

"Evie. *Evie!* Pole."

And apparently no sense of spatial awareness.

Maria's warning registers too late, and my face and the hard metal lamppost meet with such a force it knocks me onto my behind, my body and my head hitting the sidewalk and an expansive puddle.

The pride-shattering clang of aluminum clattering to the cobblestones follows.

Crap. My cheese.

"Shit, O'Shea." Liam's dark figure looms over me. My vision blurs. Pain surges through my head.

2

Glazed and Confused

THE SIDEWALK'S COLD REACH works its tendrils under my coat and wraps around my spine. Goosebumps rise on my skin as a wild, sporadic, no-sense-of-coherency rhythm beats forcefully against my chest.

Am I dying? Is this Hell?

Blinking away the watery film hazing my vision, Wonder Boy's impressive scowl is brought into focus, the grim expression at odds with the Cheshire grin seared into my memory. He scratches at his stubble, arguing with Eli a few paces away.

Bile pools in my throat. I've stared at Liam for longer than medically advisable, but I can't pull my focus off him.

He's here, the boy I married at age five in the wedding of the century and divorced at age seven when he had the audacity to throw a football at me while I was reading *Eloise in Paris* on the porch. He muddied the whole damn book. Our relationship never recovered.

Hades masquerading as Hercules, and only I could see it.

That was part of the game—rile me up and then act the part of the angel when I bit back so, even victorious, I lost.

Here's looking at you, debutante ball.

A stone sinks into the pit of my stomach. Haunting memories I spent years burying with pastries and a healthy dosing of ganache threaten to claw their way to the surface with his sudden presence in my life.

Think of something—anything, really—except that cursed ball.

"Why don't you give in and admit I've won, Peaches? Aren't you tired of the chase?" Liam's voice teases in my brain. Oh dammit. Well, at least it's something else.

The night before I left for Paris, Liam's forearm rested above my head in the corner of our college bar, a triumphant smirk plastered on his face as if he knew how badly I wanted him. Against my better judgment, my chin tilted up, lips parted, heartbeat and breath turned heavy and erratic. My body forever betrayed the history I knew well.

I wanted Liam Kelly leaning in for a different reason, something fierce. I wanted there to be more behind his teasing. After years of battling the boy next door, someone who made my blood boil and my head ache, my traitorous body's decision our junior year of high school to suddenly all-but-swoon in his presence wasn't appreciated, nor was his growing new torture tactic, replacing his annoying-but-harmless pranks with something far more devastating.

I wasn't "tired of the chase." I'd burned the fuck out, always finishing second with my family's affection, brother's attention, academics, and other school accolades. My chronic illness automatically placed me a good five steps behind him, navigating life through the heavy filter of endometriosis-induced chronic fatigue and missing a week of classes monthly on account of my period. I pushed myself until I collapsed from exhaustion, only to lose to a boy who approached everything with a lazy smile and a charming cheek dimple.

And yet, as burned out as I felt, the fire still flickered. However dangerous it was. Like nothing could ever smother the intense reaction he elicited whenever he was around.

He fanned the flame too far at the bar, leaning in and taunting me, and the naive, annoyingly optimistic twenty-year-old version of myself snapped, declaring loudly in his smug-ass face how I was leaving for France to become someone, and he'd stay the conceited, irritating, selfish ass he always was.

He pulled away and feigned being wounded, but he'd burned me enough to know better than to trust whatever appearance he flashed to the world.

"We'll see, Peaches," was all he said with a jaded expression before stomping away.

The old story should have ended there.

This ambush is an entirely unnecessary epilogue written by Eli Blythe and probably Caleb, considering our weird phone call.

"Hey, dear. Are you okay?" Maria brushes a piece of hair out of my face.

The curls atop Eli's head bounce with the sudden jerk of his chin in my direction. He quits arguing with Liam and marches toward me. I offer a faint smile. Suddenly, everything good and cheesy in my stomach violently churns. *Shit*. I press my scraped hands into the wet cobblestones, ignoring the stinging pain, and urgently stand. Emptying the contents of my stomach into a nearby trashcan, I startle an unfortunate passerby.

"Désolée," I murmur. My insides twist again. Fingers trail the back of my neck, gathering my hair as my muscles clench and release a second time. This doesn't ease the sharp sting of betrayal, but Eli's never been the hair-holding kind of friend, so I appreciate this sudden shift of consideration.

"Good?" My heart stutters as the rough sandpaper voice, *decidedly not Eli's,* slides against my ear.

My spine stiffens. "Yup," I squeak, cursing the gods of chaos for never looking favorably on me. Of course our first interaction in six years is unfolding disastrously for me.

Readying to meet his smug-ass gloating face, I take one last collecting breath and turn around for Judgement Day.

A hint of mischief flickers across Liam's features, but otherwise, they remain soft and apologetic. Huh. That's new. "I didn't know," he whispers.

"I believe you." The words fall out of me, ignoring the cornerstone tenet of our interactions. *Never trust a word that leaves that man's mouth.*

I must have whacked my noggin harder than I thought.

Liam cocks his head to the side. A crooked grin rakes across his face, and he offers up the can of cheese. "Oh, and you dropped this."

My stomach churns again, and I shake my head. There's another one in my purse for later, anyway. "I'm—I'm good."

The quirk of his lips falters, and he reaches around me and tosses the can in the trash. His chest bumps into mine, and I hit the edge of the waste bin. My arms flail in a way I thought only happened in cartoons as the massive gravitational pull of my ass threatens to bring me down again. Liam's sturdy hand falls to my back and stabilizes me, saving me from becoming one with the trash I really am.

"Steady there," he says, fingers splayed, burning away the chill of the sidewalk. Soft crinkles edge the corners of his eyes as he peers down at me. "You took quite the hit."

That probably explains why my insides are humming at a frequency I haven't felt in years.

"I—uhm. I need to—there's a certain—" I sigh, frustrated my tongue has picked this exact moment to take a vacation (hopefully it decided to go someplace nice like...Nice...). "I'm going to go yell at Ignatius," I say, stepping around him and peeking back bashfully. "Thanks for—you know." I gesture at the trashcan.

He dips his head, sliding his hands into his pockets. "Yeah. Of course."

The defeated manner of his tone pricks my chest, and I toss another glance his way before marching over to Eli. His gaze cuts to mine, and his lips part as if to say more. My heartbeat falters, and I pull my attention away, directing it at the guilty party who has gone unpunished for far too long.

"Remind me to never listen to your brother again." Eli groans, scrubbing his hands over his face.

"I shouldn't have to remind you at all," I grumble, pouncing back on my heels as my path of destruction is suddenly interrupted by one of the greatest dangers to pedestrians in Paris—a tourist on wheels, phone out, navigating their way over to the Iron Lady. Go home, the bitter, angry old man part of me jaws.

"For the record, your brother's very persuasive." Eli nervously laughs. The general merriment held in his emerald eyes diminishes, and he glances down at my hand balled to a fist at my side. "So if you feel stabby, take it out on him, please."

Freakin' Caleb. Of course my brother tried to pull this off. Liam's more like a sibling to him than I am, really. The two were inseparable growing up next door, playing football in our backyard, video games in our basement, or spending hours in Caleb's bedroom, music blaring and eating all the damn food in the house.

At the same time, I was relegated to the porch because, according to sweet Caroline, ladies don't play football, video games, or eat. It was never apparent to me what ladies did exactly, besides bitterly observing two boys enjoying life and getting stood up by them at debutante balls. But whatever it was, it rendered me nothing more than a pretty little thing Caleb needed to protect. And somebody Liam constantly bothered, tossing me into the backyard pool fully clothed, covering me with brownie batter, and still hanging out at our house when Caleb, two years older than us, scurried off to college.

Phone calls with my brother typically end with him pleading for me to talk to Liam because "He's perfect for you, kiddo. Come on."

But Caleb always missed a vital piece of the puzzle. As unappealing as a relationship with the god of the Underworld sounded, there was zero chance the Wonder Boy of Tallow, Massachusetts, Mr. Prom King himself would have been interested in the nothing-burger that was and honestly still is, me. Not with the list of inadequacies my mother would be all-too-happy to point out.

"His matchmaking ass is going to pay for this."

Maria clears her throat. She's typically Team Be-the-Bigger-Person, and I love her, but boo. "I'm going to meander inside and find something to clean your hands up with," she announces, heading for the door of American Press.

"Donuts," I holler at her, remembering my raison d'être. "The happy kind."

Pink with sprinkles, my favorite.

Maria assesses me one last time, lips quirked to the side. "This isn't the right time for donuts, dear."

Lies. Any time is the right time for donuts.

"I'll save it for later."

"I'll go in and help," Eli offers, leaving me alone to stand smashed up face-to-gorgeous face with Liam.

What? No. Pleasedon'tleavemealonewithhimyoubothsuck.

Liam watches with the same helpless expression. His shoulders collapse as the Duplicitous Duo disappears inside. "Shit, Evie." He grabs the crook of my elbow and guides me over to a red woven café chair. "I swear, the guys didn't tell me anything. They just said you wanted to see me."

I snort, but my nose took a beating in the face-meet-pole incident, too, so the attempted scoff vaguely resembles the startled hiss of a cat instead.

"Yeah, I don't know why that wasn't immediately a red flag for me either."

Falling into the chair, my eyes narrow at his broad shoulders, tight waist, and tall frame. Damn you, reality. I can't ignore it. The man's a freakin' Dorito.

I hoped he'd have lost this particular charm. Maybe a tooth knocked loose from a high tackle during his college football career. Crooked nose. Dorian Gray's black magic finally caught up to him. Something.

But nope, he's standing in front of me, like a Wall Street head of business, annoyingly attractive adult.

My heart constricts. I'm accustomed to an alternate presence as far as Liam is concerned, one full of backward baseball caps, crewneck sweatshirts, and a devilish set to his mouth. But here, now? Liam looks far less like the lazy god of debauchery and far more like the god of sun and light I mocked him for pretending to be.

And it's . . .

Unsettling.

He carefully tugs on my hand, tsking at the wreckage. Worry lines edge the grim set of his mouth, and he takes a handkerchief out of his pocket and tenderly wipes my palm.

And so is whatever it is he's doing.

He kneels, dipping his knee into a puddle, and I wince. While my knowledge of men's fashion is limited, his suit *looks* expensive, and he's ruining it.

"Did that hurt?" He pauses, and a gentle crease forms between his brows.

"You're ruining your pants," I stammer. Our gazes collide, and I am thoroughly sucker punched. Flecks of gold rim his pupils, glittering in the warm sun now breaking through the low-hanging clouds.

"Oh." He peeks down at his wet knee. "So I am." He shrugs, bringing his attention back to me. "How's your head? Does it feel like you have any open wounds?"

Just the one that opened a wormhole to an alternate reality where you're a concerned gentleman.

"Oh, I'm fine." His iris contains actual splotches of sunshine.

His hand lands on the back of my head, pulling me closer to him.

Sandalwood curls around me, enveloping me in a weird sense of familiar terror, and I call to it like a bug long since destined for the zapper.

My eyes tighten closed.

"I think you're—*shit*." He taps my cheek. "Hey, O'Shea, come on, stay with me."

A wave of dizziness takes hold of me as a clusterfuck of questions spirals inside. Why does he sound so anxious? I lean forward. My head meets his chest, and I melt into his frame. Stiffening on contact, two firm hands grip my shoulders and set me right.

"I'm sure you want to cuddle me, Peaches, but I'm going to need you to stay upright and keep your eyes open, okay?"

"Okay, sunshine, I'll try," I say sleepily, leaning back into his warm orbit.

"Oh, this is bad." A deep mirthless chuckle shakes his chest, vibrating against my own. "Seriously. Keep them open for me."

Nodding, I pry my heavy lids open.

"Thank you." He exhales and raises his pointer finger to my face. "I need you to follow this, okay?"

"What are you checking for?" I ask, attempting to follow the track of his finger.

"At this point, it's more a confirmation than anything. You're obviously concussed."

I scoff at the complete self-possession in his voice—like nails on a chalkboard after all these years. "Glad you haven't lost that unfounded confidence of yours."

"You just retched into a trashcan."

"That happens with great frequency, actually. I'm going to need more proof for a substantiated claim."

"Well, I didn't want to use this against you so soon, but you *did* just call me sunshine." The ghost of a smile tugs on the worried lines of his mouth, pulling away.

Did I say that out loud? "Oh. Yup. Knocked senselessly, I agree."

"Glad we're on the same page for once." His grin spreads wider across his face, and the dimples of doom blackhole their way onto his cheeks.

"Hi." I blink.

"Hey, Peaches."

"You're in Paris."

"I am." He breathes out.

"And you work with Eli?"

"I do." He stands and wipes his hands on his pants.

"For . . .?"

Liam threads his hand through his dark golden-brown hair, rendering his neat coif completely undone. "Right, so he really hasn't told you anything?"

I shake my head. No, but I understand why.

"The creamery, actually. Dad bought a French cheese company to enter the international market, and Eli and I are handling the merger."

Kelly's Creamery—the family business, the job that kept his mom and dad working late and left Liam over at our house for family dinners.

"But you loathed that place entirely."

"It grew on me." He shrugs. His stare sits on me for a half second longer than is necessary, and I shift in my seat under the intensity of it all. "So where's the nearest hospital?" He pulls his focus away and scans the area, bouncing on his toes. "Or do we take you somewhere else? Do they have urgent cares?"

Is he kidding me? I'm fine. I'm not wasting one of my decent days at the hospital. "Yeah, I'm not going to the hospital."

"Evie—"

The loud blare of a disgruntled driver's horn interrupts us. Liam jumps. I don't budge. Car horns are white noise for me—another soothing sound of the city to add to the ambient music soundtrack.

"It's not up for discussion."

"You're right. It's not. You're going to the hospital."

"I don't get why you think this is your call."

"Because you're concussed. Your judgment is impaired, and your brother would hate me if I let you go home like this."

"He wouldn't care," I mumble. "Don't worry. You've done worse, and you were still everybody's Wonder Boy."

A muscle flicks in Liam's jaw.

"What?" I huff.

"You never let anything go, do you?"

In general, sure. I let things go.

But the aftermath of that damn ball complicated my entire life and destroyed my relationship with my mother. Pair that with my increasing headache, pressure on my temple, and barbed-wire abdomen—like seriously, allowances should be made to grump here.

"I'll let it go when the ripple effects of your prank stop impacting my life."

He stuffs his hands in his pockets with an agitated head shake. "I should have stayed at the apartment. This was a mistake."

"And miss the spectacular production I put on for you? Come on, you can't say you didn't enjoy that just a little."

Liam's gaze cuts to mine. "Believe it or not, I don't derive pleasure from you getting hurt."

My insides squirm as a furious blaze in his stare pins me to my seat. "Well, that'd be new," I mutter.

"No, actually, Peaches, it wouldn't be," he says with a sigh.

I rub my temple with my forefinger as a motorbike careens by on the cobblestoned street. A tense silence settles in its wake around us.

"I'm sorry." I relent. "Ignore me. I'm probably just grumpy because I was promised donuts and got a head wound instead."

He snorts. "Fair. I guess I'd be grumpy too."

My fingers twitch through another beat of awkward silence until a low, rueful chuckle suddenly shakes Liam's frame. And then stops. And then starts again.

"What?" I half laugh.

"Nothing. It's just—" He drags his knuckles over his scruff, focused on the ground. "What did you think would happen when you tried to nope the situation?"

"I panicked!"

"You were horrified."

He doesn't pick his eyes up to meet mine, and my gaze slides down his slumped shoulders and drawn-in figure, like he's disappointed that was my reaction to seeing him. But what else did he expect after everything?

I blink. I'm reading too much into this for someone with impaired cognition.

"Ah, see? We left you two alone, and you're both alive and unharmed. That's a good sign." Eli joins us with a proud smile, hands full of napkins, sans donut. I direct a scowl in his direction while Liam simultaneously gestures to my head. Eli's smile falters. "Okay. Fair. How are you feeling?"

Maria also lacks the desired confection, exiting American Press with water bottles in her hands instead of happiness and sprinkles.

"Oh, fine. A little rest at home should do the trick." I avoid Liam's stare, standing and stretching.

"After she gets checked out at the hospital," Wonder Boy adds.

"Still going to pass, thanks, though." I face him.

He steps forward. A tug I haven't felt in ages in my gut pulls taut, and I fight the instinct to close the little distance between us. "I'm not above hoisting you over my shoulder if I have to."

I swallow. My palms turn sweaty, and I wipe them on my dress, wincing through the scrapes dragging along the fabric. "I'm too wet." My tongue fumbles in my throat while my brain screams *elaborate*! "To go to the hospital—because it rained. On me." I glance around at all my dry friends. "And apparently nobody else."

He frowns, the harsh lines ill-suiting him, but concedes with a nod and a sigh.

My heart glitches at his weary surrender. Liam . . . has never admitted defeat . . . ever . . .

Mercifully, Maria grabs my shoulders and shifts me away before I can overanalyze whatever that was. "We really should bring you to a hospital, dear," she says, pouring water on a napkin and wiping my cheek. "But let's get you home and change into some dry clothes first, and then I'll bring you." She considers me with all the maternal concern her mama bear soul can never overcome, no matter how much grief I give her.

Eli oscillates between Liam and me with a hasty, pleading smile. "Deal?"

"Deal," I mutter.

"That's fair," Liam adds softly.

"Good." Eli strides over to a trashcan to throw out the napkins and grimaces at its contents—apologies to whoever empties that poor bin later. "You'll need to change anyway," he says to Liam.

Liam nods, pulling at the cuff of his white shirt, splattered with blood from my scraped palms. "Yeah, probably not a great first impression, huh?"

"Certainly could help set the mood if you're going for the ruthless cheese empire-building vibe," I awkwardly joke.

An upward curve lifts the corners of Liam's lips as he shakes his head. "We'll try again some other time?" Eli flashes his puppy-dog eyes, dissipating any feelings of rage I want to direct his way.

I sigh. "Yeah, another time."

"Great." He steps forward for a hug—a chokehold, really, his signature squeeze. "I'm sorry I'm an ass who listened to your brother."

"You are, and you owe me, but I missed you and your powerful hugs."

"I missed you too." He rocks me back and forth as his arms tighten around me and near chest-bursting territory. "Text me when you get out."

"Deal."

Looming next to us, Liam stands with his hands stuffed in his pockets.

"Well . . . bye," I say, twiddling my fingers. Should I hug him? I super hugged Eli, so it'd be rude not to, right? I step forward.

"It was nice to see you, Evie." He comes in hot, hand out for a handshake, but I go all in on the hug and my quick-decision motor skills misfire. Oh, why the hell did I go all in on the hug? Seriously? Of course we were on handshake terms.

"Oh—" His eyes widen, and he clears his throat.

I drop my arms, going in for the handshake as he opens his arms for the embrace. Enter the dance of the handshake-hug. Which is totally fine and not awkward at all. I relent, arms wide, and let him lean in for the hug. Maria giggles. Eli smirks. My cheeks burn, and I'm a train wreck. He holds me tight. Firm. Warm. He's everything—late nights chasing fireflies, picking lilacs in blossom, boombox blaring, singing and dancing in the rain, and utter defeat and humiliation. He, frankly, is home. And I'm suddenly sick.

We release each other, and I tuck my hair behind my ear. A peal of nervous laughter vaguely resembling the barking of a seal escapes me. Love that look for me.

"Home then hospital, right?" He peers down at me, arms crossed.

"Yes, Mr. Kelly."

He bristles under the appellation but doesn't say anything else, pivoting on his heel and walking in the opposite direction with Eli.

"Ready?" Maria pulls on my elbow.

"Yeah." Lamenting my loss of donuts, I glance back one last time at American Press. A sharp ache pricks my chest as soft honey meets my stare. Liam's head is cocked back, and he's focused on me with parted lips. He registers my return and shoots his head forward, trudging away from the donuts and general happiness.

Well, that was weird. I shrug it off, linking arms with Maria.

"I know this is one of your complaints with him, dear, but Liam seemed like a very kind man," she hums, flashing a smile. Whatever she's trying to hint at, she's wrong.

"Give it time," I murmur back. I've let myself believe he had a soul on far too many occasions, and I don't have the energy to repair another broken heart.

My palm rubs a circle over my heart, now thrumming wildly against my chest. I would say, who am I kidding? How can someone break something that's already been shattered and buried? But I can't shake the nagging feeling that Liam's presence just jumpstarted something I thought I'd let die long ago.

Something that was always unwilfully his.

3

Sweet Caroline

I NEED TO COOL it on the Cheez Whiz.

If the swelling pressure in my abdomen is any indication, I've already downed one shot too many. Slinking toward the edge of my shabby moss-colored couch, I force a stretch well beyond my arm's natural length. My fingertips brush against the cool metal of the American oddity resting just out of reach on the floor. *Come to Mama.* The bristles of the shag rug below tickle the deep heart line on my palm, inching ever closer to my final hit.

Almost. There.

My out-of-whack hormones scream *yes, yes, yes,* while my actual body pleads *no, no, no.*

Finally, my fingers curl around the cylindrical tube of faux cheesy goodness, securing it in their grasp.

Victory is mine.

I tilt my head, lifting it from its thoroughly smooshed-into-the-couch position, and bring the nozzle to my lips.

A disheartening hiss follows, and I shake the can. Dammit. Empty.

With a huff, I let it fall to the floor.

Huh, maybe that's why it was there in the first place.

I'm. So. Bored.

I can't watch TV. I can't blog.

All I can do is think.

And eat.

Well, I could eat. But I apparently already did that so successfully there's no more bread.

Or cheese.

Or croissants.

There is an apple.

But I'm not *that* bored.

Maria's out running errands, buying bread, and hopefully cheese, though not the kind my lonely heart desires. I'm stuck on day four of doctor-ordered concussion protocol, curled up with my heating pad, a. k.a. Channing Tatum, which is giving me a lap dance hotter than *Magic Mike XXL*.

I'm in my PJs, which doesn't sound wicked exciting. But it is. Because Maria believes people shouldn't wear pajamas between six in the morning and ten at night. And she's very vocal about it. She thinks her presence is occasion enough to wear proper clothing, and well, I love her, but boo. Even sweatpants will elicit a stare and a pursed-lip look. Like, *Oh, I didn't know we were giving up today.*

Since I'm injured, I get a pass, which is why I'm currently in an *"All I do is wine, wine, wine. No matter what"* shirt. And a pair of old booty shorts with pizzas all over them—the butt says "pizza." It's the pièce de résistance of my old, ratty clothes. The shorts are clinging on for dear life. But again, the butt says "pizza," so never letting go, Jack.

Unlike Rose, I mean it. No banishing them to a cold, watery grave for me.

My eyes scan the tiny main room of our apartment as I search for a distraction.

Supplies for Maria's wedding planning business are strewn through-out the flat. My baking supplies overwhelm the kitchen and an adjacent area nearby. Confetti from the gift box Caleb and Holly sent has wafted all over the floor, couch, TV stand, and our white gateleg table. The Martha Stewart rave aesthetic is strong today.

I finally settle on a pile of mail sitting on my cheap Ikea coffee table with empty baguette sleeves and all the crumbs, forcing myself to sit and sift through the mess. A highly anticipated glossy cardstock peeks beneath what's most likely a bill. *Oh?* Has my April postcard arrived already? Practically beaming, I pluck the cherished card out from the pile. Huh. It's early. These usually come during the middle of the month.

They're always the same—a candid picture of some weird place from my hometown, edited to look like a meme with the words *"Greetings from Tallow, Massachusetts"* worked into the picture. I snort at this month's photo. It's Rohr's Diner, my favorite. Whoever took this nailed the vibe. The whole diner is blanketed in a gradient wash of orange, brown, and a coffee-stained beige. Halloween decorations grace the center of the tables, even though the specials board says it's March. Snow falls outside the diner window. A patron directs their gaze toward it with a humorously steep pile of pancakes in front of them. A speech bubble over their head reads, *The weather is wicked nice this time of the year, isn't it?* And their boothmate, blessed with an enormous burger, says, *Perfect weather for an iced Dunks.*

Snow place like home is scrawled underneath.

I flip the postcard over to read the typed message accompanying the photo, a smile permanently fashioned on my face.

April News Report from Tallow, Massachusetts.
Deciding to grab life by the horns, Bonnie, the more adventurous of Mr. Shigle's cows, went on the "lamb." It took three cops in a high-steaks chase to get her back behind the fence.

The Maces bought a school bus and turned it into a chicken coop. Classes are going well. Six out of ten chickens surveyed agreed their favorite course is eggonomics. One chicken interviewed was eggspelled. And the other three stared at me with a beady gaze suggesting fowl play would soon be at hand. I fled the coop shortly after.

Nearing the end of tapping season. The following postcard will report the winner of the annual pancake and syrup competition.

Though it's hard to beleaf anyone can stack up to Rohr's.

We all miss you a waffle lot.

Sorry, that got sappy.

Yours affectionately,

—Completely mortified at that last pun but rather proud of the chicken ones.

My focus tightens, zeroing in on the postcard for clues, an errant reflection maybe, *something*. Five years and I still don't have any leads on the sender's identity. Whoever they are doesn't want me to figure it out. I've called the Tallow Post Office, and they've said as much. I thought it was Eli, having received the first one after a long homesick cry, but he denies it—and he's hardly a pun guy.

"The Imperial March" from *Star Wars* pricks my ears, and the screen on my phone illuminates, rattling my coffee table without warning. I ruffle through the empty baguette sleeves to find it.

What could she want?

Incoming: Caroline O'Shea—DO NOT ANSWER UNLESS YOU DESIRE PAIN.

My thumb hovers over the answering button. Whatever it is, I'll have to talk to her at some point. It might as well be now.

Drawing a collecting breath, I lay back on the couch and bring my phone to my ear. "Hello?"

"Oh! Hi, sweetheart." My mother coughs, mid-sip of something. She probably anticipated going to voice mail.

My foot flicks in the air as I wait for her signature passive-aggressive tirade to commence.

She clears her throat. "Am I catching you at a bad time?"

"No, no—just resting on the couch," I say, studying the postcard and smiling.

"Oh yes, Mrs. Kelly said Liam told her you had an incident the other day. Said you practically fainted when you saw him."

"Of course he did."

"So darling, about the wedding—"

My jaw tightens. "Mm-hmm."

"Are you done with your dramatics over the whole situation?"

Resting the postcard on my stomach, I inhale and attempt to keep my voice even. "I don't know what you could possibly mean, Mother. A lady's never the source of drama. You taught me that."

"Evelina." Mother, too, keeps her voice even.

"It was a rather quick announcement, and my work prohibits me from traveling easily. But I'm working on it."

I've purposefully kept my job vague. If Caroline knew I left the University of Alabama—my parents' alma mater where "the good girls go for husbands"—for my abysmal existence as a food and travel blogger and part-time bartender—well, that guilt trip would rival summiting Mt. Everest with its cruel bite and icy environment.

To be fair, my existence wasn't nearly this mediocre at first. I was on track for the head pâtissière at a local pâtisserie for a half second. But then, two years ago, the consistent pain in my lower abdomen I'd been battling for ten years became excruciating, and I had to leave my job and steady paycheck behind, dashing any hopes to someday open my own shop.

At first, my blog picked up, exploding after a drunken creation of mine went viral. The cupcake donut. Pinterest went crazy for it, traffic came to my blog in droves, and I was able to sell ad space and sponsorships.

But lately, the lack of sunshine in my life has leaked into my blog, and it's consequently been floundering.

I try to hide that everything sucks from my followers, but even Maria, the Queen of Sugarcoating, says it's becoming noticeable, and my income is dwindling as a result.

A month ago, I started working at the pub Maria's boyfriend, Declan, owns with his twin brother, Fionn, to compensate. The job's fine. I shouldn't complain. Declan and Fionn understand what I'm dealing with and never suggest I'm lazy when I need a second to rest, which is a chronically ill dream. But I need to renew my visa soon, and the state of my occupational life is unsettling, at best. I'm worried my lack of serious employment and funds will complicate my renewal this time.

And Caroline and I need this ocean. I can't move back.

"Ah, yes. Your work as a bartender."

My foot freezes. No. She doesn't know. How could she?

"It was rather embarrassing when I chatted with Natale Kelly yesterday to find she knew more about my daughter's life than I did."

Of course she does. *Liam.*

I gaze at the cracked wooden beams lining the slanted ceiling, running my hands through my long strawberry-blonde hair. My fingers snag in a knot, and I grumpily work it out.

Wonder Boy's been here for four freakin' days. Four! And he's already wreaking havoc on my carefully crafted peace. The man's a freakin' methodical menace.

"I'm sorry Liam's still such a chatterbox about things that are none of his business." I pull at the knot; the tug forces a more substantial headache to surge at the base of my temple, but anything is less painful than this conversation, so I'll take it.

A strangled scoff cracks through the phone speaker. "He was worried."

"Oh, please. That man has never worried about anything but himself."

I can practically hear the self-preening happening on the other line, her fingers sweeping through her hair in a far more graceful manner than my own, maybe a tug at a hemline or the straightening of a sleeve. Or, heaven forbid, the dreaded clutching of a pearl. My mother never raises her voice, but I've edged her to the line plenty of times.

"Mark my words, Evelina. Someday this ugly habit of yours to hold a grudge will permanently damage your life."

"Was there a reason for your call besides this super pleasant tête-à-tête? For whatever reason, my head's suddenly throbbing, and I could use a rest."

"Come to the wedding. It's your brother's big day. Be the good girl we raised you to be."

Unfortunately for us both, my mother's idolized version of a perfect daughter—the well-mannered debutante and sorority girl—never manifested itself within me.

"I think I'll pass." I knee-jerk into a "no," swallowing down the bile burning in the back of my throat. A frustrated tear pricks the edge of my eye. I want to be there for Caleb, but I don't have the reserves to handle this—handle *her*—right now.

"Be thankful your nana isn't around anymore. Gosh, it'd break her heart witnessing you miss a moment so precious to the family."

A heaviness sits on my chest, forcing lumbering breaths. I exhale. Once. Twice.

My foot twitches.

Nana.

Lord, does this woman know how to play her cards.

But she's right. There wouldn't be a discussion if she was still around. I'd be there.

I pinch the bridge of my nose, regretting the minor aggression against my bruised appendage.

With a sigh, I relent. "I'll call Caleb and coordinate buying tickets with him tomorrow."

"Oh, excellent, honey. I knew you'd come to your senses. I'll talk to Holly about ordering your dress. Are you still a size six?"

I was never a size six.

I raise my postcard to study it again, drawing my focus away from the flood of emotions threatening to burst out of me. The "high steaks" pun releases some much-needed dopamine, calming my system.

I could figure out who's sending these when I'm back in Tallow. Stalk a Staples, maybe, I don't know, but it'd give me something to look forward to.

Oh, I should get waffles too.

"Twelve, actually."

"Okay, well, they run large, so I'll order you an eight."

When has a bridesmaid's dress in the history of bridesmaid dresses ever "run large"? Nope, can't risk her messing with my waffles plans.

"You know what—I'll call Holly and discuss ordering my dress from here. Okay? I think she wanted Clare and me to pick our own, and I venture Paris has better options than little ol' Tallow, Mass."

"Oh, yes—I suppose you're right."

"Okay, well, I really have to go."

I swing my legs off the couch and trudge into the bedroom to clip the new card on the string of twinkling fairy lights, vines, and postcards lining the wall over my platform bed. It's almost time to string up another row.

"One more thing, dear."

Of course there is.

"Mm-hmm."

I pluck the October postcard from its clip. A smile forms on my face, even though this conversation makes me want to bash my head through this fragile, poorly insulated wall. Best to wait for this concussion to heal before I cause another one.

October recounted the state fairs. The picture on the front captured a squirrel hidden in a pumpkin patch—*just a small-town squirrel, living in a comely gourd* printed underneath.

"I have a few options for your date," my mother drawls on as I half-listen, half-investigate my postcards. "Tyler Higgins grew into those teeth of his, and he's over six feet." Ah yes, the six-foot line of demarcation for potential suitors. Caroline was "forced" to eliminate much of the male population because, heaven forbid, I emasculate a man with my five-ten stature. "Or Charlie Bennet. He's tall and took a liking to you in high school. I'm sure we could persuade him to escort you if you apologize for your little mishap."

"It wasn't a mishap. Charlie Bennet tried to grab my boob at lunch, and I shooed his hand away with a plastic fork. He over-dramatized the whole damn incident if you ask me."

"The boy had a black eye, sweetheart."

"I stick by my *I didn't give him that* statement." I just kind of stabbed his hand.

Another sigh. "I'll ask Tyler's mother if she thinks he'd be interested. He's a doctor, well a veterinarian, but I suppose we can't be picky with your little condition."

My hand freezes on a postcard. She's baiting me.

"I'm sorry your daughter's a hard sell now that she's damaged goods."

"No, Evelina, that's not fair. All I'm saying is certain things might be challenging for you, so you really shouldn't waste time sitting idly by. You should be out pursuing good boys like—"

"Liam," I cut her off. It became clear at a young age my mother would have sold her soul to the Devil if it meant he would date me.

Either she did, and the Devil didn't hold true to his promises, or she never had a soul worth selling. I could never tell.

A long awkward pause hangs between us.

"I think at this point, you should aim a little lower, sweetheart. No use in getting your hopes up again or wasting time over something that will never happen."

What—and I cannot stress this enough—the actual fuck.

"Can't wait to see you soon! Really, super excited, but oh shoot, I have to go!"

"Evie—"

I hang up. A firm lump lodges itself in the back of my throat. Our tiny Paris apartment's close-knit walls narrow, slowly shrinking the space until the walls collapse in on themselves. I pace back and forth between the living room and my bedroom. The wooden floorboards groan under my agitation. I need to get out of here.

The front door swings open. Maria, arms full of reusable shopping bags, enters. "I've got—" Her bright face falls. "Oh, dear, what's wrong."

"I need to go for a walk." I pick up my chin, marching into my bedroom.

The bags drop on the floor. "Are you feeling well enough for that?"

I grab the first set of leggings I find and a flowy dress piled in a heap on the floor. Confetti cascades to the ground when I shake it out. "I'm fine."

"Evie, it's only been a few days, and it's awfully sunny."

"My mom called," I say, tossing some of the clothes on the floor to the side. Where did I put my jacket? "And I answered."

"Oh, yes—well, a walk sounds lovely. Do you want me to go too?"

"No, I need to be alone, but thank you." I force a smile, plucking the coat off the desk chair.

"I'll start dinner, then. Remember we invited Eli and Liam over along with Declan and Fionn."

Shit. "Any chance . . ."

"You can't uninvite him."

I tip my head back with a sigh. "Hell, this better be a cleansing walk, then. I'll hurry back soon to help," I grump, stuffing my feet into a pair of well-loved ballet flats and leaving.

Coat. Shoes. Stairs. Métro. That's been the natural rhythm of my life for the past six years. A torn, tattered advertisement for a sale at Printemps, heavily graffitied, stares at me on the Métro platform. It's been here as long as I have. No one's changed it.

Over the years, it's lost bits of itself, flaking away, revealing more of the gray concrete underneath. The wording, too, has dwindled away, "soldes" reduced to "lde," and the "Printemps" turning into "mps," with graffiti scrawled haphazardly over the remaining poster.

Honestly, mood. That's what *my little condition* will do.

Twelve years with this damn disease now. Weathered, tattered, torn, unchanging, littered with unsolicited graffiti, chipping away into gray.

I was so naive when I moved here, full of hope and false promises, thinking whatever pain I had would remain manageable. Bitterness washes over me recalling my past, how I was so blissfully unaware that my disease would progress over time, and all the blood, sweat, and tears I poured into achieving my pastry chef dreams would be ripped away in a slow, agonizing defeat.

Maybe if I'd known, I would have done something different. Maybe if I'd known, I would have traveled more and spent less time grinding at work. The *what-if* talons threaten to shred my guilt-ridden conscience, and I shake my head to free myself from the spiral.

Damn, eight minutes for the next train. Ugh. Not wanting to dwell on depressing existential poster metaphors, I pull out my phone to doom scroll while I wait.

UNKNOWN: Hello, Evie. This is Liam Kelly. Eli gave me your phone number. He told me we were invited over for dinner

tonight. **Wanted to confirm the invite was actually extended to both of us.**

I snort. After Caroline's phone call, I should be frustrated with him, but seriously, who texts like that? Oh. Actually—

ME: I'm sorry, but who the hell texts like this?

LIAM: A ray of sunshine.

ME: Okay, I didn't denote a particular part of the sun to you. But if I did, you'd definitely be the sunspot.

LIAM: Because I'm magnetic? Aww, Peaches, I'm flattered.

Did not anticipate him to know anything about sunspots, okay.

ME: No, because you'd be a blight on an otherwise warm and happy sun.

LIAM: ...

LIAM: Yeah, I'm going to go out on a limb and venture that was a "no" on the dinner invite.

I'd be an asshole to uninvite him, Maria said as much.

ME: You can come.

ME: But you owe me cheese.

LIAM: Why do I owe you cheese?

ME: I talked with Caroline.

LIAM: And that's the sunspot's fault because ...

ME: She very intentionally didn't know I was a bartender.

LIAM: Damn it. Do you want the fancy shit or that stuff in a can?

LIAM: Oh, maybe I'll spring for two cans.

ME: You're a terrible person. I hope you accidentally fall off a bridge.

ME: There are plenty to choose from.

LIAM: So I've read. Your blog article on them was interesting.

The train arrives.

Passengers load.

And unload.

Moving in a whir around me.

The train departs.

And I stand, feet planted on the platform.

He's read my blog?

I blink. I don't—

ME: Why are you reading my blog?

The dots dance on the screen and disappear. Then reappear. Then disappear. Then reappear. I hold my breath—what sick joke is he planning?

LIAM: Heading into a meeting. See you tonight.

That was weird.

ME: REMEMBER THE CHEESE!

Over thirty bridges rest within the city limits of Paris, each with its own unique personality and history. Pont Neuf, my favorite and current destination, is the oldest bridge in Paris, with construction on it beginning in the late 1500s. Ornately crafted mascarons—stone masks depicting mythological beings—adorn the beige side of the bridge, staring menacingly at passing travelers on the Seine.

Study any painting of Pont Neuf, and it becomes obvious: it's the center of everything. A statue of Henry IV (assassinated by a Medici, as was custom at the time) riding a horse stands erect in the middle, facing Place Dauphine—one of the oldest squares in Paris.

Carved out between two sets of buildings and flanked by two roads on the other side, Place Dauphine's my comfort place. It looks out over the Palais de Justice of Paris, once a royal palace, then a holding area for the prisoners of the French Revolution, and now part historical monument, part working courthouse. I love it. It's the embodiment of

Paris, beautiful and romantic, but its history is brimming with a dark, creepy undercurrent. Like my soul. Like life. It's the spot I go to when I need a reminder I'm small potatoes, and so are my problems. Thousands of lifetimes happened here before me: some not so pleasant, some wonderful. All bigger than me on a bench feeling shitty for myself.

The cold comfort of the bench chills me through my leggings as my attention rests on the columns and statues outside the cour d'appel. Madame du Barry, the maîtresse-en-titre of Louis XV, stayed imprisoned within these walls once. Red Skelton, Lucille Ball, and Gene Kelly all starred in a satire that revolved around her. It was one of Nana's favorites—and a big reason why I adore this spot. I sense her presence strongest here.

She's why I'm in Paris.

My lungs fill to capacity on an inhale as I rest my palms on the edge of the bench, feet stretched out on the gravel path. Head tilted upward, I soak in the warm sun peeking through the branches of an overhanging chestnut tree.

Nana. My life source. An extreme lover of old movies. We started devouring them our first winter in New England. Born and raised a Georgia peach, the stark contrast in climates between the northern and southern parts of the United States puzzled me. What *did* someone do with all that cold? Nana, who moved with us when my father's work relocated him, knew exactly what to do, inviting the rambunctious boy next door to observe "his relative" on screen and sip hot cocoa. Liam, seemingly absent of any grandparents, claimed Gene Kelly—and Nana—as his own, a declaration I found rather rude since I didn't have much to share myself.

Nana's other love—Paris—became ours, something Liam didn't share. She promised to take me someday, but futures I soon learned never do pan out how we imagine they should. And I was left dreaming of my own Paris adventure long after Nana left us all.

When she passed, I was twelve, and I grew overly attached to the classic films featuring Paris in her hard-felt absence. Audrey Hepburn's *How to Steal a Million, Charade, Funny Face,* and *Paris When It Sizzles,* in particular. But *An American in Paris* had its own unique charm too. Paris grew into a fairy tale, a place where romance, art, architecture, history, and philosophy all melded together in perfect harmony. A place of seductive glamor. How could you not fall in love with Paris during musical numbers like "I Got Rhythm" and "Bonjour, Paris"?

While I tried to bury my Paris dreams for more practical ones, after a particularly miserable semester at Alabama, I found myself at the study abroad office on campus, Ernest Hemingway's words circulating through my brain.

"There are only two places in the world where we can live happy—at home and in Paris."

If happiness didn't exist at home, maybe it was time to change my outlook, throw up my windows, and let in *la vie en rose,* just like my dear Audrey Hepburn taught me to do in *Sabrina.*

Paris was, after all, always a good idea.

And Audrey Hepburn was—and is—an infallible source I could never question.

I relocated the following term and never returned. I found something akin to—but not quite—happiness in this place. Peace, maybe? Contentedness? Pleasure? I never found a good word for it. But it was better than *miserable.*

The snap of a twig nearby and a familiar "shit" force me to open my eyes and reluctantly face the culprit.

A large, Dorito-of-a-man I could do without seeing stands on the balls of his feet a few steps behind me, slowly retreating—a hot beverage of sorts in his hand and a box from one of my favorite boulangeries, Castelblangeois, balanced in the other.

4

(You Drive Me) Glazy

LIAM KELLY—FOR ALL INTENTS and purposes—started out as your stereotypical sweet and charming boy next door. So naturally, I locked that shit down, marrying him at the very mature age of five in a floral crown Nana and I crafted with lilacs and ribbons and Belle's yellow dress from *Beauty and the Beast*. Liam, wearing a Nomar Garciaparra Red Sox jersey, waited for me at the end of an easel-papered aisle, a huge grin fashioned on his face.

Nana officiated. Caleb gave me away. And my bunny, Sir Stick E. Buns, ate a carrot.

After the ceremony, Liam and I split a pink-frosted donut with sprinkles on a blue gingham blanket in my backyard. I laid down, feet flicking in the air. He sidled up next to me and laced his fingers with mine while the rays of the mid-afternoon sun cast a warming glow on everything it touched.

"You know when the sun shines on you like that, your hair gets all sparkly, and you look like a fairy princess," he said.

I smiled, basking in the glow of admiration. My mother made sure I knew I was a pretty little thing, but hearing it from Liam felt different.

His stare lingered on my face. "Mom says I'll have to marry you a second time when we're older to make it lethal."

"Nana said that too." I flipped over on my stomach and reached for the bowl of peaches covered in sugary syrup not too far away. My mom only prepared them extra sweet when she was proud of me. "We should have a big bowl of peaches then too," I hummed, taking a bite.

The snap of a disposable Kodak camera followed. Liam always had one in his hands, running around the backyard and sneaking shots at Nana, who would loudly order him to stop if he didn't want to break his camera with her old mug. "Oh, we should have donuts too," he said, winding the wheel on the top right corner.

"Obviously." I laughed. "You have to have donuts at your wedding; it's an addition."

"To what?" *Snap. Wind.*

"I don't know. I think it means everybody does it, so we have to too."

"That makes sense." He captured another picture of me. "You're so smart."

I blushed, greedily heaping peaches onto my spoon. Nana was the only one who ever called me smart.

Sweet syrup dribbled down my chin, and Liam offered me a napkin. "Thank you," I muffled through my bite.

"Nana said taking care of you is my full-time job now."

"Like forever?"

"Guess so." He shrugged, running a piece of ribbon from the crown through his fingers. "But I don't mind."

Warmth bloomed in my chest. My mom was sugary-peaches proud, and Liam thought I was a fairy princess.

It was all downhill after that.

I tilt my head toward the sun, blinking through the branches of a chestnut tree, and ignore the nettling earworm that my life peaked at the age of five. Drawing in a cleansing breath, I collect myself before acknowledging Liam.

"I'd prefer it if your stalker tendencies could remain dormant while you're visiting my city, Mr. Kelly."

"I'd be a pretty lousy stalker this out in the open," he says, blinking himself out of a daze. A small child on a scooter undercuts his path. He jumps back, the box wobbling in his grasp, and he comes perilously close to dropping everything.

"Never stopped you in the past." I shrug. "You always bumble more than usual when I catch you."

"I was never stalking you." Liam sighs, placing his food, coffee, and briefcase down next to me. "That was always a weird fantasy of yours."

"Trust me—my fantasies of you aren't weird." Open mouth. Wince. Repeat.

He quirks an eyebrow. "Good to know."

"They're . . . bloody."

"Ah. And obviously that's not weird," he says, an easy smile playing on his lips. His deft fingers work at undoing the button on the cuff of his white-collared shirt.

The steadiness of my pulse gives way to chaos as he rolls his sleeve up past his elbow and his sun-kissed olive complexion shines in the mid-afternoon light.

He still wears his shirt sleeves like Gene Kelly—high and tight. Neat. That doesn't make me weak in the knees at all. Le nope. His corded forearms are leaving me completely unaffected. It's fine. I'm fine.

The unsettling stomachache reserved for him flutters to focus, right on schedule.

It's really not fair that just his presence and a slight lift of his sleeves have this much of an effect on me.

Seriously, I'm as bad as a Victorian man seeing a woman's ankles for the first time.

"Not with our history." I fold my hands in my lap, eyes falling to the box on the bench. He's far too trusting in this situation—I could grab this box of happiness and make a mad dash to freedom. Be out of this dangerous situation with a satiated appetite in no time.

"One. I want one concrete example where I 'stalked' you."

"Just one?"

He gestures for me to proceed and crosses his arms in front of his chest. The stretch pulls his white shirt taut across muscles he has no business possessing.

In high school, I accepted that my body's traitorous attraction to him shifted the playing field in his favor. Liam didn't suffer a thousand restless nights, tossing and turning, imagining what my lips felt like pressed to his. And he certainly didn't know the horrors of coming face-to-face with him in the morning after having a vivid, punishing dream. But still. He could tone it down. It's quite frankly indecent and rude for a man with a face like that to have *those*.

"Okay, well, off the top of my head, there's the time you followed me halfway across the country for college."

He tsks, peering at me beneath thickly hooded lashes. "Correct me if I'm wrong here, Peaches, but I believe I accepted first. So by that logic, *you* followed *me*, you little creeper." He reaches out and ruffles my hair.

"Oh, bullshit. You had so many other colleges to choose from." I swat his hand away. "You knew with Caroline I only had one choice."

This is the dynamic I remember. Whatever *that* was a few days ago, it was for show.

Or I temporarily opened a wormhole. I've seen too many Hallmark movies to rule out the power of the head wound/alternate reality dynamic.

"Sorry I didn't turn down a full scholarship and a chance to play football at Alabama so you could find some unsuspecting man to marry," he says, bending down to grab his coffee and toast me. "That worked out well, by the way."

The gold flecks sparkle, colliding with my scowl as he sips his coffee with a devilish grin peeking beyond the lid.

I flinch at the poke to my open wound, carefully hiding the crack. "How's your budding career in the NFL going? What team drafted you again?" I bat my eyelashes.

His stupid grin slides into a full agitated glare. "I tore my ACL senior year. Don't pretend like you don't know."

"Believe it or not, Mr. Kelly, since I moved to Paris, I haven't thought about you at all." I pick a fake crumb off my leggings at my slight stretching of the truth. I thought of him more than I care to admit, but when everything crashed and burned spectacularly in my life, I blocked Liam on social media as an act of self-preservation. "And it has been glorious."

"Ah. Well. Not being accused of having some nefarious motive every time I take a breath has been nice too." He turns his back to me, directing his attention over the park.

Spotted with chestnut trees, Place Dauphine is one of the quieter squares at this time of the year when cherry blossoms bloom and cover Paris in a pink decadence. Of course, chestnut trees have a certain charm, but they're understated compared to the plumes of blush-colored petals dusting Notre Dame and the gardens at Palais-Royal in April.

I peek at him, allowing myself a moment to observe him when he's not watching me. It's safe if I don't let my gaze linger too long. My heart rate dangerously escalates when I do that.

His shoulders rise and fall as he regards a group of elderly men playing pétanque in the distance. The tension in his back doesn't release after his second exaggerated inhale.

Huh. I don't usually get to *him*.

"Sorry, Peaches, that wasn't the right way to greet you. Old habit," he says over his shoulder.

My elevated, erratic heartbeat swells at this change of character. The Liam Kelly I knew never apologized.

He passes a hand through his hair, rounding back to me, and an errant tendril sweeps across his forehead, further adding to his rakish vibes. I blink.

He really is like staring directly at the sun—radiant and enchanting, sure, but I'm more likely to end this whole interaction well and burnt.

A soft twinkle sits in the recesses of Liam's gaze, pinned on me, and I shift on the bench. There's something almost sincere about the rueful way he's staring at me that makes me want to believe maybe he does apologize now.

"It's fine." I sigh, too tired to care if he's playing mind games with me. Let him try to ruin me again. I've got nothing left for him to take. "Just admit you lied and somehow creepily followed me here, and all will be forgiven."

"I panicked and lied about the meeting, but I didn't know you'd be here." The bench creaks as he lowers his six-foot-four frame on it.

"What are you doing?" I shriek, garnering stares and an exasperated "américaine."

"I'm sitting here. All the other benches are taken." A low, amused rumble shakes his chest. "My word, you're still a feral little thing, aren't you?"

"Yes, now find another person to bother." Sweat coats my palms from clenching them so tightly, and I unfurl my fists, wiping them clean on my pants. "You've already messed my day up enough as is."

"Look, I'm sorry I'm still the worst, but if we could agree to a ten-minute ceasefire so I can eat, that would be great. I'm tired and would rather not sit next to a stranger." The agitated set to his jaw tightens as he holds his cup and fumbles to open the box.

The self-deprecation pricks something in my chest. "Ceasefire granted." I sigh, plucking the cup from his grasp to save him from spilling it. "But no talking. I came here for peace and quiet."

"Fine by me." His knee bounces, shaking his box. I wince for the integrity of whatever is inside. "What are you doing here, anyway? Shouldn't you be resting?" His gaze lingers on my profile, and I shoot him some serious worry-about-yourself side-eye.

"Shutting up." He raises his hands in mock surrender.

Crinkled boulangerie paper beckons my attention as Liam opens the box. I'm overly nosy when it comes to all things bread and pastries.

A niçoise sandwich—tuna with hardboiled eggs—rests inside the hallowed wrapping. Good, solid, practical—

He shovels a fork full of the sandwich filling, sans bread, into his mouth.

What the hell is he doing? No. He's not—

He does it a second time.

I control my own peace. I control my—Oh, to hell with the ceasefire. I can't allow this harsh slap in the collective French face to occur without consequence.

"What in Sam's name are you doing?" I grit out.

He pauses mid-dig. "I'm eating lunch?"

"You're eating a sandwich . . . with a fork!"

"Oh, yeah. I thought I ordered the salad, but the cashier gave me this, and I didn't try to fix it." He shrugs like this is a totally valid reason.

My brain whirs like a cartoon scribble trying to formulate a coherent thought, but all that's circulating there is "You're eating . . . a sandwich . . . with a fork."

"I don't eat carbs?" Pink rises on the tips of his ears. If he didn't want to be attacked over this, he picked the wrong damn bench.

"Oh my god." I groan, scrubbing my hands over my face. "I didn't think it was humanly possible to be more annoyed with you."

"I thought we weren't supposed to be talking."

"That was before you committed French heresy. I literally cannot even with you."

He puts his fork down and sighs. "I'm sure you really can even."

"Nope. Literally impossible."

"You're overreacting—it's just bread."

"Just bread? *Just. Bread?*" The words roll off my tongue with significant friction. "Is the Eiffel Tower *just* a structure? Is Notre Dame *just* a church? No! This isn't *just* bread. This is French bread in Paris! Seriously, this is the most offensive thing you've ever done. Worse than the time you cut my hair—"

"I was seven."

"Or chopped the head off Samantha."

"Who the hell's Samantha?"

"My American Girl doll."

"Ah. Eleven. And I built a working guillotine. Can you blame me?"

"Yes! I can! Do you know how expensive those dolls are? Nana bought it for me right before her diagnosis—"

"I get it." He puts a hand up to halt my response. "I was a little shit."

"You were a big one, too," I mumble.

"Wow, okay." He tilts his head back and laughs. "If I take a bite of the damn bread, will you stop whatever new game this is?"

"It would certainly help the situation, yes."

The veins on his arms protrude. With a narrowed intensity on my face, he raises the sandwich slowly to his mouth and takes a bite of the whole thing, bread and all.

I huff. "Thank you."

"Don't mention it," he grunts back.

A miniature soccer ball rolls to a stop at my feet. I nudge it back to a girl waiting expectantly with a shy smile a few feet off. She picks it up and runs away, curls gathered in a big pink bow cascading down her back, her ruffled skirt bouncing at her knees, white tights peeking out underneath. Impeccably dressed children are a direct shot to the ovaries for me.

They're also the only kind of children Paris produces.

All I'm trying to say is certain things might be more challenging for you, so you really shouldn't waste time sitting idly by.

That frequently used Caroline O'Shea mantra is half the reason I ran to Paris. My diagnosis was an impediment our mother/daughter relationship could never overcome. It was a unique gift of hers to cycle any conversation back to where she thought my value lay and how I had somehow managed to diminish it.

Sharing I learned how to make macarons turned into the shame that I'd probably never have a family to enjoy them. Visiting the Eiffel Tower for the first time resulted in uncontrollable sobs because how could I ever know the joy of hearing such a happy story from my child when I did things like go to the Eiffel Tower alone?

All of it was stupid.

Yeah, endometriosis and my uterine fibroids put me at a higher risk for complications with my fertility. Sure, it meant it would probably be more challenging for me, the odds were lower, and I considered the possibility of infertility more than a person without these conditions would. And yes, the actual act of procreating was rather unpleasant for me. But still, nothing would be certain until the future became the present, so why worry now?

And second, I am and would always be so much more than my ability to create tiny humans inside of me. Separation from her hysterics had proven as much to me.

Sure, I need to do *something*, but if it's not bringing life into the world, that's okay.

Though lately, doing something—*anything*—has become equally tricky.

In my introspective trance, Liam turns his back to me, sneaking another bite of his whole sandwich.

Oh, hell no. He can't hide away I clearly won.

Resting my elbows on my knees, I stare at him with a teasing smile. "Told you," I sing.

He drops his shoulders. "You were right."

"Of course I was!" I shout, eyes still laser-focused on this momentous occasion. "It's bread. In France!"

"What are you—" He glances down at my cocky smile, back at the sandwich, and then at my face. "You're going to stare at me eating this whole thing, aren't you?"

"I'm savoring the moment."

He reaches into his briefcase and pulls out a brown bag. "Why don't you savor this instead, weirdo." He smirks, tossing it at me.

"What's this?"

"It was supposed to be a peace offering tonight with the cheese, but I'd rather use it now."

I peek in the bag, and a pink frosted donut with rainbow sprinkles greets me. My favorite. I hazard a glance back at him and then back into the bag.

The Admiral Ackbar alarm sirens in my head.

It's a trap.

He snorts. "I didn't poison it."

"Oh, I wasn't—I didn't—"

"That's exactly what you were thinking," he mutters, like he's irritated my brain ventured in that direction.

"Thank you, Liam. This was really nice. Peace offering accepted."

Left leg still bouncing, he shrugs it off with a bite of his sandwich.

"You know, Castelblangeois is one of my favorite places, actually," I say, ripping off a piece of donut. The pink icing melts in my mouth, and I close my eyes, reveling in the overwhelming sweetness. "It's funny. I usually stop and grab a jambon-beurre before coming here on days like this."

If you're feeling down and out or need a place to think, there is precious little a sandwich from Castelblangeois and a park bench at Place Dauphine cannot cure.

Oh—my eyes snap open.

"Blog thirty-six," I blurt.

He arches an eyebrow and wipes his hands.

"You went to Castelblangeois, and you're having lunch at Place Dauphine—that's blog entry thirty-six."

He dips his head, ceding the fact. "Yeah, it is."

My heart cinches; he's practicing Evie O'Shea's "Break in Case of a Hard Day" protocol.

"Are you okay?" The words stumble out with an odd, unfamiliar concern. The sudden widening of his eyes suggests he's surprised by the question. "That post touches on going somewhere when you're down, so I assume . . ."

A smile cuts across his face, but it doesn't quite reach his eyes. "Yeah, I'm fine. Just frustrated and wanted to breathe."

Ah well, I'm sure I helped that.

"Work?"

"Nah." He shakes his head. "Work's fine." He clears his throat and focuses on two pigeons sizing each other up not too far away. "A dynamic in my life is getting old, but I don't know how to fix it."

Mood. That's why I'm here, too, isn't it?

Honestly, he could be referring to a dynamic with a parent too. Not that Liam shared that kind of stuff with me, but I remember his dad pushed things on Liam he didn't necessarily love and blocked him in other ways. Like when Caleb wanted Liam to join the basketball team, but his dad kept pushing winter football programs on him instead.

Growing up, Liam hated the creamery, so it makes absolutely no sense to me how he ended up the vice president of it now. Though, truthfully, not a lot of whoever I'm sharing this bench with makes sense.

"Have you thought about running away to Paris?"

He snorts. "No, but it's an interesting solution."

"Italy's lovely too; your mom's parents were from Naples, right? I bet you'd fit right in—although eating carbs there is a must. Oh, maybe the south of France would suit you better. Yes, somewhere in Provence. You'd be sunning and enjoying life in no time."

"Seriously, Peaches, don't worry. I'm fine." He gently pats my hand like he knows I'm actually worried and passes me a napkin, standing.

"Thank you," I mumble, wiping my cheek free of icing while he takes my empty bag and tosses it and his box in a green trashcan nearby.

He laughs. "You inhaled that."

"I like donuts," I say, cheeks full of doughy goodness.

"I'll have to remember that for future screwups."

My nose scrunches up under the pressure of a wide-spreading grin. "It would definitely buy you infinite grace if that's your aim."

"Noted." A corner of his mouth curls up, and his dimple softly pricks his cheek. "So, what are you doing here? If this is your thinking place."

"Oh, yeah." I forgot why I was here in the first place. "My mom guilt-tripped me into going to the wedding now that she knows how expendable my job really is—and then immediately made me regret my decision."

"Ah—hence the apolocheese."

I quirk a brow. "Really?"

"I thought it was grate."

"Are we about to fondue this?"

Pun-offs were a Nana O'Shea specialty. It was the one thing I was ridiculously good at, so, of course, Liam never played.

He shrugs. "In queso missed it, we already are."

"Unbrielievable."

"Hey, that was pretty gouda."

"Yeah—but now I've got nothing cheddar than that." I worry my bottom lip with my teeth, careful not to expose the cheek-busting grin threatening to explode across my face. I don't know if I'm an overly nostalgic person in general, but with Nana, the limit doesn't exist. If I could, I'd bury myself in a cocoon of her everlasting warmth.

He blinks. "Yeah, you win. You clearly have a punning problem."

"Huh. My first victory."

"Oh, come on." He sits, sipping his coffee. "You've won plenty."

I cross my arms, slowly raising a brow in challenge. I wouldn't exactly call my victory count plentiful, as the number hovers approximately at zero. "Please refresh my memory."

"Well." He hesitates and rubs the stubble on his cheek. "You—There was the time . . . *you told me to eat a sandwich, and I liked it?*"

"Oh yes, I remember that like it was yesterday," I say, satisfied he's at least able to recognize reality and have the decency to sound a bit embarrassed. "But mark my words, Mr. Kelly, the tides are changing. Victorious cheese puns are just the beginning for me."

He shakes his head, smiling into his cup. "I have no doubt you could win whatever you want with me, Peaches."

A familiar warmth blooms in my chest and rattles my nerves. This isn't a feeling I typically associate with Liam. No, this feeling is reserved for people I like. *Danger. Danger.* I shift further away on the bench for safe measure, tucking my hands under my butt and letting my legs lightly swing. "Do you remember Tyler Higgins?"

"High school quarterback, Tyler Higgins? Yeah, what about him?"

"My mom wants him to take me to the wedding."

"You know we nicknamed him President Party Pooper for a reason, right?"

"So?" I shrug. "Not everyone is blessed with the social advantages of black magic. Some of us have to charm others naturally."

"Still, that'd be a cruel thing to do to the poor guy. You should go with someone more on your level."

"I can behave for the night," I say bashfully. The warmth wilts inside my chest as quickly as it bloomed. Well, at least this feels more natural anyway.

"You shouldn't have to *behave* with whoever you're with." A hint of annoyance flashes over his features. "You'll be bored stiff with him."

"I was under the impression stiff was the objective."

He doesn't acknowledge the joke. Moving on, then.

I shift on the bench. "Well, it was either him or Charlie Bennet, so . . ."

"He was an ass to you. Why would you want to—"

"I don't want to do anything, but he's over six feet, and I'm in a bind with my mom."

"Does your mom want him to get another black eye?"

"Contrary to popular belief, I didn't give him that."

"I know. I did," he says calmly, sipping his coffee like this isn't a serious news bomb he's dropping into the conversation.

"You did?" My breath snags in my throat as I try to fully comprehend what he's saying.

The pocket full of sunshine.

King of Whittemore High School.

Wonder Boy.

Punched Charlie Bennet?

Because of something he did to *me*?

"But why?"

His finger edges the rim of his cup, and he shrugs. "Because he was lying to the locker room about whatever happened between you two and you were—" His voice trails off. "Caleb's little sister. It's what he would have done if he wasn't off at college. Coach wasn't happy, but it was fine."

"Oh my god." I jump, and the motion startles Liam. "*That* was why you had a one-game suspension?" Senior year of high school, Liam missed a game because *reasons*. I never learned the true story, but he was grumpy and broody the two weeks leading up to the homecoming game and dance.

The week before the dance, a rumor spread that I was off-limits because of something Liam said, like he decided he couldn't be the only one in a bad mood and wanted to drag me down with him. The one offer I had received was rescinded, and no one else bothered to ask me.

I marched over to his house to tell him I didn't want to go to the stupid thing anyway and pitied the miserable soul he planned on taking while he leaned shirtless in his doorframe with a pointed intensity on my face.

"*You feel better, Peaches?*" he asked as I caught my breath and nodded. "*Great. You can hurry home now.*" He shooed me away with the flick of his wrist like I was a peasant girl who deigned to bother the prince. Then shut the door on my burning cheeks.

The night of the dance, I wasn't allowed to watch TV. Between sort of stabbing Charlie Bennet and the horror of no one asking me to homecoming, Caroline couldn't allow such frivolities. *I never should've let Nana show them to you. Those movies of yours give you the wrong idea.* Like somehow, these mid-century films were too progressive.

Liam was surprisingly home, watching *Take Me Out to the Ball-game,* his personal Gene Kelly favorite, in his bedroom. He caught me staring, elbows perched on the ledge of my window to get a better look, and opened his own. I braced myself for a zinger, but he didn't say anything. Suddenly, the movie grew louder, the TV moved closer, and neither of us acknowledged the olive branch.

"Uhm yeah. That's why." The tips of Liam's ears redden. "Why do you need a date for the wedding anyway?"

"Caroline." I sigh. "She's very much of the one-track mind that it would be complete and utter humiliation for the family if I showed up alone—and I'm trying to keep the peace and not ruin Caleb's big day."

"Ah." Liam leans back and focuses his attention across the street. "So why don't I take you?"

My heart stammers.

"Huh?"

"Why don't I take you? Save your brother and Holly a plate and keep your mom's embarrassment at bay—"

Go with Liam? My past-high-school self pauses her iPod Nano playing a mix of Dashboard Confessional and Yellowcard for the fifty-thousandth time and squeals. *Wait, what did he ask us? Say yes. Say yes. He's dreamy,* she screams, trapped inside her anxiety-ridden, still-trying-to-perfect-her-top-eight-on-MySpace cage.

Okay, Lizzie McGuire doodle, chill. Your naive ass got us in enough trouble already.

Heat rises on my cheeks, and I nervously tuck my hair behind my ear, fingers brushing the bruise on my forehead.

His brow furrows. "Did you get checked out?" He leans in, and my eyes flash to his mouth.

"Kiss Me" shuffles on the Nano in my mind because sixteen-year-old me isn't the jaded spinster I am desperately proud of becoming.

"Yes, Mr. Kelly, I did, and I have a concussion."

"Is that so?" He smirks knowingly, fingers lightly trailing the spot.

"And your know-it-all expression really makes me want to go to the wedding with you."

"Come on." His eye crinkles deepen, pulling me further into his orbit. "We can call a truce for the night, or I can let you win everything, whatever you want."

His knee brushes against mine, and fireworks careen out from the point of contact, spiraling inside in an explosion of vivid color. My inability to control this little crush and an open bar would be a recipe for disaster. No, best to guard ourselves now.

"Thank you, but I've accepted this offer before, and it didn't exactly turn out well for me," I manage, flinching at how harsh that sounded.

Liam blinks. "Right, we're still on that then." He clears his throat and glances at his watch.

"No, it's just—" A tiny fire flickers in my stomach, recalling Caroline telling me to *"aim a little lower, sweetheart,"* because of what *he did*. I shouldn't have to get over something currently wreaking havoc on my life, and I shouldn't feel guilty about my boundaries. "I don't understand how you expect me to trust you after everything."

"But Charlie gets a pass because . . ." Liam narrows a pointed gaze on my face.

"I'm not seriously asking Charlie either, okay? Does that smooth your damn ego?"

"Right, let's forget I offered." He stands, avoiding my eyes, and tosses his cup in the trash. "Thanks for putting up with my company, Peaches."

Pangs of guilt prick my chest, though I told them to quit it.

"Hey." I catch his wrist. "There's a pretty good crêperie at the other end of the square. I could treat you."

He stares blankly at my hand grasping his. Probably confused at my one-eighty. Hi, yes, let me bite your head off and then buy you crêpes because balance.

"Thanks, but I've bugged you enough today. Enjoy your crêpe in peace." He pulls away, flexing his hand at his side. The hint of something resembling hurt flashes briefly across his face, but it's gone as quickly as it appeared. "I'll send the cheese along with Eli tonight."

My face drops. "You aren't coming?"

He sighs, scrubbing a hand over his face. "I don't know, Evie. What do you want me to do?"

"I don't—" I stutter. Whatever is happening between us, this isn't the dynamic I'm used to, and it's weird. It's like an old nostalgic part of my life is back in a new, unfamiliar way, like a pair of Converse that doesn't fit right anymore. "I need some time to get used to you being here. I'm sorry."

"I get it. I'm sorry you needed one, but someone should have given you a heads-up. Look, I have a lot of work to catch up on anyway, so why don't I raincheck tonight, and I'll catch you another time, okay?"

"Yeah, right. Okay." I nod, trying not to crumble from the overwhelming guilt as his footsteps crunch further away.

"Mark my words, Evelina. Someday, this ugly habit of yours to hold a grudge will permanently damage your life."

I drag a cleansing breath through my lungs and commence sitting on a bench to think, take two.

That flash of *something* in Liam's eyes stays with me.

Maybe I need another cleansing breath.

Inhale. Exhale.

Better?

Nope.

Screw it. I need a cleansing crêpe.

5

Never-Ending Circles

WHEN I WAS SEVENTEEN, my mother, the always-extra human, decided she simply could not send me off to college without a proper presentation into society. Unfortunately for us both, our little backwoods town in Massachusetts didn't have an establishment that held such functions, so she, much to the chagrin of everyone, made one.

The town, and my classmates, have never recovered from the forced horror.

The night of the ball, she hugged my shoulders, beaming with pride as she inspected me through the reflection of a backstage mirror. I had found a white-bodiced dress with a sizeable poofy skirt and black brocade, reminiscent of the Givenchy dress Audrey Hepburn wore in *Sabrina*. A compromise of sorts. I'd play along if I could cosplay as Audrey for the night.

"You are absolutely gorgeous. Liam's going to die when he sees you." She pulled the strings on my bodice tight to allow for minimal breathing for the remainder of the evening while I applied a peach shade of lip gloss with shaking hands and smacked my lips together.

My mother, not giving homecoming a chance to replay itself, asked Liam herself to take me.

An agreement on his part seemed suspicious at first but over the last month of planning for the ball, Liam and I traded our sharp, cutting banter and fiery rivalry for sweet smiles and compliments that left me giddy. Dreaming of sunlight and full-body shimmers well into the night, I hoped our game would soon permanently end, and a new story would bloom in its place.

"I've never been prouder of you, sweetheart." My mother kissed my cheek and left to look over the other girls. I stared at my reflection, daydreaming about Liam's reaction to it all.

Would his jaw drop? His heart thud against his chest like mine did whenever he glanced my way? Did the same pesky butterflies cause him gastrointestinal distress whenever I was around? Or the jolts of electricity that shot up my arm when we touched, did they go both ways?

They had to, right?

People didn't feel this head-over-feet, stupid in love with no return.

That would be a cruel and bleak reality, and the gullible daydreamer I was still saw life through an old Hollywood lens, full of glamor and kisses, where everything turned out flawlessly in the end.

Except, Liam Kelly never actually came to escort me. I had forgotten my rules and let my guard down.

It was all one long, elaborate joke.

Me walking out on stage alone was the punchline.

My mother never forgave me. "*Obviously, you didn't do enough to keep his attention, or this never would have happened.*"

And I never let my guard down again, ignoring whatever pull I felt to the contrary.

Maria's glossy black heels clop over the polished white marble tiles of the bridal gown boutique as she rushes back and forth past prints of Degas's ballerinas in gilded frames. A crystal chandelier casts its light on Eli's slumped figure, the epitome of an unwilling participant hunched in a white wicker chair.

"I swear to god Elijah Ignatius Blythe, if you don't hold that phone upright—" snaps Clara "Clare" Williams, Holly's little sister and the third and final member of our high school brat pack. The phone, in Eli's distracted possession, has tilted downward at least twenty times in the last five minutes, and apparently, she's not standing for his mediocre FaceTiming skills any longer. "I'm never making another pie for you ever again."

"I like Evie's pie better anyway," he mutters, eyes glued to his own phone perched on his left knee, a lazy smile spreading wide across his face.

She gasps. "How dare you."

"Oh hush, you know my pies are fire," I tease. "But who are you texting, bud?" I smirk, assessing a blush-colored chiffon dress in the mirror, the fifth bridesmaid dress of the day. It's draped over my curvy figure somewhat flatteringly with a drawn waist, flutter sleeves, and a long flowing skirt. Overall, it's nothing remarkable. The color is on the wrong side of washing out my already porcelain skin. But it's comfortable and would hide any case of endo belly that will occur given the stressful circumstances.

The last thing I need is to overhear some distant relative asking my mother if I'm expecting . . . again.

"Unfortunately, no. Evelina would need to find a man first. And even then, there's little hope, bless her heart."

A sharp twinge tortures my left ovary—a quick stab and twist of a knife. I press in on that side and breathe, dropping my mask slightly.

One. Two.

It doesn't go away, but I have a life to live, so I can only devote two seconds of my sanity to caring. There's always a pain. Just some are more manageable than others.

I've had to learn to cope and surrender my energy reserves to ignoring them, since living life in the fetal position isn't an option long-term.

But now and again, the resolve fails, and I am acutely aware of my situation—the draining on my mental health falters, and I wear myself thin. Today is one of those days.

Eli ignores my question, pushing up the sleeves of the black sweater I made him change into earlier when he met Maria and me outside his apartment in flannel and a Boston Red Sox hat. The colorful ink on his right arm peeks through. My gaze narrows to the spot below his elbow where my name sits nestled among Patriots Super Bowl logos and shamrocks. I was joking when I suggested it, but Eli was drunk, and now a part of me lives on his arm forever.

He glances up from his phone, eyes traveling to the same spot mine have landed. "This is definitely one of those times I regret having that."

"Rude," I huff back. "And don't change the subject. Who are you texting with your goofy grin?"

Eli straightens with a sigh. "Fionn, actually." The edges of his ears prick red as a flush creeps across his face. I squeal. I took it as a good sign when Fionn asked to walk Eli home the other night from dinner, and he agreed, but not glued-to-the-phone-with-a-shy-smile good.

"Oh! Who's Fionn?" Clare shouts.

"He's my Irish, Hugh-Grant-look-a-like friend, with the fluffiest hair. And he's super nice. Oh my goodness, my heart is bursting." I bounce on my toes.

"Yes!" Clare perks up. "'Bout damn time, Ignatius."

"Yeah, you both need to seriously chill. Nothing's going to happen." He sighs, slouching in his chair with resignation.

"But why?" I whine.

"Because Liam and I go back to Mass in a month, and I'm not starting anything with a deadline."

"Oh pooh—screw the future." I wave him off.

A rare scowl forms on Eli's face.

"Come on, please." I fold my hands in hopeful prayer. "Have a little Paris romance with an Irishman that looks like Hugh Grant. What's the worst that could happen?"

"Yeah, Paris romance, Irish Hugh Grant!" Clare reinforces.

"I'm not having this discussion in a bridal shop." He tucks his phone into his pocket and stands, pointing my phone's camera at me and fulfilling his duty as the official FaceTimer for the first time in the past hour. "You like that one?"

"I don't know." I turn to the side and attempt to flatten my stomach. The endo belly is real. "What do you think, Clare?"

"Ignatius needs to trim his nose hairs. You turned the camera to face you again, bud."

"Oh, shit, sorry." He fumbles.

"Ah, much better," Clare says. "Oh, hmm. The cut is flattering, but I don't know about that color. I think Holly wanted a dustier rose. What does Maria think?"

"She's pulling some more dresses, but I like it. It hides the bloat and is pretty comfortable."

"Yes! That material is great for that. Holly and I also decided on chiffon dresses to hide the baby bumps a bit."

A large, strangled cough rattles Eli's six-foot frame.

I still. "I'm sorry, your what?"

"Oh, that reminds me. We're going to throw a dual baby/bridal shower for her, I know that's a little bizarre, but we wanted you there for both. When is your flight home?" Clare continues to prattle off questions, probably on some laminated checklist, oblivious that I'm learning there will be baby bumps to hide for the first time.

My heart hammers against my chest, pumping heat through my veins in a wild panic. Oh hell, why didn't I figure that out sooner? They went from engagement to a wedding date in three months, for heaven's sake.

"I—" I attempt to steady my erratic breathing as my airways constrict to a thin, barely navigable passage. Well, at least I'll test drive the panic attack features of this dress. "I haven't purchased my plane ticket yet."

"Oh, well, no worries then. Let me know when you do so I can send out those invitations."

"Yeah, of course."

"Speaking of, do you want your name on the invites too? Like should we both host the shower?"

"Uhm." Placing my hands on the back of my head, I pace the length of the platform, attempting to give my lungs the space to breathe.

Eli lowers the phone.

"What am I saying? I'm sorry," Clare continues, I assume catching on. "Of course you'll host it with me. We can talk theme later—" *Or not.* "But actually, Paris is perfect. It works for a bridal shower and a baby shower. Maybe you could grab some souvenirs for decorations and prizes? I swear to god, Ignatius, keep it on her beautiful face."

I could speak up, but causing more of a scene in this public space while entirely overwhelmed and wheezing doesn't exactly appeal to me.

"Sorry, my arm's tired." He offers me a lopsided smile, and the usual shimmer in his bright green eyes slowly fades.

Maria marches in, arms full of dresses. "I found some more—oh, dear, what happened here?"

"Found the dress, I think," I choke out, forcing an unnatural upward curve of my lips.

Eli clears his throat. "Oh, shoot. Clare? Evie's battery is wicked low. I'll have to let you go."

"Is everything okay? What's going on?"

"Everything's fine. The little shit doesn't charge her phone. Really going to die—bye." He hangs up, handing me the phone.

"Clare's pregnant?" I manage through warring emotions.

"Ugh, yeah, she is."

"And Holly too?"

"Yeah." He sighs, rubbing the back of his head. "Clare was first, but Holly and Caleb apparently liked the idea of having a cousin their age."

"Oh. Shit." Maria gasps. "Well, alright, let's get you out of here. We can come back another day."

I drag another breath through my lungs.

"And everyone knew?"

"No, not everyone." Eli shakes his head. "They still haven't told your mom because they're worried how her response will affect you."

"Why didn't Caleb tell me?"

"I don't know—he was supposed to while we were here so we—I—could support you."

Maria loosens my zipper, allowing oxygen to return with the expanded space. A heavy weariness bears down on my legs, and I sit on the platform's ledge, resting my head in my hands.

"It's okay, dear. Deep breaths."

"Caroline's going to be insufferable."

"I know, but you're not going there for her. You're going there for your brother. And Holly. You love Holly."

I do. And this is ridiculously exciting news. My brother and his future wife, and somebody else I care deeply for are all starting huge, wonderful chapters in their lives. And I am so very happy for them.

Or I will be. Once the shock of the news wears off.

First, I get to be the loser having a panic attack because this is my life. That's part of the curse. Even the happiest news gets tainted.

Of course, after the panic attack, I will spiral further down the self-pity rabbit hole and feel terrible that I'm a selfish ass who wallows when someone else has the best news ever, and everyone has to handle me with kid gloves because I'm not well-adjusted like adults should be. And then I will have to allow for some time to grapple with the overwhelming thought that this is it for me, none of this ends. None of this gets easier. I just have to get tougher.

Hell, I am so tired of having to be tougher.

But then I'll be happy for all parties involved. Really.

"Hey." A little kick to my foot from Eli pauses the spiral. "Let's get out of here and grab some ice cream or something. Didn't you tell me the Ben and Jerry's was somehow better over here?"

"Oh. Yup. The wine's cheap too." I gather myself, standing.

"You want me to take this dress to the counter and check out?" Maria asks, dragging the zipper the rest of the way open.

I worry my lip, wiping at the tears collecting under my eyes. I need heavier armor if I'm going to survive my mother now.

"Let's try a few more. Maybe we can find something chicer." I hold my chin up. I'm sure that confident pre-shattered debutante is in there somewhere—and hell, I'll need all the fake confidence I can get.

The brass tones of the "Imperial March" flood my apartment, a sense of dread settling in me. I take another swig of my five-euro bottle of wine and rip off a hunk of a freshly baked baguette—the only pain I care to experience. An empty carcass of a Ben and Jerry's pint keeps me company since I pushed Maria and Eli out of the apartment to visit Declan and Fionn with a convincing *"Will you please go? I'm fine."*

Two text messages from Caroline populate on my phone. Not the salt in the wound I need right now.

I take another swig. Fine was a bit of an exaggeration, but it is my mess to deal with. I'm not going to let my pity party affect those around me.

Another text notification from her appears.

Screw it. Rip the Band-Aid off and read them.

CAROLINE: Tyler Higgins regretfully must do a load of laundry on the day of the wedding.

CAROLINE: And Charlie Bennet is married. Though I don't remember seeing an announcement in the newspaper, so I don't know how valid that excuse is.

CAROLINE: Going to ask at book club if anyone knows any proper suitors for you.

Excellent, I can hear the sales pitch now. *"Do any of you have a son desperate enough to overlook the glaring issues with my daughter? I need someone to take her to a wedding so she doesn't disgrace the family name with her perceived spinsterhood."*

Who am I kidding? There's no sales pitch. She's the one offering payment right now.

My fingers itch over the buttons. I will need something to distract Caroline with when my high school best friend announces she's expecting. You'd think older brother announcing their first grandchild would do the trick, but knowing my mother's disposition, it's going to make it worse. Just two examples of people succeeding in the only parts of life that have ever mattered to her when I'm practically drowning in failure.

But a *suitor*, if I could have part of the equation, maybe that'd neutralize the stench of disappointment enough to placate Caroline. It'd be worth a shot, anyway, right? It's probably the half bottle of wine I've already consumed talking, but saying something along those lines sounds brilliant. I close my eyes, breathe twice, pop them open, and text.

ME: Thanks so much for thinking of me, but you know, I actually found my own date.

You're the worst.

ME: Love you!

Self-advocation. Not my personal strong suit.

CAROLINE: Over six feet?

Oh gosh, the way this doesn't actually matter to me.

ME: Yes. He fits the list. Solid marriage material!

Way to have a spine, Evie. Really, well done.

CAROLINE: Well, quit teasing me, hunny. Who is it?

A figment of my imagination! We'll get along smashingly well.

I take another swig of the wine, but the bottle is bone dry. Oh. So half a bottle was a bit of an underestimate then.

ME: I want to keep him a secret a little longer, but you'll find out soon.

CAROLINE: Looking forward to it. So proud of you.

Well, at least one of us is.

Son of a biscuit, the pit in my stomach expands. The immediate satisfaction my little falsehood provided gives way to the consequences of the impulse.

I do, actually, have to find a date.

And after the whole debutante fiasco, there's minimal chance of weaseling out of this with an *"Oh, he couldn't come."*

Unfortunately, no one's really coming to mind for a solid stand-in.

Clare might know someone, though. Maybe I should call her.

Thumb hovering over the call button, I take a deep breath and press. "Evie, Evie twice in one day," she sings after two rings, brightening my melancholy mood. "What's up, princess? You get the plane tickets?"

"Oh—no." I wallowed in self-pity instead. "But I will. When I'm less . . . cloudy. I actually need help."

"Okay, shoot."

"Who do we know that fits Caroline's Suitors for Evie List and would be willing to go on a date to the wedding with me?"

"No offense, but isn't that list like, tall and breathes at this point?"

"You make solid points." The list had dwindled significantly over the past five or so years.

"I thought Liam was supposed to ask you."

I sputter. He was *supposed* to? As in his invitation at the park was pre-meditated and not a spur-of-the-moment thing?

Doesn't matter. I shake my head, my mind churning like a kaleidoscope through the various implications of Clare's word choice. Who am I kidding? Caleb is probably behind this, too. Best not to read too into it. "Yes, and I'm sure he would have followed through with the arrangement too."

"Oh hush, that was, what, nine years ago? And I still contend something happened."

"He told me it was all a giant practical joke."

"Yeah, after you made it pretty clear what you thought of him. The poor boy was probably saving face."

"Unlikely."

"Ugh," she grunts. "You and Ignatius are the worst. You deserve each other."

"Harsh." I laugh. "And I'm totally not as bad as him. I'm not worried about getting attached; I'm worried I'll get screwed."

"From what I've heard, you may find that very enjoyable coming from him."

"Unless he has a magic penis, that's doubtful considering my situation." I shift on the couch, wincing as the words leave my mouth, my filter all but eradicated courtesy of the cheap bottle of wine I apparently inhaled. "And there's already enough people who think there's a link etween having sex with demons and my disease. Best not to add to their ammo." An uneasy chuckle rattles my chest as a similarly awkward one sounds through the speaker. Making any situation impossibly uncomfortable when I don't want to dwell on my inadequacies is a particular skill of mine.

"I still can't believe that bullshit theory exists."

"Some dude did a whole study on if people with endometriosis were scientifically more attractive than people without, instead of working on understanding the disease or finding a cure for it, so I mean, sure. Why not have some medical professionals floating demon sex theories too."

Clare sighs. "I'm sorry, boo. If I could toss a bucket of water and melt them all, I would."

"Your willingness to go all Dorothy on their ass is noted and appreciated." I snort.

"Good. But in all seriousness, Evie. If Liam asks you to the wedding, promise me you won't get all defensive and you'll at least consider it."

"He already did," I mumble.

"I'm sorry, what was that?"

"He already asked me."

"And we're having this conversation because . . ."

"I don't know." I groan, stretching my feet out wide on the couch. "It won't work with him. My mom needs to feel like there's a chance it could become more to satisfy her, and it'd be rather obvious Liam's escorting me out of obligation." Especially after she made her feelings on the plausibility of this situation ever occurring crystal clear in our previous conversation.

"Play it up, make her believe your dynamic has changed. You're in the City of Love with him for a month, for Pete's sake. It's realistic! He's objectively gorgeous, played college football, he's super nice—"

"Is he, though?"

"Yes, yes, he is. I'm sorry to break it to you, but years of my sister dating your brother and his best friend have only solidified my you're holding a weird grudge over nothing stance."

"My grudge is totally valid, but let's say I'm entertaining the idea—who else could we throw in for options?"

"I love you. You're a freakin' catch, but honestly, no one. Everyone's still terrified of your mom after that debutante fiasco and the weird ad she took out a few years ago."

"Hell." I rub my temple with my forefinger. "I had almost scrubbed that damn ad from my memory." Two years ago, an avalanche of direct messages from random guys in town offering me less than gentlemanly services had me scrambling for a culprit. For a brief second, I thought Liam may have landed the ultimate prank, but it seems Caroline and her inability to handle me turning twenty-five without a relationship resulted in the weirdest birthday newspaper announcement in existence. I was fortunate newspapers were a dying medium, even then.

"It was an excellent picture of you." Clare unhelpfully supplies.

"It should have been. It was photoshopped." I bitterly laugh. "But you're right, I won't even be able to get a mercy date with anyone after that."

"Evie. Ask. Liam. Or tell him you changed your mind, whatever, but he's the answer to your problems here. He loves your family and knows what he's getting into, and you can sell it. End of discussion."

"You're bossy today, mama." I giggle. Oh, that was a lot of wine.

A tense silence pulls our lines taut. I've called Clare "mama" countless times, but today it's awkward.

"I'm really happy for you, you know that, right? I didn't say that earlier, but I'm going to spoil the shit out of that baby."

"I know. I'm sorry, Eli texted me after. I didn't know Caleb hadn't told you yet, and I was in the planning zone. That was such a shitty way to find out."

"We handled it." I sigh, twirling the bottle.

"You're okay?"

"Yeah, fine, promise."

The low voice of Clare's husband, Josh, rumbles in the background.

"Oh, I gotta let you go, but seriously. Liam—make it work."

"I'll think on it." I hesitate. "Love you."

"Eee. Love you too. See you sooooooooon," she sings before hanging up.

I hug my trusty heating pad to my crampy mid-section before slinking off the couch, reluctantly leaving my heated solace behind.

The pain from earlier never quite took the hint that I had enough to spiral over without its nagging presence—the freakin' audacity.

Groaning, I enter my bedroom. It's so damn messy. Books are scattered over every flat surface: my bureau, my nightstand, and my tiny desk that, in theory, is for working on the blog, but in practice, has become a flat surface to hold all the things. My clothes are flung haphazardly on top of the books, on the floor, anywhere that isn't my closet or bureau. I pluck a pair of black leggings dangling for dear life off a side of the desk and a long white button-up tunic nearby.

The minor scars on my abdomen from what should have been a "You might have endo" exploratory surgery, but quickly turned into, "Oh shit, you have way more crap going on down there than expected" surgery are fading a bit, which is appreciated. They're tiny. Minimal in size—but in reality, they're huge. They're validation.

One moment changes everything. Validates everything. Doctors who have told you your whole life you're mentally unstable or have a low pain tolerance, that it's just painful periods (that one's hard to swallow when you're very aware it happens almost every day) suddenly tell you you're one in ten, ushering you into a forced kinship nobody wants to be a part of.

Endo warrior. That's the nickname they give us. Sure, I would prefer a cure, but there's no time for that when you have an erectile dysfunction crisis looming. Stodgy old cis men must be able to get it up at all costs!

It always devolves into an erectile dysfunction rant, doesn't it? That's part of the experience: that you have a soul-crushing ailment and the research on it is minimal and the journey to diagnosis is degrading and doctors are typically assholes to you. And you have to keep on keeping on until you find the Unicorn Doctor, Magic Vagina Fairy, whatever name you prefer, who believes you and wants to help you get better and fights for you.

And for many endo warriors, that means years and years of journeying first.

Tossing my jacket on, I text Eli.

ME: Is Liam home?

ELI: Yeah, he should be—what's up, little shit?

ME: I need to talk to him about something, and I'm in the area.

ELI: Please don't murder him.

ME: Going to try my best not to. Hope you're having fun with Fionn!

Two ballet flats and a brief tipsy wobble later, I'm out the door. I can do this.

Eli and Liam's apartment is a fifty-minute walk from mine, which is precisely what I need. Time. Because I'm about to humiliate myself, and I'd like to spend a little more time with my pride before handing it over in a crumpled heap to Liam.

I haven't seen him in the three days since the bench incident. He didn't come to dinner, which I mean, he said he was busy, so I'm probably reading way too much into it. No way a little snide comment on my part affected him, right? I don't know. I tried to compose a text apologizing, but it didn't come out right, so I stopped trying and ate things instead.

By the time I hit Pont de la Concorde, I'm seriously regretting my decision to walk. One, because I'm tired and in pain and exercise doesn't give me the endorphins it used to, I swear.

And two—because, tut, tut. It looks like rain.

I hurry my steps, but I maybe take a solid five more before the clouds open up and downpour all over my hopes and dreams. I jog the rest of the way to Liam's apartment, thoroughly soaked and cursing the gods of chaos for what feels like the thousandth time this week. Climbing up the five flights of stairs, I attempt to gather my thoughts, but I am so thoroughly flustered from the cold rain, and honestly still tipsy, that I don't know what I'm going to say.

Taking a collecting breath before knocking, I resign myself to say whatever comes to me in the moment. That always works out well.

Footsteps pound on the other side.

Locks turn.

A barefooted Liam Kelly opens the door. Gray sweatpants hang low on his hips. I don't want to look higher; from what I gather out of my peripheral vision it spells doom. But I very well can't stare at his pants either. Swallowing back my nerves, I bring my gaze up, over the sleek lines of an Adonis V winking at me from above his waistband. In an instant, my ovaries commandeer Operation Look at Liam's Face, and my eyes travel at an agonizingly slow speed up the rest of his bare chest. Deep shadows highlight his taut obliques and hard, tanned abdominal muscles in the low hallway lighting—like we're in an outtake for some ridiculous action movie about Sparta.

I want to yell at the white T-shirt hung futilely over his shoulder.

You have one job!

But all words have dried up on my tongue.

"Evie?" A jet-black stare meets mine, threatening to devour me whole before his gaze slowly rakes down the length of my body, erasing any coherent thought I have in the process.

"I need you," I blurt.

Liam blinks. Once. Twice.

And then promptly shuts the door in my face.

6

Hole in my Heart

"SERIOUSLY?" I SHOUT, STARING at a wooden knot on the heavy antique door that was just mercilessly slammed in my face. After navigating a quiet life on the Seine for the past six years, strategically avoiding any of the drama I left behind, the avalanche of nostalgic turmoil in the past week threatens to bury me alive.

My brain is shouting *For the love of God, woman, leave.*

But it is no longer in control. The connection to the rational part of my mind snapped along with my last shred of hope, with the slamming of that door, leaving behind unfiltered access to the chaos gremlin housing a daily talk show in my brain.

Talk Soup with Gremmy, Live—In today's episode, Evie officially broke and is in the worst place possible for it to all go down.

"Why don't you give him a chance, Evie?" I say, imitating Clare's sweet innocent tone out loud to no one in particular.

"I don't know, Clare, maybe because I've been screwed over one too many times."

"I think screwing Liam Kelly sounds nice. Maybe you should give it a try, Evie."

"Uhm. No thanks, I'm sure he's very selfish in bed, so I think I'll pass."

"Oh, whatever would make your silly little head think that?"

"Great question, Clare. Well, this slammed door in my face is a great example. Would you like me to elaborate further?"

A click and turn of the doorknob followed by the whoosh of the door sliding open straightens my spine.

Liam peers down at me. A muscle in his jaw flicks angrily before setting tight.

"You know, call me old-fashioned, but for whatever reason, you having a fake conversation on my stoop where you insult my bedroom habits isn't the charming conversation starter you think it is."

Heat rushes from the base of my neck to my cheeks as reality comes crashing back over me in an unyielding tidal wave. I step back. I just—*shit*—did I word vomit all of that?

If he wasn't already, I'm sure he's very intimidated by how successful and together I've become.

He leans casually against the threshold of his apartment, studying a speck of dirt under his nails like he's already lost interest in this conversation. "Although, you're welcome to come in for a demonstration of how unselfish I can be," he says, nonchalantly tossing the invitation into the void between us.

Unfortunately, my body hasn't gotten the *he-doesn't-mean-it* memo. Want gathers deep in the pit of my stomach, and heat stains my cheeks at the images his throw-away comment inspires.

With Herculean effort, I force my jaw out of its gaping position and manage, "It's not a stoop."

He picks his gaze up with a raised brow. "What?"

Oh. Dammit. The stoop route was a bold strategy.

"You said I had a fake conversation on your stoop, but a stoop implies stairs and a platform."

"Yes, Peaches, and what did you use to get up here?" he asks in a slow, deliberate manner like he's interacting with a child, although I guess I did just act like one, so fair.

"Outside. I feel like stoops have to be outside." At this point, I'm grasping at straws, but arguing about stoops is better than acknowledging the word vomit from hell I just spewed, or the fact that Liam is now leaning in a doorjamb shirtless, arms crossed, muscles flexed, like he's some smug movie star who knows he gets the girl in the end. Le nope, not dealing with that mess.

He massages the bridge of his nose. "Evie, what do you want?"

Oh. Okay. Old Liam would have let the argument go a bit.

"Clare had this suggestion—well, multiple suggestions—but—" Yeah. No. I can't—I can't be here with him looking like that while I'm untethered. "It doesn't matter anymore. I give up." I sigh, shuffling back to the spiral staircase I barely conquered on my ascent, dust kicking up around my feet.

"Where are you going?" he asks, straightening his stance.

"Home. Away. I don't know. But not here." *It never should have been here.* I grab the banister with both hands, forcing a step down as the pain in my abdomen radiates past the crook of my inner thigh and shoots down my leg into my calf. I plant my left leg on a lower step, and a strong tremor works its tendrils through while I transfer my weight on it. A sharp intake rattles my teeth, bringing my right foot down to the next step, and I twist my face into a neutral, pain-free expression.

"You said you needed me."

"Yes, and your response was to shut the door in my face, so clearly that was a mistake."

"I didn't—"

"Don't even try to convince me that isn't what happened."

"I needed a second."

"Why?" I stop, humoring him.

His bored stare drops as he motions to my shirt with wild eyes. A string of consonants emits from his lips like somehow he's equally tortured right now.

Glancing down, an internal light bulb sheds some illumination—however dimly—on the situation. My white shirt is plastered to my skin, the black bra underneath fully visible, breasts spilling over because it's one of those days. And apparently in my tipsy state, I didn't even bother to button it up the whole way before I left.

My fingers tremble trying to fasten the neglected buttons. "I'm sorry, I—uhm—yeah, nobody wants to see that."

"That's not the problem." Liam groans, digging the palms of his hands into his eyes like he's trying to unsee everything.

"Forget it. This was easily the stupidest idea in the history of ideas anyway." I shake my head and take another step.

"So you're just going to leave, then?" I swear there's a half second where this anxious energy flickers across Liam's features, but I don't know. I'm not in the right head space to overanalyze his facial expressions.

"That is a thing I'm going to do, yes," I huff, descending a few more. *Shit, that smarts.*

"Evie." He picks his lean up off the door. "How are you planning on walking home if you can't manage the stairs right now?"

I wave him off. "It's fine, I've walked home in worse shape." Would sitting and resting be super helpful? Sure, but I'll do whatever it takes to exit this situation quickly. "I'm sorry to have bothered you. There's a lot going on right now, and I'm obviously not thinking."

Liam clasps the edge of the railing, locking his elbows as he leans over it, his dark brows slanted into a frown. "I'm sorry about how you found out about Clare and Holly." The gentle apologetic tone halts my retreat. "I wanted him to tell you a month ago, but you know Caleb, he was worried and thought it'd be better if you had more support around you."

"You've known for a month?" My voice breaks.

"A little longer than that, but yeah." He releases the tension in his corded muscles, resting his forearms on the railing and peering down at my face. "Truly, Evie, I'm really sorry. That was a shit thing to hide."

"I could have handled it."

"Oh, I know." I glance at him still hanging over the banister, a crooked smile quirking his lips, his left dimple imprinting his cheek. "If anyone else saw this side of you, I'm sure they'd realize you're tougher than they give you credit for."

A sharp stab and twist of the knife almost doubles me over. I crunch, ever so slightly wincing while still maintaining the mask I've trained myself to use to keep the miserable feelings subtle. Either people care too much about your pain and you have to endure false pity while they tell you you're strong, a warrior, and handling things with grace, unconsciously heaping pressure to maintain composure to meet their expectations, or they think you have a low tolerance and need you to quiet your drama queen tendencies.

Either reaction gets old real fast, and both recenter and detract from the validity of my own pain. Sometimes I want the freedom to be and not be strong or a warrior, and I sure as hell don't want to be graceful.

Liam's brow furrows. "Come inside, Peaches."

"I'm fine." I dismiss him with a wave of my hand. "Your concern here is not needed."

"Glad to hear it. But seriously, get your stubborn ass into the apartment so we can talk about whatever it is you do need."

I press down on the pain radiating to my side. "Don't suppose there's a chance you two have any tea, do you?"

Liam mercifully pulls his shirt on, sheathing his rippling muscles and providing me with some much-needed cloud cover. "We do, actually. You can teach me how to use the electric kettle the apartment came with?"

I nod, pivoting back up the stairs. My knee buckles with the movement, the spasming muscles not appreciating the sudden twisting motion. I stumble backward. My foot misses the edge of the stair, and I
collapse onto a landing. The fall breaks whatever spirit I have left, and
I scrunch up against the wall as a giant uncontrollable sob floods out of
me.

Everything is one big giant clusterfuck, and I'm using too much of my
energy controlling my pain to handle any of this.

"Shit, O'Shea. You okay?" Soft steps pad down the stairs.

A deep heaviness turns my limbs to lead and I bury my head in my
hands. "Just leave me alone. I'm fine."

Liam sighs, and a warm, firm hand grips under my legs as a strong
arm gathers my back and lifts me up off the ground. I wrap my hand
around his neck, burying my head into his chest. My pride is thoroughly
decimated anyway.

"It's okay. Let it out. I've got you."

"Oh god, I must look awful if you're being this nice to me."

There's a stilted breath from him before he responds, "Not any more
so than usual."

"Jerkface."

"Pain in my ass," he whispers into my neck, a smile lacing his words.

"I'm the pain in the ass?" I hiccup. "Seriously? You're so firmly lodged
up there."

"You thought I was a ray of sunshine last week."

I snort, the sobs quieting to a trickle. "I plead head wound."

"Speaking of which." He pads up another step. "I know you get all
weak-kneed when you're around me, Peaches, but I'd appreciate it if you
could quit falling all the time. I have fragile nerves."

I lift my head and peer at him. "And I'm affecting them?"

"You are. I was a nervous wreck after you ran into that pole."

"Oh, poor baby, that must have been harrowing for you."

"Traumatic. So if you could get your shit together, that'd be great."

A weird mix of laughter and crying shakes my chest. "I'm sorry, I can't help it. The will to live just leaves my body when you're around."

He pushes the door wide with his foot. "Is that so?"

"Mm-hmm. Absolute soul sucker." The tremors slow as a soft giggle bubbles out of me. I bury into his neck. Sandalwood enters my bloodstream and sends shockwaves spiraling through my body.

"You're awfully cheeky for somebody in such a vulnerable position." He fumbles with his grasp, and I shriek.

"You wouldn't drop me."

"Oh no?" He wiggles his brow, tightening his grip, and the placement of his hand on the back of my thigh sears into my skin. "That almost sounds like you trust me."

"To not be one hundred percent a shitty person. Yes. I trust you that much."

Liam traipses along the original chevron wood flooring down a long white hallway adorned with Haussmannian molding before turning left into a living room with a charcoal couch.

"I feel like that's progress." He flashes a lopsided smile at me, hovering over the couch. His eyes flicker to my mouth. I swallow, my breath matching the slightly elevated rhythm of his, while a flutter in my stomach mixes among the general, painful chaos down there.

He clears his throat, eyes widening, before placing me gently on a sofa cushion. "You want me to call Eli?"

I shake my head. "Thank you, but he's out with Fionn, and I don't want to ruin that. I'm fine. Promise."

He scratches at the scruff on his cheek and nods. "I'll go get you some dry clothes. The kitchen's back there." He motions behind me before trudging into an adjacent room.

"Clothes? Oh no. Seriously, I just need to talk to you quickly, maybe drink some tea, and then I'll be on my way. No need to fuss."

"You have to be freezing in those," he yells from his room.

"Oh, I'm fine. Really." I allow a shiver to pass while he's out of sight.

Liam sighs, peeking his head out from his bedroom. "Peaches, if you want to have this conversation, have a little mercy on me, please." His eyes stay pinned on my face like he doesn't dare put them anywhere else.

If I had a modicum of self-confidence left, I could see how some would interpret the anguished expression on his face as a man desperate for relief of some kind, but I've done this dance long enough with him to know he probably just doesn't want Caleb's little sister's unmentionables prominently displayed in his apartment.

I nod, as a full-bodied shiver I can no longer hide takes possession of my body.

He smirks, shaking his head. "Fine my ass. Put these on," he says, tossing a bundle of clothes my way.

I hold up the long sleeve shirt—it's from his time playing football at Alabama State, "Kelly" printed on the sleeve. "Are you kidding me?" I bust out laughing.

"Yes. Well, no. I don't have a lot of options, but I can't say I won't thoroughly enjoy winning this one."

I groan, dragging my spasming body off his couch. A modern kitchen sits behind me with white marble countertops and a professional stove. The pilot lights flicker with temptation. I could do some serious damage baking in here. "I thought I was supposed to do the winning now."

"Oh no, that offer's only good for my wedding dates."

I snort to myself, filling the kettle with water. "So, funny story—" I start, turning to put the kettle back on its base. I jump at Liam's figure hovering over my shoulder. "What are you doing?"

"You were going to teach me how to use that."

"Oh, right."

I step around him, settling the kettle onto the base, and wait for the satisfying click. A simple "on" and "off" switch sits at the bottom.

Wonder Boy couldn't have figured this out on his own? I peek at him. His face earnestly rests on mine. I pivot back around, a little befuddled by this whole thing, and flick the switch. "Voila." I make a big show with my hands.

"Right." He blushes, and his eyes fall on the clothes he handed me. "Why don't you use the bathroom in my bedroom? I can't guarantee Eli's is clean."

"Thank you." I glance up at him, moistening my dry lips. His lips part slightly as if in response before he dips his head and steps aside.

"How do I know when it's done?" he hollers as I saunter away.

"It literally turns itself off."

"Huh." He laughs to himself. "You're kind of useful, buddy."

"Are you talking to the kettle?" I enter his bedroom.

"Just letting off some steam, don't mind me."

"Oh man, how long have you had that one brewing?"

"Not long. Puns are kind of my cup of tea."

I pause. Crap. "You win."

"Aww, I had a few more to spout off."

"I'm not humoring your punning problem anymore," I shout.

"Well, isn't a certain pot calling the kettle black?"

"Consider this slammed door my response." I smile, shutting the bathroom door behind me.

Like the kitchen, Liam's bathroom is modern, with slate gray tiles lining the back wall and a tall glass standing shower flush against it. A large frameless mirror hangs over a square sink. I step toward it, preparing myself for the worst.

A figure vaguely resembling Amy Adams in a punk rock phase stares back at me in the mirror. Shit. I brush the hair sticking to my ashen face off my cheek and turn the knobs on the faucet to wash off the raccooning under my blood-red eyes. So much for the waterproof mascara.

After a thorough scrub, I pull on the oversized flannel pajama pants he gave me and the long sleeve shirt, laughing at myself in the mirror. Girls used to make shirts with Liam's name on them, but he always offered me this one, saying "his girl" deserved something official.

"I'd have to lose something pretty terrible to wear that shit," I'd say with a death glare, determined to suppress any butterflies that may have felt alternatively. If Liam knew how dangerously close I was to the edge even after everything—to the line between hating or loving someone with every passionate fiber of my being, I could only imagine how he would have manipulated the situation and strung me along to his advantage again.

Hand resting on the bathroom handle, I take a moment to breathe. Once I bring up the subject of pretending to date, there won't be a "going back." And the border between the land of love and hate I've so painstakingly maintained will all but blur from my perspective.

But Caleb deserves peace at his wedding, and I can't give that to him like this.

So long dignity, I think, slipping back into the living room.

Liam's knee bounces as I approach him already sitting on the couch. My steaming cup of tea rests on a large glass coffee table nearby.

"I didn't freak you out, did I?" I pull at the hem of the shirt.

He shakes his head. "Just the normal amount."

"Well, that's good anyway." I pause and sit down on the other end of the couch, picking up my tea. "Thanks for this."

Liam's focus stays heavy on me as I prolong the inevitable. "So, what did you want to talk about?"

"Oh. Right. Well . . ." I inhale the steam and breathe. "So this is going to sound—well, to be honest, I don't know how it's going to sound to you, but due to recent developments regarding Caleb's wedding, I may require some assistance."

"And this would be—"

"I need a date for the wedding."

He crosses his arms, his grim mouth twisting into a wry smile. "I thought you were going with Tyler Higgins."

"He, unfortunately, has an inflexible laundry schedule and cannot be bothered."

A crease forms between Liam's eyebrows.

"I don't know." I huff. "Obviously, he didn't want to take me."

"Why do you suddenly trust me to take you?"

I pick at some fuzz on my lap and shrug.

He snorts, shaking his head. "You don't. You're just desperate."

"Basically." I shift.

He surveys my face, searching for what I don't know, but the heavy attention is unnerving, and I fidget some more. "Yeah, fine, I'll take you. But that's not what got you so worked up, is it?"

"There's a little more—" I buy myself some time with a sip of tea. "It would be helpful to have something drawing my mother's focus away from certain aspects of my life. And Clare had this idea—I don't know, it feels kind of weird to ask—but wouldyoupretendtodatemewhilewere-inthestates."

Liam's brow furrows deeper. "You're going to have to use actual pauses between words if you want me to understand you."

"This is hard!" I moan, pushing him with my foot.

He snatches it before I can do any damage, bringing it to his lap. "Take a deep breath and start again." His thumb rubs firm circles into the sole of my foot.

I close my eyes. A low hum vibrates my chest. Gosh, that feels good, that feels—my eyes snap open. "What are you doing?"

"I'm trying to get you to relax." He rubs a thumb over the inside of my arch, and I bite down the tiny moan threatening to pass over my lips at the relief it provides.

"Since when has that been a concern of yours?"

His jaw sets tight when he picks his gaze up to meet mine. "You want me to stop?"

No. Please don't.

I shake my head.

"Thought so." His mouth twitches and he gestures for me to raise my other foot to his lap. "Why are you here, Peaches?"

"Oh, yeah, that." My teeth graze over my bottom lip. Melting into the couch, an alarming warmth begins pooling in the pit of my stomach. "Clare thought if we came back with some story about Paris being a great place to reconnect and we fooled people into thinking we were sort of dating, that it would balance out my mom's hysterics on certain subjects enough for me to get through the wedding with my sanity relatively intact."

The circles slow. Liam eyes me suspiciously. "You really think your mom will be that bad about everything that you're willing to torture yourself over it?"

"I do. Like I've told you plenty of times, she's very different with you than she is with me."

"What's your idea of sort of dating?"

"Honestly, whatever you're comfortable with. If you want to just go as my date to the wedding, that's fine, but the more involved and into each other we appear to be while I'm there, the better. We can fake a breakup once I'm back in Paris—long distances not being manageable, etc. And I can deal with her ire from afar like I have been." A big yawn passes through me. I'm oddly relaxed for how weird this conversation is. "Shit, your hands are magic."

"You should see what else they can do," he says in a low, husky register that has gooseflesh pebbling my skin in an instant.

The comment takes me by surprise mid-swallow, and I choke on a minuscule sip of tea. A spasm of coughs rattles my chest while I try to regain control, embarrassed by how overdramatic this entire display is for such a tiny comment. A strong hand raps my back. The warmth of his side hits mine, and I jump at the fluttery sensation it provides.

He sighs. "You're not thinking this through, Peaches."

"I have though, I swear." I heave in a few breaths, finally returning to a somewhat composed demeanor. Composed for me, anyway.

"I will have to actually flirt with you without you breaking into a coughing fit for this to work."

"I can handle it."

"You almost murdered me the other day because I ate a sandwich with a fork."

"If you don't see the problem with that, I don't know what to tell you."

Another yawn stretches through my body.

"Tell you what—watch a movie with me, think it through some more, and we can talk about it after, okay?"

I nod. He pulls the blanket down over the couch and boots up the TV.

"Hepburn or Kelly?" He smiles.

"Mm, you pick," I hum, gathering the blanket tight to my chest. My eyes are weary with sleep, but I'm confident they'll perk up once the movie starts. "But not—"

"I know, I know." He puts his hand out to stop me, scrolling through the options on whatever streaming service he's on. "Never *Roman Holiday*. I'll never understand why you hate that movie."

"Okay, first off, hate is too strong a word to describe my feelings towards anything Audrey Hepburn. I love ninety-eight percent of that movie, in fact. I dislike the ending because I'm a happily ever after or get the fuck out kind of gal with my fiction."

I'll never forget the one and only time I watched Gregory Peck walk down the long hallway, heart racing. I kept peeking at Nana. *"She's going to run down the hallway, right? Any minute now, she's going to come."* But she never did, and no one holds a grudge formed at the age of seven quite like me.

Liam arches a brow while he's scrolling. "And you don't think *Roman Holiday* has a happy ending?"

"No. The formula is simple and infallible. Does the couple end up together?"

"Well, no—but her speech about always cherishing her visit to Rome, that's a happyish ending."

"That's an unsatisfying ending; that's what that is. How would you like it if you ran around a city with someone, fell in love, and then all you had was a memory to look back on? No fight, no reason you couldn't be together besides circumstance or duty or some other stupid thing like that. Love's supposed to conquer all! Even the monarchy!"

Liam draws his lips together thoughtfully. "I don't know. I think going about your life knowing someone loves you and living off that one perfect memory seems good enough."

"In real life I could accept that, maybe. But a movie? When there's a chance to control the outcome? I'm not settling for good enough." I shake my head. "Life sucks hard most of the time. Let me escape into a promised land where everything works out in the end."

Liam cocks his head, studying me.

"What?" I squirm.

"Nothing. I'm just not used to you sounding like me. That's all."

"Oh, I'm sorry, I think you're mistaken because I didn't hear an ounce of unfounded arrogance in my voice." I flutter my eyelashes, and he snorts.

"'Kay, smartass. All I meant is that the Evie O'Shea I knew thought life was this grand magical adventure, fully equipped with sparkles and rainbows, and that sounded more like something the brooding, life-is-pointless boy next door would say." He presses play on the screen.

"Oh." I shift in my seat, unsure if Liam's disappointed I think like this now or if that even matters. "Consider it another win to add to your victory column, then, I guess."

"That's not something I wanted to win," he mumbles, the beginning score to *Singin' in the Rain* drowning out most of his soft reply. My eyelids flicker shut as the opening music lulls me close to sleep, but I fight the pull to dreamland. If I let my head drop, I'll likely land on Liam's lap the way I'm leaning.

"Let yourself fall, Peaches. It's okay. I'll catch you," he says with an unfamiliar softness.

And against my better judgment and all my instincts screaming otherwise, I relent to the softness and give in to the lean, for now.

7

Sugar Pie Honey Buns

"WHY WON'T YOU GIVE in and admit I've won, Peaches? Aren't you tired of the chase?"

Liam's breath falls hot against my ear and lights a fire deep in the pit of my stomach.

"Do you honestly think you can make it through all this without me figuring out the truth?" His body hovers above me, his right hand fisting the sheet by my head. A finger grazes my abdomen, and I shiver under the trail it leaves, fumbling for words. I try to open my mouth, but the three-word phrase that dances on the tip of my tongue isn't meant for his ears, so I clamp it closed instead.

"It's really cute you're pretending like you don't want this for real."

He dips and presses his lips to the side of my mouth. I whimper, desperate to taste him for real. I'm famished—starved—I need his kiss.

"If you show me how much you want me, Peaches, we don't have to do this dance anymore. The torture ends."

His fingers brush against my waistband.

The fireworks I thought had long burnt out inside of me crackle back to life as his touch grazes along my skin.

I try to open my mouth to tell him I want him, that I need him right now—but I can't find the words. Fear rips them away, and I just lie breathless on the bed.

"I can see how much you want me, Evie. Why do you keep trying to hide it?" I meet his eyes, shimmering brilliantly in a halo of sunlight. I don't know where we are, but it feels dangerously like home.

The speed of my breath increases, and any form of communication on my part is completely eradicated. I reach for his lips, but he pulls away, a cocky smile spread wide across his face, dimpling his cheeks to catastrophic levels. "Say the words."

"I hate you."

He tsks. "We both know that's not true, Peaches. Look at you. It's been a week and you can barely contain yourself around me. So say it."

"I love you, okay? I always have."

"Oh. Shit." I wake up in cold sweat, catching my breath and wiping an errant tendril stuck to my sweaty face.

The light streams in through the cracks of an old wooden blind. Edging off the bed, the chill of the cold hardwood greets my toes as they press against it before rising.

The low cadence of Liam's professional voice in a nearby room reverberates through the bare white walls, sending vibrations along the floorboards and tingling my spine. Gooseflesh prickles the nape of my neck, and I huddle into myself. I haven't had a dream like that in a good long while. I walk into his bathroom to splash my face with cold water but find little relief; the crimson stain on my cheek might be permanent.

"Get it together," I scold myself in the mirror. "What you say and do in dreamworld can't be held against you."

Making his bed buys me a few more seconds of calm to collect my thoughts. I pull the sheet up and swallow the ball lodged in my throat. Caught in a haze of the waking sleep and a thick fog of wine, Liam managed to get me as far as his bed before I passed out. I rub my temple as a dull ache permeates my skull. I'm never drinking wine again.

Corners properly pressed, I drag a slow, steady breath through my lungs, eyes roaming Liam's spartan room. The only pieces of furniture beyond the bed are a dresser and a workout bench in the corner, with weights collected there.

My stomach rumbles—apparently anti-live-in-this-room-forever.

Reluctantly, I inch out into the hallway, preparing for the awkward.

Hunched over the dining table clad in a black Henley, Liam's broad figure sends another—it's way too early for these nerves—bolt of electricity to my system.

That's certainly one way to wake up.

Focus aimed at a collection of papers spread out on the table, he runs a hand through his hair, a highlighter clenched between his teeth. My fingers itch to do the same, and I ball them at my side.

A soft pattering in my chest follows the initial surge, and I pause, enjoying the brief moment where I can be an unobserved spectator.

Maybe I can back out now and admit he was right. I wasn't thinking the whole fake dating through.

His gaze picks up, meeting mine as a soft dimple pricks his right cheek. "Morning," he says before bringing his attention back to his work.

The gentle pattering intensifies.

"Morning."

"There's a coffee and a plate for you in the kitchen."

"Oh, you didn't have to—" I pull at my fingers, slowly slinking toward the door.

"You're welcome." The corners of his mouth tug upward into an infuriating smirk, focus still trained on whatever is in front of him.

"Thank you," I exhale. It'd be rude to leave now if he plated me breakfast.

Entering the kitchen, the tiny flutters in my chest give way to forceful thuds as my eyes fall on a white china plate sitting on the island. A pink-frosted donut with rainbow sprinkles, a pain au chocolat, and a peach tartlet are all delicately placed next to a cup of steaming coffee.

"All of these—" I pause, clearing my throat and hoping next time I speak I don't sound quite so much like a frightened schoolgirl. "Are all of these for me?"

Liam grunts in the affirmative.

Yeah, that noise certainly isn't going to help this situation.

"Did you have breakfast? Can I get you anything?"

"A yogurt from the fridge would be great if you don't mind."

"Sure." I clear my throat again.

"You okay in there?"

"Oh yeah, fine." Heat rises to my cheeks, and I fan away the color. I can't leave anytime soon with this display of treats. He had to make multiple stops for these.

Collecting myself the best I can before wandering back out, I attempt to balance the yogurt, coffee, and treats within my trembling grasp and slowly approach the long maple dining room table.

Liam drags his highlighter across the paper, his other hand still mussing up his hair, and my grasp wobbles.

"I—you know, that island in the kitchen had a stool, and it looked nice and comfortable." I continue hovering awkwardly over the table. Papers are scattered everywhere, there's a growing pressure between my legs that needs relieving, and it looks like I'll be in the way. "And you're clearly busy—so I'm going to wander back into the kitchen and use it—"

He shifts some papers. "Sit and eat, Peaches," he says gently and makes another stroke with his highlighter on the document.

I plop into the chair.

Without looking, he reaches for his yogurt and spoon. A crease furrows between his eyebrows.

I can't see a hint of the carefree, lazy facade anywhere—the one that used to annoy me to no end, the one I hated. I search for it, desperately needing something to cling onto that will cool me down.

"Is this for work?" I ask, eyes roaming over the scattering of papers on the table.

"Kind of. It's my final thesis for my master's." He flashes a puzzled look at the paper in front of him. "Or it will be. Once I figure out what I'm doing."

My attention falls back to the pain au chocolat. Honeycomb flakes grace the inside of the pastry, and I vibrate with excitement. Finding a perfectly laminated pastry is such a rush.

Baking is my preferred art form, for the simple reason that it requires all the senses to be enjoyed. Monet is impressive and all, but have you ever licked a Monet? I imagine it'd be musty. And licking Monets is generally frowned upon. But a pastry. You can feel the buttery flakes coat your fingertips. Smell the flour and butter melding to their euphoric thin-layer final state. Hear the crunch of the top layer as you rip a piece off. And finally, taste the rich dark hunk of chocolate dancing on your tongue as the buttery flakes melt away on your tastebuds.

I roll the piece of pastry over in my mouth, savoring the moment, eyes closed, lips curled up. A soft hum rattles the back of my throat.

Swallowing, I open my eyes for a sip of coffee and catch Liam watching me with curiosity.

My cheeks burn under his assessing gaze, and I shift in my seat. "What are you getting your master's for?"

"Business analytics," he says dryly, returning to his work.

"Ah, I was looking at some of those classes when I was thinking about opening my shop, but that plan's cooked now."

He picks his head up. "That's not the plan anymore?"

I shrug, plopping another piece of pastry into my mouth. "I've kind of given up planning anything, to be honest. I don't know. Every time I have a goal, stuff just gets in the way. It's better not to get my hopes up and be disappointed at this point. Keep my dreams . . . *dreams.*" I blush, meeting his eyes trained on me with a gentle intensity. "I know, I know, doesn't sound like the Evie you used to know."

"We all change." He offers a crooked smile and closes his highlighter. "Are you looking for another job at a pâtisserie then?"

"Oh. No." I lower my attention to my plate. "I don't know what I'm doing, honestly. Working full-time for someone else feels impossible when I'm not sure how my body will be every day. That's why I had to leave my last job, and my body hasn't really gotten better since. I just got better at managing some of it." I don't know why I'm opening up about this to Liam when I haven't talked about this with Maria. Maybe it's because I've grown too tired of carrying this heaviness alone or maybe I figure if I disclose this bit, I can keep the far more dangerous truth buried down a little longer. Either way, there's something about this alternate dynamic we've fallen into the past few days that's almost inviting me to be vulnerable.

"With my last boss, explaining how I could be seemingly fine one minute and in excruciating pain with no warning a second later was hard. Like this one time, I was piping macarons and a bad flare gripped everything."

I shift, feeling the phantom talons now. "I remember needing to lean on the counter to stay upright, but I didn't want to draw attention to myself. People are always weird about pain, so I never really told anyone. I asked to go on my break, but my boss said no and called me lazy. I pushed through the rest of the piping, and when it was time for them to rest, I went into the bathroom. Vomited. Brushed my teeth. Popped some ibuprofen and got back to work. He yelled at me for being delicate and unreliable for the rest of the shift because I could have used that time to get ahead instead.

"When my shift ended, I folded up my apron and barely made it back to my apartment before I blacked out. Anyway—" I awkwardly laugh. That was way too much unloading this early in the morning. "Do you like doing this stuff?" I pick up a sheet lying on the table, trying to make sense of the slashes and marks on the paper. I may speak a second language, but it's definitely not this one.

"Oh, yeah, it's fine." He blinks, opening his mouth as if to say something, but he closes it, offering a tight-lipped smile.

A loud vibration rattles the table, and I jump as papers rustle to my right.

"I charged your phone." Liam nods toward the commotion.

"Oh, thank you, that was clutch. Maria probably thinks I'm in a ditch." I reach for it, frowning at my receipts.

Caroline.

CAROLINE: Are you doing anything special for your birthday next week? Can't believe you'll be the same age I was when I had you. Your father and I were already married for eight years by now, how funny!

I slump in my chair. "It's five in the morning her time, and she's already chosen passive-aggressive violence," I mumble.

"You okay?"

"Yeah." I toss my phone across the table so it can't hurt me anymore. "Just Caroline's patented seemingly innocuous statements that stab you in the subtext."

"Ah."

I rub my temple with a forefinger. I hadn't even thought about how my birthday would affect my visit. Turning twenty-seven is whatever, but on Caroline's Hopes and Dreams for Her Daughter Checklist, I might as well be an elderly Rose Dawson Calvert on the ship going *"It's been eighty-four years."*

Whether I think I can handle this or not, dream me was right. I am desperate and I do need help.

"So." I drag out the "o," still biding my time. "Have you thought about what I asked you last night?"

Liam leans back. His eyes narrow to mine as he considers me. "I have. Have you?"

Thought about it. Had vivid dreams about it. Tomato-tomahtoe. I nod, finally taking a sip of my coffee and biting back a grimace. This coffee was made for the sugar and cream-loving American I used to be. Not the dark-as-my-soul ex-patriot I've become. "I still think it would help keep the peace while I'm home."

He places his elbows on the table, clasping his hands in front of his face. A weird, mischievous smirk hangs firmly in place. "If you're sure, I'm in, provided you agree to my conditions."

Of course there'd be conditions.

I train my features to neutral and wave him to continue.

"I don't want to risk someone figuring out we're faking it," he says, sliding open the cover of his yogurt and dipping his spoon in.

"Right, that's kind of the point."

"But I don't know how you expect to do that when you still don't trust me."

"I trust you enough."

He snorts. "No, you don't." He brings a spoonful of yogurt to his lips and wraps his mouth around the head. His eyes raise and collide with mine as he licks the back of the spoon with broad strokes. I'm too poorly caffeinated to maintain composure while his tongue is out and doing *that*. His brow furrows, and he reaches out and touches the back of his hand to my forehead. "Hey, you okay?"

"What are you doing?"

"Checking for a fever."

"I'm fine."

"You look flushed. I don't want you making a decision like this when you're ill and your judgment is cloudy."

"Of sound mind and body." I cross my heart and will the images of his tongue away, summoning split meringues and curdled whipped cream.

"Were you ever?" He angles his body forward, his pouty, upward curving lips hovering far too close to mine. I give in to the pull for half a second before my breath hitches, and I shake myself back to reality.

"I was until you showed up last week." My eyes flit away, avoiding the dangerous gold flecks in his eyes.

"I can really feel the trust here, good."

I pick up my eyes and glare at him. "I'm sure my mother is so desperate for this to be an actual thing it'll be easy to convince her. It's fine."

"Evie, you can't maintain eye contact with me for longer than two seconds. In what world is how much you hate me going to translate as a convincing relationship?"

"I don't hate you," I mumble, which forces Liam to cock his head to the side. But it's the inconvenient truth, I don't hate him, not like this, not now. "But the eye contact thing is entirely your fault. Nobody else looks at me as intensely as you do."

"I look at you how you should be looked at." He shrugs.

"If your only hesitation is me actually pulling this off, I swear I can do it."

A fingertip gently brushes my chin, tilting it upward. Liam unleashes a full-bodied stare, flecks and all. The intensity of his narrowed eyes hurries my breaths, and I last maybe two point five seconds before I pull my attention back down to my pastries.

"Did you see the lamination on this pastry? It's super well done, definitely someone who makes pain au chocolats on the regular." I pick at the pastry, running a finger through the inner layers. "You know rumor has it Marie Antoinette introduced the croissant—what this evolves from—to France. When you think about it, her demise was a rather miserable thank you considering it's such an important part of French culture now."

"Is that so?" Liam leans back, grabbing his chest and chuckling. It's this annoying thing he does when he thinks something is particularly funny—and it's usually me. The gold flecks dance with amusement as he shakes his head. "I knew you weren't thinking this through."

"Fine," I grunt. "Then what do you suggest we do?"

"You need to go through a deprogramming or something."

"For what?" I flail my hands, and precious flakes from the viennoiserie fly everywhere.

"That." He snorts. "I don't know how many times I have to tell you I'm not the enemy before you believe it, but if we're going to do this, you need to practice pretending you can tolerate my presence, because a lot of people who aren't your mom will be watching us."

I gulp down a portion of my breakfast. I *wasn't* thinking this through. Because pretending I actually like Liam is a complete violation of all my safety guidelines wrapped in a tiny package of doom, covered in a veiled layer of how-to-get-Caroline-off-your-back-and-cause-five-hundred-other-problems-for-yourself paper. At least it's gilded paper, and I imagine the box is gorgeous. It's the kind of wrapping where the person is anxious to open it because it looks so stunning, maybe even carefully removes the bow and goes, "I don't want to ruin the paper, it's so pretty," and pretends they want to save it for later, and then they open it up and inside there's a can of tuna or something. I don't know.

"How would—what's your idea?" I finally ask.

"I thought maybe we could set aside a few days to practice, feel each other out before we return for the wedding. Take some of the pressure off."

A weird nervous energy hums through me, and I tuck my lip under my teeth, almost baring down hard enough to draw blood. Pressure needs to be relieved, but I don't think spending more time with Liam will help.

"That sounds fair." I nod. "But you said conditions, as in plural, so what else were you thinking?"

Liam slides a card over to me as a sardonic smile curls up on his lips. "Our dating backstory. Nonnegotiable."

"Yeah, you didn't overthink this last night or anything," I say, eyeing the index card suspiciously.

"Couch wasn't super comfy."

I scan the words scrawled across the index card, narrowing in on the one that threatens to speed up my heart rate to catastrophic proportions. *Love.* "Are you freakin' kidding me! No. No way."

He tsks, and his mouth wraps around the head of the spoon for another bite of yogurt. My stare rests on his lips, and my throat dries up. Okay, seriously, how much yogurt is in that cup? "Those are my terms."

"I've"—I gaze down at the words—"always been in love with you but didn't know how to tell you? So I wore a mask of negativity to hide it?"

"Wracked with nerves every time you saw me." He clasps his hands in front of him, directing his stare to the ceiling with a dopey lovesick look.

"So when Eli said he was visiting with you, I begged, *begged*—really?—that we meet up, and after ten years of pent-up agony and unrequited love, I blacked out upon finally seeing you." I pick up my head and glare. "Ha. Ha."

"Love hit you full force, poor thing."

"Finally, I confessed to you that I am, and have always been, head over heels in love with you and no longer want to hide my true feelings—" My voice escalates several octaves higher than it usually rests. "I'm not doing this."

"Yeah, I figured. I just wanted to hear you get up into your squeaky panicked register," he says nonchalantly, scraping his yogurt cup clean.

I blink at him in disbelief. "Forget it. You were right. I clearly wasn't thinking. I'll brave Caleb's wedding alone." I stand abruptly and my chair tips over with a thud.

Liam shoots up with me, lightly grasping my arm. Jolts of electricity ignite through my system at an alarming speed. "I was kidding, Peaches. Having a backstory really isn't a condition."

"I mean, it's not a bad idea, really—to have one. But this *particular* one does nothing for my situation. My mom already thinks I'm a pathetic loser. Pining won't add anything."

He frowns, reaching beyond me, and his chest bumps into mine as he grabs the card. "Then it's mine."

"What?" I gasp, stepping back on my heel. "Are you trying to get me into my panicked voice again?"

"Not intentionally, no. But if you're this stressed about going home, maybe this would give you a positive distraction."

Liam pining over me? Really tempting.

"I don't understand why you're putting so much thought into this. It's not like you're getting anything out of this."

Seriously. I half expected him to negotiate the situation in his favor, but not like this. All he's done is make it so I have to spend more time with him.

His lips tip into a crooked smile, dimpling his left cheek. "Because I've been in love with you since we were five, and you're finally giving me a chance to get close to you."

A panicked laugh tightens my chest. "What? Why would you say that? What?"

"Just getting into character, Peaches, relax." He taps the index card wedged between his fingers and winks. "Honestly, if it helps keep the peace around your brother's wedding, I don't mind."

Okay, *that* I buy.

"So you're serious about this? You really think you can play the tortured lover part?"

"I wouldn't worry about me." His stare shifts from playful to serious. The energy in the room changes along with it, and my fingers twitch through the heavy static, filling the air and suffocating my lungs. "But you, I'm worried you're not going to make it through this. You're already acting weirder than usual."

"I'm not acting weird. You're the one being weird."

"Come on. Your comebacks are better than that."

I take another step, and my back finds the wall. "I can handle it." I half-smile, fighting back the charged magnetism building up inside. "But I'm serious. If you think I need to practice, I'm a little skeptical *that you* can fake something being hard for you. I feel like a lifetime of unrequited love would break someone with your general disposition."

"You think I need practice?" He mirrors my steps.

"Your life's track record has yet to prove you can play the part. But please, feel free to prove me wrong."

"How do you know I'm not playing right now? Maybe I'm really good at hiding it."

"It'd be pretty obvious you were cracking."

"Maybe it is, and you're not that observant." He steps closer, placing his hands on either side of me and forming a cage with his body. Last night's dream flashes in my mind again, and my chest heaves against his. "Maybe I accepted a long time ago I was always going to be miserably in love when it came to you and learned to mask the crack."

He brushes a portion of my loose hair over my shoulder. Shivers ripple down the nape of my neck in the wake of his grazing fingers as waves crash against my reserve. Whatever fortress I had built to survive this is in serious trouble of crumbling under the growing storm. Remember why the fort was built. *Remember the ball. Remember the ball.*

"Oh yes, suddenly your prank at the ball makes perfect sense. People love to humiliate the ones they're madly in love with."

His jaw tightens. "It wasn't a prank. Something happened."

I roll my eyes. "Yeah, okay, bud. Sure."

"I'm serious." The dark intensity that meets my gaze when he says this makes my heartbeat skip, over and over with the thrashing waves.

"You said it was a prank."

"No, actually, I just didn't correct you."

"But why?"

Liam leans closer, lips slightly parted. My breath hitches and I tilt my chin toward him, reduced to nothing more than the girl at the bar, hoping I misread our situation. Because no matter how hard I try, I can never shake the feeling we were destined for something greater than what we settled into. His long-hooded lashes brush against his cheek, shadowing his already shrouded face.

"Because you needed a villain that day more than you needed the truth."

"What if that's not what I needed—" My ability to form any coherent sentence suffers as Liam draws closer. His lips rest a fingerbreadth away. The growing static floods my entire being until I'm drowning in need. The need to feel his lips on mine. The need to have his warmth on me. To no longer find myself wrapped in his scent but to be buried in it instead. Maybe tortured lover wasn't that far off a role for me. "What if—"

Oh. Shit. *He's playing.* The rational part of my brain finally foghorns its way through. *This isn't real. For this to be believable, you'll need a cover story for that night.* Right. "Shit, you're good," I manage, blinking my way back to reality.

"Evie, I—"

The rattle of the doorknob on the front door jolts us both upright as Eli stumbles in.

A crease forms between his eyebrows while he's gawking at us, caught like a deer in the headlights in the back of the room.

"And that." I nervously laugh, pressing a hand to Liam's chest. "That's roughly how Rodin posed his models for *The Kiss.* Thanks so much for asking about my favorite art blog post."

Liam smirks, rubbing the scruff on his cheek. "Fascinating."

"No. Shit. You finally told her?" A wide smile spreads across Eli's face.

"Tell me what?"

Liam shakes his head, clearing his throat and adjusting his shirt. "Evie asked me to take her to the wedding, and given the circumstances, she thought it might be a good idea if we convinced everyone that more was going on. We were just messing around to make sure it was realistic."

"And posing like Paolo and Francesca is the perfect way to do that!" I add.

"Right. . . " Eli rubs the back of his head. "Well, I'm tired, so I'm going to get some sleep, and you two carry on with whatever weird-ass thing you're doing or not doing. Lunch date after I nap?" he asks, walking by.

"Sure," I manage, eyes flickering to Liam's, trying to shake out of whatever the hell that was.

Eli's door shuts with a mumbled "freakin' weirdos." I stifle a giggle, still frozen against the wall while Liam marches back to his seat.

"Are you free tomorrow?" he asks.

"To-tomorrow?" I stammer.

"For a date." He opens his highlighter and focuses back down at his work like he's ridiculously unaffected by what just happened. "I have a meeting in the morning if you're free. We can take a picture and you can post it on your blog. I assume your mom still follows that."

"I have to work tomorrow through the weekend, but I'm free Monday."

"Great." He shifts in his seat. "If you want, I can join you and Eli later for the picture. Get the ball rolling."

"Oh, yeah, that sounds good." I swallow.

What the hell did I get myself into?

8

Donut Dream It's Over

"Do you want to try the whole thing or the abbreviated version?" Maria quirks a brow as we halt in front of the eastern arm of the Panthéon. Corinthian columns loom overhead, bathed in the warm, shimmering light of the mid-afternoon sun.

She's asking about our Friday ritual. A long, leisurely stroll to the bar reserved for each other. A tradition we started when Maria, a lovestruck college student, determined that the local grumpy bar owner was "the one."

Eventually, Declan opened up and said, "Your face, I like it," and other such swoony sentiments, and the two of them have been inseparable ever since.

Usually, I don't have much to share, and Maria happily regales me with stories about Declan or muses over a planning snafu while I quietly soak in the unbridled beauty of Parisian architecture.

But today.

I am frightened.

Because the second-degree regarding my recent chaotic decisions is coming, and I don't want to acknowledge the answers.

For the first time since the shorter route's creation, I'm almost okay taking it.

Even if it means cutting out my favorite part: beginning our stroll along the Seine at Pont de l'Archevêché, a narrow three-arched bridge draped in metallic padlocks that blink alive, catching cascading sunbeams on days like today—a microcosm of heaven.

It's a place where Gene Kelly and Leslie Caron danced in *An American in Paris*.

And then Audrey Hepburn reminisced over the dance number in *Charade* with Cary Grant.

If I could have my own Evie and Nana Center of Paris marker, it would be there.

Unfortunately, as far as this walk is concerned, my endo isn't a fan.

Sudden flare-ups are all-too-common lately, and I don't want to risk one striking too far from The Quays.

"Abbreviated would be best."

A tiny wrinkle settles between Maria's brow, the only hint of worry she ever allows to show. "Sounds good," she hums, wrapping her arm around mine. Our legs press together, and she jolts away, experiencing what I attempted to ignore.

My pants are buzzing.

Left pocket specifically.

The *Dance of the Bumble Bee*.

Except nothing in these rapid-fire text messages is sweet.

All stingers, no honey.

"Why on earth is that on vibrate?"

"It's only been like this the last two minutes or so." I sigh, sliding my phone out of my pocket to silence the ringer. "Caroline must have seen the post."

Early this morning, I uploaded a candid Eli snapped yesterday of Liam laughing while we shared an éclair on the Champs de Mars to my blog and Instagram.

Eiffel for you under Paris skies captioned underneath with a smattering of hashtags.

Did writing that caption physically hurt?

Yup.

Does it already have grotesquely more likes than any of my other posts with super exciting tidbits about the history of Paris?

You betcha.

Dimples, corny-ass pun, and the Eiffel Tower in the background for the ultra-filtered high-life social media win and low-key real-life panic attack.

It was, surprisingly, a rather convincing picture of two people in love. A comment on how easy it is to fool the general public on social media, nothing more. Paused for eternity in a little square, Liam's arm is wrapped around me, his hand falling to my waist and pulling me in. Laugh lines edge his eyes, and his dimples pucker his cheeks.

In my infinite chill, as we were about to pose for the picture, I nicknamed the pastry "Fred Éclair" and made it dance before promptly taking a huge I'm-uncomfortable bite. Liam erupted at that moment with a glorious, genuine laugh. And as he wiped some tears from his eyes, a terrifying realization slammed into me while a wide uncontained smile simultaneously took real estate on my face. I would do just about anything to make him laugh like that again. Unguarded. Joyful. Sunshine.

It was, truthfully, the only usable picture of the bunch. After Liam settled, his body language went rigid with all the signature "I'd rather be touching just about anyone else" signs. Throat mid-nervous swallow. Unbridled terror flashing through his eyes. You name it, he may have been more uncomfortable than me.

I unlock my screen, and notification after notification from my mother mocks me. Total buzzkill.

CAROLINE: Are you still planning on staying here for Caleb's wedding, or will you be spending your time at Liam's apartment?

The text sits on top of a good fifteen other questions ranging from Did you mean to buy a size twelve dress? to I scheduled you a hair appointment for when you're home. Did you ask for that haircut or was something lost in translation?

I control my own peace, I repeat to the rhythm of Maria's heels clopping on the concrete sidewalk. My free hand runs through my hair, smoothing down my flyaways.

Dammit. She's seriously controlling me from over three thousand miles away.

Thanks for nothing, social media.

Flanked by opposing structures of learning, the Sorbonne and the Lycée Louis-le-Grand, I pause, clearing the notifications off my screen and drawing new life from these tale-as-old-as-time buildings.

Hopefully I didn't miss anything important in the bevy of text messages.

CAROLINE: Your bra is supposed to support YOU, honey, not gravity.

These "helpful" tips are why I don't post photos of myself. It's a lot harder to criticize an old building. Though I'm sure Caroline would find a way.

"These slabs would pop more if they were a brighter white. And honestly, does this foundation need to be this wide?"

Chuckling to myself, I snap a picture of the limestone lining the Sorbonne clock tower. A group of students lean against the outside of the building, smoking, directing non-descript bored stares my way.

Shut up. Bricks can be funny.

"How's your mom taking the news?" Maria asks as I swipe away a few more texts and notifications from Instagram.

Migrating_Coconut24: Oh, he's cute.

Grumpy_Giraffe: Those toned forearms, though.

TheFumblingTraveler: Ugh, yas queen! So jealous of your life! Keep slaying it in Paris.

A quick snort puffs out my nostrils. I doubt they'd say that if they were privy to my reality, but in my experience, social media is 95 percent bullshit and filters anyway. Maybe for some it's therapeutic? Like controlling your life is damn near impossible, but at least you can manage what other people see? A false sense of security, maybe? Whatever the reason, it'd benefit all parties involved if people could see that no one has their shit together.

"As expected, excited and overly 'helpful,' but this version of Caroline I can handle."

I blink as my thumb hovers over another text.

LIAM: Be honest, how many texts has your mom sent you about us?

ME: Like twenty?

LIAM: Hmm.

ME: ???

I push myself off the building to resume our trek. My eyes anxiously hang on my screen, waiting for his response.

LIAM: Nothing, only she's sent me a solid twenty too. Thought you would have more. Must be going soft.

ME: I'm sorry. You have twenty texts … From MY mom????

Internally, an agonizing scream boils to a whistle as I pass a corner toy store. Board games and a colossal Eiffel Tower 3D puzzle sit in the window. I don't need to look up to know the rest of the nineteenth-century building is immaculate with black iron balconies twisting into delicate spirals gracing its side. It *should* lift my spirits, but I've grown cruelly accustomed to the little, utterly divine aspects of Paris.

What a pity.

LIAM: Still don't think she's really your mom, but sure.

ME: Dude, we've been over this. Julia Child is NOT my mother.

Look up, a grumpy voice whispers in my mind. *You're missing Paris.* But here I am, eyes glued down.

LIAM: You can't convince me otherwise. I mean . . . she's tall, loves French culture and butter . . .

ME: And old AF when I was born.

LIAM: If Julia Child could make the perfect soufflé, she could give birth old.

ME: She would have been in her seventies!

LIAM: Fine just shit all over my theory to give you the best mom ever.

ME: You're ridiculous.

LIAM: *shrug emoji* I can live with ridiculous.

"What?" Maria smirks as a soft titter escapes me.

"Oh. Nothing." I shove my phone back into my pocket and sigh. "Liam, well, he's kind of weird sometimes, isn't he?"

Passing Église Saint-Séverin, Maria slows, knowing the deal. I freakin' love this church. Roman meets gothic meets late-gothic architecture. Flying buttresses and gargoyles, mixed with stained glass windows, cover every inch of the outside, and a small, modern playground sits on the corner of the park area, wrapping around the church. A relic of the past, a player in the present. Proof that the present is a minuscule moment in reality, never fixed. We are the past. We become the future in a literal blink of an eye. Life continues on.

Out of the corner of my eye, I catch a big grin plastered on Maria's face—a dangerous gleam in her icy blue stare.

"Hey, Evie?" she asks in her I'm-about-to-ask-you-a-leading-question-and-shatter-everything-you-know-about-life-in-the-process voice. It's the voice she used when I was struggling to manage to work full-time, and she found me passed out on the bathroom floor. *"Do you think this is a sustainable way to live, dear? Or do you think it's time to find a vocation that fits your flares better?"*

"Yes?" I tepidly approach her sweet, sing-songy ruse, which undoubtedly proves she's about to hurl a QMD (question of mass destruction) my way.

"Liam is particularly goofy sometimes, don't you think?"

"Yes, I just said that—"

"And from the stories you've shared recently, he has taken a liking to puns all of a sudden." She restarts our trek to The Quays.

"Well, yes . . ." I say, chewing the inside of my cheek. Whatever this is, Maria better not ruin puns for me.

"And as far as people you know from back home are concerned, he's the only person you haven't considered who could be sending you these personalized postcards, right?"

"I mean with good reason, though," I say with the conviction of a monumental executive telling Lina Lamont she has a beautiful voice. I have allowed my brain to question this exactly once. And the ramifications of tainting the one thing that brings me joy with the possibility of this being an elaborate prank grew too strong, so I closed it down and never let myself travel that path again. "But he hates me," I manage.

"Does he, though?"

"Yes, we have an understanding that our animosity is mutual."

"Do you, though?"

I clear my throat, hoping it doesn't close. I'm allergic to stressful lines of questioning, and honestly, after our past few interactions, after the way he's taken care of me, Maria's making some valid points. At the very least, I can confirm he doesn't hate me.

"You're so off. Get out of here." I laugh, deflecting and turning my attention to the window of a pâtisserie to hide the flush creeping up my neck. Like hell I'm going to give her the satisfaction of knowing she might be onto something.

Maria's eyes widen in the reflection and an annoying, albeit infectious smile spreads across her face. Dammit, I forgot how reflective materials work.

"You want it to be him!" She claps.

"What?" I rake my hand through my loose strawberry curls, pivoting back to her and praying Saint Honoré, patron saint of bakers everywhere, will take pity and rescue me from this situation. "That's beyond ridiculous. Why would I? What?"

"Yeah, that was convincing." She snorts.

"Doesn't make you less wrong," I grumble.

"Evelina Rose O'Shea." Maria puts her hands on her hips. "What's my job?"

"Annoying meddling stupid head." I roll my eyes so far in the back of my head, I'm sure I can see my brain. It's a rather dark place, not much happening.

"Oh no, that's my hobby." She chuckles. "In case you missed it, I'm a wedding planner. And what do you say I have a second sense for?"

"People in love." I shift to avoid a bike chained to a side rail on the sidewalk. A mass of tourists perusing the boarded menu of a red-painted café forms a narrow wedge ahead of us. Maria steps in front of me, and we pass through the tourist sieve single file.

"Best man for the Lafeyette wedding?" she shouts back at me.

"Married to the bride now—pardon—" My shoulder digs into the back of a halted photographer, attention devoted to a cherry blossom tree juxtaposed against a cream background.

"How long did it take to call that?"

"One cake testing," I moan, sidestepping a dog defecating, with an owner, sans poop bag—jerk.

"And the Delacroix wedding?"

"Okay, I get it. You're good at your job. But seriously—he's not—I'm not—" I stumble. "If you saw him when Eli busted in, it was like a freakin' light switch. The man can turn it on and off whenever he wants. That's not real. That's acting."

"Okay, but hear me out." Maria and I pause at a cross signal. A smattering of languages crowds around us. Swedish, English, French, Italian, Japanese, and Arabic meld into one harmonic, indistinguishable chatter. She leans in closer to my ear. "What if he's used to it?"

"No," I say flatly. "Just no."

"Oh my goodness. His backstory. It's real!" Maria does the Swedish version of a happy dance, which is a tiny, almost imperceptible shoulder shimmy. It draws the attention of a group of elderly women with necks wound tightly in scarves, whispering amongst themselves and peering down at one of their phones. Americans. Probably New Yorkers. Not their first visit.

"Evie, seriously! He's so in love with you but doesn't know what to do." Maria squeals.

"Excuse me." A lady with a chic grey bob puts her hand out to stop us before we cross, her thick brusque voice confirming my New York suspicions.

"The Eiffel Tower's west of here." I gesture, not missing a beat. "Follow the bridges. Big iron structure, can't miss it."

She purses her lips. "I know where the tower is. We actually have a question regarding your blog."

"My blog?" I stammer.

"Yes, I couldn't help but overhear, you're the Evie from *L'Evie en Rosé*, correct?" she asks, flashing her phone where the picture of Liam and me sits on top of the page. Oh. Well, this is certainly a first.

"The one and only." Maria perks up.

"My friends and I have been following one of your self-guided tours today, but we're currently deciding where to eat. Do you have any recommendations around here?"

I chew on my lip, thinking. "To be honest, most of the restaurants in this general area cater to tourists and are kind of bleh, but if you travel down this side road"—I point back toward Shakespeare and Co. and the adjacent park—"there's a decent boulangerie. Well, two actually. Skip the first one, and stop at the second. You can eat inside or retrace your steps and eat at Square René Viviani and have a nice view of some cherry blossoms and Notre Dame."

"Oh, that sounds lovely!" Another woman in the group with white curly hair claps. "How lucky we ran into you! Really!"

A third woman, stuffed in her oversized scarf, leans, and her shoulder brushes mine as a strong dose of Chanel Number Five hits my nostrils. "We're enjoying your 'Book Lover' homage tour. You should map out some more of these for our next trip."

"Will do." I blush. "Oh, there's another church on the backside of the square too. Église Saint-Julien-Le-Pauvre, not much on the outside, but worth a gander inside if you like twelfth-century architecture."

"Perfect. See? That wrong turn was a blessing." The curly white-haired lady laughs. "Oh, and honey, if she's talking about the boy you posted to your blog this morning, listen to your friend: he has every marker of a man in love, and he's pretty cute too."

"Agreed, but not as cute as my Andrew, if you're ever in Ohio," the stuffed scarf supplies.

"Andrew's in jail, Beatrice. Stop trying to pawn him off on unsuspecting woman."

"He'll be out in two more years on good behavior, and he's a doctor."

"No, he's not, Bea." The gray-haired lady groans. "That's why he's in jail." She rolls her eyes. "Sorry, we'll let you two be on your way, but thank you again."

"What a nice little pick-me-up." Maria huddles back into me.

"Yeah—that was something." I glance back at the three ladies heading toward Shakespeare and Co.

"And they agreed with me. The man's in love and clueless."

"He's anything but clueless." I shake my head.

Maria hasn't been around Liam enough to understand how calculated that man's actions are, even if they come across as effortless. Changed, grown up, whatever he is now, I'm still not ready to declare him naive about anything.

I've given him the benefit of the doubt too many times, and it always blew up in my face, like when he failed multiple math quizzes and I agreed to tutor him before an exam. The black holes on his cheeks, full pouty lips, and flirty touches under the disguise of forced proximity distracted me well into the dead of night as I fantasized about realities that were just that. Fantasies.

Unsurprisingly, I failed a math and chemistry exam and underperformed on an English paper the following week under the heavy fog of my daydreams. At the same time, he aced them all and passed me to finish the semester top of the class again.

A **Had fun. Let me know if I can tutor you next semester, Peaches** text sat on my phone for a good few days before I sent back a clever "Fuck you" response.

He was too with it in math to have *actually* failed those quizzes. And the consequence of my services couldn't have been a coincidence. He knew I'd fall prey to his charms.

The blare of a car horn blankets all other sounds around us. "Besides, he could have made a move multiple times and took advantage of the situations in different ways instead. It's more likely he's playing the long game like he always does, lulling me into this weird state of comfort before pouncing and shattering my heart."

Much more likely, actually . . .

"Or, every time he gets close, something happens, and now he's traumatized." She brings her palm to her chest, feigning a swoon. I swear she's a theatrical Southern belle sometimes.

"Your helpless romantic is showing. He was the Devil."

"And yet, here you are with him as your faux beau," Maria says as the walk signal turns and we cross the street toward the Seine.

"Yes, and that's all he's going to be. Stop trying to fill my head with your delusions on love." I grump as we descend the stairs near Pont St. Michel to start our stroll along the Seine.

It's the dreaming part that's dangerous.

Collecting myself in the mid-afternoon sun, I breathe in the river air as light dances off the wake of passing boats full of tourists and attempt to ignore the severe side-eye Maria is sending.

"Any chance there's a bigger reason behind your reluctance to admit I could be right?" She smirks.

"No," I say, exasperated about being psychoanalyzed on my way to work. "There's no logical way thinking he's sending me postcards or has feelings for me ends well."

"Look, I love you, and all I'm saying is I've seen more life in you the past few weeks than the past few years, and I don't think it'd be terrible if you let yourself fall a bit. It might shake things up, shed new light on some old, weathered perspectives," her overly romantic self says, sending googly eyes at a couple showcasing some serious PDA on a bench. I fashion a similar loving gaze toward Pont Neuf coming into focus in the distance, where the affections of my stone-cold heart lie—old architecture with thousands of stories to tell. "Seriously, when was the last time you opened yourself up to the possibility of falling in love?"

Sometimes, I wish Maria and I were surface-level friends.

Because she's honestly the worst.

And so is that question.

The simple answer is—I haven't been open. Not here in Paris, anyway. Not even with my boyfriend Michel during my first year here. Ironic considering it's the city of love. But the truth is, I let the hopeless romantic in me die a while back.

I'd love to pretend I built up a wall after the debutante fiasco or some other negative experience turned me away, but it didn't. I was still a wide-eyed optimist up until the end.

The end.

What a pathetically depressive term I've given it.

My diagnosis. The line of demarcation where my past life ended and a new one began.

One where I let love die without noticing it.

Without properly mourning it.

Until now.

I never have time to notice anything.

But if I learned anything with Michel, it's that it's not worth the time and effort to get emotionally intimate with someone when I know the physical intimacy is going to hurt like heck and ruin everything anyway.

I raise my eyes, letting them roam around the overhang, steadying my breaths. The urge to push Maria into the Seine for digging up all these buried wounds strengthens.

"It's not that simple," I say softly. "I'm already so tired, and my endo will complicate things."

"What do you mean?"

Tears well in my eyes, and I blink them back. "I never wanted my endo. I mean, who would? But I didn't have a choice, and it has to come with me in whatever relationship I have. How can I justify that? And who the hell would want to take that on? It's better for everyone if I keep my hopes low and not try."

Maria freezes, hands on hips. "Evelina Rose O'Shea," she says in her sternest voice possible. Which is not stern. Not at all. "You can't possibly believe that."

"It's the truth." I shrug. Am I maybe dipping into my self-loathing part of the month? It's possible—actually, it's definitely that—but still, when I'm here, these thoughts feel as natural as two plus two equals four, even if I try to tell myself they'll pass and I'll secretly like myself again eventually.

"Oh no. No. No. No," Maria sputters, shaking her head and marching away. "No!" She pauses again, tossing her hands in the air in frustration—but sure, I'm the melodramatic one—before turning back to me. "Evie, seriously, you're gorgeous, brilliant, funny—sure, sometimes I don't get your jokes, but hey, you try! You love your people fiercely, and you're one of the toughest, strongest women I've ever met—who has a shitty thing and handles it with so many of the adverbs I know you don't like me using. But dammit, I'm going to because you are. You are strong and handle this with so much grace every day. I thought you didn't want to get hurt—but this—nope, consider this me putting my foot down."

I snort. "I don't think you can categorize anything I've done in the past week as graceful."

"It's true, though! And anyone you choose to give your love to will be the luckiest person alive. Understood?"

"Uhm, yeah," I say, blinking back tears as Maria's compliment overwhelms me in the feels. Her words blossom in my chest, emphasizing how hollow I'd let my cavity become.

Clearing my throat, I force out a tiny, "How are you and Declan doing?" Buying myself time to process something, *everything*.

A glow sinks deep into Maria's pink cheeks right on schedule. As much as her romantic tendencies irk me, a large portion of me envies her ability to give her heart over entirely to whomever she's with. Even if it ended in messy nights with ice cream and running mascara in the past, she's always risen from the ashes stronger.

An uncharacteristic swallow and deep breath from Maria forces a quirked brow on my end.

The swallow, deep breath is never a good sign.

This is having to tell a destination wedding bride you can't legally get married in Paris as a visitor territory.

"We're good, actually. I wanted to talk to you about something." She drags another large gulp of air through her lungs. "But maybe right now isn't the right time."

"I'm fine," I lie, begging for something else to hyper-focus on.

"He—uhm—he asked me to move in with him."

"Oh?" My hand twitches as we pass another couple kissing on the edge of the Seine. Stupid, stupid love. I knew this was coming. But yeah, this is a gut punch for me.

Maria's my platonic soulmate. It's like she's breaking up with me but saying we should still be friends.

"And I know it would leave you hanging with rent and your shop. So I told him we'd need to wait. Let you get settled."

Hah. Settled. Getting settled is a lifetime away for me, if ever. I can't do that to them. She can't wait for me.

"You do you, don't worry about me. I'll land on both feet. Always do," I say, climbing the stairs near Pont Neuf. Back on the sidewalk, the noises of the city crash over us. "As long as you make time for your old spinster here." Wrapping my arm around Maria, I lean in and kiss her cheek. "I will be happy for you and support your decision, whatever you choose."

"We'll see. It won't be immediate anyway." She huddles tighter as we cross the road, traveling under a decorated archway that leads to a narrow alley and The Quays. "And as long as my old spinster friend is happy with her situation because I'm fairly certain there's a man moonstruck in love with her if she wanted it."

I shake my head, biting down the upward curl of my lips. She couldn't be more off.

"Are you at least looking forward to the wedding now?"

"Not really." An illuminated Guinness sign hovers overhead as an Irish flag flaps in the wind in front of the pub. "I'm hoping Caroline will stay quiet about certain things now, but you know me, stress and self-advocating are my downfalls."

"A little romance might help lighten the mood." Maria waggles a brow at me, reaching for the door and opening it.

My face falls flat as I go in. "You're not the funny one, dear."

"Hey, wicked harsh!" Maria mocks back and follows me in.

Declan greets her the minute we enter. His grim expression melts, meeting her softer one.

"You think I'm funny, right?" She frowns and buries herself into the arms of the six-foot Irish man.

His gaze darts to mine, a slight panic flashing through his usually stoic slate gray eyes.

I raise my shoulders in return.

"Of course, mo ghrá," he says, kissing the top of her head.

"Hah." She muffles into his chest.

"Yes, clearly an unbiased opinion. You were right," I tease, heading to the back. An avalanche of questions regarding postcards, romance, and other such miserable concepts berate me with the accompanying quiet.

Sighing while I organize the contents of my apron, two thoughts poke through the chaos, thundering the loudest.

How long have I been surviving without living?

And how long has my heart just been left to pump blood?

Oh, damn it, well, that's not a depressing way to start work or anything.

Ugh. Maria's the worst.

9

Donut Speak

WHEN IT'S TIME FOR a break from behind the bar, I lean against the cool limestone wall in the side alley of The Quays and soak in the ultimate view of the Seine from the shadows.

Golden strands ripple in the wake of a dinner cruise floating slowly under the archways of Pont Neuf as the faint romantic lilt of an accordion plays "La Vie en Rose" somewhere in the distance.

Light mist hangs in the raw spring air, puckering my skin with goose-flesh. Huddling further into myself, I inhale the sweet aroma of fresh crêpes from a nearby stand and find some semblance of peace on the crystallizing exhale, releasing the heaviness that's loomed over me since my earlier conversation with Maria.

I may have let a part of my heart die, but simple moments like these remind me there's still breath worth stealing from these lungs.

"Bonjour, Paris," I whisper into the night, my soft swoon mixing with the brusque tone of two Americans arguing around the corner at the front of the building.

A familiar agitated voice rattles my nervous system, killing any sense of serenity my calming breaths acquired.

Honestly, I should have guessed Eli would pay the bar a visit given his blossoming romance with Fionn, but if he could send a girl some warning given his chosen company, I'd appreciate it.

"Dude, you were on your phone all day. Put it away," Eli says.

A heavy sigh I was unaware Liam used on anyone else follows. "Sorry. Last one, and then I'll shut it off for the night."

"Fine, I'll be inside with your girl."

Apparently, Eli's clever nickname maintained its charm from yesterday.

"Yeah, that's why we're here. I can't believe it's been a week, and you're already in knitwear for someone."

"Shut up. It's cold," Eli says, his embarrassment betraying itself in his tone. Eli's a lot like Maria, where he falls hard, fast, and deep. But where Maria maintains composure with her feelings, Eli becomes possessed by the spirit of a golden retriever puppy with high energy that cannot be left alone. I haven't had a front-row seat to his disaster in love show in a while, so I'm excited to see how this pans out.

The condescending scoff I know intimately rattles the back of Liam's throat. "And your flannels weren't warm at all."

"You're always such a dick before we see Evie." Eli chuckles.

"I'm always a dick. It doesn't have anything to do with her."

Well, at least he's self-aware.

"You're definitely more of a dick when she's around."

"Just go inside," Liam says, almost sounding defeated.

"You have a plan for getting through all this dating shit with her?"

Ice freezes my veins, shocking my system in a cold panic as Eli's question wafts around the corner.

My footing slips, and my back slides further down the wall before I catch myself. A bevy of pebbles knocks loose from the sudden shift and clatter to a rest in front of me. Fuck.

I glance at the corner, hoping my commotion didn't attract their attention, relaxing slightly when the shadows don't draw any closer.

The whine of an ill-timed ambulance drowns out most of Liam's response but straining my ears, I pick up the words, "don't fucking know" and "get her to trust me and finally get that damn wall down so I can . . ." Can what? Can what? The ambulance fades, the words *torment* and *like the past* hitting my ears with a deafening blow.

"Good luck with that." Eli laughs. "I think she might actually kill you this time."

"Hasn't happened yet."

Who's the naive one now? the smug, younger doodle version of myself snarks in my brain.

"But he changed," I whisper under my breath. "He bought us pastries. Multiple pastries."

Chatter from inside The Quays swells and then fades behind the heavy oak barrier while the sounds of the city trickle back in. Training my ears, I search for a calming sound to cling to, narrowing in on the distant accordion melodically playing "La Mer."

Calm fails to find me, and my breath grows more erratic with each passing moment. Giving up on serenity, I rely heavily on the wall behind me for emotional support.

Fuck—and I cannot stress this last part enough—me.

How am I allegedly an adult and still falling for the same bewitching behaviors seventeen-year-old me did?

A yogurt cup rendered me undone, for Pete's sake.

And it wasn't even flavored.

It's just—

What psychopath buys a woman copious amounts of pastries if they're going to screw them over?

"That ass!" I cry, puffs of frustration drifting away with what little peace I gathered.

Kicked gravel rolls across the alley's entrance. Liam's long ominous shadow grows closer, strolling along the sidewalk.

Merde.

He peeks around the corner. Light cascading down from a lamppost illuminates the befuddled expression on his face, and I press further into the shadows.

Come on, emotional support wall and obscurity, please don't let me down.

"Evie?" he whispers in the dark.

My insides churn as his broad figure nears in a few short strides.

Clearing my throat, I step from my shrouded darkness, managing a tiny unconvincing, "Oh—hi."

"Uhm, hey," he says, rubbing the back of his head and glancing over to the corner where he and Eli were talking. "How long have you been back here?"

"Not long."

His shoulders relax, and a sense of relief washes over his features.

Oh, no. Your plan's still busted, Wonder Boy.

"I mean, I wasn't—I was already—" I ball my fist at my side to hold back a tremor while an odd mix of rage and disappointment spirals inside. I wanted to give him a second chance, truly. But he's still the same pain in my ass he always was; he just wears suits now.

Not that he's in a suit this very moment. No, that would have some-how been better for me than *this*. Because the black collared shirt he's sporting with his sleeves rolled up past his elbows and his dark wash jeans are scrambling my brain. Again, I want to look at his jacket draped over his corded forearm muscles and say, "Really, buddy help a girl out here."

He's gorg—*Sweet baby Debbie, Evie. Focus.*

How does he still have this chaotic effect on me? It's like a constant battle between reality and my masochistic dreams that sees the bottle labeled "poison" and thinks, *But could we still have a taste?*

"I'm on break, and this is my favorite spot. I didn't mean to creep or anything," I finish nowhere near confidently, but they were words arranged in a generally agreed-upon manner, so there's that.

"I'm used to you following me around like a creeper. It's fine." He smirks and stuffs his hands in his pockets.

I roll my eyes, folding my arms in front of my chest. "The way you must think your smirk is charming, the amount you employ it. But black magic doesn't work on me, in case you've forgotten."

Hi. Liar.

"Oh, now see, that's something we'll have to practice because you'll need to at least pretend like my magic works on you." His lips tug upward in a dangerous smile as his eyes rake over me. A hypnotic gleam flares in the recesses of his gaze, sparking a blazing fire in its wake. Like I needed a reminder I made a deal with the Devil, and now my insides are hell.

"I can pretend that you cursed me."

"I think we could work with that—" He rests his hand to the side of my head, hovering far too close for my protective shields to stay firmly in place. His teeth graze across the lower portion of his lip, and I fight back the pull to do the same, caught under the spell of his bewitching stare. "Yes, I cursed you, and now my lips on your skin are all you can think about."

"You'd have to be desperate to put them there," I whisper, my lips aching for his to brush against mine. Maybe he really is casting a curse.

"Dying, Peaches. Show me you're dying too."

My mask slips enough to elicit a "there you go, good" from Liam, his breath prickling the hairs on the nape of my neck.

My entire being calls to him.

Don't. Trust. This.

Fight the lean.

"See this—" I wag a shaky finger. "I'm not falling for it this time. I'm officially calling this whole thing off. Whatever you're up to, I don't want to deal with the ramifications. Consider your prank busted."

"My prank?" He blinks, and a false doe-like innocence twists his silhouette into an almost saintly demeanor. It's the patented look he'd plaster on the minute my mother entered a room, and the blame landed on me for whatever *he did.*

"Evelina, why did you go in the pool with all your clothes on?"

"Why are you covered in pie, sweetheart?"

"If you didn't want the book covered in mud, I don't understand why you read it so close to their football game."

"Oh heavens, why did you think cutting a random section of your hair was a good idea?"

"Yes, whatever you're up to that's making you do shit like this—it's over."

He steps back, stumbling as if the force of my statement physically gut-punched him and searching my face—for what, I don't know—but I steel away, the nerves coursing through at the light jolt that permeates my being whenever his amber eyes meet mine.

"Honestly, Peaches. I don't know what you're talking about."

"I heard what you said with Eli. He asked if you had a plan for dealing with me—and you said you were trying to get my wall down so you can torment me again, or something like that. Well jokes on you buddy because the wall's way freakin' high now."

"Or something like that," he repeats with a shake of his head. A muscle flicks angrily in Liam's jaw as he pins a heated stare on me. "I take it you missed some of what I said, huh?"

"I heard enough."

"You really didn't." He chuckles bitterly. "Un-fucking-believable. I almost thought we were getting somewhere."

"Oh please. You're just upset I spoiled whatever you had planned."

"Are you kidding me?" he asks in a low, resentful rumble, reminiscent of the night before I left for Paris when I found myself in a similar position. "Is that seriously what you still think of me?"

I shrug him off, staring past his shoulder, keeping everything inside cold and devoid of feeling.

This is how I stay safe from him.

But the heat radiating off Liam threatens to melt away my reserves, and I'm severely out of practice feigning disinterest in this type of situation.

"Tell me, Evie. What exactly was my plan? Take you to your brother's wedding—and what? Embarrass you in a place you already had a mental breakdown about going to? Because apparently, I'm that much of an unfeeling ass? And what about Eli? He was just going to let—whatever—happen to his best friend?" Liam's chest heaves, and his eyes blaze in the low light of the alley.

I've never seen Liam mad. Annoyed? Sure. Hundreds of times. But not—*this*.

The way he's staring at me, lit with passion, burning heat with a pronounced rise and fall of his chest, it's intoxicating. It heightens the tugging sensation that tortures my insides whenever he's near and scatters my thoughts in dangerous directions.

What would he do if I gave in and leaned? Would his lips crash into mine, while he buried my back into the wall with a demanding embrace? Or would he maybe enter with a gentle caress instead and work into something more? Who am I kidding? He'd probably be repulsed. Or find a way to use it to his advantage and string me along like the lovesick puppet I'm dangerously close to becoming if I ever let my guard down.

"No. I don't know. I haven't had time to think it out yet." I wipe my clammy hands on my apron, pulling my attention off his lips. *Focus, Evie.* "But given our history—"

"Oh yes, let's talk about our history"—he steps forward, narrowing his fiery gaze—"because I'd like to know why every time we get remotely close, you shut down like this."

Picking my lean up off the wall, I mimic his powerful stride, strangling a gasp in my throat at the sudden proximity. *Bad idea.* "Maybe if you hadn't taken advantage of my trust in the past, I wouldn't be so defensive." I tilt my chin up and unleash the full force of my glower, hoping he misses the desire broadcasted through my gaze.

It's infuriating.

He's infuriating.

Liam's body sways forward, bumping into my chest and clearing my mind. The rigid, humorless line of his mouth parts slightly.

My chin raises the final fraction, leaving my lips recklessly close to his.

"I thought you'd at least make it forty-eight hours before you ran."

"I'm not running. I'm being practical." My pulse thuds in my ears. My lips tingle, craving his. The temptation is far too close to be sensible for much longer.

"You're always running, and I'm tired of chasing you."

He thinks he's chasing *me?* The mirror images from the night before I left for Paris pull me between the past and the present. I was so sure he was going to kiss me that night, so sure I wanted it—and yet—

Liam's eyes flicker to my mouth, and I let myself believe he might be under the influences of a similar spell for half a second. Maybe Maria's right, and he's fighting against the same intoxicating pull, drowning in the same overwhelming pool of need.

But he didn't kiss me that night. He taunted me and told me to admit defeat. Right?

"You're never going to see anything else, are you?" he asks. Cool mint and heat curl around me as we exchange breaths. Neurons and synapses misfire, and any chance I have to make sense of this goes up in a puff of smoke. "After everything this week, you were still so quick to villainize me." His eyes search my face for something. *I'm sorry* dances on the tip of my tongue, but I swallow it back down. "Nothing I do is ever going to change that."

"I can—I could—" My tongue fumbles over itself as I desperately wish it was doing something else right now. *It's not him you don't trust.* I shoo the revelation away, but it's too late and far too right.

His lips part as if to say more, but he shakes his head instead. His spine stiffens. The space between us grows again, and I'm left to catch my breath in the emptiness between us.

"Right, well, I'm sure you need to go back to work." He nods, his granite expression faltering slightly. Like it's a mask he's warring to keep in place. But I can't tell if I'm imagining something I want or not. "I'm sorry for keeping you as long as I did."

He tosses his jacket on, and my back finds its emotional support wall for balance while he walks away.

A chorus of "The Fields of Athenry" hits my ears, sliding back into the main room of The Quays. Drunken men huddle in celebration after an apparent rugby match win. Or are they upset they lost? The line is fine and relatively undefined regarding their demeanor either way.

Sighing, I stop at one of the repurposed oak barrels Declan converted into tabletops and stack a round of shot glasses together, cleaning up in the wake of the mass of men emptying out onto the street. Marching back up to the unpretentious counter where Eli's waiting, I duck as an errant dart throw from a ruddy-nosed man in a rugby sweater narrowly misses my head.

"There she is." Eli smiles. My hands fumble over the dirty glasses, placing them into the gray plastic dishwasher rack. "Any chance you've seen Liam? I lost him."

"Scared him off." I shrug. "What do you want to drink?"

Dragging his gaze over to the drafts, he furrows his brow and studies the taps. "No Sams?"

"No, sorry."

"Guinness then, I guess."

"I'll take a Kronenburg too—when you get a second, Evie." Fionn approaches the bar and sits beside Eli, flashing a broad, dangerous grin. A pink tinge colors Eli's cheeks right on schedule.

"You got it," I say, maintaining a visual of the two love birds out of the corner of my eye. If I bury myself into the adorable interaction unfolding, I can suppress the ugly, anxious thoughts whirling inside my mind.

I almost kissed Liam Kelly. I *wanted* to kiss Liam Kelly.

More than usual.

More than I ever have in the ten years we've played this game.

Undeniable sparks fill a well I've left empty for years with rapid urgency.

Hi sparks, can you not? Thanks.

"Are you coming out with us tonight?" Fionn asks Eli. His fingers lightly brush Eli's arm, pretending to reach for something. I angle the Guinness and hold the glass at a forty-five-degree angle. Steadying my breath, I focus on the hallowed ritual. Hops and chocolate mix together, providing a brief respite from the otherwise musty odor of The Quays.

"Oh, I don't know." Eli's attention oscillates between the door and me, topping the Guinness off with a foam layer. "Wait, did you seriously scare him off?"

Pursing my lips, I grab another glass and head back to the Kronenburg tap, choosing to ignore Eli since his line of questioning threatens to further exacerbate my nerves.

"Evie."

I let my shoulders drop. "We had a disagreement. Like we always do—no big deal."

"Right." He arches a brow as I lay their glasses in front of them. "And he left?"

"Maybe he had more work to do, and the two are completely unrelated."

A lone stool scratches in the distance in the far too quiet bar.

Eli sips his beer, wiping the foam mustache forming over his top lip, clearly not buying my shit. "Evie, what the hell did you say to him?"

Fionn's spine straightens at his brusque tone. "I should—er—go check with Declan and see if he needs any help." He stands, patting my shoulder, and strides to the backroom.

Eli's eyes remain on me, a disgruntled snarl resting on his face.

"Oh, quit the intimidation tactics. I've seen you fight a tree and lose." I wave him off. There's a spot on the counter that needs a serious rub down, and I channel my energy, hoping to eradicate the ring. "I just told him I wanted to call off our whole arrangement."

"And . . ."

"And nothing, that's it."

"Bullshit, he wouldn't leave if that's all that happened."

"I may have been outside when you talked about his plan to deal with me and called him out," I mumble.

"His plan to—" Eli's brow furrows deeper. His eyes widen with realization, and then a deep, amused chuckle rumbles in his chest.

And then stops.

"What?" I sigh.

"You couldn't have heard the whole thing if that's what you got out of it."

I pause wiping the counter and glance at Eli. "He said that too."

"Maybe you should trust him, then."

"Or . . . you could be a good friend and tell me what I missed if it was so crucial."

"Nuh-uh. Nope. This is between you two. Ask him directly if you want that answer."

"Why do I keep you around if you're always this damn useless?" I grump.

"Because I'm easy on the eyes and a fucking delight." Eli shrugs, taking another sip of his beer.

"And obviously humble."

"Can't stay humble in the City of Champions." He rolls up his sleeves and flashes his Superbowl, World Series, NBA Championship, and Stanley Cup tattoos.

"Yes, and you were integral to all those wins." I reach out and tousle his curls with my hand.

"Get out of here." He bats me away. "But seriously, Evie, why would I be in on some prank after last week? Like if you can't trust him, at least trust me."

"Fine. Maybe I panicked and jumped to conclusions."

"Oh no, you definitely did." A few more laughs bubble out of Eli sipping his beer. "Welcome to the Train Wrecks in Love Club, kid." He raises his glass to me.

"I accept the train wreck part, but I'm not in love with that spawn." Heat rises to my cheeks as I recall my dream at Liam's. I'll take my dream-state proclamation to the grave. Besides, Eli's the one who gets overwhelmed with feelings and does stuff like this. Not me.

At least, it *wasn't* me for the longest time. I thought I had everything together in high school and college, but now? It's possible Liam's presence has highlighted how much I've broken down in the past five years and stopped growing.

Something had to go seriously south if Eli's claiming maturity over me.

I open my mouth to tell Eli I'll apologize to Liam when I'm home and can gather my thoughts enough for a decent text, but a sudden, shrill "Eevee, hi," steals the air from my lungs and arrests Eli's laugh in an instant.

Only one person butchers my name like that no matter how many times I correct her; it's a short "e" like "heavy" without the "h" and not a Pokémon. Eyes widening, terrorized by the impending situation, I manage a quick "Run. Run now" to Eli and gather whatever reserves I have left for another battle.

10

Sugar and Spice

THE DETERMINED CLACK OF heels striding over the worn-out floor-boards draws closer. Harmony, another reminder of the woman I used to be. Back to the impending doom, I breathe and gather my weapons for battle.

Clack.

Harmony and I met my first year here. She was everything Caroline wanted in a dutiful daughter. So naturally, still clinging to the dream that I could please my mother if I tried hard enough, I wanted to be Harmony.

Like a lost puppy, I followed her everywhere, staying out until five in the morning, going out to clubs, and snapping photos of us dressed in the latest fashions around different parts of the city.

The endo was present but manageable, and I could hide and drag through the pain without letting anyone in on the reality of living with the disease.

As the endo became a more prominent player in my life, though, Harmony's role as the main character in my story diminished, my disease demanding the title, and her interest in me waned.

I invited her over for movies with Maria, but she didn't "get" Gene Kelly, and she kept relating Audrey Hepburn to Blair Waldorf in *Gossip Girl*, which felt sacrilegious to me.

She started throwing solutions at me while whining that I wasn't fun anymore, pointing out my lack of organic food, exercise, gluten intake, etc., as possible culprits, like having this disease without a cure was my fault.

Clack.

Maybe I should have forced Eli to stay for moral support instead of sacrificing myself for the cause, but hopefully his hasty retreat led him into the arms of Fionn, and he can thank me for my offering at his wedding one day.

The clacks echo in the empty landscape of my mind until they are no more, replaced by nimble fingers drumming on the counter.

Steady, aim—"Harmony, hi!" Armed with a fake smile, I turn to greet my passive-aggressor. "Oh my goodness, how are you?"

"Oh, you know, the usual." She flips her mahogany curls over her shoulder, meeting my cheek for a kiss. "Radiating positive vibes and gathering the goodness flowing in from all directions in my life. What about you?" she squeaks, booping my nose. "I've missed your cute ass."

That's unlikely.

On her last visit to The Quays six months ago, Harmony informed me that "my little downer" harshed her vibe, and she needed to "withdraw from our relationship" to fill her life with positivity.

I was devastated for two seconds and then got over it.

"Oh, I'm doing fine. Great, really," I lie.

Harmony furrows her immaculately manicured brows. "Your little issue is still giving you problems, huh?"

My incurable disease? Why yes, yes, it is.

"Here and there." I shrug, grabbing a short glass. "You want your usual?"

Nodding, she pulls out one of the bar stools in an apparent attempt to keep me company while I muddle some berries in a shaker for a Black Rose, an ombre drink filterable to absolute Nashville perfection.

In other words, Harmony in hard liquor form.

When Harmony used to visit, she'd be accompanied by a gaggle of friends who honked and preened their feathers at the other side of the bar while I endured their hushed whispers and blatant stares alone. So this solo act has me on red alert.

"Oh! Before I forget," she chirps, "I've been doing yoga over at Bois de Boulogne" —my spine stiffens, endo cure suggestion incoming in *five, four, three, two*— "and there's a woman there who follows my blog. Get. This. Her sister's friend's cousin had an issue with her periods, and she started going to these classes—which are totes cute, by the way. The instructor trained in the foothills of Mount Shasta, so like very legit—"

"Isn't that in California?"

"Exactly. Anyway, my sister's friend's cousin says it's like she has a whole new body. Totally cured."

"How fortunate for her," I manage through bared teeth. Hopefully, it comes across as an innocent smile, and she misses the maniacal forest witch possessing my soul.

Harmony summoned her.

I swear all it takes is a fixer or dreamer to mention one of the Holy Trinity of Cures—yoga, diets, and supplements. And bam! I'm one eye of newt short from cursing Harmony with a perpetual bad hair day.

Shaking Harmony's drink a bit more aggressively than necessary, I bite back a cackle and ponder the true reason for her presence here.

"So . . ." she drawls, tracing a spot on the counter with her finger. "What's up with that cute guy you posted earlier on the 'gram?"

Ah. There we go.

"Like, are you two serious?"

"Oh. Uhm." I settle the shaker, unsure how to proceed here. I *should* tell her the picture was a plant. Her entire Instagram is a fictitious account of a chic bohemian lifestyle she barely lives. But after years of her belittling every aspect of my life—well, it's farther along the complete and total humiliation spectrum than I care to venture.

"It's still new, but maybe?" Best to toe the line with half-truths here, less likely to be caught in a complete lie that way. "We grew up together, but there was always *something* there—at least for me." *Something* is the only word I have in my vocabulary to describe it. I grab the mesh strainer and steady my hand, pouring out Harmony's drink.

"So were you two talking before he got here, then?"

"No, actually. Liam coming was a bit of a surprise." I blush. "But once I ran into him, we fell back into our natural patterns like no time had passed. He surprised me a few days ago with a picnic at Place Dauphine, and then I stayed at his apartment yesterday."

"Already?" Harmony squeals. "Oh my gosh, you must really like him then. I remember in college, your one boyfriend—what was his name?"

"Michel," I say through clenched teeth. Nothing good can come out of this trip down memory lane. Michel was patient and understanding when we discovered intimacy was painful for me, but in the end, it was too hard for us to overcome, so we parted ways after a few months. After that, relationships didn't make sense to me, with painful intercourse looming overhead like a dark cloud bound to rain blue lady balls at any given moment.

"He complained all the time you wouldn't put out, and after him, you weren't interested in anyone."

"Liam's special."

"He's way hotter than Michel, so good for you for reaching up." She boops my nose again, and I'm one boop away from booping her nose with my fist.

"He's very handsome." I force a smile. "But he's really sweet when he wants to be too." *Which isn't often.* My lips twist into a more natural grin at this play on words.

"Oh my god, you're practically beaming. This is so cute."

I keep my mouth snapped shut to suffocate a startled laugh. I'll have to brag to Liam about this minor victory later. Obviously, he was mistaken with his concerns that I couldn't pull this off because, hello, somebody give me an Oscar. I'm nailing it here.

Not that he'll want to talk to me.

Internally groaning, I toss a yellow straw into Harmony's drink. Drafting him an apology won't be easy, but Eli's right, I jumped to conclusions I shouldn't have and I owe him one.

Dipping my head to reach into the mini fridge for a sprig of rosemary, my cogs whir together as I figure out how to approach that very awkward situation. At least I have some time.

"And he visits you at work. Definitely a keeper." Harmony sighs, pressing her palm to her heart.

No. My head shoots up, slamming into the overhanging counter. Son of a biscuit, that hurt.

"Seriously, Eevee, don't mess this up, or I'm going to steal him from you." She scrunches up her nose and playfully nudges me.

I rub my temple, eyes watering, and frantically search the bar. A non-committal "arghskfk" emits from the back of my throat.

Wonder Boy bows under a hanging beam, scanning the room. His looming demeanor suggests he's still agitated and a tad broody. Not a great combination for me.

Mindlessly dropping the sprig of rosemary into Harmony's glass, I shift it over to her and shuffle out from behind the counter. "Excuse me, I should—" I motion toward Liam, cursing under my breath. "If that man could leave well enough alone—just once in his damn life."

My hand rubs the egg forming on my noggin. Maybe I can convince him to exit without ever talking to Harmony. The less those two interact, the better, considering I just gave Liam a loaded weapon to embarrass me with.

"I'm not dating that troll."

Or *"Is she still telling that creepy story? It's adorable that she thinks she has a chance."*

Or some other variation of the actual truth is bound to slip out of his lips if I let it. And after the alley, I wouldn't blame him for wanting to get even.

"I went to get your corsage," he blurts, throwing me off-balance.

"Huh?" I blink.

"Your corsage." He threads a hand through his hair. A crease forms between his brows, and he pauses, gingerly reaching for the spot where I hit my head. "What happened now?" His fingers trail the bump, and I forget I'm in panic mode for half a second.

Frozen, I gape at my assured destruction manifested in human form, delicately rubbing a bruise on my head. Why—what—who is this man?

"I'm fine." I pull his hand down, but in my haze, I don't release it. "Could we talk outside for a minute?"

He nods and turns, but before we reach the door, a shrill "Aww, you can't leave without introducing me to your beau first" stops me in my tracks.

Shit. My momentary lapse of wherewithal gave the Goddess Divine of Moonbeams and Sparkles time to pounce, and now I'm about to pay for it, suddenly lodged in a shit sandwich of awkward.

In other words, I'm in a bit of a pickle.

That really didn't cut the mustard.

For God's Sake, Evie, focus or you're toast.

Liam's gaze oscillates between Harmony, me, and our hands clutching each other. His trembles in my grasp, and I release it, ready to open my mouth and explain the whole "beau" thing but find a dry desert in place of a voice.

"Liam, right?" Harmony bats her fake eyelashes, pressing her cherry red lips to the skinny straw in her glass. "I'm Harmony." She offers out a dead fish of a hand. In his stupor, he doesn't extend his own.

"Eevee was just bragging about how she has the sweetest, dreamiest boyfriend, so obviously, I had to come and introduce myself."

"Couldn't be me." Liam arches a brow, his stare colliding with mine before raking down my body, setting every inch of me ablaze. "You called me sweet, really?" he asks, a faint smirk playing on his lips.

Unbridled panic flashes through my eyes. I'm a good two seconds away from total humiliation, and I deserve it. If I had told Harmony the truth, I wouldn't have set Liam up for this opportunity.

"I believe my exact words were, 'he's really sweet when he wants to be.'" I nervously laugh.

"When he wants to be, right. That makes more sense. And the dreamy part?" He cocks his head to the side, crossing his arms and leaning against one of the oak barrels.

"Oh! I added that myself," Harmony interrupts. "But you could tell the way her eyes lit up that she's got it bad for her boyfriend."

The corners of Liam's lips twitch with amusement as a mischievous glint twinkles in the recess of his gaze. "Huh. I'm glad to hear that because, well, you know our Peaches here. Sometimes she plays it so close to the vest I have my doubts she even likes me."

"What? Of course, I like you. Why would your silly little head think otherwise?" I flash him a tight smile, trying to settle the endless pit of anxiety and doom roiling in the depths of my stomach.

"Insecurity of mine." He shrugs. "I do have a question about this boyfriend part, though."

"Oh, this is awkward," Harmony says gleefully. Okay. Seriously. Chill. At least pretend like you'll miss me after this kill shot.

Gathering the strength of Marshal Michel Nay, I face the firing squad, ready to take a bullet to the heart. An impish grin spreads wide across Liam's face, popping the dimples of doom. I doubt Marshal Nay dealt with such a mirthful executioner, but here I am, waiting for my impending social death at the hands of Hades once more.

"I mean, I feel like I've been pretty clear with my intentions, and maybe I was reading this wrong—" Reaching for me, he hooks a finger through a belt loop on my jeggings and pulls me into his orbit. "But I didn't think you were warming up to the idea too."

Nervous laughter bubbles out of me as I attempt to collect myself and steady my wildly beating heart. He's managed to catch me off guard with the direction he's chosen to take this, and I've never been great with improv.

"Oh yeah, very warm on the boyfriend idea, hot even! Hot for boyfriend! Not that I'm hot for you . . . but that would be okay if I were because . . ." I sigh, my brain finally catching up with my tongue. "Sorry, my poor heart and brain still get so flustered this close, but I'm sure you get what I'm trying to say, right . . . sunshine?"

I press a hand to his chest, and his muscles tighten a fraction. The slow, steady heartbeat I expected to find underneath my palm greets me in a wild, staccato fashion.

Confused by his willingness to play this charade—by the rhythm of his heart—I glance up at his face, only to find a smug, challenging gleam washed over him.

His hand falls on my back and rubs soft circles into it. With each stroke of his thumb my nerves slowly melt away. "We're still working on the whole verbal communication thing." He winks at Harmony over my shoulder.

"It's true. I'm more of a doer," I manage.

A little snort shoots through his nostrils, and he coughs into his hand to cover it up. I flash a look that says "smooth," and he raises a brow to say "same" back.

"Actions are great, but I'm a fan of fostering solid communication in my relationships," Harmony butts in, gathering near Liam's side. "It's the oxygen every couple needs for survival. I always say that if you want to breathe easily, you need to have positive open airways at all times." She finishes with an exaggerated inhale and an upward salute highlighting her chest.

I blink, officially uncomfortable for her.

"Harmony's making an excellent point, dearest." *Yeah, I'm sure she's making two, actually.* Liam flashes a toothy, devastating grin. An outsider might think it's charming, but there's a faint twitch where he's holding back a chuckle that tells me the whole thing's laced with mockery.

"One I will surely take into advisement in the future, sunshine. Promise," I force out.

"Never put off for the future what you can do today, silly." Harmony leans over to boop my nose again and lets her chest brush Liam's arm. "If he's not sure you want a relationship with him, you should water his garden with positive thoughts and affirmations. I always make sure my gardens are thriving oases, or else why be in a relationship? Right, Liam?"

"I *could* use a little watering," Liam says with a phony hopeful look directed at me, waiting expectantly. As if to say, and this is the time you run.

Harmony's banking on that reaction too. She knows me too well. When vulnerability is part of the equation, I recede. It's why she's chosen to pull these specific affirmations out of her perfectly toned ass.

But Liam's challenging stare nettles me enough to force the opposite reaction than what's expected of me.

Stepping in between his legs, I play with the button on his shirt, biting back the cutting remark dancing on the tip of my tongue. I clear my throat and slide my gaze to his, letting the instinct to lean lead for once. "I'm so sorry, I just thought it was perfectly obvious how much I adore you," I end, batting my eyelashes for good measure.

"I'm sure I've just been getting your signals mixed." Liam smiles back. "You know I've never read your subtleties well, Peaches. But truthfully, I have felt a little fragile about our relationship lately. If you cared to, I don't know, maybe you could elaborate on the adoring part and help a guy out." He unleashes a set of puppy dog eyes on me like he's some lovesick man who desperately needs to know he's not on the raw end of unrequited love. The look of need hanging in his eyes tugs on something deep inside me, begging me to give him some kind of satisfaction.

Nope. Don't like that.

My jaw tightens a fraction, but I keep the smile plastered on my face. "Of course, if you're so insecure about it. I'd be happy to reassure you of my affections."

"Great, I'm looking forward to it."

"Wonderful," I grit.

With a flick of his wrist, he motions for me to proceed. I flash him a pointed you're-pushing-it,-buddy look, but he remains undeterred, acknowledging my annoyance with a slight raise of his shoulders.

It's time to go all in or bust.

I reach for his left hand, delicately resting it in my grasp. Drawing slow circles into his palm with the pad of my thumb, I gather what I'm going to say. Again, my lack of improvisational skills means leaning closer to the side of truth will serve me best.

"I'm sorry if I don't communicate my feelings well, but the truth is, most of the time, I don't have the words to describe how you make me feel. But you're the only one who manages to stir these strong emotions in me, and—I don't know." I shrug. A light tremor in his grip gives me pause, and I meet his eyes, catching a brief nervous shiver. It draws me closer, curious to uncover the crack in his usual confident demeanor. "But if I can assure you of anything, just know, I've been dreaming about there being an us for as long as I can remember, and I have a sneaking suspicion that's not going to change anytime soon."

The tightness in my chest lightens like a burden I've carried for years has finally been released, even if it's under false pretenses.

Liam considers me with a hooded stare. He struggles to open his mouth as if what he has to say carries similar weight. "I—"

"Oh, is that why you haven't dated anyone in five years?" Harmony cuts him off with a patented, seemingly benign question laced with passive-aggressive poison. "Because I just assumed you were too tall for anyone over here to be interested."

I don't bite, stuck in a trance, dying to hear what he was about to say. My gut screams it was important, and I almost ask him *you were saying?* But this close, the pull to Liam's orbit controls my breaths, my chest rises and falls at a speed to match his own, and I get lost in the arcing energy between us.

A loose curl falls to my cheek. I let my grip on his hand drop and whisk it behind my ear as his hand lifts to do the same.

His fingers brush over my skin, sending a rush of shivers down the nape of my neck in their wake.

My lips part.

His left dimple makes a subtle appearance. He leans, and I forget the basic mechanics of operating my respiratory system independently. His stubble presses against my cheek, his breath hot against the nape of my neck. Maybe he feels the same way, maybe—"Say you have to get back to work, and the torture ends, Peaches," he whispers.

His warmth withdraws, and my entire being yearns to follow.

Maybe, nothing. Hope deflates with his words. I don't know why he's helping me, but I can't let myself get lost in some unfulfilled high school fantasy of mine. People don't use the word torture for something they enjoy unless they're masochists.

"I, uhm—I should get back to the bar." I hastily smile, slowly detaching my fingers from his and smoothing down my apron.

"I have to go meet a friend too," Harmony says with less pep than usual. "But a bunch of us are going barhopping if you want to come, Liam."

Liam's eyes meet mine briefly. His thumb rubs the skin on his palm where I touched it, and he swallows, peeking over my shoulder at Harmony and opening his mouth to reply.

"I get off in an hour, Harmony. Why don't we meet up with you then?" I intercept, wincing as the words leave my mouth. I had accepted, in some capacity, that Eli was right and I should trust Liam more. But my kneejerk reaction is still to expect the worst, and Liam running around Paris with Harmony after I all but declared my fake undying love to him, well, there are very few scenarios where that ends well for me, and a great many ending with Liam jumping ship for far less troubled, far more harmonious waters.

Waters that don't come with a propensity to accuse him of malicious ulterior motives at the drop of a hat.

I don't know how many times I have to tell you I'm not the enemy before you actually believe it.

You're never going to see anything else, are you?

Liam's words over the past week play in my mind, and I sigh. The fi st thing he did when he came in here was check on my head, and then he rescued me from an awkward situation, however annoyingly he accomplished it. He's not the Liam I used to know. That much is certain.

I glance at Harmony, now a clear relic of my past. And I'm not the Evie I used to be either.

I need to break the habit of coming at him with my former expectations, for my sanity's sake, sure. But I also try not to be a terrible person, and I can't say with certainty that I've been the best version of myself the past few weeks around him.

Harmony's expression sours into her patented sparkling scowl, but I've left her little room to maneuver her way out of my suggestion. "Oh yeah—no, that sounds great."

"Super," I say through a tight-lipped smile.

"See you then." She presses her cheek to mine and clacks right out the door.

I ignore the glare from Liam searing into the back of my skull. "I'm starting to think you might be a masochist, Peaches."

I bite down the shiver at his word choice.

"With you?" I toss over my shoulder. "Always." I smooth down my flyaways and return to work, hoping the next hour never comes.

11

A Spoonful of Sugar

"FOR THE LOVE OF god, Liam Kelly, will you please stop grinning like some lovestruck fool?" I flash a scowl his way, arms crossed, leaning against the unsavory silver pole in the middle of the Métro car headed for Trocadéro, a platform with the ultimate view of the Eiffel Tower at night.

A languished expression remains plastered on Liam's face, and after watching him wear it for the past hour, I'm ready to wipe it right off.

He's annoyingly convincing in his role already.

Which *should* be a good thing.

But I, apparently, can't handle it. At least my body can't. It doesn't care that this is fake, or that I remind it of that fact on the regular—the butterflies still cause massive gastrointestinal distress whenever his teeth graze across his lower lip, or he looks at me with an unfamiliar softness.

I need a break.

"What? Can't a fella be happy to be taking a stroll with his darling girlfriend?" Liam places his palm over his heart, his thumb still rubbing where I drew circles on it. It's something he's done a lot since Harmony left.

"Did I cut you?" I ask, motioning to his hand.

"Huh?" He blinks, apparently taken aback by the sudden shift in questioning.

"Your palm, you've been rubbing it since I grabbed it earlier with Harmony, and I'm worried I might have cut you or something." The announcement for our stop repeats in the background.

"Oh." His eyes widen, and his thumb halts as he puts his hand back to his side and flexes it. "Just a tic, you're fine."

The cabin slows to a stop. I assess him skeptically. It's a new tic then because I've certainly never noticed it. "As long as I didn't hurt you."

The doors slide open, and we step out of the cabin on the poorly lit concrete platform. "All good, baby." He winks. "But I appreciate the concern."

I glare, an irrational part of me sparking alive—like I shouldn't like him calling me baby, and yet . . . "No, no freaking way am I letting baby pass your lips in reference again to me. Off-limits."

"What would you prefer me to call you, then?" He scratches at the scuff on his cheek. A phantom memory of the rough hair sliding over my skin sends a shiver down my spine. "Sugar?"

"I'm sorry, are you a forty-year-old man with a toupee and too much chest hair?"

"Damn. You caught me. Don't tell Natale, though. We have a good mom/son dynamic going."

I hold back my snort because the last thing this man needs is encouragement. Unfortunately, the snort ends up sticking to the back of my throat, and I soon reenact cat-coughs-up-hairball in an Oscar-worthy performance.

His lips tip into a knowing smirk as he springs up the staircase two at a time. I sigh, breathing through the pain radiating in the crook of my thigh after working on my feet, and ignore how this moment is a metaphor for our entire life.

"Sweetheart?" He pauses a few steps to the top. With his left dimple imprinting on his cheek, he offers out his hand to me.

"That's a Caroline-ism." I reach out, needing the stability. "Thank you."

We march past a hundred tiny glittering Eiffel Towers spread out for sale along the sidewalk, and the grump in me intensifies. Well, really, the pain does. I release his hand and stride forward, hiding my face while I breathe through the spasm. It feels like my uterus is about to go "so long suckers, it's been real" and plop out of me onto the slick square tiles below.

My stress level's becoming more of a problem because it intensifies my flares, which adds more stress, so . . . I'm flaring more. It's a vicious circle nearly impossible to escape, but if I don't figure it out soon, I'm doomed to flare at catastrophic levels during my brother's wedding in three weeks, which is less than ideal. Nobody wants a bridesmaid curled up in the fetal position during the procession.

"Would 'Duck' fit the bill?" Liam continues behind me. My patience is way too thin for this, and I round on him with a glare. "Okay, so duck puts you in a *fowl* mood, got it." He puts his arms up in surrender.

My lips twitch, my love of puns at war with my general sour disposition. "I'm delighted that my misfortune is bringing you so much joy, and I admit I deserve it, but if you could drop the act for five minutes so I can breathe before I take on Harmony Part Deux, I'd appreciate it."

"I'm not reveling in your misfortune, Peaches."

"Then what would you call this—" I gesture between us, raising my voice over the chaotic chatter falling around us, close to one of Paris's most popular tourist destinations.

He rubs the back of his head and peeks at me with one eye. "Flirting?"

I blink. "You're flirting with me?"

"Apparently not very well," he mumbles, stuffing his hands in his pocket and glancing at an illuminated disc hovering near another local vendor selling gadgets, Eiffel Tower statues, keychains, and the like to gathering tourists.

My gaze oscillates between the growing commotion and the flush creeping across Liam's cheeks, accentuated in the casting light of a nearby streetlamp. If this is what Liam flirting looks like, he's been flirting with me for our entire lives. "Like for practice?"

"I figured with this crowd, Harmony might see us before we see her. Probably a good idea to keep the ruse up, just in case, right?"

Crossing my arms in front of my chest, I raise a skeptical brow. "I believe your card said something about being head-over-heels in love with me, not for you to maintain your typical teasing demeanor."

"And I vaguely recall you recently scolding me in a Métro car to stop 'grinning like some lovestruck fool,' so why don't you figure out what you want, Peaches, and then let me know."

Liam's not wrong. I've actually scolded him multiple times tonight, and he's still standing here, a willing participant with no tangible benefits I can point to. Keeping the peace at home is one thing, but on this side of the Atlantic, all I can see is this just being one giant headache for him.

"Why are you helping me, really?" I say, my voice so small I fear it'll be carried away by the wind before it reaches his ears.

A smile rests on his face, and he shrugs. "I guess I just figure I owe you."

My heart stops, and a soft "oh" passes over my lips.

His stare stays connected to mine, and he clears his throat. "So tell me, Peaches, how are we playing this?"

Like you've been equally tortured for all these years. A giddy, dizzying feeling rushes over me at the ridiculous request forming in my brain, but I bury it back down. Liam actually acting like he's head-over-heels isn't realistic when he looks like *that*, and I have the charm and body type of a potato. "Well"—I pull at the tips of my fingers—"Caroline *did* tell me to 'aim a little lower' when it came to you, and Harmony congratulated me on 'reaching up' so I guess the doting, worships-the-ground-I-walk-on boyfriend dynamic's a bit unrealistic anyway. We can say we're just enjoying each other's company for a change."

Liam's brows squish together. "I'm sorry—your mother said what?"

I toe the ground with my shoe. "To aim a little lower, it's not a big deal. I mean, she's right, anyway, so I get it."

"I don't think *I* do, though."

"People won't buy you falling first, that's all. So if you don't want to get caught, we shouldn't push it."

He crosses his arms in front of his chest and slowly raises a brow. "Well, now I think you're doubting my acting skills."

"I saw you in our school performance of *Chicken Little*. I was very unconvinced the sky was falling." I ruefully chuckle, eyes glued to the black and white checkered tiles.

"Evie—" Two fingers delicately lift my chin. "Why would your mom say something like that? Does this have to do with what she thinks happened the night of the ball?"

"Oh, well, yeah." I swallow. "Sort of." I don't want to throw the ball in his face any more than I have tonight since it's becoming abundantly clear that I'm holding a hollow grudge at best.

"Okay, so I'm the one who messed all of this up. Let me play the part of adoring boyfriend and fix it." He brushes a loose tendril off my cheek. His fingers leave embers in their wake that dance along my jawline. The dizzying spell I was under gives way to a more profound ache, begging for release, like the cavity in my chest can't handle the pressure.

"If—you insist—" I stutter. He never could say no to a challenge.

"If you believe the shit they're selling, I do." He withdraws his hand from my cheek. "As long as you're comfortable with it."

"I mean, who could say no to a little flattery?" I blush.

"Great, then it's settled. I'll adore the fuck out of you, and everyone can go screw—" He gestures for our walk to continue, and I nod, taking in the stone expression on his face. An unexplained tension holds his shoulders high as he strides forward.

"Liam?"

He glances down at me.

"You know you aren't obligated to do this, right? I appreciate it, and I'm sorry for what I said in the alley, but I can find another way to get through this."

"I know, Peaches, don't worry."

He gives my hand a reassuring squeeze before returning his attention to navigating the throngs of people on the platform while mine stays glued to the harsh worry lines rimming the edge of his mouth. A sudden halt in our steps jerks me back to alert, and I pull my eyes off his gold flecks and soft pillow lips to find the Eiffel Tower shining in the distance.

Illuminated throughout, it stands sharply against the black expanse of sky. Light and shadows meld together to turn the harsh iron latticework into a crocheted piece of lace, delicately weaving the golden strands together through the darkness.

Liam's mouth hangs slightly agape, attention devoted to the tower. Pride warms my chest to be a part of this with him. No one forgets their first time.

Montmartre at midnight. That was mine.

The hopeless romantic that I was, I opted to hike the stairs of Sacré-Coeur, pivoting for a glance of the city at the top. The soft serenade of a violin playing "Sous le Ciel de Paris" in a nearby apartment accompanied the reveal, stealing my breath and my heart in an instant.

The soft voice of a street performer nearby breaks me out of my revelry as it floats over the general chaos of this platform. I strain my ears trying to pick up the song. It's vaguely familiar, but maybe the acoustic guitar is throwing me off. Almost like it's—yup, that's the Rick Astley song. Nice. Very Parisian.

I stand at Liam's side, watching him in whatever semblance of a moment he has through the music choice. The harsh worried lines rimming his mouth relax, and a heaviness in my chest lightens.

"Nana would have loved this," he whispers.

"She really would have." I breathe out. My gaze roams over the illuminated waters of the garden fountains below the platform.

"Are we getting RickRolled right now?" he asks, a strong dose of humor in his voice, eyes still trained forward.

"Yes. Yes, we are. I'm so sorry that's what's playing during your first time."

"Company isn't half bad."

Liam's pinky finger brushes against mine, lightly curling around it. I fight the pull to glance down, keeping my gaze out in front of us, roaming over the groups of tourists posing for pictures. Couples. Families. Friends. Girls' night out. An engagement unfolding. Chaos whirls around us, and yet there's a beat of silence in our little bubble. A tiny truce.

Anxiety roils in the pit of my stomach. He's right, Nana would have loved this, but she would have hated us.

Who Liam and I became.

How so many things came between us. That we're all but strangers at best and the greatest adversaries at our worst.

It's okay that you like being alone, Evelina, but that boy needs you as much as you'll need him when I'm not here anymore. Life will throw curveballs at you all along your journey, but if you have your friends and you support each other, every little thing will turn out alright.

I'm not sure Nana knew the curveballs life would hurl my way would be more like getting pelted with paintballs repeatedly without any protective gear, but I can't help but feel like she has a hand in all this—in pushing us back together, here. When I need him now more than ever to get through this wedding.

"Thank you for coming to my rescue multiple times, especially after I was horrid to you." I sigh. "I'm going to try my best not to jump to conclusions anymore, I promise. If you owe me anything, I at least owe you that."

He smiles softly, and his left dimple puckers his cheek. "Can't say I was exactly a knight in shining armor with that rescue but you're welcome."

"I'd have been worried there was an invasion-of-the-body-snatchers situation unraveling if you didn't tease me while you were helping. But I'm sorry for getting us into another situation, I'm sure this isn't what you wanted to do on your Friday night."

"Honestly, standing here with you right now kind of makes up for it, even if I had told Harmony this morning I had work to do tonight."

My brows furrow. "How—but—you met her tonight."

Liam threads a hand through his hair, still not acknowledging our interlocked fingers. "She DM'd me on Instagram earlier, followed it from the tag in the photo or something. Said if I wanted someone to show me around Paris, she would be more than happy to."

A jealous heat flushes through my body. Harmony came into the bar pretending to be so happy for my relationship, and the whole time she sat there, she'd already planted the seeds to steal Liam away. I'd say it's reassuring to find at least one person from my past hasn't changed but— "That bitch." The words bypass my filter with mortifying speed. Heat rises to my cheeks, and my embarrassment makes it damn near impossible to meet Liam's eyes.

We're not together. This reaction is entirely unwarranted.

"I'm so sorry," I say, finally forcing my gaze his way. "I know this isn't real and I have no right to be jealous. It's just, she doesn't know that."

He snorts. "You can let her know I'm very taken if you want, Peaches."

"You know what? Maybe I will." I fight back the muscles wanting to tense around our locked fingers. Harmony's just like the girls who swarmed Liam at the college bar. The type of person who felt confident enough to wear figure-flattering outfits because they didn't have to worry about their endo belly and sported perfectly tousled hair because they had the energy to expend on it. An ugly, unsettling feeling swelled in my chest, knowing they were everything I wasn't, everything Caroline wanted me to be, and Liam didn't desert and torture.

A knot in my stomach deepens. Regardless of what I thought at the bar—and let's be honest, when Liam's involved, I'm *not* thinking much these days—it'd be selfish of me to cockblock him with my problems if he really were interested. "I appreciate your dedication to our situation, but you didn't have to say no if you wanted to go—I mean, she's totally your type, and I shouldn't have tried to get in the way."

Liam slides his amber eyes on me, pulling his attention off the tower. "You think *that's* my type?"

"Maybe not to a T, but come on, it's Harmony. She's gorgeous."

"That's not really where my attention was, so I'll take your word for it."

"That's fair. You were probably too busy focusing on getting out of the situation as fast as possible, huh?"

He snorts. "No, Peaches, that wasn't where it was either."

"Where exactly was your attention, then?" A nervous, chaotic energy whirls through me, and I'm surprised I summoned the courage to ask that question out loud.

In a perfect, romantic mirror of this world, he'd grab my hand, swing me into him, bring his hand up to my cheek, and with a desperate softness, whisper "on you."

A shiver flashes through his soft gaze resting on my face. Like he knows what I want, and he can't provide me with that kind of satisfaction because this is the real world where dreams go to die.

"Why would you ask that?" He glances over my shoulder, unable to meet my eyes, and I chide myself for making this even more awkward.

Any response halts with a firm tug on my hand that pulls me into his orbit. His right hand softly caresses my cheek, and I blink back to reality. Nothing changes. My cheek still rests delicately in the palm of his hand. Shimmers stream down my spine. Butterflies flutter around in a free-for-all.

"It's always right here," he says.

My heart stops dead. Cause of death, impossible swooning.

"I don't get it—" A familiar voice carries over the chatter around us, and my shoulders deflate.

This is an act.

This is an act for Harmony.

He's acting.

Maybe if I repeat that enough times I'll actually remember.

"She used to be cute, I guess. But now it's like if Shrek and Strawberry Shortcake had a baby, and he's gorgeous," Harmony practically shouts. She was never great with voice modulation and lost in the crowd, there's no way she knows how close she is.

"She probably gives good head," the second voice supplies with a cackle.

I glance over my shoulder. Oh holy Jean Hagen, no.

Standing five feet behind me, clad in a champagne sequins dress, hitting just above the knee, is a familiar face that's haunted my dreams, murdering both me and the French language on several occasions in the past week.

Harmony 2.0.

The Métro rider less affectionately known as Red Beret. Hell, I can't deal with two Harmonies tonight.

They're still searching for us. We have time.

"Hide me," I whisper, regretting this entire escapade.

Liam tugs on my hand, pulling me toward the platform's edge lined with statues on towering pedestals. He cages me with his body against one of the bases as I fight back the tears burning inside my lids. I can't hold them back much longer. I'm too tired, overwhelmed, and frankly, still in pain. So I'm going to have to accept that sometimes crying happens.

"Ignore them." He wipes a tear away with his thumb.

"They're not wrong." I laugh, trying to regain my composure. I've cried more in front of Liam in the past week than I ever let myself in the past.

"Seriously, Peaches. You're beautiful."

I snort. Liam's nailing the adoring boyfriend part, but apparently there's still some work to be had on my end accepting said admiration.

It's not a particularly familiar experience of mine, especially given the mother I have, so it might take some time.

"Evie, look at me." A sharp, frustrated edge in his voice prompts me to listen.

Breath steals from my lungs the second I meet his eyes. Cast in the glow of an overhead streetlamp, the gold flecks held within dance with a passion that could rival Gene Kelly.

"I'm looking at you," I rasp.

"Good, and do you see what you do to me?"

My heartbeat pounds in the hollow of my throat. I want this for real, but there's no way I could actually have that effect on him. He's just trying to right an old wrong. "Drive you up a wall."

"You have no idea how true that is." He brushes a tear off my cheek, and my lashes flutter closed at the sparking sensation his skin against mine produces. "How you continuously sucker punch me with those big blue eyes."

He brushes another tear falling on my right side. "And that damn hair of yours that still sparkles in the sun and drives me wild."

The ache inside dips into something more profound. Richer. These are all the things that Caroline says are wrong with me, and his voice is treating them like they're treasures, like they're worth revering.

"I expect you to be very mature about this information in the future," he whispers. "But Evie, I shut a door in your face the other day because I was hard, and I panicked."

I stutter, blinking at this admission. "I'm sorry—I'm—uhm—I'm going to need you to repeat that. You, what?"

The tips of his ears turn red, and he mouths, "I got a boner."

My head tilts back, releasing a boisterous, cathartic laugh, and Liam beams down at me. And for a microsecond, I see the reality Nana wanted for us. The one where he's a safe haven instead of a threat. Where when I cry, he's there to cheer me up instead of being the original instigator.

"That's the story you're going with? I didn't know ogres and bonnet-wearing dolls were your things."

"You're so fucking stubborn it's ridiculous." He sighs. "Maybe I should tell Harmony the story instead."

"Don't you dare. I'm Harmonied out."

"And honestly—" Harmony's voice grows closer. "Those big-ass cakes are her brand or whatever, but she doesn't have to eat the entire thing herself—"

"On second thought, share away," I grit out.

"Oh, okay, good." He shoots his head toward their voices, opening his mouth.

"I was joking!" I panic and pull at his shirt, tugging him back toward me.

He comes to a rest, inches from my lips. My breath hitches. His eyes flicker to my mouth. My chin tilts a fraction, our lips almost brushing together. He just has to finish the lean.

He closes his eyes with a pained expression, "Evie, listen—"

"There you two are," Harmony sounds over Liam's shoulder. "We almost missed you."

"Oh, Harmony. Hi." I rise on my toes, peering over his broad figure.

"This is my friend Samantha," Harmony says. "She's new to the city, but she reached out, and I just had to take her under my wing."

Samantha narrows her gaze at me. I bury into Liam's shadow, hoping the combination of poor lighting and a six-four figure obscures me from recognition, and deflate when her face illuminates with dawning.

"Oh my god." She laughs. "Harmony, I think that's totally Cheese Girl."

Liam, still caging me, raises a single brow and mouths, "Cheese girl?"

"I may have done shots of Cheez Whiz on the Métro," I say in a hushed explanation. "It was not a particularly proud moment, and I don't wish to revisit it."

"It is. That's the girl that choked on Cheez Whiz."

"Can't say I'm surprised." Harmony snorts. "Eevee's habits were always interesting."

Liam nuzzles closer into my neck and all but growls, "God, I love the way you work a can of cheese."

The two women blink at his backside as if to say we knew something was clearly wrong since you've chosen this weird Shrek meets Strawberry Shortcake hybrid, but we didn't realize it was this bad.

"You do love your cheese." I pat his chest and press a kiss to the tip of his nose. "I call it his little feta-ish." I wink conspiratorially at Harmony.

He bites on his knuckle, suffocating a laugh but still looking oddly aroused, his stare heavy and dark under his thick-hooded lashes.

Danger. Danger. My internal alarm sirens.

"Will you look at the time? The tower's ready to sparkle," I sing, gesturing for him to turn. "Oh, actually. Harmony, would you mind taking a photo of us for Instagram?"

Harmony rolls her eyes but nods. "Lord knows your traffic needs it."

Forcing a smile, I hand my phone over to her and follow Liam to an empty-ish space a few feet away. The Eiffel Tower looms overhead, glittering in the night sky as Liam snakes his arm around my waist, his splayed fingers burning an imprint into my side. Harmony holds the phone horizontally and takes a photo.

"This pose is boring," Samantha yells. "Y'all need to kiss. It'd be gold on Insta with the sparkles."

Harmony shoots her some serious side-eye. *Oh, poor sweet Samantha, we hardly knew your actual name.*

Liam tenses next to me. Samantha's not wrong (though I fear a name isn't the only lived experience she and my American girl doll are about to share), kissing in front of the Eiffel Tower is the perfect picture. But I don't want to push Liam further out of his comfort zone than he already is.

"I'm fine with it if you are," he whispers.

"Are you sure?"

"It's just a kiss." He shrugs.

Right, just a kiss, that's it. Not the thing I've been fantasizing about my entire life or anything.

"We're on a time limit with the sparkles, guys," Harmony shouts.

I nod. "Just a kiss, totally fine," I repeat, more so to myself. "It is the better photo."

"Then we probably should do it."

"Yeah." I shake my hands out at my side with a little shimmy. "We should."

Liam wraps an arm around me, resting his hand on the small of my back and igniting the embers that always burn brighter when he's near. He dips his head, bringing his lips to my ear. "Slight note. Maybe don't do your nervous energy dance before we kiss next time." He kisses my cheek, and my eyes flutter closed at the sensation. Shimmers radiate from the side of my face, heating the rest of me in an instant. "I'm going to kiss you for real now, Peaches."

I nod, blinking my lids back open.

My skin hums with anticipation as our proximity narrows, until my chest presses against his hard wall of muscle. He gently cradles the back of my head, tangling in my mess of strawberry curls.

I try to keep the impending breath hitch silent. Try to hide the fact that everything inside is screaming *Oh my god, we're about to kiss Liam Kelly.*

Liam's eyes lock on mine with a dark intensity I thought was reserved for dreamland, and he lowers his head with slightly parted lips that brush against mine. Air steals from my lungs with the contact. Weak-kneed, I'm grateful for the support of his arm against my back.

But this kiss, this soft gentle caress, I need so much more than this. My masochistic tendencies were wrong. We were never going to be okay with just a taste. Suddenly, an impulsive, far too ignored part of me breaks free from its cage as if his mouth's imprint held the key, and I wrap a hand around his neck, tugging him deeper against my mouth and ravishing him with a hungry embrace. Whatever senseless instinct kicked in, it takes a few beats for the rest of me to catch up and register what is happening.

I am *kissing* Liam Kelly.

Hard.

And nothing's ever felt so utterly sweet passing over my lips.

Liam hasn't melted into the kiss like my body aches for him to do, and the genuine fear I'm overstepping consumes me.

Maybe I should stop, maybe—

A raw guttural sound rumbles Liam's chest. He pulls me tighter into him, and warmth spirals across my skin. I relax, and our bodies mold together like a Rodin sculpture. My panic and hesitation smooth away with every pass of his hand on my back as Liam builds a masterpiece, curve by sculpted curve.

My lips part as if on their own accord, and my head tilts, seeking better access. With each soft caress, I beg to be handled with less care, aching for the rough broad strokes of an Impressionist desperate to catch the fleeting light of a moment as ten years of pent-up whatever releases into sheer reckless abandon.

My hand slides to the back of his head, fingers threading through his hair's soft, thick strands. I've imagined this hundreds of times, how his hair would feel tangled in my grasp, how his mouth would feel pressed against mine. But in my dreams, I never imagined my insides coming to life like they're live in technicolor for the first time. Not to mention the unquenchable fire burning in the pit of my stomach. Its hunger propels me further to an abyss that looks much more like Heaven than Hell.

Our bodies become a single unit of tangled breaths and racing hearts as Liam deepens the kiss. Yes, this right here. This reality is better than any daydream. His tongue urges my lips further apart, and I feel his desire down to my marrow, mingling with my own. Molecules rearrange to become one. I arch against him, asking for some sort of confirmation that I'm not imagining this.

He wants me too.

Liam obliges, sweeping over my mouth and feeding years of starvation with an embrace that threatens to devour me whole.

"Okay, we got it." Harmony's voice floods back into my reality. "You guys can quit mauling each other."

Right.

Right.

Opening my eyes, I reluctantly pull away before I'm fully addicted to Liam. He leans again for half a second but stills. His forehead falls to mine.

"I think she knows I'm very taken now, Peaches," he murmurs, hovering over me with heavy eyelids and swollen lips.

"And you doubted I could fake it," I whisper. My fingers stay frozen, threaded through his disheveled hair. I honestly cannot think of a time he's looked more utterly divine than in this moment cast in the light of the Eiffel Tower.

"You win," he says on an exhale. He narrows on my lips, and mine part again in response.

Divine and dangerous.

"How did the sparkles come out?" I nervously laugh, turning my attention to Harmony, straightening my clothing and smoothing down my hair. "I'm never sure in the dark."

"Perfect, honestly, dream kiss," she says, glancing at my phone with a frown and shoving it back into my hand. "So we actually got a text from a friend to go over to their apartment for a party, so we're going to have to leave you guys here." She grimaces with an oh-this-is-awkward face.

Strong arms fall over the tops of my shoulders, pulling me tightly into a firm wall of muscle. "You want to go back to my apartment?" Liam asks in a low husky whisper. His fingers lightly trail up my arm, sending way too many goosebumps in their wake.

"That sounds good." Ignoring the butterfly garden fluttering in my stomach, I scroll through Harmony's rapid-fire collection of photos, stopping at one toward the end. The look cut across Liam's face in the picture causes a slight pause. I want to squeeze my two fingers and zoom in, but he's hovering over my shoulder.

"You want my jacket? You're shivering," he whispers in my ear.

"I'm fine. Thanks for taking this, Harmony. Did you want one with you and Samantha, was it?"

"Oh, uhm." She flashes another glance at Liam. "We're good, actually. We'll catch you." She leans in for a bise and doesn't spare him another glance as she leaves.

Well, that was weird.

When Harmony's out of sight, the fingers grazing my arms stop, and I am released from a wall of warmth. I face Liam. He's rubbing the back of his head, gaze roaming toward the musician who RickRolled us earlier strumming out "Fix You."

He catches my eyes on him and offers me a smile. "Want me to walk you home?"

"Oh—no. It's. You've. I need to. I'm just going to—" I straighten my shirt, that final picture burning in my pocket.

He dips his head. "I get it. It's fine."

"I'll see you Monday?" I pull at the tips of my fingers. Electricity hums through me in a restless current. What would happen if I leaned in for another round? Everything in his kiss felt real, but what if I'm wrong? What if I'm misreading this like I always have? What if he really is that good of an actor, and I come across like a clueless Lina Lamont, convinced he couldn't kiss me like that and not mean it just a teensy-weensy bit? "If you want. I mean, if the offer still stands for another practice date."

"Yeah." He nods. "Monday's good."

"Awesome. I'm looking forward to it."

He snorts. "Harmony's gone, Peaches. You don't have to torture yourself anymore."

"I'm not." I bounce on my toes, glancing over a growing crowd around the platform. Right, so there's my answer then. "I meant what I said earlier, about trying not to jump to the wrong conclusions anymore. So I'm looking forward to catching up and getting to know you again. If you want."

"Oh." His eyes widen, and a soft smile pricks the edges of his cheeks. "Yeah. I'd like that a lot, actually."

"Great. Then. Well. Bye." I shoot him some weird finger guns, backing away, expecting his boisterous laughter to accompany me.

But when I glance his way again, he's just staring out at the tower, one hand stuffed in his pocket, a warm smile plastered on his face, fingers tracing his lips.

And I fight back the urge to do the same.

12

Donuts and Kisses

THE DONUT CUPCAKE CHANGED my life.

Two years ago, my drunken concept for a confetti cake donut with buttercream filling and a white chocolate glaze slathered in rainbow sprinkles exploded my blog and my life. Ever since, people frequent *L'Evie en Rosé* for the donut cupcake, but they stay for my mish-mosh of French restaurant reviews, at-home recipes, and quirky Paris travel guides.

Until this weekend, when traffic erupted, not because of some recipe or well-planned tour, but because of a photo.

The Eiffel Tower held in a sparkle in the background.

Liam's mouth molded to mine, casting a spell.

My foot perpetually popped.

My mom is on cloud nine.

People are obsessed. And unfortunately, so is Maria.

"People don't just kiss like that. You see the way he's holding you? That's not acting."

It's a hard point to argue against when my lips tingle, recalling his pressed to mine like it was more than an exchange of breaths. It was a joining of the two.

If I still believed in fairytales, I'd say it had all the makings of a happily ever after.

Fortunately, my self-preservation instincts know better. Embers can flick and reignite all they want, but in the end, a fire consumes and burns everything in its path, only leaving behind the ashes of what once was. Feeding the fire never ends well.

Stress-baking is always a good idea, though, because when I'm done I have a plate of tasty treats to feed my soul with. I shake myself out of my spiral, stacking pink, white, and red macarons on a porcelain, gold-rimmed dish on my balcony. Tiny flowers embellish the tops of the shells in honor of the cherry blossoms bursting to life around the city.

Placing a glass of rosé and cheese in the background for aesthetic purposes, I snap a rapid-fire roll of photos for the blog's cover photo. My hands tremble, my nerves recognizing what my brain refuses to. I'm going on a date with Liam today, and my body isn't over our kiss on Friday. Unfortunate, considering everything that transpired three days ago was fake.

It sure *felt* like more, though.

The picture at the end of the camera roll, now permanently ingrained into the back of my skull, calls to me. His forehead pressed to mine, lips swollen, hovering like they're desperate for more. My fingers itch. Maybe I could peek at it one more time.

Philomène, our resident pigeon, perches precariously nearby, staring into my soul with the silent judgment only a bird can muster.

"I know it's just a picture. No need to get your feathers in a bunch. I'll settle." I down the glass of rosé. "I'm sure I'm reading too much into this anyway. He's a good actor. I don't know why that's surprising. He's good at everything."

My feathered friend coos, waddling around the balcony, pecking sporadically at the ground, until her beady eyes land on my plate, darkening with desire.

"Keep your eyes off my goods, Philomène Wilhelmine de la Roche. I'm serious." I pick the plate up off the table, balancing it over my phone, and she cocks her head to the side. "Don't look at me like that. You know I don't share food."

"Are you . . . talking to a *bird?*"

A deep voice sneaks up behind me.

"Sweet baby Debbie, don't take the mixer!" I shout with a jump. My hands flail. My macarons toss in the air, dropping to the ground with my phone and heart in a thud. My gaze oscillates between my fallen treats and Liam, who's trying his darndest not to laugh. The mirthful set of his lips sits at odds with his sharp tailored suit pants, white-collared shirt, and tie.

Swiftly, I pick up my phone and lock the screen to black. "You scared me." I place my palm over my heart and rub it. I don't know if I'm close to cardiac arrest because of his sneak attack or him. "I'm sorry, I lost track of time. Is it one already?"

"Yeah, a little after." He bends to pick my fallen pastries up.

"Leave them." I sigh, trudging back into the apartment. "They're Philomène's now."

"Philomène?"

"The bird I was talking to."

A bouquet of lilacs rests on the almond flour-covered butcherblock countertop. My pulse thuds in my ears. Don't read too much into this. Maria could have stopped and left them there. I pour myself a larger glass of rosé, attempting to soothe my nerves.

Why did I think I'd be able to handle interacting with Liam after knowing what kissing him felt like?

"How'd you get in here, anyway?" I grab a dishcloth, wiping the almond flour off the counter.

"Maria let me in. I guess she stopped in and then left again." He rubs his neck.

I pause my wipe down, catching deep circles under his eyes, accentuated in the kitchen light. His usual neat layer of scruff shadows his cheekbones in a scraggly, unkempt mess. Something is off. My chest tightens with the accompanying thought. Liam never used to open up to me about whatever was bothering him, even on the rare occasions when I asked. He'd grumble and brood, isolating himself instead.

True, our dynamic has shifted these past two weeks, but I don't know if he'd consider more than a surface inquiry into his wellbeing an intrusion or not, and I don't want to risk upsetting our progress now.

"Oh, these are for you." Liam grabs the bouquet, and the cellophane rustles in his grip. "I thought you could take a picture of them for Instagram."

"Thank you. That's a good idea—easy way to continue the narrative." I blush, reaching out to accept them. My fingers brush against Liam's on the exchange, begging to linger there. The brief contact sends sparks flying straight into the deepening ache in my chest. Our eyes connect, and he looks at me as if he desperately wants to say or do *something*.

I sway. Lips part.

Shit. Blinking myself out of the rom-com in my mind, I hastily pull my fingers off his and take possession of the flowers.

"Hi," he says on an exhale, a light laugh rattling his chest while I emit a similar nervous one. "How are you today?"

"Oh fine," I squeak, inhaling the sweet floral scent of the lilacs, hoping to steady my pounding heart and breathless lungs.

He zeroes in on my face like he doesn't buy my response.

And, well, it's a patented Evie O'Shea half-truth, so fair.

Fine, except there's a throbbing pain searing into the back of my skull and a matching one hovering slightly above the uterus, and this is a "good" day.

"Do you want help cleaning up?" Liam asks, glancing around the destruction Hurricane Evie left behind.

"No, thank you. I'm almost done." I pour the remaining rosé into a glass for Liam and hand him a wedge of cheese, shooing him out of our narrow kitchen. We need a ten-foot barrier of space, or I'm liable to do something reckless, like grab his loosened tie and pull him to my lips. "Seriously, shoo." I motion to the table again.

"I'm going. I'm going. Believe me, I know better than to get in your way in the kitchen." The corner of Liam's mouth tips into the beginnings of a smile. He takes the glass and plate from me and heads to the gateleg table, where scatterings of pages for the pastry shop litter the top like a graveyard to my deadened dream. I haven't looked at or moved them for months, only having the brain power for survival and not much else. "So what's the plan for today, Peaches?"

I shrug, feigning like I didn't stay awake the past two nights planning a fake date for us.

Best not to appear too eager and freak him out.

"I thought we could meander and find a good area with cherry blossoms to picnic under, like Square Gabriel-Pierné or Palais-Royal. But we'll have to go grab some picnic food now."

"That sounds good." He smiles softly at me, propping his hand on the table and leaning against it. A paper from the table flutters to the floor. He retrieves it, studying it as he straightens. "These for the shop?"

"They were, yeah."

"Mind if I peek?"

"No, go right ahead. Just fair warning, it's kind of a mess."

Fifteen minutes later, the kitchen is finally in an acceptable state. "I need to rinse off and change."

"'Kay," Liam says, focused on whatever sheet he has in front of him.

Post-wash and dress, I exit the bathroom, adorned in my signature chiffon billowy shirt dress and leggings. At this point, the outfit is more a uniform than a choice. "I could go for a crêpe if you're up for some carbs."

A dizzying wave crashes into me when I catch sight of Liam hunched over the table, mindlessly running his hand through his hair, tie on the table, the top two buttons undone on his collar, sleeves rolled up to his elbows. I pause, off-balance.

A fire lights in the pit of my stomach, and I get the sense it's going to burn relentlessly until it consumes every part of me. Never satisfied, always hungry.

This, this feeling right here, is why I clung so fiercely to the fragments of a hollow grudge.

Because now that all the bitter resentment is gone, I have to deal with my feelings for Liam. There isn't a shield to protect me anymore. It's just me, staring deep into the abyss, our kiss the other night pushing me precariously close to the edge.

Liam picks his head up, and my one-track mind makes a beeline for his lips. I fight the pull to brush a finger over my bottom lip as the tingles radiate down my spine. His mouth moves, but I'm not registering a single sound leaving his lips right now.

"Huh?"

His brow furrows. "I said that sounds good? You okay, Peaches?"

"Oh yeah. Fine." I hastily clear my throat, pulling my attention away from the danger zone and focusing it elsewhere. Somewhere safe.

Eye contact?

Mirthful lines edge the corners of his lids. My pulse thuds in my ears.

Chest?

Nope. Remember the white partially unbuttoned shirt. Do not attempt.

His wrist must be safe, though, right? Wrists aren't sexy. Except his wrist is so very close to his forearms, and those are . . . my eyes fall on his corded forearms, a constant source of misery in my life.

Oh. Hell. What was I thinking kissing this man? I. Am. Doomed.

"Seriously, you feeling okay?"

"Probably just overdid it with the wine on an empty stomach." I half-smile. "A crêpe should do the trick."

Liam's mouth twists into a grim line as he assesses me. "We don't have to do this if you don't want to. I don't want to stress you out more than you already are. I think we proved Friday we'll be fine."

"Oh." A pang of disappointment pricks my chest. Of course, this should be good news. The less time I spend with Liam, the better for my nerves. Except, now that it's had a taste, the masochist in me wants this. Desperately. "I mean, I don't think building up some stories is a bad idea. If you're too busy, I get it, though. It's just not stressing me out, promise."

Liam snorts. "Right, you're not acting like you're stressed at all."

"Stressed in general, sure, but believe it or not, what we're doing isn't the culprit." It's what we're not doing and how much I want you to wrap your hand around my waist and pull me into you that's bothering me. But eating a crêpe. I can handle that.

He slides his hands into his pockets, and the dimples of doom say hello. "Whatever you want to do, I'm yours, Peaches."

If only he knew how badly I wanted that to be true.

Abutting the seventeenth-century architecture of the Institute de France, Square Gabriel-Pierné, named after a famous composer of the early 1900s, is happily settled in the Saint-Germain-de-Prés neighborhood on Rue de Seine. Stone book-shaped benches honoring the well-known bookstores and libraries in the area are nestled under canopies of cherry blossoms in this quiet, tucked away park, making it the perfect Parisian hideaway.

"Have you talked to your brother yet?" Liam asks, handing me the gooier of the two Nutella crêpes once I've settled into the bench. Overhead, a branch of a cherry tree bows under the weight of its pink blossoms nearing peak bloom. A delicate sweetness catches on the wind, spreading the faint floral aroma around the park.

"Only briefly."

Liam sits next to me. His warmth radiates along my side, and I focus on a couple at the other end of the park snapping a photo of a pigeon to steady my excitement. I've never understood why tourists are so keen to take pictures of the birds. I guess I'd understand it if Parisian pigeons wore berets and ate mini croissants, but unless I'm missing something, they unfortunately don't.

"He's wicked excited," Liam says, taking his first bite.

"That could be a problem." I sigh. "I'm worried that if he thinks playing matchmaker paid off, he's going to set me up with every friend of his visiting Paris."

"Nah, I wouldn't worry. Caleb doesn't have that many friends." Liam's lips quirk, and a brief appearance of the dimpled doom-maker arrives.

"What did he say when you talked to him?"

He shrugs. "Brief congratulations and a quick if-you-hurt-my-sister-I-break-your-thumbs thing."

"No way." I almost shriek. Heat rushes to my cheeks, and I burrow into my scarf. "Please tell me you're joking."

"Not the first time I've gotten it." He waves off my mortification.

"I'm sorry. What?" I keep my voice even, though I want to pop a blood vessel. My brother shouldn't get to prioritize spending time with Liam, ignore me, and pull this macho bullshit too. "Why isn't he texting me threatening messages? You're the favorite."

"I think your brother secretly likes you better." He winks. "He just has a funny way of showing it."

"Oh yes, heaven forbid he show his true feelings to me."

"What would we have fought over if he did?"

"Being lifelong friends, can you imagine the actual horror?" A broad grin stretches across my face.

"I don't think it would have been that bad."

"Why, Liam Kelly, I think that was almost a compliment." I place my palm over my heart. "Thank you for watering the garden. I think it's blooming already."

He snorts, taking another bite of gooey goodness. "Anytime you need watering, let me know."

"Absolutely, whenever I need someone to get me wet, you'll be the first person I call." I catch him mid-bite, and he starts to choke. With a way-too-proud-of-myself snicker, my palm falls to his back and gives it a good thwack.

"Hell, Peaches." He coughs. "You can't do that to a guy when he's got his mouth full." I giggle, and he shakes his head, standing and wiping his hands. "I don't think I've ever heard you make so many dirty jokes. Paris has changed you."

"It's because you've been granted access to my authentic self without Caroline hovering over my shoulder. Consider yourself lucky. Very few people are privy to this side of me." I finish my crêpe, savoring the warm cocoa beans and hazelnuts dancing on my tongue for a moment, and stand.

He draws his lips in thoughtfully. "I'll have to add it to my list."

"What list?"

"Moments with you I don't take for granted."

My heart jerks against the tethers I tried to implement on this walk for safety. "Are there a lot of moments on that list?"

He shrugs. "Briefly stolen smiles, finger grazing, typical boy next door pining for the backstory."

Right. The backstory. The backstory for Liam. The backstory chosen specifically for Liam. Liam's backstory. My brain malfunctions into a Kuzco's poison meme, trying to calm High School Me that wanted to jump to the fastest OH MY GOD, HE LIKES YOU conclusion.

"Got it. Want to wander toward Palais-Royal?" I ask, wiping my sweaty palms on my trench coat.

He nods, his brows furrowing in concern at my face. I haven't kept track of whatever it's doing, but it's probably not subtle how nervous I am.

Marching down a set of stairs along the Seine, we head west toward Palais-Royal, walking in relative silence. This section of the river is a popular destination for tour cruises and floating restaurants to load and unload passengers. Hence, it's thick with tourists, and we frequently separate to navigate them.

Finally, the thick of the crowd thins to a few couples sitting on the edge of the bank, enjoying a rare spot of sunshine and bottles of wine. Water laps up against the stone in the wake of a passing boat.

Liam's phone rings for the fifth time on this walk.

"You want to get that?" I nod to his pocket.

"Nah, just let me silence it." He pulls it out, shaking his head.

"Everything okay?"

"Everything's great, actually." He smiles slightly, but the way his lips curve, it's unfamiliar, peaceful and relaxed, almost. "What's that?" Liam points his chin across the river at a palace running perpendicular to Pont du Carrousel, a three-arched bridge connecting the north and south bank.

"The Louvre. That's not a bad place to cross and walk to Palais-Royal if you want to explore the gardens."

"We can just do that?"

"Yeah, you can drive through it, too, actually."

"Huh," he muses to himself. "Wild." He shakes his head and laughs. And for an American, it is wild. Because places like Paris are bursting with so many former lives that they needed to find a way to merge the former ones with the present.

Living in history is natural here.

It's a big reason I've needed Paris these past few years. Because when the present is a dumpster fire and the future feels an awful lot like a land of broken dreams, being surrounded by a world gone by is like being wrapped tight in a reminder that life is relentless in its existence and hardship, but people are remarkably resilient.

We cross under the archways of Pavillon de la Trémoille, and the beige brick with ornate moldings and black lampposts all melded into one expansive backdrop gives me pause.

"Hold on," I order as a motorbike careens by on our right. "This would be a really great photo." I fumble to find my phone in my purse. Glancing up, I catch a fleck of Nutella on Liam's chin. "Oh, you've got—let me get that first—" I reach up, wiping it off with my finger. Without conscious thought, I keep my eyes trained on Liam's and lick it off, blushing with surprise when I catch up with my actions. Where did I find the audacity to flirt? I clear my throat. "We should—we should be practicing, right?"

He nods, and his pupils darken. "How am I supposed to react when you do something like that? Coach me through it."

A dozen filthy suggestions rifle through my brain. Probably best to keep those to myself.

"What would you want to do?"

He shakes his head. "Nothing you'd be okay with."

"Oh, I wouldn't be so sure." I take a step back and hit the stone wall of the Pavillon behind me.

"But you bring up a good point. We should probably discuss boundaries and expectations so nobody gets caught off guard," I say.

Heat tinges my cheeks as I recall Liam's rigid figure when I all but took his lips hostage with mine, but I continue. "Paris is a big city. But Harmony lives in the Latin Quarter, too, and we run in similar circles, so we might be on the same street or Métro car, and with your height and my hair, it's highly likely that Harmony could see us and not the other way around. Which will be a lot like Tallow, given our history people will be staring." I puff out my cheeks. "Okay, I'm getting sidetracked, but I'm not keen on risking Harmony finding out this is fake. She's patronizing, and I've embarrassed myself enough in front of her as is. So if you wanted, I thought maybe it wouldn't be a bad idea to just go all in now—give you full permission to do *whatever* you'd do if we were really dating *whenever* . . . for authenticity, and so we don't get caught here."

My eyes cast down. *Nailed it.*

Two fingers trail my chin and pick up my gaze. "Are you sure? That's a dangerous thing to grant me."

"I trust you." I swallow, drowning in his scent, lungs tight, unable to draw a single life-giving breath. Maybe that's the idea, and this is an elaborate death-by-suffocation murder plot.

He cocks his head, resting his forearm near my head on the wall. "That would be a first."

His eyes flicker to my lips.

"Desperate times call for desperate measures," I whisper. And I *am* desperate. "And I mean, it wasn't *awful* on Friday."

"Not awful." He snorts. "The highest form of praise coming from you. But just to ensure I understand this right: We're dating, no breaking—that's what you want from here on out. Kissing, touching, the whole thing."

I nod.

"What about in our apartments?"

"If it works for you, I think it'll be more convincing if we maintain it everywhere, really smooth out the rough edges so we don't get caught back home."

"Even kissing?"

"I mean, I could probably use some more practice to shake the nervous energy dance out of my system. And it'd probably be better for the end product if it looked like something we've done more than once."

Don't be suspicious. Don't be suspicious.

He smiles slightly, fingering a fallen curl brushing my cheek. "Anything for the end product."

"Great." I offer a tight-lipped smile. "That's settled, then." I pat his chest and pick my lean up off the wall, walking a few paces ahead. "Did you want to wander through the gardens first or the glass pyramid?"

A hand falls to the crook of my elbow and tugs me back.

"What are you doing?"

"We kiss all the time; this isn't out of the ordinary." The flecks in his eyes swirl, casting an incantation with a low growl. His brow slowly raises in a question. "Right, Peaches?"

"Right. Right. We kiss all the time," I parrot, stuck in his trance.

He moves a piece of hair off my cheek, tracing the curve of my jaw with his finger. "I can't get enough of you."

"I'm falling deeper with every pass of your lips." The truth bypasses my filter. My lungs squeeze, all but exploding in my chest.

He lowers his head, and his soft, warm mouth covers mine. It takes me a second to catch up before my eyes drift closed, focused on that single point of gentle, sliding contact.

His hands grip my waist, bringing me flush against his body as he tilts his head to take the kiss deeper, sending my stomach into a free fall. I grant him access and wrap my arms around his neck, desperate for something to anchor me. A deep rumble in his chest reaches my ears, and his hold tightens, leaving me with no choice but to press closer until we're a single entwined body. A second, a minute, an hour passes—and he slowly pulls away, leaving me in a breathless haze. Then he's there again, nudging my lips back to his, lightly brushing against them before completely stepping back.

He scrubs a hand down his face, and for a second, I think he's as dazed as I am, but then a spark flashes in his eye. A devastating grin slowly spreads across his face. He turns, tossing over his shoulder, "I think a walk through the gardens sounds nice."

My trembling fingers lightly trace the hum of electricity on my lips, coursing in the wake of his kiss. I smooth out my trench coat and try to regain composure. After our initial kiss, I hoped my body's overwhelming reaction to his would filter its way out of my system, but everything has only heightened.

I have to admit it: kissing Liam Kelly was the final nail in my lovesick coffin. Here lies resistance. It was futile.

"Seriously?" I holler, catching up to the broad shoulders strolling ahead of me, hands fastened behind his muscular back as he admires the palace. "Your affinity for teasing me truly knows no bounds if you would still tease me like that as your girlfriend."

A dark, heavy stare meets mine. He slowly raises a rakish brow. "I imagine it knows some." He lowers his lips to my ear. "I'd do much worse if we weren't in public, Peaches, but then you wouldn't be faking anything."

A shiver works down my spine as he pulls away. "So confident." I click my tongue.

He shakes his head. "Determined."

I swallow, unsure what to make of that statement, of the challenging glint in his eyes. Is he *actually* flirting with me?

Any brain-to-mouth filter I possess goes up in smoke. "Well, maybe you should take me back to the apartment then," I say, matching the pits of hell with a devilish stare all my own.

"I swear they're in here." I chuckle, hands trembling, digging through my purse for my keys. "I mean, I locked the door so they—"

Liam reaches into the pocket of my trench coat, his stare pinned to me, and pulls them out.

"Right."

"You sure you want to do this?"

I nod with a swallow, plucking the key from his grasp and pivoting to unlock the door.

Liam's fingers graze the back of my neck, gathering my hair to one side, and then he presses a kiss on my bare skin, wrapping a hand around my waist.

"I can't concentrate when you do that." I fumble with the key, electricity flooding my system and jumbling my motor skills.

"Oh, does this fluster you, Evie?" he says, far too pleased with himself.

"I'll be flustering your ass in a moment," I grumble.

A loud mirthful laugh erupts behind me, giving me enough time for key meet hole. A satisfying click follows, and I exhale, opening the door. "I *should* be rethinking this." I shake my head, kicking off my shoes.

"But you aren't?" He studies me.

"Unfortunately, no." I slam Liam's back against the door. He grabs my hips, fingers firm and sure, and pulls me close.

"Good," he breathes out before our lips crash into each other. None of the electricity arcing between us has dissipated, and this feels less and less like a show and more like a conversation.

The poet Alfred de Musset once said, *"the only true language in the world is a kiss,"* and as Liam's other hand tangles in my mess of strawberry curls, I can't help but think that's what this is. So many things left unsaid bubble to the surface, baring themselves in the warm sunlight of this embrace. Like somehow, our kisses were inevitable. The magnetic pull would never relent until our lips were finally molded together.

A soft moan emits from my throat as his tongue sweeps inside my mouth. If the first few kisses were an act to satiate a pang of hunger, this—this is an imprint. It's like he's claiming my mouth for his own, saying no one else will do from here on out.

A shiver works through me, and I catch my breath. I close my eyes, focusing on the butterflies, the goosebumps, the fire ripping through me and consuming the usual hell.

I. Feel. Good.

You're screwed, the chaos gremlin says almost gleefully in my head.

I tell it to shut up so I can focus on everything going on here—the heat of him, the spiral of my pulse, the eagerness of his kiss.

His tongue urges my lips apart, shifting, growing in desire and need. My fingers hungrily work on undoing the buttons on his shirt. A muffled groan leaves him while he grips my waist to place me up on the counter. He pulls away, dragging his teeth along my bottom lip.

His fingers swiftly undo the buttons on my shirt as he lays a cascade of kisses along the nape of my neck and down my shoulder in a desperate exploration of my body. One hand runs slowly up the outside of my leg. My breath hitches, and my back arches, pressing further into him.

"Hi," I breathe. Smooth.

"Hi." Liam smiles, pausing for a brief moment before he moves to the other shoulder.

Okay. Let's try that again.

He works up my neck, his hands forcefully moving over my back.

Oh, come on, is this man going to kiss my lips again soon? I'm dying here.

"Lips, please." The words escape me. His exploration stills, and I'm greeted with a crooked grin.

"You miss me, Peaches?" he asks, brushing the pad of his thumb over my limp bottom lip. I'm too dazed and confused to be sufficiently snarky even though I really want to bite back. Unfortunately, I also want to bite him, and the war of dichotomies battling inside overwhelms me, so I nod compliantly in response.

"Huh. Well, today's a day of firsts here, isn't it?"

And okay.

"Shut up and kiss me, asshole."

"There we go!" Liam laughs, cradling my face with his hand. An incantation swirls in his eyes as he leans in slowly, trailing a finger under my shirt and dragging it down my side. A brain-numbing chill takes possession of my entire being.

Finally, Liam returns to my mouth, firm and demanding. Warmth floods me with a passion I'd laid to rest long ago. Resurrected with a press of the lips, the brush of his finger, the scent of his skin. I can't get close enough.

My legs wrap around his waist and tighten around him, reaching official koala status. His arms fall behind my back, lifting me up and bringing me into my bedroom. Suddenly, Liam's footing stumbles, foiled by my mess of a room. We collapse on the floor into a mound of dirty laundry. His lumbering figure falls on top of me.

"Ow." A giant, tension-releasing laugh escapes me.

"Are you okay?" He lays kisses on the side that crashed into the floor, and my heart flutters.

"I'm fine." I anxiously giggle, the panic of what we're doing seeping in. Whatever was about to happen was a bad idea. Liam doesn't need to learn the truth about my intimacy struggles, fake relationship or not. It's embarrassing.

His eyes widen as they take in my bedroom, landing on the wall decorated with postcards in the back. He inhales sharply, as if he hurt something in the fall, and stands.

I pick myself up off the ground and assess him. I wish I could read him better than I do. It's like there are parts of Liam that I can read like the back of my hand with buttons and levers I know how to push and pull to my advantage. But there are times like this when he's a complete enigma to me. Maria thinks he's the one sending me these. But his gaze is roaming over my wall with wonder, which wouldn't make sense if he knew about them already.

A loud vibration rattles inside Liam's pocket. "I put this in 'do not disturb' for a reason," he mutters, pulling out his phone. His eyes widen, narrowing on the screen, and he rakes a frustrated hand through his hair with a tiny groan. "Ah, shit, Evie, my dad scheduled a meeting for me today, but Alice forgot to put it on my calendar, and it's across town. I gotta—" He glances at his crumpled mess of a shirt and sighs.

"Oh yeah, no—I totally get that. That was probably enough practice for one day anyway."

Liam's face falls, and my brow furrows as I study the transformation. "Right. Solid practice. Good job, *team*." He hesitates, offering his hand for a high-five, which I almost whiff on, swinging my hand to meet his.

"I'm sure we'll get less awkward eventually." I blush.

"That's why we're practicing, right?"

"Right." A tight smile stretches across my face.

He pauses, hanging on to the top of the doorframe. His half-unbuttoned shirt exposes the top of his ridges, stretched taut in this position. "Can I see you again soon?"

"Yeah, of course. Whenever you're free, I'll brie around."

Must. Stop. Making. Cheese. Puns. After. Making. Out. With. A. Man.

"Great." He releases the door frame and stares for half a second. "Okay, well then—I'm going to—" He shakes his head and steps forward, laying a soft, breathless kiss on my lips, like he's savoring the moment. "Just in case you change your mind between now and then." His thumb brushes my cheek.

His phone chimes again, and he groans.

"I won't. Go do your big adult things." I raise on my tiptoes and press another quick kiss to his nose.

He nods, turning away and grumbling, "Being an adult is the worst."

Honestly, mood.

13

Pour Some Sugar on Me

I'M FLARING HARDER THAN Tom Hanks on a deserted island.

And I need to find a way to push through it to finish my Thursday baking session for the blog.

I lay out several empty white bowls on the countertop, label each a color of the rainbow, and attach a corresponding sticky note to the front—a strategy I employed long ago to combat the severe brain fog plaguing me. The less recall needed, the better. Sighing, I slowly breathe through the pressure swelling in my abdomen, covering my stomach like a pair of high-waisted barbed-wire underwear.

If I went out in public like this, some tourist would undoubtedly ask when I'm due, and I'd give them hard-to-follow directions to the Eiffel Tower because I'm petty.

The hot water bottle wrapped around my distended abdomen slips slightly, and I tighten the strap holding it in place. It's on the edge of too hot and burning my skin, but today's flare is a good ten out of ten pain-wise, so the extra heat is appreciated and desperately needed.

At this point, ibuprofen isn't going to cut it. I'll have to take my heavier pain meds, but trying to bake under the influence of my narcotics usually gives Maria a heart attack, so I'll have to wait until I'm done for more substantial relief.

My round ligament convulses on my left side, pulling my ovary with it since endo bound them in an unholy union. I uncrunch my middle, stretching as lightning-like pains streak through my ass and down my thigh, radiating to my calf. Endo is hardcore bullying my bowel today. Honestly, total crap.

Maria descends the loft staircase where her makeshift office lays, and I pray what happens next is silent.

Unfortunately, it is not.

At all.

And a big, comical wet fart worthy of a sound effect board is broadcasted throughout the apartment.

Maria doesn't break her stride as I break wind. "Oh, is it that time of the month, dear?" she asks, raising on her tiptoes and pulling down the "Evie's Farting Like a Fratboy After a Night of Pizza and Beer" box of supplies with various candles and deodorizers from over the fridge.

"Unfortunately," I groan, pressing on my abdomen. I push right on the tender spot, massaging it a bit, and the sudden prick from the pressure takes my breath away.

Maria pauses her spray down of the apartment and narrows her gaze. "Do you think you should be baking? If you get behind on your pain meds, you won't be able to control it later."

"So I'll suffer a little more." I wave her off. "At least this will be done."

"Evie," she says, dipping into stern mama bear territory. "Don't overdo it."

"Scout's honor, I'll behave," I mumble, focus still trained on the recipe.

"Mm-hmm, sure."

Given my general stubborn disposition, her skepticism is valid, albeit an annoying reminder I have a condition that requires rest, even when I have a million things I'd rather be accomplishing.

Last year, clinging to the remnants of my tattered dreams, I went through a phase where I tried to plow past my pain and ignore it. After so many people in my life—doctors, family members, acquaintances, and alleged friends—told me my pain was mental, how could I not? Out of self-preservation, my body responded by blacking out whenever my blood pressure elevated to dangerous levels.

It took a stern talking to by a medical professional for me to learn not to push my body to syncope anymore, but still, this Type A personality doesn't suffer suffering well. I have things to do, pastries to bake for the blog, and an income needed to survive, pain or not.

Maria's gaze stays heavy on me.

Picking up my eyes to meet hers, I sigh. "It would behoove me to get another recipe on the blog. Traffic has picked up because of the pictures, and I need to utilize the algorithm."

"Fair," she says, entering our tiny kitchen area and spraying directly behind me. "That picture is pretty damn cute if I can toot your traffic horn."

A sharp staccato knock on the front door echoes through the apartment, reverberating off the tight walls inside and halting any response I had to her ridiculous joke.

Maria pauses her tidying. "Are you expecting Eli?"

"Not today. I texted him that I wasn't feeling well."

And then texted Maria asking for her to grab bread while she was out because priorities.

Maria peeks into the keyhole, and a broad smile sweeps across her face. "Seems your boyfriend didn't get the message."

The regular pitter-patter rhythm of my heart drops like an EDM classic now thrumming against my chest.

No.

No.

Panic toot.

No.

"You should answer it." She says, walking away from the door and grinning rather wickedly.

"But—farts." I reach for her, clinging to my fart-filled air as she moves beyond my grasp.

"I'm sorry, I need to do this thing over here, and I simply cannot be bothered."

"You're a real Benedict Arnold, you know that?"

"I don't know who that is, but if this Benedict Arnold fellow gets you out of your funk, I'll take it."

"I'm not in a funk. I'm—"

Another knock.

"Coming." I sigh, shifting the deadbolt and slowly cracking the door open.

"Hey, Peaches." Liam greets me on the other side in a dark charcoal suit.

"Hi." I blink at the crusty baguette gripped firmly in his hand. "What are you doing here?"

"You asked for bread?"

Warm flour mixes with the plethora of scents wafting around our apartment. It's fresh. And the sight of it is stronger than any arrow Cupid could aim my way.

"When?" I all but squeak. I only sent one text message this morning asking for bread, and it was way more forthcoming about my bowel situation than I would ever want to be with the man who got the nickname *Toots* to stick Senior year.

"Maybe an hour ago? Sorry it took so long. I was in a meeting."

"But I—" I stammer. "I texted Maria. She bought me bread."

"No, you didn't. I just got you a stick because you always want one," Maria adds from her bedroom. Apparently, she's too busy to save me from my ass but has plenty of time for eavesdropping.

I wince, worst fears confirmed, glancing at his phone and holding in another panic toot. "Please tell me I didn't send you—"

"My ass is bleeding, and I'm dying. Can you grab me a baguette so I can lube it up with Nutella and shove it down my throat? Thank Xanadu, I don't have a gag reflex. *Raised hands* *Raised hands* Love you!" His gold flecks mischievously reconnect with mine. "I don't know what I love most, the gag reflex tidbit or that last part."

"The last little bit should have been a hint it wasn't for you," I grumble, willing the heat in my cheeks to settle as a bit of gas escapes.

"I didn't know if it was part of our agreement. Speaking of which—can I?" He motions inside the apartment, but I don't want him walking where I crop-dusted.

"Don't you have work or something more important to worry about?"

He shrugs, stuffing his phone back into his pocket. "I finished what I needed to so I could come here."

"To bring me bread?"

"Ass bleeding doesn't sound pleasant."

I hug my water bottle tighter against my abdomen. "Not my favorite."

Maria sighs, exiting her bedroom. "Evie, why haven't you let him in yet? Come. Come."

Begrudgingly, I open the door wider, discreetly fanning behind me, and allow Liam entrance. "He's not staying. Just came to check on me on his way elsewhere."

I'm not trying to be rude or ungrateful here. But I'm on the precipice of my day breaking in one of two ways. Either my flare will be manageable, and I'll be able to control it well enough after baking. Or I'm about to have a no-relief, torture, and agony kind of day filled with graceless, vulnerable moments and farts.

I'm not ready for Liam to see that part of me, and I need the freedom to be a mess today.

"Evie."

"Maria."

"You need to take your big meds."

"Yes."

"And I have to go meet a new client. Please, for the sake of your friend and our apartment, ask him to stay."

I scowl. Maria's only pulling this guilt trip because she's playing matchmaker. I can handle anything that today will throw my way just fine. Always do.

"Think of the eyebrows, dear."

Oh. Low blow.

"That was one time, and they grew back!" I grit out.

Maria continues to match my stare, and my shoulders deflate. "Fine. Liam, would it be a terrible imposition to ask you to stay with me for a few hours?"

"How can I say no when you seem so eager to have me?" The corners of his lips tip into the beginnings of a smile.

I gesture with both hands at him like, "You see what you're asking me to put up with!" But Maria ignores me.

"I'd love to take care of you, Peaches. No imposition at all," he says a bit softer, and I shoot a confused look his way at the tenderness of that statement. Nobody said anything about taking care of me. Just to be here to stave off another EyebrowGate.

"Thank you." Maria sighs, sliding into her high heels. "I feel much better leaving now. Make sure she shuts off the gas line, doesn't climb anything, and doesn't attempt to use knives. Love you, bye." The breeze of the shutting door brushes my cheek, and I'm left standing in the entryway with Liam.

A tension-filled silence settles around us, and I bounce on my toes. "You mind if you get those dirty?" I gesture to his clothes.

He glances down; a worry line forms a crease between his brows. "No?"

"I think I have another apron in the bedroom, just in case."

His eyes snap back to mine, and the wrinkle eases. "You want to bake with me?" he asks in a soft, hopeful tone.

Given our history—his surprise is justified. When we were younger, Sunday baking was a Nana specialty. Chocolate chip cookies, brownies, mayonnaise cake, whatever sweet treat Nana wanted for the week, we baked and packed, sending half to the Kellys and keeping half for ourselves. Nana always invited Liam to bake with us, but his chaotic energy to my prim demeanor was like mixing oil and vinegar, so eventually, she put me at one half of the island with my own station and him at another. I never let him come to my side. Not that it stopped him. I usually got a dough bomb or batter splattered all over my face at one point or another.

I begged Nana to let it just be us, but she'd always maintain a similar mantra: *"Someday, you'll need that boy as much as he needs you now."*

I finally pull my eyes off Liam's bottom lip, desperate to feel them brush against mine, and answer his question. "I mean, you're here. And baking together would probably make for a cute story we could tell if you wanted."

"Yeah, no, baking sounds great. If you're feeling up to it."

"Feeling up to doing something and needing to do it rarely align properly." I shrug. "Hold on. I'll go get the spare."

Wading through my pile of a room, I use the time searching for my pink apron to gather the single wit I still possess and, honestly, release a bit of gas. I'm not in a space to pretend I'm not in immense pain, so trusting Liam with my vulnerability it is.

Gross.

But he stopped his work to bring me over a baguette, which is a genuinely wonderful thing to do, so maybe it won't be that bad.

Back in the kitchen, Liam's forearms draw me into his orbit like a tractor beam as he rolls his sleeves up to his elbows, his suit jacket now draped across a kitchen chair.

I toss the apron at him and grab my own to protect my cooling hot water bottle.

A sharp intake snaps my attention to Liam, sporting pink frills and somehow maintaining that devastating lazy charm. He clears his throat, but his stare remains heavy on me. "I didn't know you had Nana's."

"Oh, yeah." I fumble with the strings to the Tiffany blue apron. "I like having her with me when I'm doing this," I hum. Moving over to the counter with the bowls, I straighten the labels underneath, content that each station has its ingredients, bowls, etc., ready for me to begin.

As messy as my actual life has become, the kitchen is one of the places I have some semblance of control, so this part is therapeutic for me. Even if pushing through agonizing cramps isn't.

"Some things never change." Liam snorts over my shoulder.

"I don't know. We've been in the kitchen for a full five minutes, and I don't have brownie batter coating my hair yet, so—" I turn to face him, forgetting that this glorified galley kitchen space is tight. My back hits the counter, leaning distance away from Liam's chest. "Something's . . . changed."

"That's just because I haven't found the brownie batter." Liam's eyes light, scanning over the eggs, flour, and other baking ingredients. "Is that what we're making?"

"Oh, no. We're making a twist on a Charlotte Royale." I skitter further away to recheck the recipe and give my stammering heart a fighting chance. "Hopefully it'll have the perfect *Pinterest eat-your-heart-out* vibe."

I rest my elbows on the counter just as a cramp spasms through my lower abdomen, and I stretch and wince.

"You think maybe you should be resting instead, Peaches?"

"I'm fine. You think you should be resting, though?" I motion to his haggard appearance, the dark circles deepening under his eyes, the stubble growing closer to a beard.

Liam worries his bottom lip, not meeting my concerned considera-tion. "I've just had a few restless nights, nothing to stress over."

"Great, then we're both fine, and the sponge is baking and needs to be rolled hot anyway." I focus back on the recipe. "Let's see, I made the jam, so I think all that's left is the buttercream, bavarois, rolling and cooling the sponge, and then assembling it with sprinkles."

He crosses his arms, pulling the pink frills tight. "Oh, is that all?"

"I'll be gentle." I tap his cheek.

He catches my hand and presses a kiss into my palm. "It's not me I'm worried about."

The warmth in my chest radiates outward until every inch of me is covered in a pleasing tingle. His fingers graze my forearm and roll up my sleeves while a gentle intensity rests on my face. "I'm fine, I promise."

Heat curls down my arm. I reluctantly pull away and dance around him to get to the stove. Starting the bavarois filling, I mix the framboise, gelatin, and peaches in a bowl and grab a pan to heat the milk over the burner.

"What can I do, Peaches?"

"Oh, uhm." I pause my stirring. I'm so used to the solo baking act, I don't quite know what to do with Liam or how he could be helpful. "What's your skill level with all this?"

"Hasn't progressed much since I was twelve." He peeks at me bashful-ly, stuffing his hands into his pockets.

His sagging shoulders and what he's left unsaid tug at my heartstrings. Since Nana.

"Oh, well, that's okay. I'm sure there's something. There's a checklist by the mixer if you want to look over it and see if there's anything you're comfortable doing."

He nods, shifting his attention to the flour-dusted paper. "What kind of photos do you need?"

"Just a few of the mixing bowls and ingredients while I work through the recipe, you know, the standard baking blog stuff. But that would be really helpful if you don't mind, I hate having to stop to take those, and my phone usually ends up covered in batter at the end."

"Yeah, I think that might be the only thing I can handle here. What the hell is a bavarois?" he asks, pulling his phone out of his pocket.

"A Bavarian cream." I glance over my shoulder and catch Liam's camera angled at me. "I didn't mean for you to take photos of me!" I shriek, his thumb pressing on the screen in that instant.

"What?" He blinks innocently back.

"I look like death."

He peers at his screen, then back at me. "You just look like Evie to me." He shrugs.

"Glad to know I look like a mess all the time to you." I wave an accusatory wooden spoon at him, and flecks of cream dot his cheeks.

"Not what I said." He sighs, wiping the side of his face. "Would you quit waving that thing at me? I'm trying to focus."

The spoon in my hand slips. Liam snaps another photo. "Pun intended?" I ask, trying to keep my cool.

"Aren't they always?" He hovers over my shoulder, grabbing a picture of the bowl. His chest is inches from pressing into my back and a shiver works down my spine at his proximity.

Never telling Maria about any of this. If she had a theory about him sending the postcards before, this would confirm it for her. As hesitant as I am to allow my brain to entertain that thought, it's hard when my alternate options are dwindling to not at least consider it.

The latest one *did* come early.

And his pun game has grown significantly compared to our childhood.

But that would mean he's been doing something selfless and kind since I left.

Since the night I called him a selfish ass that would never change.

Sweet and kind weren't his M.O, even if I'm starting to seriously believe they might be now.

My spine stiffens as his chest presses into my back. "Hey? You okay?" Liam's mouth dips toward my ears as his free hand falls on my hip and gently tugs me towards him.

"Huh? Oh yeah, fine," I autopilot. "Why?"

"I know you're the professional, but you're stirring that like a robot."

"Oh." I force my spine to relax. "Helps keep the milk from curdling."

"Right," Liam says skeptically.

Just having a crisis of faith and questioning everything I thought I knew about everything, ah yes, the Socratic Stirring Method.

Missed the opportunity to make an obscure philosophical joke, to be honest.

My hot water bottle slips, and he tightens the strings, letting his hand rest on the small of my back. Sunkissed shivers shoot from his fingertips up my spine. "Am I too close? I can step back."

The words tickle the hairs on the nape of my neck. I'm never going to get any of this under control.

Doomed. I am doomed.

"Oh, no, you're fine." I manage a calm, even tone as his warmth envelops my back, inviting me to lean and use his body for support for a moment. I give in, burrowing myself in the familiar scent that has become more of a comfort than my wildest dreams could have imagined. Whisking the yolks for the bavarois in a separate bowl, his hand lightly strokes the top of my arm, fingers leaving goosebumps in their wake.

If I'm not careful, I could get used to baking like this.

Butterflies fill my lower abdomen, mixing with the pokes and prods, slowly creeping in a band across the area.

I'll worry about those later.

Images of Liam and I baking and kissing in technicolor take center stage.

The timer for the sponge blinks me back to reality. Sensing my growing hope, a sharp tendril seizes everything inside and bends me in half.

A tiny whimper I try to bite back escapes my lips.

"What do you need?"

"I'm fine," I manage through another spasm.

He sighs, grabbing my elbow and turning me. "Peaches, come on, we don't have to do this now."

I wince at the exasperation in his voice. I get it. I'm not exactly pleased with my situation either. But this is why I don't start new relationships anymore, platonic or romantic, and why my social circle is minuscule and embarrassingly lacks anyone I didn't meet in my dorm room my first ear here. Endo is exhausting. But it's a part of my reality. We're a package deal.

And as far as modern medicine is concerned, it always will be in some capacity, or at least until they've solved every minute cis male ailment first.

Here's looking at you, pill for bent penis. Didn't see you there past the rapid tears collecting because of hormones.

"Evie." This time Liam's voice meets me in a softer register. "Please sit and rest."

"No, I can do this—" I wipe at my tears.

"I'm not doubting—"

"I need to get the sponge out of the oven."

"I've got it, Peaches. Please, for me."

"We should make the buttercream while the sponge settles." I sniffle, dancing around Liam and getting two sticks of room-softened butter into the stainless-steel mixer bowl.

The butter needs a good five minutes on low to grow soft and fluffy, so I busy myself finding the powdered sugar and ignoring the fact that I randomly started crying about—what I don't even know. Bent penis, maybe?

Well, no use crying over bent penis, I always say. Carry on then.

Liam regards me like I'm the porcelain doll everyone in my family treated me like, and it stings my pride. The hurt must be washed all over my face because he furrows his brow, rubbing the back of his head. "Look, Peaches."

"Want to add the sugar?" I nervously laugh, shoving the canister into his hand. I can't handle Liam feeling sorry for me. Because that means recognizing that I have something that some people pity, and I don't open that door. We don't think about that. We muscle through. Conceal.

Sighing, he nods while his lips remain curled in a defeated frown.

I scrape the mixer bowl with a rubber spatula, gathering all the creamy butter into the center.

"Good to go." I step aside, holding the bowl of sifted powdered sugar. Liam dips the canister, scooping out a generous heap.

A little too generous for a first churn.

Covering my mouth, I mask my gasp.

"What?" He assesses me with a wary set to his mouth.

"Nothing," I gleefully squeak, stepping back. "Just turn the mixer on."

"Yeah, that's not suspicious." He arches a brow, but I don't give away anything more, so he shrugs and flicks on the mixer to full speed, much to my evil, vengeful delight.

A plume of powdered sugar shoots back at him as I giggle.

He blinks through the snowy mess coating his face and sticking to his eyelashes before turning his full attention to me. "Oh, I see how it is. You think this is funny, huh?"

"Revenge has never tasted so sweet." Licking a few flecks of sugar off my finger, I savor the moment fifteen years in the making.

"You sure you thought this through, Peaches?" he asks, eyeing the bowl of powdered sugar still in my grasp. A villainous grin slowly rakes across his face.

Uh. Oh.

I shuffle my feet, juke this way and dart the other, trying to escape his clutches, but his looming figure blocks the only way out, further highlighting my lack of escape plan.

With a squeal, my rear hits the wall, and I resort to tossing sugar at him like it's Holy Water. "No. Back, Hades."

"You want me to be the Lord of the Underworld again?" he asks, eyes trained on mine with a playful intensity.

"No, bad." I panic, my ever-present pokes and prods mixing with a wave of dizzying giddiness. "I want you to be the lovesick boyfriend you signed up to be."

He cocks his head, reaching into the bowl. "This isn't what that looks like?"

I go to block what is coming at me, but I still have the bowl and a general lack of understanding of how holding things work, and in an instant, all the powdered sugar dumps over my face and down the front of my apron.

Stunned, I blink in disbelief as a boisterous laugh rattles Liam's chest. His eyes crinkle. His dimples pop. And I'm far too close to handle any of this properly.

"I don't know how I thought I'd get out of this clean with you." I huff, wiping my cheek, but my hands are coated with sugar too, so it smears more.

"Oh no. This one's your own damn fault. Don't you dare try to pin it on me." He chuckles, reaching for a towel and wetting it. He turns back and wipes my forehead with it, that same dangerous mirthful set to his lips.

"Your aura made me do it."

"My aura?" He gently wipes down my cheek.

"Mm-hmm, it's kind of the worst."

"And here I was thinking I was growing on you."

"Like a fungus, maybe."

"Like a fungus," he repeats with a snort and a slow stroke down my chin and neck. My breath grows ragged, and I grip the bowl—the only barrier between our bodies pressing together.

The playful charge in the room shifts. He brings the towel over my lips, and my breath hitches in response.

His hand stills, his gaze darkens, frozen on my mouth.

"I find Italian mushrooms particularly palatable at times, though," I rasp.

"Is that so?" He slowly raises a brow. "And would this be one of those times?"

I nod in response, consumed by the deep ache in my chest to feel his lips pressed against mine.

Gently, he plucks the near-empty bowl from my hand and steps forward, a questioning stare pinned on my face, searching for something. I fumble, placing my hot water bottle on the counter in anticipation before he lowers his head and slants his mouth to meet mine. His hand slides to the back of my neck. Carefully, he captures my lips with a warm embrace. Sweet and tender, his other hand falls to my hip, pulling me closer to him. A stabbing pain punctuates the movement, but I've wanted this for too damn long to surrender to my endo.

I catch his lip with my teeth, challenging him, and he responds, slamming my back against the wall and pinning my hands above my head with one of his own.

Breathless, I feel my chest heave against his as he leaves my mouth, kissing along my jawline and down the nape of my neck.

The mixer roars in the back, angry it's been left unattended for so long. "I should get that," I say through shallow breaths.

"Leave it." He presses another kiss to my lips, and I almost oblige him, leaving the buttercream to die.

"I can't—" I grab his arms and walk him toward the counter, flicking the switch as a charged silence fills the new space. Liam's back hits the counter. I undo his apron, slowly peeling it off him before relinquishing my attention to his buttons. Shirt free, I work a hand up, feeling the rough and lean ridges of his abdomen, so different from my soft curves. Power slices through me as I raise on my toes, inches from his lips, and his part as if on command at my proximity. His warm mouth grazes my lips in surrender, and then, as if he remembers this is some new competition we're playing, he recaptures mine.

"We're going to ruin the sponge if I don't curl it soon," I whisper.

"I'll make you another one." His mouth brushes against mine with his response, urgent and desperate.

"I don't know. It's a complicated sponge," I tease, dragging a finger slowly down his chest and tracing the sculpted v along his pant line. His body quivers under my touch.

"Evie, please." The ragged plea in his voice catches me off guard, and I meet his eyes. Air steals from my lungs at the look of longing held there like this is as much a fantasy of his as it's always been of mine.

"You'll have to beat the egg whites until they're stiff."

"I'll beat whatever the hell you want," he says between heaving breaths.

I bite back the snicker.

"Come here with your dirty-ass mind." He wraps an arm around my back and hoists me up on the counter, untying and removing my apron. His hand runs under my shirt, and I try not to wince, knowing it's running over a mess of scar tissue and dermal fibrosis where he has nothing but rugged ridges and smooth skin.

Liam's fingers shoot off my stomach with a gasp. "Shit, Evie, your stomach is burning."

"I'm so sorry. I had my hot water bottle close to scalding because it's the only way to keep my flare under control. I didn't think—" I blink back to my mess of reality. We knocked over the colored bowls at some point, and a rainbow is dripping down to the floor, scattering among a rash of sprinkles. "I wasn't thinking."

"Right. Apparently I wasn't either." He smiles bashfully. "Let's get you down from there, huh?" He offers out his hand.

"Oh, uhm. Yeah. I got it." I go to pop down, but the movement of the past few minutes was too much for a day like today, so I stay put for a few moments longer.

And then, because my uterus is a thief of joy who simply cannot go more than five minutes without being the center of attention. It screams. Rather loudly. Everything inside of me roars with pain. Spots cloud my vision as a not-so-pleasant breathless wave takes hold of my body, and I fight to manage the words, "I'm blacking out."

14

All I Do(nut) Is Dream of You

STRONG HANDS GRIP THE top of my arms as spots cloud my vision, and my head swirls like it's disconnected from the rest of me.

The spasm sinks its claws frrther into my lower left side and rips my breath away before it reaches my lrngs.

"What do you need?" Liam whispers against my forehead.

My head falls on his chest, and I relax a fraction.

The spots clear, but the someone-gave-Stab-by-the-Uterus-a-knife-and-now-she's-living-up-to-her-namesake sensation doesn't dissipate.

"I need help getting down."

He grabs my hand and lowers me off the counter. Flour and sugar cover me from head to toe. I sigh. I don't have the spoons—the energy reserves—for a shower, but sticky sheets don't sound pleasant either.

My legs wobble when they meet the floor, and Liam wraps his arm around my waist.

"I'm so sorry. You didn't sign up for this. You should leave," I whisper under my breath.

Liam laughs against my chest. "Like hell I will."

"I can take care of myself."

"I know you can, but I *want* to help you." The teasing lilt of Liam's words vanishes as his arm tightens around me.

"Oh." I pause, studying him. His brow is furrowed in concern, lips slightly parted, but it's not the usual look some cast down on me—it's not pity. It's like—he's feeling part of this too. I don't know how else to explain it.

I should start moving *somewhere* that isn't the mess of a kitchen, but the pain is close to curling me up into a ball, and I'm going to puke shortly. I bite down the litany of curse words dancing on my tongue.

"Let it out, Peaches. I'm not going to judge you." He brushes the hair off my face. "Whatever you need to do, just do it."

Gasping, another tendril grips my lower half, and a rash of cramps shoot through my uterus and down my leg. I waffle between begging for mercy and cursing this miserable existence but settle on a string of expletives slipping past my lips.

I look up and blush, panic seeping in. This is going to be the day from hell.

"Feel better?" Liam's left cheek imprints slightly.

"Infinitesimally."

Another twist works its tendrils through, taking my entire pelvic floor hostage. Nausea increases with the pain. I'm a minute from releasing the contents of my stomach in front of Liam again. Spots dot my vision, and I stumble, pushing his hands off—*shit, at least make sure it's in the toilet and not on him. I race*—which is more like an all-mind-consuming, herculean shuffle—into the bathroom just in time to vomit into the toilet. Hands graze the edge of my neck, and I groan, releasing more before the tension relaxes a fraction. If he could just not see me hurl once, that'd be great.

"I'm sure you're relieved this is fake right now." I sigh, leaning against the wall. I may have to live on this floor for the rest of my life.

A nervous look cuts across his face, and he worries his bottom lip with his teeth.

I peek at him, maybe even fake this is too much for him. "What?"

"Nothing." He shakes himself out of whatever that was. "You think you can manage a quick shower before we get you into bed?" He tucks a piece of hair behind my ear and smiles softly at me like he didn't just see me retch in a toilet, and it makes me question my previous thought. *Or maybe something more is going on.*

I nod. Really, I need to eat and take my painkillers and try to get this under control before another spasm has my head in the toilet again, but powdered sugar and sticky sheets take priority right now.

"Where are your pajamas?"

Blushing, I think of the easiest place to point him in my mess of a bedroom. "The desk is probably your best bet. I should have a pair of Caleb's pajama pants I stole near there and some bigger Alabama shirts if you want to change too."

He pushes up off the floor, offering his hand and pulling me up.

After a quick sugary rinse, I manage to slightly dry myself with shaking hands and brush my teeth. There's a soft knock on the door, and I wrap the towel around my waist and chest and open it.

Liam blinks, holding my clothes. "I, uhm, I was just going to pass these to you."

His cheeks redden with a nervous bob of his throat as his eyes rest heavily on my face.

"Right." I reach out for the clothes, and the knot in my poorly secured towel starts to fall. My eyes widen. I hastily fumble to catch the towel, but it falls before he closes the door with a startled clearing of his throat.

"Sorry!" I squeak. I toss the loose shirt that says "donut worry be happy" over my top half, careful not to catch my bloated reflection in the mirror. I don't need the extra mindfuck today. Pulling the pajamas over my still damp legs, I stumble. I didn't have the energy to fully dry myself, but now I'm paying the price on the back end. My leg snags in the long pants, and I wobble and lose my balance, crashing onto the floor. Oh, son of a biscuit.

Footsteps rush to the door. "Evie? Are you okay?"

"Fine, I just fell." I go to push up off the floor, but I don't have anything to hold on to, and my legs are too shaky. I crawl toward the tub to get some leverage and knock over the shampoo and conditioner bottle in my desperate climb.

"What are you—are you decent?"

"Am I ever?" I laugh, trying to use the tub's ledge to push myself up. My foot catches my pant leg, pulling me back down and forcing me to swallow my pride. "I need help."

"Thank you," he breathes out, opening the door. Strong arms wrap around my waist from behind, and he stands me upright. I turn. The pant leg that didn't trip me is stuck further up on my leg, but I'm anxious to bend and kickstart another flare, so I guess that's the style now.

"I'll get it," he says, bending toward the offending leg. His fingers graze my leg, rolling my pant leg down. "Jesus, Peaches, you're still soaking wet."

"I didn't have the energy to dry them all the way." I blush.

His scowl softens. "Can you manage to sit on the edge of the tub?"

I nod, lowering to the edge, and he grabs a towel and kneels.

He rolls both pant legs back up, wrapping the towel around my calf and gently wiping beads of water off. It reminds me of this scene from *Summer Stock*, so quietly sweet, where Gene Kelly does something similar for Judy Garland.

The words *Summer Stock* pass over my lips.

"Huh?" Liam peeks up at me under his thick black lashes.

"I was thinking about that scene in *Summer Stock* right before the show starts."

"Oh." He peers down at the towel in his hand. "Yeah, I guess it is like that. Are you going to start belting out 'Get Happy,' too?"

"No, I'm very against the whole just forget about your troubles and be happy mantra. When your troubles don't want to forget you, it's hard to do." I snort.

"To be fair, you are very unforgettable," he says, clearing his throat. "Since I assume I'm trouble."

"Not lately. No."

Liam's finger errantly grazes my skin as he moves further up my leg, and my insides scream like we're a regency romance couple touching without gloves for the first time, although the images this accidental contact is inspiring of Liam rising on his knees and ravishing my mouth would undoubtedly make Jane Austen blush.

I should probably consider dating *someone* after this whole thing if my body is this desperate to be touched by another human.

It's not just another human. It's Liam.

My gaze drags down past the worry creasing his brow and over his lips, pressed into a concentrated thin line.

Clad in an old Alabama shirt and flannel pajama pants, he should look more like the man I used to know.

But that man's face was harsh angles and teasing glints, and here he's all soft concern, kneeling before me. I don't know. Maybe he's just getting into character and doing what he thinks a doting boyfriend would do, or maybe it is something more.

Either way, I shouldn't try to figure this out on a day when my brain is thicketed in a deep fog and I could fall asleep right here.

His eyes pick up and meet mine with curiosity. "You still with me, Peaches?"

"Still here." I force a smile that's tight and unnatural. "Thank you."

"Yeah, of course. Let's get you into bed before another wave hits." He supports my arm, walking me across the living room and into my bedroom. His eyes flicker briefly over the postcards hanging on the back wall.

Ask him, screams a voice from the back of my skull, but the ache in my abdomen is increasing exponentially, and it would behoove me to find my heating pad and settle into bed before doom part two emerges. We disconnect, and I wade through my mess of a room. Since I use my heating pad almost daily, you'd think it'd be easier to find, but it's like keys at the bottom of a purse. The minute I relinquish my grip on it, it buries itself into the depths of my room, never to be found again. I shift things around, and a pile of books and paperwork crashes to the floor in a dramatic thud, making me jump back just in time to save my toes.

"Peaches, what are you doing?"

"I'm trying to find my heating pad."

"I'll get it. Lay your ass down." He shoots a cutting glare in my direction.

"I want to say no, but your stern face scares me."

"Good. Bed. Now." He points over to the bed, and I salute him.

Marching over, my feet trip on a cord, and I pause. "Channing Tatum, you sneaky bastard." I shake my head, rescuing my life source from the abyss.

"Wait. Did you just call your heating pad Channing Tatum?"

"Yes, because naming random shit is one of the few joys I have left in life, and this beautiful object gives the best damn lap dances. Do not judge me." I point an accusatory heating pad in his direction.

He puts his hands up in surrender. "I would never dream of doing something so hazardous to my wellbeing—I'm just jealous Channing Tatum gives you lap dances, that's all."

"You want to give me a lap dance?" The accompanying blush that creeps across my face can't be subtle, if the searing heat burning my cheeks is any indication.

"I don't think your cheeks could handle it, Peaches."

"Typical unfounded confidence." I shake my head, sitting on the edge of the bed. Liam leans down and plugs my heating pad in while I try not to stare at his own set of cheeks. God bless the squats that man must do.

"I think some of it is founded." He quirks a brow at my face as he returns with the pad.

Busted.

With the heat on my abdomen, the tension lightens a fraction, and I breathe a little lighter. There's still hope I'm going to get this under control.

"You want some tea?"

"Yes, please."

Reaching into the drawer next to the bed, I pull out the "break in case of emergency" pill bottle as Liam leaves the bedroom. "Can you bring the bread and Nutella too?" I holler.

"Sure."

"And a knife. Please."

"That depends. Are you going to stab me with it?"

"I make it a point not to stab people who bring me Nutella."

"Good to know. I'll have to keep some of those travel pouches in my pocket just in case." Dishes clatter in the sink while the water runs far too long in the kitchen.

Oh no. I'm still having trouble swallowing my pride enough to be okay with what happened in the bathroom. I can't add cleaning up after me to the ever-growing list of things Liam's done for me today too.

"Don't you dare try to clean up. I'll do it after I sleep this off a bit."

Another clink. Another clatter.

"I have the Nutella. I can do what I want."

Damn it. I didn't think this through. Equipped with his dimples of doom and Nutella, that man will practically be invincible now. I need to correct the situation.

"You're precariously close to becoming an exception to the rule."

"And you're precariously close to not having any Nutella."

I bite back a grin and pretend I'm suddenly overcome with my ailments, coughing into my hand, which doesn't even make sense, but I never did say I was good at improvisation. "But I'm so sick, and the only prescription is more Nutella."

Liam snorts, returning to the room and balancing the tea, Nutella, and a plate in his hands, the bread tucked inside a sleeve under his armpit. "Shit, Peaches. That sounds miserable. Almost like you should stay in bed and let someone care for you for the rest of the day."

I narrow my eyes, conflicted. On the one hand, I can totally drag my way through everything just fine; on the other hand—Nutella and not having to leave the comfort of my heating pad. Which is going to win. Every. Damn. Time.

"Fine, if you want to take care of me so badly, who am I to prevent you from your oddly placed happiness?" I pull the little lap desk I have resting on the floor near the crook of the bed and put it on my lap.

He places everything down with a phony, "Dreams do come true." And I have to hold down my laugh or risk spilling my tea everywhere.

I am lucky at how today's unfolding, though. Sometimes the heat doesn't work, and I can't get myself under control long enough to eat and take the pain meds, but I can at least manage that today. I just have to wait a little longer, and a warm dulling of my body and mind will give me the relief I was begging for an hour ago.

I grab the tea and inhale the steam, letting it settle my nerves.

"I'll be out on the couch doing some work if you need anything," he says once I'm relaxed a fraction more in bed.

"Oh. I mean—I'm going to put *An American in Paris* on if you wanted—I could give you the lap desk when I'm done eating, and you could work in here?"

Liam cocks his head to the side. "Do you want me in here?"

I shrug, slathering the Nutella on a piece of bread. "I may secretly enjoy your company."

"You sure that concussion is healed? You sound delirious."

"Oh no. It's definitely not." I pat next to me on the bed. "But come sit anyway, Wonder Boy." I smirk. There's a decided new warmth in that nickname, and it summons his eye crinkles as he settles next to me.

The happy chimes of Gershwin's opening score to *An American in Paris* play on the TV, and an icy shiver shakes my entire core.

Struggling, I try to pull the blankets up under the lap desk.

"Are you cold?" Liam asks.

"I get these weird cold flashes during my flares. It's fine." I sip my tea, savoring the warmth sliding down my throat.

"You can steal some of my body heat. If you think it would help."

I glance up at him. His honey eyes stare softly at me under a blanket of inky black lashes. His dimples slightly prick his cheeks in a closed-lip smile. If I didn't have a barrier of tea and bread around me, I sense that he'd dip his head and kiss me again. "I've honestly never tried it before. But it might?"

Scooting over, Liam wraps an arm around me. His hand falls on my right shoulder as warmth radiates down my left side, burning at every point of contact. He pulls me in tighter, and his firm grip keeps the shivers from thoroughly shaking everything on the bed.

His head turns, his lips resting a fingerbreadth away from my ear, and warm excitement spirals through me as I recall how they felt pressed against my skin. Gooseflesh pebbles on my skin, and I don't think it's from my shivers this time.

"Is this helping at all?" he asks.

His hot breath pricks the nape of my neck. My body practically calls to it. Like there really was a spellbinding moment in our exchange of breaths, and now I'm doomed to answer it every time we're near each other.

"Yeah, actually." I stuff some bread and Nutella in my mouth, hoping to satiate my craving for something sweet.

Liam draws soft circles on the top of my arm as "I've Got Rhythm" starts up on the screen, and Gene spins his arms like an airplane propeller.

"Remember when we got so dizzy trying to do that we fell face-first into a pile of mud?" he asks, a smile curling on his lips.

"Oh yeah. It took my mom a good hour to scrub me clean that night."

"I don't doubt it. I think I had mud in my ears for a good week after that. Got a wicked bad ear infection."

I swallow, picking at the crumbs of bread on my plate. For all I thought I knew about Liam, his home life was never one of them.

"Your parents weren't home to help?"

"No, they weren't really around a lot." His soft smile falters slightly. Maybe I should stop there, but he's being open, and I'm curious to get to know this part of him.

"How was that for you?"

I couldn't imagine a quiet, lonely house. Not without the chaos of Caleb's or Nana's singing, even my mom—as much as she causes so much strife—and her homemade meals.

"It wasn't ideal, but I had pretty good neighbors who took me in and shared their Nana." He pulls me in closer.

"She knew you needed her." I sigh. "Trust me, it wasn't my choice."

"I still appreciated it," he says, stroking my arm with his fingers.

I put my tea on the nearby table, passing the lapdesk over to his side, and relax back into his arms. Confident he can't see my face, I tilt my gaze to my twinkle lights and postcards, giving the blissed-out expression warring for real estate safe harbor. Butterflies swirl and swarm in my abdomen, and for once, it doesn't scare me. It emboldens me.

I'm not misreading this. I can't be.

"Liam?"

"Mm?" he hums.

"Why have you been sending me these postcards?"

He tenses, and a light chuckle rattles his chest. "You figured that out, huh?"

"I had my suspicions, but that pun in the kitchen showed your hand, yes."

"I hope that doesn't ruin them for you," he says with a sigh.

Two weeks ago, maybe the revelation that the *yours affectionately* signature featured at the end of each postcard belonged to Liam would have freaked me out a great deal. But today, all it does is warm my insides with an incandescent light, providing me with something that feels dangerously like hope. It's the hope that propels me to ask him a leading question. "No, it doesn't ruin them, but I'd love to know why you've been sending them." I shift a little closer to him.

He swallows before scratching the scruff on his cheek with his free hand. "I don't know. I was at a bar with Eli one day when you called. You were crying, and I could hear how homesick you were. Eli tried to get you to look on the brighter side of your decision and list some positives about Paris, and your immediate response was, 'Well, I mean, anything's better than having to deal with Liam Kelly on a regular basis, so at least there's that.' And all I could think about was how miserable I must have made it for you here if you sounded so unhappy and still thought you were better off than when you were with me.

"The words you threw at me at the bar had stuck with me, but I saw then how selfish I must have been if I didn't notice how miserable you were, or what you were going through. And then I thought about how I had broken my promise to Nana to take care of you."

"Liam, you were five." I fight the pull to capture his face with my hands and tell him to forget I ever said any of that. I wouldn't remember which call he was referring to, except Eli forced me to physically write down my reasons for being in Paris, and it sits in the top drawer of my desk to this day.

And it's true: *Liam isn't here* does feature prominently on the list.

Sometimes when I don't know why I'm here, I pull it out and remind myself about all the reasons I adore Paris. The glamor. The history. The ocean away from my mother.

But I also know why I made that phone call that day. Michel and I had just broken up. I was overwhelmed with the reality of my body not performing well in a relationship when Caleb started dating Holly and posting pictures of his double dates with Clare. It was an avalanche of things I couldn't do, and I crumbled under its weight.

He clears his throat. "I was twelve the second time I made the promise, not that that's much older. But I did such a shitty job, anyway. So I don't know, I didn't expect the postcards to go so long, or that you had them—like this—but Eli said they made you smile, so I figured I'd go along with it until they didn't."

"They really did help," I whisper. Those postcards got me through some dark moments in the last few years. Through hopeless flares, leaving my job, anniversaries of Nana's death, and fights with my mom. I'd always return to them for comfort and a nice warm pun-hug.

"I don't know how I'll ever be able to thank you for them." Maybe Maria was right about it all. Maybe there's a story behind the ball, and maybe I'll ask him—someday, when my brain isn't fading to dreamland. My eyes flicker, heavy with sleep.

"You don't owe me anything. They're just a part of the Grovel-for-Evie's-Friendship apology tour."

My heart skitters against my ribs. *Friend.* An uglier word has never hit my ears.

"Is that what you want? After this? To be friends?" I turn into his shoulder, finding his lips resting an inch away.

He tucks his lip between his teeth, and the column of his throat bobs with a swallow. "If that was something you wanted."

I blink. Friends don't usually suck other friends' faces, yet I want to do that with Liam, desperately. I open my mouth, feeling brave, feeling like maybe I could tell him I want something more than *friend*. But all I get out is "No" before an encore of twists and stabs punctuates the dull pain that's been present under the protection of the heating pad. "Oh, fucking hell." I crunch, grabbing my abdomen and slinking down in the bed to laying position.

A contraction rips through. False labor pains are a cruel joke, but they're happening far too regularly lately.

I'm tired, too tired of this portable torture chamber for a body, and I start sobbing. It's all I've thought about lately; it's even consuming my daydreams, and I'm just done.

I curl further into the fetal position, pressing the heating pad to my stomach. Cold sweat beads on my forehead from the pain. Nausea intensifies, and my heart races at a dangerous level. I beg internally for a relief I know will only come when it's good and ready. Shit. I shake, stretching out my legs and writhing because, at this point, I'm disconnected from my actions, desperately finding any way to lie that will relieve this even just a bit. Seconds that feel like an eternity pass, and the pain only deepens, curling me further into a ball. "I can't do this anymore," I whisper.

Liam rubs circles on my back. "I've got you. Deep breaths."

Another throbbing contraction rips through the already intense cramping. "I can't keep doing this."

The stabbing continues. I jump and shift, praying for mercy. Something, anything, soon. Hopefully the pain meds will kick in quicker than usual because I don't know how much more of this I can take. I'm drawing on negative.

Liam doesn't say anything more while I sob and writhe. He just keeps a grounding touch on me as the pain fades, ever so slightly, until it's still present, but something I'm equipped to manage, and I relax a fraction.

"I might fall asleep like this." I sniffle, sinking into the crook of his arm and resting my head on his chest.

"I hope you do." His finger delicately trails my back.

"But you have work to do. I'm getting in the way."

"Don't worry about me, Peaches." He lays a kiss on my forehead. "I just want you to get some relief, and if that's sleeping like this—trust me, I'll be okay."

My eyelids fall heavy as my tightened muscles release a fraction. The Vicodin finally kicks in. I direct my thoughts to dreamland and find the all-too-common thought I've had lately. Not some fantastical Hollywood starlet notion or Chris Evans entering my baking shop. But a simple, just-as-outlandish thought these days.

I wake up, and I'm not in pain.

How visionary.

"Hey, Liam?"

"Mmm?" he hums, still drawing lazy circles on my back.

"You know when you're trying to fall asleep. Do you ever try to control your dreams?"

"Sometimes. Why?"

"It's nothing. I've just been thinking about that lately. When I was younger, I used to fall asleep with dreams of being a pop star or a famous athlete."

He snorts. "You can't walk without causing physical harm to yourself."

"Dreams don't have to be realistic." I laugh. "That's precisely why they're dreams. But as I got older, they shifted. At night, I'd wrap myself in a reverie about walking down the Champs-Élysées in a Givenchy dress, living my best Audrey Hepburn life. Or I'd dance with a Gene Kelly doppelgänger, twirling in the moonlight along the Seine. But lately, when I'm falling asleep, the extraordinary fantasy that finds me is that I'll wake up and I won't be in pain."

His hand stills its circles on my arm. I don't know why I'm opening up this much. It's probably a side effect of the pain meds or my hormones (let's be honest, it's always the hormones). Or maybe it's because we've taken giant steps over a relationship line the past few days. Whatever the reason, I trust him with everything.

"Because the truth is, my body can't go on vacation from my disease. There's no pretending it doesn't exist, and feeling like a healthy twenty-something, even for a day, is as bizarre to me now as finding my own Gene Kelly. But that's such bullshit, because when I spiral like this, I have to admit that I've even let it take my daydreams, you know?"

"I don't," he whispers and clears his throat. "I can't pretend to know what you're going through or what living like this every day must feel like. But I know you deserve your daydreams. You deserve to find your Gene Kelly, Peaches. Please don't let it take that. Your ability to dream big and believe in the unbelievable were such big parts of who you were."

The hollow cavity in my chest cracks open with his words, filling endlessly with all things old Hollywood glitz and glamor, warm nights and fireflies, and picnics with peaches, because that's what Liam is to me when the shield is down. Maybe he is magical after all.

"That was a very lovely thing to say. Thank you for not being a fixer."

"I'm not quite sure what that means, but no problem, Peaches." He kisses the top of my head, and the warm fuzzies intensify.

"Most people try to fix the mess, but you don't."

"That's because there isn't a mess to fix. This is your life."

"That's also very true." Another yawn passes through, and I burrow deeper into Liam. "I'm stealing more of your heat."

"Steal away," he whispers into my hair.

The blanket drops from my shoulder, and Liam gently pulls it back up, letting his fingers rest there.

My eyelids grow heavy. I drift in and out of consciousness, drawing closer into Liam but a nagging thought tugs on my conscience and keeps me from dreamland. "Liam? I didn't mean what I said that day I called Eli. There are a lot of things I can think of that are worse than dealing with you."

"Don't worry about that right now, Peaches." His fingers brush a strand of hair off my face, and warmth spirals through right on schedule. "Just get to sleep, okay?"

"Okay, sunshine."

I fall asleep to the rhythm of his chest matching mine. Images of today flicker through, the desperation in his voice while we were kissing, him on his knees in the bathroom, the postcards, the gentle kiss on the top of my head just now. Maybe it's time to finally trust him with the whole truth. The truth I'm finally ready to admit to myself:

That more than any dream about Gene Kelly, my biggest dream has always been him.

15

Donut You Forget about Me

FOLLOW YOUR DREAMS.

Try.

Don't let endo take this from you too.

Past Me can be the absolute worst sometimes. Especially on a good day when I willfully ignore the whole *you're still chronically ill, even if you feel okay and you're-going-to-crash-and-burn-again-soon* reality.

I narrow my gaze at a sheet dotted with facts and figures I found in the avalanche of paperwork that nearly crushed my toes two days ago in my flare. It's an application for a small business grant that I almost finished before I let it die in my graveyard of a room. Wrapped in the adult equivalent of a diaper because I'm bleeding from multiple places thanks to my period, couch-bound again, and bored, I decided maybe I should at least read over this stuff before the deadline passes next month. Not like there's much else I can do right now anyway.

Truthfully, the grant is a great opportunity, but if I got it, the shop would have to be somewhere in the US. At this point, with an expiring visa and Maria moving out, I shouldn't turn my nose up at anything.

Rain patters along the windowsill, and I snuggle into my heating pad. The extra heat is appreciated on this freezing spring day as I stare at various forms spread across my coffee table in an unwelcomed state. I would much prefer it to be littered with an abundance of baguette sleeves instead of *this*.

Hell on paper.

Math.

Logic.

Quantifying my self-worth.

Fighting for my dreams seems an awful lot like hard, tedious work.

What a scam.

Sighing, I read over my lists of expenses. The word "storefront" sits at the top with a blank space.

I can't fill in an estimation until I know *where* I would want to open the shop, but that answer isn't so simple. It's what tripped me up and forced me to put the application aside the first time. Massachusetts seems out of the question, given its proximity to my mother. Still, the thought of starting over without anyone I know in a different state is a terribly lonely prospect, even for this hermit.

How does one even make friends as an adult? Not to mention my giant impediment of a disease. I'd have to start every new friendship with a disclaimer like "Hi, my name is Evie, and I have endometriosis, so when I bail on social plans, please do not think I'm flaky or ghosting you. I probably like your company a lot." Or else deal with the anxiety that I will eventually flake, and they'll never know why.

Chill, Evie. My palms shake, and I breathe, calming my racing thoughts. I'm spiraling unnecessarily over hypotheticals. Time for a break.

My phone chimes as if in agreement.

LIAM: Hey. How are you feeling today?

My heart summersaults at the sight of his name on my screen.

Two days ago, when I woke up after my drug-induced nap on his chest, I had a sneaking suspicion that Liam's arms could shelter me from just about anything. His thumb lightly stroked my hand as a low hum vibrated in my chest. I was going to tell him—maybe not everything, but enough for him to know he no longer felt like a storm I had to weather, but the safe harbor I looked forward to returning to. But I didn't have a chance because Maria's return to the apartment sprung Liam from my bed. A heavy weariness sat in his shoulders, and he vacated the premises in a haste once he made sure I was okay.

I didn't tell Maria on our walk yesterday how I ended up falling asleep on him.

Or that I confirmed he's the one who's been sending me the postcards. Even though I'm dying to dissect both with her.

She'd be overly insufferable with her "encouragement" to tell him the whole truth, and I need time to marinate on the situation and come to my own decision. I'm going to tell him everything, I think. Probably. No, I definitely will. I just need to collect my thoughts a bit more.

ME: Much better, actually. Looks like the doctor's orders were just what I needed.

LIAM: Glad to hear it. Are you home right now?

ME: Yeah, what's up?

LIAM: We're supposed to make a business plan for my final project, and I'm struggling to make a fake one. I was wondering if I could borrow the information I looked over on Monday for your shop. I'll give you everything when I'm done if it's helpful.

Glancing at the pile of papers on my table and rubbing my temple to abate a growing headache, I clack out the only logical response to this.

ME: Hell yeah, you can have it. When did you want to pick it up?

LIAM: I'm close by if now's okay.

ME: Oh yeah, no, that's fine.

Don't sound too eager. Don't sound too eager.

I drag myself off the couch to change, digging through my pile of clothes, but not even two minutes later, a knock on the door results in a rake of nervous flutters that travel the length of my body. He must have been outside when he texted me. Well, shoot. I straighten my baggy graphic shirt with Audrey Hepburn on it and a pair of booty shorts I changed into after my morning shower to prevent another falling-while-pantsing incident.

Running my hand over my hair piled high on my head, I accept my hot mess fate. There's no hope I can improve that bird's nest in my few steps to the door. "Hey, there. That was fast," I say, opening the door.

Liam greets me on the other side, wet and shivering. Beads of water slowly drip from his pitch black hair sticking to his forehead. The bags under his eyes have deepened, and my heart stutters as I take in his increasingly unkempt beard and chattering teeth. He doesn't say anything. His attention lands on my legs with a swallow before raising to meet my eyes again with a heavy stare, devoid of his usual confidence.

Something is off. He's not okay. Gooseflesh pebbles the skin on the nape of my neck at the thought.

"Get your ass in here," I chide, pulling him inside. "I'll get you a towel and start you some tea. What the hell were you thinking coming here without a jacket on a day like today?"

He stumbles over the threshold. His lumbering figure crashes into mine, and he rests a hand on my hip to stabilize us.

"Okay, I didn't pull you that hard." I laugh, my breath coming in short bursts this close to him. "But, hi."

"Hello." His hand tightens its grip, pulling me against his chest, and his eyes lock on my lips. I wrap my fingers around his neck and jolt at the ice-cold skin that greets me.

"You're freezing. I need to get you that towel."

"I'm fine."

"No, that's my line." I smirk. "And you aren't fine. You look terrible."
I rub the back of my hand over his scruff. "What's going on? I'm worried
about you."

"Peaches, leave it."

"No way. You just spent a whole day taking ridiculously good care of
me, and I can't even be concerned? I'm not okay with that dynamic."

His eyelashes fall softly against his cheeks as my hand slides to the back
of his neck, my fingers threading through a few strands of his silky hair.
Gently, he grasps my hand and pulls it back down. "I can't keep doing
this, Evie." He releases me, stepping back and distancing himself.

"Doing what?"

"Whatever the hell this is." He gestures between us. "I haven't slept
since this damn thing started."

Guilt falls like a stone in the pit of my stomach. He's this miserable
because of me?

"So let's call it off, then. I'll figure something else out. Not a big deal."
My heart fractures at the suggestion, but it's the right call, even if I'm
killing the only chance I have to be this close to him. He's the priority.
He has to be.

He shakes his head. "I don't want to call this off."

"Okay . . . Do you want to pull back? Stop the kissing?"

"No, I don't want that." He paces slightly, raking an agitated hand
through his hair.

I don't know what's going on, but Liam's acting like he's a wild animal
that's been kept in a cage for far too long, and it's starting to put me on
edge. "Then what do you want, Liam? Help me out. Whatever it is, I'll
do it."

"I want you." The words rip out of him in a brief low-pitched growl.

His eyes darken, cutting to me. I've never seen Liam like this, dis-
tressed, inhuman, and unguarded. His words and hungry gaze slam into
me with such a force that I step back on my heel, eyes wide and face

undoubtedly paling from the draining blood. His eyes widen before the stony, bored face I know intimately slams down over him and shields his features.

I was ready to accept that Liam might actually have feelings in *some* capacity, but not whatever that was. He couldn't—no. There's no way. "Are we practicing?" I whisper.

Liam keeps his eyes down, and a small, rueful smile quirking his lips. "No, Peaches, there's nothing to practice."

"I'm sorry, I don't get—"

Bashfully, he meets my stare. "The backstory was real, Evie. I'm in love with you. I always have been," he continues with a trembling voice. "You know, you were right. I thought I could handle this. Thought, hell, I pretended not to care for so long, what's a little pretending the other way? Should be easier, right? But this broke me. Your fucking lips broke me."

Every inch of me itches to close what little space is left between us and throw my arms around him in a wild embrace, but my brain is being held captive by the words pouring out of his mouth, and I can't find the courage to move. Worried he'll stop, worried I fell asleep on the couch and none of this is real.

"Because I've wanted you since before I knew what wanting someone felt like, and finally having you and knowing it wasn't real? That's worse than not having you at all.

"So I've been overanalyzing every fucking moment of this. Wondering if there was a spark of hope in the way you looked at me or if what we were doing meant anything to you. I thought maybe if we spent enough time together, you'd at least see we could be friends, but when you didn't even want that—" He scrubs a hand over his face. "I don't know what I'm saying anymore. I should—I should probably go, sorry to bother you."

Every word out of Liam's mouth shakes me down to the marrow. *He's in love with me. He wants me. He's agonized over the very same things I have.*

And this is real? *Say something!* My brain is a jumbled chaos of starter sentences, and none seem right.

He takes a step toward the door, and I panic. "Don't you fucking dare. Yeah, that was a lot to dump on me, but it was more than I could ever dream of you saying, so if you can just give my brain a second to process that you love me too—"

Liam turns, and my eyes widen at the unconscious slip.

He meets my gaze. "I'm sorry. Did you say 'too'?"

"No," I panic, covering my mouth.

He just poured his heart out to you, asshat.

"Evie—" Liam steps forward, eyes wild. "Why did you say too?"

"I mean, I feel like that statement's pretty self-explanatory."

Oh, for the love of sprinkles, woman. Tell. Him.

"Not in this case, Peaches." He takes another step forward, and his lithe body takes on an almost wolfish prowl. "Because I've been under the impression you've hated me with every fiber of your being for the last ten or so years, while I suffered through an acute form of unrequited love—so I'd really like you to elaborate on that 'too.'"

"It may have come to my attention recently that I harbor a significant amount of positive feelings for you and probably have for some time."

"In other words . . ."

"I'm in love with you too, okay? I was going to tell you in bed before my uterus decided to go all exploding shattered glass on my insides. *That's* why I didn't want to be friends because, no offense, but being friends sounds unbearable after knowing how earth-shaking your lips feel against mine—and that terrified me. What I feel when you're around? That's always terrified me.

"No one else elicits the kind of feelings in me that you do, the desire, the passion, the overwhelming need to smash your face with both my fist and my lips at the same time. How every time you touch me, I run the risk of being putty in your hands. I've tried to keep my heart safe from you, but you had it in a death grip before I knew I'd given it to you, and I don't know that I want it back anymore—because I think, for the first time in maybe ever, I like that I'm in love with you.

"I like that I'm staying up and thinking about how your mouth feels against mine and how you took care of me when I was sick. I love that you wrote me postcards for years, just to make me smile, and I love how you look at me—like you see my faults and think they're actually these beautiful, magical parts of me."

"They are. You are." Liam blinks. "Magic." He steps us backward, and my back finds the counter.

"What are you doing?" I manage with a shallow breath.

"Checking something," he says, eyes wide with disbelief. "Don't run from me this time, Peaches. Keep the wall down."

"I'm here." I swallow. "Unguarded."

Slowly, he raises a finger, dragging it across my collarbone, and my flesh pebbles under his touch. My legs slowly turn to jelly. A warmth pools in the pit of my stomach. My chest rises and falls in a needy rhythm. I'm electric with anticipation for a kiss and damn near exploding. His gaze searches my face, and a tiny "huh," escapes him, that broad smile deepening to catastrophic proportions.

"This is mine?" He dips his finger, tracing the skin guarding my heart. Want gathers beneath his touch.

"Desperately," I manage, my eyes fluttering to a close. I'll never know how he can elicit such a strong reaction with just his finger.

"How desperate, Peaches?" He leans toward my lips, hovering torturously close, letting them brush, but never fully giving in to the embrace.

The need arcing between us is unbearable. Release, I want release. I lean forward, and he follows the dance. Oh, hell.

"If you think I'm going to let you tease me like this—I've squashed this before, I'll do it again," I scold.

"Oh, see, that's not fair." His nose brushes against my cheek, angling like he's finally going to put me out of my misery and kiss me. "Because I've tried to kill this Evie, trust me, and I never quite found the trick."

"And yet here you are torturing me when you could be showering me with affection."

"If you don't think I'm not going to enjoy every second"—he lays a kiss on my jaw—"of knowing you want me, too, then you don't know me as well as I thought you did."

"Oh, believe me, the knowledge that you'd make me a lovesick puppet—" I pause as he runs a finger up my side and I lose a breath. This man is going to be the death of me. "If...if you knew, is what's kept it locked up so tight for years. I was just hoping if your affections are as you claimed, you might"—he presses a kiss to the corner of my lips, and it slices through any remaining lucid thought— "that maybe you would be more inclined to lavish me instead of this extended torture."

"I can't do both, puppet?"

"I swear to go—"

He cuts me off, pressing his lips firm against my mouth. Shivers of desire race through as he crushes his body against mine. The tension of anticipation slakes away, and we mold into one in the following embrace. My breath catches, and Liam takes the opportunity to deepen the kiss, thoroughly wrecking me with a spine-tingling, hungry pass of his lips.

Warmth spirals through me, curling my toes. Nothing has ever felt as free as this kiss, like before we were doing everything with an elephant of false pretenses on our backs, and now it's just us being honest for once in our damn lives.

My hands fall to his shirt, soggy and freezing, plastered to every ounce of his skin, and the need to have a living, breathing Liam Kelly wins out over my urge to keep kissing him. I pull away. "You still need a towel."

He hovers, lips swollen, a glorious half-dazed expression washed over his face. Maybe I wasn't misreading his decimated appearance at the Eiffel Tower.

"I'm not really thinking about towels right now, Peaches."

I bite the lower portion of my lip, the need to take care of him and kiss him senselessly at odds with each other.

"Especially when you do that," he groans, reaching for me. Pushing up off the counter, I walk us backward, never breaking the kiss, toward the bathroom doorframe. I miss a bit and whack my back and head against the wood. He cradles my noggin with a "fuck's sake," still greedily devouring my lips.

I snatch a towel and back him up again, thankful for once this apartment's square footage is so tiny. We walk in tandem to my bedroom, and I finally pull away. Grabbing the folds of his shirt, I tug it up over his head, running the towel over his chest and ridges. His body shakes, and my scowl returns.

"Coming here without your jacket." I tsk. "What were you thinking? Look at you. You're still shivering."

"I wasn't thinking, and that's not why I'm shivering." He smirks, catching my wrist as it passes over him with the towel. He brings me up against the bed, and the crook of my knees hits the mattress. I allow myself to collapse, dragging him on top of me. He brushes his lips to mine, but when I reach out and touch his skin, it's still too cold for my liking.

"Get your ass under the blankets, mister."

"Such a bossy caretaker, my goodness." He nibbles my earlobe.

"I'm serious." I giggle, pushing him away. "I'll let you steal my body heat if that's any kind of incentive, but go. Now." I wiggle off the covers and snap my fingers. He raises his hands in surrender, getting into the bed and burrowing under the blankets.

There's a camisole underneath my shirt, and I gather the edges of my top layer to take it off for more skin contact. Raising the edge of my shirt, I inadvertently meet Liam's stare, and my heart stutters.

Gene Kelly had this face. This one look that he fashioned on his leading lady that made it seem like he'd go to the ends of the world for them. Like nothing else mattered, and he was irrevocably theirs. In my teen years, I dreamt about being on the receiving end of that face. Of having someone so far gone, they'd look at me with that soft admiration, and I'd just know that at least one person on this earth thought I was worth something. In my twenties, though, I buried that desire with my other dreams, certain that look, and most of the magic I thought existed in life, were reserved solely for Hollywood pictures.

So imagine my surprise as I inch closer to my twenty-seventh birthday, with very little magic left in the world, to have that particular attention pinned on me by none other than Liam Kelly himself.

The desire reflected in his eyes emboldens me, and I slow my stripping, winking at him when my shirt is finally off. He crooks a finger, beckoning me to the bed, propped on one elbow, the sheet falling at his hips.

I shake my head, a slight smile lifting the corner of my lips, and meticulously fold the shirt, placing it on a pile of clothes flung haphazardly on my desk.

A groan from behind deepens my smirk. "What, you know I like to keep this room tidy," I tease with a slow turn back to him.

A tortured muscle flicks in his jaw.

"Oh, I'm sorry." I put an innocent hand to my chest, highlighting my cleavage. "Do you *not* like being teased—I just assumed."

"I don't mind the teasing, Peaches. It's just—" He fists the blanket, pulling it tight to his chest and flashing a dopey needy smile at me with an overexaggerated shiver. "I'm so cold. I need you."

I tilt my head back, and a euphoric laugh rattles my chest. "Oh, you poor baby. Here, let me take care of you." I climb over him, settling into bed, and he grabs my hips, tugging me against him. His hand comes up and cups my face.

"This is real?" he asks, brushing a thumb across my cheek. A look of uncertainty flashes in the recesses of Liam's gaze as he searches my face, and my heart turns over at the vulnerability washed all over his features.

"This is real," I whisper back before crashing into his lips and claiming them for my own as much as he's ever claimed mine. Electricity arcs between us until we're nothing but tangled breaths and sizzling body heat. And we stay like that for some time, savoring a lifetime of lost kisses and untold truths.

The problem with endometriosis, nay, *one* of the problems with endometriosis, is that endometriosis doesn't care about anything. It doesn't care that it's inconvenient. It doesn't care that it's causing you a significant amount of pain every hour of every day or that it's brought you to your knees both mentally and physically. It doesn't care who you are. What you do or need to do for a living. And it doesn't care that you're in the middle of one of the most spectacular moments in your life—or maybe it does care, and it's just a bitch. Maybe it's the Regina George of diseases, who knows? I've tried to converse with it on multiple occasions, and all I've ever heard back is *stabby, stab, stab, stab.*

What I do know is that no matter how many times I try to ignore the stabbing pain, the stabbing pain doesn't seem inclined to ignore me back, and with every pass of Liam's lips on mine, two facts are becoming more and more apparent.

First, Bridget Jones's enormous white panties have nothing on me as I am still in the adult version of a diaper.

And second, being turned on freakin' kills.

Liam rolled me on my back a little while ago, his hand now exploring my body (thankfully over my pants), and with every pass, want and need are punctuated with a pin prick in my vagina. A rash of cramps through my lower half follows—I know what comes next, but I'm desperate to keep this going, the craving to feel his hands on every inch of my body still too strong, no matter what's going on down below.

Liam slides a hand up my sternum, traveling under my camisole for the first time. A shaky breath rattles my chest at the sensation of his calloused hands rubbing against my skin. "Is this okay?" he whispers. "We can slow down."

"No, I want you too—" I trail a hand on his bicep, desperate for his lips.

He obliges, pressing his hot mouth against mine, and I'm flushed with need. His hand roams higher, grabbing my breast and running a finger over my nipple.

"God, you're so perfect," he says in hushed reverie.

I moan, arching against his touch. The intensity sets everything in my malfunctioning lower half on fire as every muscle I'm in firm possession of down-there spasms. An Excalibur-worthy stab underscores the situation, and I wince.

He freezes. "What was that?"

"Nothing. I'm fine." I panic, not wanting to ruin this perfect moment.

"You winced."

"No I didn't."

"Evie, I saw you wince."

"Okay, but to be fair, I wince a lot. So please come back." I pull him toward my lips, but another spasm grips me, and I tense slightly.

He presses his forehead to mine. His need flushes hard against my thigh. "Let's take a break, Peaches."

I nod reluctantly, the pain growing more persistent.

He rolls on his back, running a hand through his hair. "Where's your heating pad?"

"Couch."

Scrubbing a hand over his face, he gets up and stumbles out the door with a pained, encumbered gait. I swallow. I can't pretend to understand what that feels like, but from all accounts I've heard, unreleased tension doesn't feel great.

Yes, yes, in general, I have little sympathy for penis pain, but Liam's—it's growing on me, and I don't like that I'm the one that caused him any kind of discomfort.

He smiles softly at me, re-entering the room, plugging in my heating pad and handing it to me before settling into bed and resting his arm behind his head. He leaves the side where I am open, and I curl up into him, pressing the pad against my abdomen.

"Thank you." I sigh. My cheek falls against his bare chest, and I graze my fingers over the exposed skin on his stomach, dipping along with the peaks and valleys of his ridges.

"Of course." He crunches, kissing my forehead. "How are you doing?"

"I'm okay."

He assesses me skeptically, and I sigh in response. Liam being able to read me the way he does might be a problem. "I'll be okay when the heat kicks in. But it's not anything to worry about, it's just my time of the month."

"We could have stopped sooner."

"I didn't want to ruin the moment. Believe it or not, I like kissing you too."

"Nope, still don't believe it." His fingers delicately stroke the back of my neck, and my fine hairs stand on end. "And you didn't ruin anything. This right here is perfect."

I pick my head up as a satisfied exhale collapses Liam's chest. A wide smile dimples his cheeks to catastrophic proportions. That look of reverence, like Gene when he's singing and dancing in the rain, sits dreamily on his face, rimming his eyes with a gorgeous revelry.

"Just promise me you'll speak up next time, Peaches."

"Who said there'll be a next time?" I tease. "Maybe I got it all out of my system."

He peeks at me with one eye and catches the grin on my face. Tucking a finger under my chin, he angles my lips to his and lays a soft, breathless whisper of a kiss there. Pulling away, my lips chase his for half a second. *Busted.* "I hate to be the one to tell you this, but I think you've got it bad there, baby." He winks, smug and satisfied. "And I intend on keeping you that way."

"I shouldn't have let you in on that secret. I could have done some serious damage letting you think it was unrequited, would've been much less of a headache for me." I pout, sticking my lip out, hoping he comes back to meet me with another soft caress.

"I'm glad it slipped." His arm tightens, bringing me closer to his chest. "I'd done a pretty good job keeping it in check all these years, but then you went and kissed me like *that* at the Eiffel Tower, and I knew I was done for."

"If it's any consolation, that kiss broke me too." I giggle, snuggling into him, a question poking the back of my mind. *All these years.* The words shouldn't be the snag they are with how he's acting. But there's one thing about our history that doesn't fit, and my gut is screaming that maybe it's the outlier, not his current sweet disposition. "Can I ask you something? You don't have to answer if you don't feel comfortable, and I promise I trust you—it's just . . ."

"You want to know what happened at the debutante ball." Liam sighs.

"Am I that predictable?"

"After today, I can't say yes to that." He laughs. "But it's probably time to have this talk anyway."

I lay my hand on his chest. He covers my hand with his, lightly stroking the top of it with his thumb. "You need anything first?" he asks into my hair. "It's kind of a long story."

"No." I shake my head, heart pounding because *I was a dick and pranked you* isn't that long of an answer, and after he showed up soaked to the bone today, looking like death, Maria's *maybe something went drastically wrong* narrative seems to be lining up more succinctly.

"So I guess the best way to start this is by admitting that I haven't been exactly truthful about what happened that night, and I'm sorry it became such a nightmare for you, too, but I never meant to hurt you. I can promise you that. I meant to be there that night. And I hoped this—" He crooks a finger between us. "I don't know, I'd started catching you looking at me differently, and I was hoping you were warming up to the idea of us too."

"I was."

"Right. I don't know if that makes this better." He laughs. "Because trust me, Peaches, if we had it my way, this would have been how we spent most of our time in college too."

But then I wouldn't have Paris or Maria. The what-ifs and could-have-beens slice through, but I don't want any of them, as lovely as they sound on the surface. I wouldn't trade a single one for Maria.

Huh. It's entirely possible that the worst night of my life also gave me some of the best parts of my reality.

"So what happened?"

"Well, I went to get your corsage," Liam repeats the words he said in a fluster at the bar before Harmony interrupted the situation. "I had one made with lilacs and some of the ribbon woven through the crown you and Nana made that time we had our play backyard wedding. I doubt you even remember that, though."

"We ate peaches on a blanket after," I add.

"We did, and I pocketed some of the ribbons from the crown and somehow still had them. Thought it'd be a good way of telling you how I really felt."

"It sounds impossibly sweet," I whisper. My pulse quickens. Something terrible must have happened if Liam didn't show after keeping a bunch of ribbons safe for twelve years.

"The lady at the florist shop gave the corsage to me with a huge smile, saying it reminded her of my father, who was always doing romantic stuff like this for my mom and that I was growing up to be the spitting image of him."

"But your dad is like five-foot-four and blond."

"Exactly." He exhales. "And you wouldn't know this, but he's not exactly a sentimental guy, either. Anyway, I must have looked wicked confused because then the florist amended she meant my biological father, not Harry."

My heart pounds against my ribcage like a chorus of timpani drums. Please tell me I haven't been holding the ultimate grudge against Liam over a day he found out Harry wasn't his biological dad. Please tell me he already knew.

"I didn't know." I breathe out, trying to lighten the tightening in my chest.

"Neither did I." He chuckles bitterly. "Apparently it was this big town secret that everybody kept from me. When I went home, I confronted my mom about it, and she broke down and explained everything to me. Explained how my biological dad was her high school sweetheart, but he was a few years older, so when she got pregnant at sixteen he was about to graduate. He had a scholarship to play basketball at Duke, which he said he would turn down, but when it came time, he chose basketball over us and left her seven months pregnant. Harry was her best friend in high school and apparently, he'd been in love with her since he was younger but didn't know what to do about it—a learned trait, I guess—constantly upstaged by whatever this other guy did. So when he left, Harry proposed, said he'd take care of us both, and they never told me the truth. I have Harry's last name, and he's the father listed on the birth certificate and everything.

"That night I said some awful things to Harry that I still regret. He was sixteen and he married my mother, quit high school, and started working at his dad's creamery, and I stood there like a spoiled brat saying that at least I finally understood why he was always so cold, and then I just went into this weird catatonic state. I don't know how to describe it, but by the time I shook myself out of it, well—"

"It was too late to go to the ball." The words fall out of my mouth, but my mind is blank, processing the bomb he's dropping on me.

"Yeah." He rubs my knuckle with my thumb. "I knew that I had blown it with you."

The night's end flashes through in my brain, the *actual* night. Heavy with anger, I always focused on my side of the story, the fist curled tight, tear-soaked mascara running down my cheeks. Complete and total humiliation coursed through every ounce of my being in a jumbled static.

After my mom ripped into me, calling me an embarrassment to the family and a disappointment of a daughter, I marched over to Liam's house to let him know what a jackass I thought he was for leading me on and then bailing on me. When I found him on the porch, I rationalized that he was waiting to gloat. But now, I see him for what he was, a dejected boy, tie askew, his eyes picking up to meet mine in a blurry state. Not the twinkling pride I reimagined. A tiny "You look pretty," fell out of his lips.

The mask didn't slam down until I reamed into him. The hard stone, the smirk, the twinkle—I can see the moment it all crashed over him.

"I was awful to you." I fight back a well of tears. I don't want to make this about me right now, but one escapes anyway, falling down my cheek.

"Hey, hey, no, it's okay." His arms tighten around me, brushing the tear away.

"You were hurting, and I was an absolute monster. Liam, I'm so sorry."

He raises my chin to meet his eyes. "I could have handled things better, too, Peaches. But I don't know . . . I think I just decided being the villain with you and fighting was a lot easier than processing anything. Like if I told you, you'd just pity me and still be sad because I ruined your big day, too. And I thought if you were angry with me, you'd have somewhere to vent your frustrations, like otherwise, the truth would have swallowed us both up."

You needed a villain more than you needed the truth.

I don't know if Liam's right about what I needed. If he was honest, maybe sitting on the porch and crying over the golden wash our parents lost that night would have healed us faster, but there's nothing I can do to change it.

"Still, I could have been a little nicer." I half laugh, half cry at the absolute mess I made for us both. "Thank you for telling me now." I brush a kiss to his lips and then press my forehead against his. "I'm really glad you came to Paris."

"Me too," he says, fighting a yawn.

His weary, tired demeanor pulls at my heartstrings. In all the chaos of the last few hours, I forgot that he hasn't slept well in at least a week, maybe longer.

"We need to get you some sleep. You look ragged. You think you can nap now?"

"Here?"

"I have a few hours left before work."

He nods, wrapping his arms around me and rolling me on my side so my back and his stomach are pressed together. He nuzzles into my neck.

"Your birthday is coming soon," he says in a groggy voice.

"Mm-hmm."

"Do you have any plans?"

"Just wherever Maria makes reservations for. Why?"

"If you're feeling up for it, you think I could take you on a real date?"

If you're feeling up for it hits the nail on the head. I want to say, yes, absolutely! But the truth is, I could flare and ruin everything again. "I can check the symptom tracker app on my phone. I don't know where I'll be in my cycle or if that day is usually good, but I'd love that otherwise."

"We can eat cake in bed if it doesn't work . . ." His voice is fading to sleep. Not even five minutes pass before his breath rises and falls with that signature heavy slumber cadence. A tightness in my chest lightens, but thoughts spiral in a frenzy in my head.

I knew Liam wasn't an ass anymore, but the thought that he maybe never was one, that maybe he's secretly sweeter and gooier than the best version of a cinnamon roll, well, I hadn't let myself entertain that thought. I wince, closing my eyes. Nana would be scolding me something proper for the way I treated him, but I can't take it back. There's only forward. Another Nana life lesson. And from here on out, I must protect the cinnamon roll at all costs.

Liam's fingers slightly graze my abdomen as his hand falls limp across it. His warmth spirals around me, but it's quickly chased away by an accompanying pain.

I sigh, falling to sleep to the images of Liam passionately kissing me and switching it off when he realized I was in pain. I hate myself for letting my body ruin that moment.

And it's going to happen again. And again. And again. It's what it does. Nothing will ever be like it would be with someone without this disease.

It's frustrating and hellish with me when it's supposed to be a release and joyous.

I squirm in bed next to the restful sleeper. He doesn't know. He's just seen the tip of the endo iceberg. It'd be selfish to be happy. A ton of self-loathing thoughts prod my conscience. But that's all they are, thoughts. They're not me.

The strong arm draped over my side tightens around me, and the warmth of the sun radiates and eradicates the dark clouds looming overhead.

There will be time to spiral over these things. I tell my mind to be quiet, deciding today that it's okay to be incandescently happy for once.

16

Donut Stop Believin'

FINGERS DELICATELY TRAIL THE edge of my abdomen. My legs tangle with Liam's in his navy sheets, and I wrestle with the fabric barrier for freedom. Finally breaking loose, I drag my foot over his lower calf, reveling in the low murmur that vibrates his body pressed tight against my back.

One week ago, I'd never awoken in the same bed with anyone I was romantic with, not even Michel, and now it's dangerously close to becoming a habit I don't want to break.

We still haven't explored each other beyond the boundaries of a few heavy kisses.

Not that I don't want to go further.

I do—*desperately*. Even the slight graze of his fingers curls my toes.

But after my ill-timed pain last week, I'm anxious to let him see me at my most vulnerable, the part where I always feel broken no matter what I do.

Liam doesn't seem to mind, or if he does, he's not acting on it, content with going as far as I take us, and his patience is becoming another virtue I add to my growing list of things I admire and love about him.

Liam's lips fall hot against my neck, and a cascade of light kisses follows.

"Morning," I happily sigh.

"Happy birthday," he hums against my ear, his raspy morning voice warming my chest better than a good cup of tea ever could.

My finger slides against the bicep curling under my neck.

In recent years, waking up with a case of the birthday-sads had become as much of a tradition as cake and my mom's passive-aggressive text messages, which always send me into a spiral over the milestones I hadn't hit yet and probably wouldn't.

Like having a decent job.

Or kids.

Everything felt stagnant—like I was falling further behind the rest of my friends, battling to just survive and keep whatever footing I had in this world and never progressing forward.

And for the longest time, this birthday in particular terrified me. It's my Charlotte Lucas birthday. I looked at it, saw the no prospects, no money, and growing to be an increasing burden on my parents' psyche lining up just so, and much like Charlotte Lucas, I was frightened.

But today—instead of doom and aging gloom, I feel good. Optimistic, even.

"Best birthday wake-up ever." I smile. He ventures under my shirt, and I lean back into him. "I think spooning is my new favorite hobby."

A ribbon of shimmers follows the wake of Liam's touch, stirring the butterflies awake. They've become a welcomed intrusion these days.

"Mine too." His fingers graze my waistband, and I tense, anxious with anticipation.

I'm not a virgin, but I might as well be an honorary one, my depth of experience being limited to a few mediocre college tries with Michel. When it was clear my body couldn't handle penetration in general, and it wasn't just the typical first-time pain, we stopped, agreeing that friendship was the best course of action. Another thing that faded quickly when I couldn't bring myself to leave the confines of my heating pad long enough for parties and other outings.

And then, that was kind of it.

I didn't put myself out there for other guys. Thought it was best not to think about that part of my life for sanity's sake. I had too many other things to worry about anyway. But Liam's been the temptation I never had, and I want to scratch that itch. Even if I'm terrified about the aftermath.

"Sorry." He retracts his fingers. "Sorry. Sorry."

"No, it's fine—I just—" My tongue ties itself into knots. How do I explain all this to him? That I'm twenty-seven today, and my list of partners is limited to one man when I was nineteen. That it hurt like hell repeatedly, and I never felt like trying again, so I'm clueless when it comes to navigating these waters.

I flip over on my other side to face him. I feel my heart stutter, still not used to how he's somehow more devastatingly gorgeous in the morning. When his hair is a mess because he runs his fingers through it unconsciously in his sleep, and the light from the window falls on his cheekbones just so, and I'm reminded that his jawline is of the "cut glass" variety. Thick black eyelashes shroud his face, and mirth lines the edge of his eyes peering back at me. Like he knows I'm lost in all of him right now and he's soaking it in. "I'm not very experienced with a lot of things, so I get anxious about them, but with you, I want to do—those things."

Liam raises an eyebrow. "You've never—"

"Oh, no. I have. A few times, with this one guy, but I wasn't exactly overwhelmed by it, or maybe I was, just in a different way—I don't know. It wasn't like what I've read about in books or seen on TV."

"We can go slow. Not a problem." He brushes a piece of hair off my cheek, leaning in and laying a soft kiss on my lips. "I need to feed you and then kick you out anyway."

"Kick me out? On my birthday? Rude."

"Well, yeah, I gotta get ready for our date tonight." He flutters his eyelashes. "You think this charm just happens naturally?"

"It's adorable you think you're charming." I giggle, wrapping my arm around his back and pulling him in for another kiss.

Oh, can I be cheeky now?

"You really think you can insult me and then just pull me in for a kiss, and it'll be okay, huh?" He halts inches from my lips with a devious smirk.

"I was admittedly entirely too confident for half a second, and now I regret things." I swallow. "But I'm hopeful you wouldn't do anything nefarious to me on my birthday."

"Definitely not," he says while his hand pins my shoulder to the bed, suggesting otherwise. "It's just clear I still have some major work to do tonight."

"That sounds vaguely threatening," I squeal as he burrows a rash of kisses into my neck.

"It should. You're screwed." His thumb rubs the fabric over my nipple, and I lose a breath. I glance up at him hovering over me on the bed. The light catches his dimple and reflects in the glittering depths of his eyes. *You love him*, screams through my mind in the quiet moment, and I let it, hugging the thought tight to my chest. "Tonight, I'm going to woo your socks off, and then you're going to be doomed with how in love with me you are, Peaches."

I already am.

He lifts my chin, tracing the curve of my jawline with his mouth.

"I was thinking of wearing heels, and I don't normally wear socks with those."

He picks his head up with a pause. "I'll have you falling head over heels then."

I tilt my head, laughing, and it grants Liam better access. "So confident."

"Determined." He winks. "I need to return the favor."

It is a rather unfortunate fact that I only own shift dresses. Nothing against them—they're my life force—but now and again occasions arise where I wish to resemble something other than a potato. Liam threatening to take me on a date so swoony that I will be forever doomed is one of those occasions.

In a panic, I clack out a shopping SOS to Maria and rush to the Marais, hoping to find something in one of the Free'p'star thrift shops. After a fitting room montage worthy of an early-2000s rom-com, we find "the one" in the third and final location.

A pink fit-and-flare dress reminiscent of another Givenchy dress that Audrey Hepburn wore. Miraculously, it's a perfect fit, like Audrey herself is looking over me with an *"I've got you, darling."*

Maria handles my makeup, my hand far too shaky thanks to an internal cocktail of excitement and anxiety.

I'm not feeling great, which for me is almost okay, but Lord knows that can switch at any moment, and I really, really, don't want to ruin tonight.

"You took something for your pain?" Her brow furrows as she applies my lipstick.

"Mm-hmm," I hum, smacking my lips together.

"And your anti-spasmodic?"

"Oh, not yet, but good call." I fluff my loose curls, standing to let Maria assess me one last time.

"Gorgeous." She pulls me into a hug. "I'm so happy you're giving this a chance."

I swallow, unable to quiet the feeling that "giving this a chance" was never an option. I got so caught up in the passion that I haven't been thinking about what happens next, just the now of everything.

Because someday, I'll have to deal with the fact that if he genuinely ants to be with me, he will have to sacrifice things that I mourn the loss of every day.

Like those easy, wild intimate moments.

A sharp pain pricks my side, and I sigh, pressing on it. Maria frowns slightly and looks to the corner of my bedroom. "Maybe bring your cane so you can stay out longer?"

I nod, tucking my anti-spasmodic medicine under my tongue, and breathe. Sometimes my ego gets the best of me, and I try to go without my cane and push too far, too stubborn for my mobility aid, but Maria's right, it'd be silly not to use it today. The cane takes the pressure off the muscles pulling on my left side. It helps me. There's nothing negative about that. Especially if it means I don't ruin whatever Liam has planned.

A knock sounds on the door, and Maria wraps a final hug around me. "Remember that you're the absolute best, and he's a lucky fucker."

I snort at her uncharacteristic cursing.

She grabs my cane and hands it to me. "Go get 'em, tiger."

After one final collecting breath, I implore my heart to settle its anticipatory meltdown, turn the knob and swing the door open, happily greeting—

Gene Kelly?

I blink, confident I'm hallucinating the khaki-clad figure in my doorjamb. But when my eyelids flutter open, my focus anxiously buzzes around a dreamlike character bowing in the open space, not knowing here to settle.

Liam peeks bashfully back at me, his hands stuffed inside a pair of pants that should be concerning in their high-waisted nature, but somehow with his tapered waist, he makes them look aggressively alluring. A yellow vest pulls tightly across his broad chest, buttoned over a white-collared, gold-striped shirt, sleeves rolled above his elbows, his corded forearms out to be adored and celebrated.

I don't know what to do. What to say. I could grab him by the pink tie peeking beneath the yellow vest and kiss the crap out of him. I want to desperately, but my hands are hanging uselessly at my sides, my palms a sweaty mess. And I probably should greet him at some point instead of mindlessly staring at him, but all I can get my mouth to do is hang open. My throat goes dry, and I lean a little heavier on my cane for support, my legs threatening to become the absolute mush my heart already turned into.

"What—" The words die on my tongue, meeting the amused sparkle in his eyes. He's too proud of the effect he's having on me, but I can't do anything to rectify that right now because all that's spiraling in my head is *he's dressed like Gene Kelly for you. Gene. Gene freakin' Kelly.*

"You look gorgeous." He exhales.

"You're—you're Gene Kelly," I sputter.

Maria squeals behind us.

He shakes his head, pointing to his chest. "No, Evie. Liam. Liam Kelly." His lips lift on one side, and I roll my eyes in return, balance restored.

"Your confidence that I wouldn't want to fight with you may have been misplaced."

He offers out his hand. "I had to do something to knock you out of your stupor. Wouldn't do to have you insufferably love stricken already."

"So confident." I click my tongue and wave at Maria swooning in the living room before shutting the door behind me.

"Determined." He winks.

Liam offers his arm as I hold the railing and carefully go one step at a time. This building is too old for an elevator, and we live on the seventh floor, which is terrible for my pelvis but also cheap. A lot of the time, it's impossible to have all the boxes checked, so I just have to cope with what I have and make do.

"I'm sorry if I'm a bit slower on the street. I just need a little extra help tonight."

His dimple pricks his cheek. "You don't need to apologize for that."

My eyes wander over his broad figure clad in a yellow vest. A silly grin spreads wide across my face, threatening to rupture my cheeks.

Insufferably love stricken may not be too far off if this is the kind of thing he's going to pull.

"Where did you even find a costume like that?" I ask as Liam leads me along the cobblestoned street. He won't let me in on our ultimate destination, and relinquishing control is taking all the self-restraint I have. What if it's too far? What if we end up in a dead spot as far as Métro stops are concerned and a flare happens? What if we're going to Montmartre and I can't handle the hills?

"I've had it for a while." His phone buzzes, and he glances at it, nudging me down a narrow street. I don't trust his navigation system, but I bite my tongue. "I just had my mom overnight it."

"Wait, how long is a while?"

The tips of Liam's ears redden, and he peeks at me. "Homecoming. Senior year of high school. Fit a bit looser then." He chuckles, stretching and pulling the vest's seams to their limits.

I stop in front of a red brick building featured prominently against the otherwise beige landscape of the Latin Quarter, almost tumbling over my cane. The clamor of laughter and dinner chatter melds with the chaos of passing traffic. I inhale. The sweet smell of something slathered in a honey butter sauce hits my nostrils. "I'm sorry, why did you have this"—I gesture to his attire—"in high school?"

"I—uhm—there was a plan, but the incident with Charlie may have ruined it."

"Oh my god, no—" I can take one I-was-a-horrible-monster moment, but two? That's not fair, universe! I rub my palm over my chest, drawing the attention of one of the sidewalk patrons. The woman's eyes scan Liam's attire with a smirk. No. Bad. My Gene Kelly. Even if I don't deserve him. "What—what was the plan?" I ask in an increasingly dry voice.

He scratches at his scruff, wincing. "I may have been changing into this to ask you to the dance when you stormed over and said you pitied the miserable person I was going to take—"

"But the rumor—"

"Yeah, no, I fucked that up." He blushes. "After I punched Charlie, my parents grounded me, so I couldn't ask you as quickly as I wanted, and I panicked and, uhm, told some of the guys on the team who mentioned they were going to ask you that you were off-limits." He winces. "I'm not proud I did that. And I'm sorry. I know that was a mess with your mom."

And that's not his fault.

The moment of clarity streaks in like an asteroid, laying waste to all it collides with. My mom's reaction to situations Liam may or may not have had a hand in creating isn't his fault.

And it's not mine either.

It's hers. She could choose to react differently, positively, and she doesn't. I shouldn't be bending to create favorable conditions for her and enabling her shitty reactions.

"Don't be." I shake my head and reach up to Liam's cheek, sweeping my thumb across it. "I'm sorry I blamed you for things that weren't your fault, and I'm sorry I jumped to the wrong conclusions, and now you're carrying guilt that's not yours to own. You are an impossibly sweet and thoughtful man, and I appreciate you. Understood?"

"That's the second time you've called me impossibly sweet. You going soft?" He raises a brow, pinning his stare on me as he presses a kiss into my palm.

"Sir, I'm the furthest thing from soft with you like this." I laugh. A harsh, cleared throat startles us both. I peek back, catching a very annoyed diner staring at us, and heat rises to my cheeks. "Désolée," I murmur, shifting down the block.

"We should probably start walking again if we want to get to our first spot on time, anyway," Liam says, pulling my hand.

"Oh yeah—" I swallow, letting Liam lead again, trying not to show my disappointment that my slower-than-usual stride is already messing with his plans.

As our walk progresses, twisting and turning through familiar alleys and boulevards, my heart quickens with every step.

I'd say there's no way he knows about my favorite spot, but he's read my blog—so it's entirely possible.

Running down the stairs to the Seine near Pont de l'Archevêche confirms my suspicions.

Gene Kelly. By the Seine. At the spot where Leslie and Gene danced in *An American in Paris,* and Audrey Hepburn and Cary Grant talked about it in *Charade.*

The sun is setting over the bridges in the distance, bursting through the clouds in one final bow as the city blinks alive in all its resplendent glory. *The golden hour.* The lights of the city glitter against the Seine, bathed in the beauty of the Parisian sky at sunset. It's as if Monet himself kissed the heavens with a quick brush stroke. Coral, saffron, lilac, and plum, swept across a cerulean canvas, reflect in a rushed gradient in the river below.

Liam pauses briefly, pulling out his phone as the words "my spot" escape my lips. He smirks to himself, and then Gene Kelly singing "I've Got a Crush on You" plays through the speaker.

It's my favorite underrated Gene Kelly song, an outtake from *An American in Paris* that Nana used to play while we were baking. I'd sit and sigh along to the lyrics, like one of the blonde triplets from *Beauty and the Beast*, daydreaming about someone singing it to me.

A strong hand wraps around my waist, and I blink back to reality. Liam grabs my free hand, and my arm with the cane falls to his back. He dips his head to my ear, singing along with the lyrics until the instrumental portion kicks in, and he slowly sways me cheek to cheek.

Tourists and Frenchmen sidestep us as I allow myself to melt into Liam, savoring the moment. He beams down at me, basking in my own glow.

"Did you know this was my favorite song?" I ask, head resting on his shoulder.

"I had my suspicions."

"How?"

"Your face used to get all dreamy when Nana played it. It was one of my favorites, too, because you'd relax when it was on."

He sings along to the refrain, his voice soft and sweet—fully living up to his promise to having me falling head over heels by the end of the night, doomed to be insufferably love stricken.

Another song starts next, and Liam continues swaying me along the Seine, lit golden in the setting sun. My own Gene Kelly, here, dancing with me.

"Thank you for this." I sigh into his shoulder.

"Anytime, Peaches." He half steps on my foot and winces. "I'm sorry I'm not the light-footed Kelly you dreamt of."

"You are, though. You were always everything."

Liam's hand pulls me in tighter. "Happy birthday, Evie."

I don't know how long Liam and I stay swaying along the Seine, my head resting on his chest. Maybe it's five more minutes, or maybe it's an eternity, and we're now ghosts of a fleeting, perfect moment. However long we linger there, Liam finally tugs my hand and brings me along back alleys and side roads toward the Latin Quarter and *another surprise*.

"It's—" I pick up my gaze, and it lands on the storefront I stopped at along Luxembourg Gardens on the day everything changed. "A storefront?" I rub my forehead in a phantom memory.

"I found a few for my master's project, but I thought this was worth showing you. The traffic here is a good mix of tourist and Parisian, and it's not that far of a walk for you either, just one Métro stop."

"You mapped out my commute? How is that helpful for your project?"

"It's not." He breathes out. "But I was looking over your numbers, and I got so excited about your idea to pair everything with cheese and rosé that I wanted to show you it was something you could do."

"I'm sorry. What's this about my cheese and rosé?"

"Pairing it with the desserts?"

I blush. "I wrote that?"

Sometimes I zone out when I look at all those facts and figures, but I feel like I should remember writing something like that.

"Yeah, in a margin."

I tilt my head back and laugh. "That was definitely just a grocery list reminder."

"Oh." He rubs the back of his neck. "I thought it was a good idea, though. People would go to a place like that."

Cheese and rosé are always a good idea.

"It is, actually."

I stare back at the storefront. Dreams I told myself a month ago I should keep buried bubble up to the surface at a dangerous not-easy-to stamp-down level. It's hard to tell them to stay quiet after a day like today, after this week, really.

Maybe some dreams really do come true.

Liam rubs my shoulder, staring at me in the window's reflection. "I always loved that you were a dreamer, Peaches. No matter how much crap I gave you for it, I want you to keep dreaming, about the silly things, about dancing with Gene Kelly, about real-life things, about the shop. You deserve to fall asleep with thoughts like that dancing up here." He presses a kiss on the top of my head.

"You sound like me now." I laugh and turn to meet him.

His thumb brushes a tear that broke rank off my cheek. "I know, and seventeen-year-old me would be upset, but if he knew I got to do this now—" Liam gently cups my face, bending and laying a whisper of a kiss on my lips. "He'd get it." He winks.

I smile against his lips. "I'll look over everything again. Thank you." With his hands still bracing my face, I close my eyes, curling my fingers around his wrists, and revel in the warmth radiating off him. "I haven't had the heart to move forward with anything for a while. I think I was orried another disappointment might break me. But with you I feel like I could take on anything, and if it didn't work out, that'd be okay. Like my heart will be happy regardless."

"I like making your heart happy," he says, brushing his lips lightly against mine before pulling away and lacing his fingers through my hands. "Which is why we're going to get donuts now."

"Gene Kelly and donuts? I hope you know what you're doing because I'm about to become pretty freaking insufferable."

"It's a burden I'll have to bear." He shakes his head and alters our path toward the café.

We cross the street, nearing American Press and the chairs where Liam took care of me. My mind flashes to his disappointed demeanor I swore I was imagining, and it tugs at my heartstrings. I wish I had been kinder that day.

The guilt of who I've been weighs heavy on my chest, and again I tell myself I can't change it, but I can make a better tomorrow.

"Wait here," I whisper, abandoning Liam in roughly the same spot he stood when I ran into him that first day.

"Where are you going?"

"Just—hold on." I clack a little further away on the cobblestone around the corner.

"Evie, if this is your way of ditching me—"

"I am no longer aware of your existence on this sidewalk and therefore will not be acknowledging any further completely unfounded accusations." I fight down the smile curling on my lips.

Turning around the corner toward Liam, I watch his face twist deeper with confusion. I proceed slower than the day I ran into him here, as the butterflies flutter relentlessly in my abdomen, increasing their frenzy as I near him.

I pause. My eyes turn up to his face and feign surprise. "Why, Liam Kelly, is that you? Here? In Paris?" I place my heart on my palm, rubbing it. "Oh dear, if you could give me a second, I suffer from these acute heart palpitations whenever I'm near you. It's this annoying side effect of my wild lifelong crush on you."

Liam snorts, his cheeks reddening from the attention. He steps toward me, wrapping an arm around my back and pressing me against him. "I'm sorry, I didn't know about the crush, or I would have put you out of your misery years ago. But hopefully, we can make up for lost time now."

"Well, that seems a bit quick and forward, but I accept—"

Liam tilts his head, and his nose brushes against my cheek. I let out an exalting breath before his lips capture mine in a slow, gentle conversation.

One filled with forgiveness for the past and joy for the future. Eventually, Liam pulls away, placing another kiss on my forehead and turning.

"I believe I promised you donuts." He offers his hand, walking me back to the storefront and gently guiding me away from a lamppost I once lost a fight with. "Careful, that could cause some serious damage."

"Really rude of them not to move out of the way, to be honest. The audacity some lampposts have."

"Planning on writing a strongly worded letter to the Council of Lampposts on the matter."

"Heard their meetings can be illuminating; maybe we should go."

Liam pauses, opening the door with a grimace. "Oh, you know, I just realized I had this load of laundry I need to change out." He backs up on his heels, and I grab his vest, pulling him inside.

"Ha. Ha. But I'm not buying it. I know you like me, bad jokes and all."

"Or in spite of," he cheeks. I glare to surrendering hands. "Kidding. Kidding."

I order a pink frosted donut and two cups of decaf coffee, leading Liam to the table where just a month ago I thought an unnecessary epilogue was being written by Caleb and Eli.

And there, under the light of a very hard, immovable lamppost and the last winks of twilight, Liam and I start our new chapter.

"To the new beginning of an old story," I toast, splitting a pink-frosted donut between us for the second time in our lives.

And hopefully the last.

Because as great as a metaphor this is, Evie doesn't share food.

Liam beams, pulling his phone out and angles it at me like he's taking a picture. I smile over my shoulder before sending a quizzical gaze at the reverie held in his eyes. He nods to the light cascading on us. "Fairy princess," is all he says before he brushes his fingertips under my chin and pulls me in for a sweet, toe-curling kiss.

I get lost in the moment, in the magic swirling around us. In the warmth and sparkles that radiate and tingle my spine with every pass of his lips.

Until a loud bang rattles my heart in my chest and forces our lips apart ith a jump. I glance down at the ground where my cane fell from where I propped it up.

I pick it up with a sigh. Even when it's not stabbing me, my endo finds a way to ruin the moment.

17

Sweet Surrender

TWO DAYS AFTER THE best birthday ever, I wake up to persistent drumming on my door. Oh hell, what time is it? I pad around for my phone nestled somewhere in the comforter, squinting with one eye at the blaring bright white light on the screen. Eleven a.m.

The pounding persists. Maria must be out. A headache shoots through the back of my skull, and a heavy, oppressive fatigue settles into my limbs. Begrudgingly, I slink out of my bed, clad in my pizza shorts and Liam's college shirt he insisted I keep because I guess he finally did win. My okay window didn't last as long as I hoped, which is unfortunate because I promised to take Eli on a tour today. Liam wanted to come, too, but I forced him to work. He's got bags under his eyes again because he's splitting his time with me and then working late into the night on his master's project and whatever other work he has to do.

I haven't seen much of Eli between his budding relationship with Fionn and my own little something, so I was looking forward to today until today became today, and now I have regrets.

I open the door, Eli's curls greeting me on the other side. "Evelina O'Shea, is that Liam's shirt?" he asks, a cheeky grin cutting across his face as he enters my apartment.

I blush, mumbling incoherent nothings into my hand and smothering a yawn. We haven't really talked about what's going on between Liam and me. Eli has been skillfully absent from the apartment the last week, but I'm sure, as Liam's roommate, he's privy to most of it.

"I had another week on the bet, but I guess Maria really is the love whisperer." He shakes his head.

I open the fridge and pour myself a glass of water to swallow my plethora of morning pills. "I wouldn't let her call you in on the bet. She manipulated the situation in her favor," I say with a gulp. "There are sandwiches and desserts in the fridge. If you want to throw them into the picnic basket I left on the counter, I'm going to change. For whatever reason, ratty pizza shorts aren't *en vogue* this season."

"They'll have their day."

"Maybe someday." I do my best Briar Rose impression while walking into my bedroom. A sudden intense stab punctuates where my ovary hangs on my left side, and I crunch.

Uh oh.

It passes quickly, though, and I shrug it off. I can handle a few pricks and prods through the day fine, but it'll probably be better not to venture too far out like I envisioned. "I wanted to take you to a park on the edge of town, but I'm not feeling great. Would you hate me if we did something closer?"

Eli scoffs. "We can picnic on the balcony if you want or wherever your heating pad reaches. I just want some Evie time. I've missed my little shit."

I glance lovingly at my heating pad, which hasn't receded into my bedroom's hellmouth. Tempting. But I haven't been able to show Eli much of Paris, and I don't want to let him down. No, I can push a little. It'll be fine.

"How do you feel about having a picnic at Palais-Royal?" I ask. "I haven't gotten there yet, and the cherry blossoms are at their peak, and I really need that picture for my blog."

The fridge door creaks open. "Oh. Pie. As long as this bad boy's coming. I really don't care."

"An impievised tour it is," I joke, tossing my tunic on.

"Huh?"

"Bad joke." I sigh. "Liam would have loved it, though."

"I hate to break it to you, but it's not the bad jokes he loves," Eli hollers from the kitchen.

"By the way, we need to discuss how you're the worst and keep everything from me—" I stick my head out of the doorframe. "Like the identity of the postcard sender."

Eli's eyes widen a fraction as his cheeks redden. He grabs a spoon drying by the sink and shovels a heaping bite of pie into his mouth, mumbling what vaguely sounds like "I can't . . . pie."

I roll my eyes, stepping into my flats and ignoring another quick stab that steals the air out of my lungs.

He takes another heaping spoonful.

"We were supposed to share that after lunch, you know." I wrap my scarf around my neck, shooting heavy daggers his way.

Hell. Another stab punctures my left ovary. My heartbeat falters, and I fight to pull a breath from my tightened airways. Sometimes before I leave the apartment, the anxiety that a flare might be imminent heightens. I guess today is just one of those days. It's okay. I'll be fine. Everything is fine.

"Sorry." He blushes, scraping the pie plate clean.

"Come on, loser." I sigh, opening the door and gesturing for him to walk through it. "We're going to look at cherry blossoms."

"This bridge used to sparkle." I lament the loss of the metallic locks to Eli on Pont des Arts, breathing in the fresh, crisp April air. "This is the original lock bridge, but the weight of all the padlocks was a danger to its structural integrity, so a few years ago, they cut them down and redid the sidewalls."

"They're beautiful," Eli mutters, face glued to his phone as we clop over the wooden boards of the bridge.

"How's it going with Fionn?" I tease, nodding to his phone. "Must be good if you're already ignoring me this bad."

"Meh." He shrugs, tossing the picnic basket over his shoulder. "He knows I'm leaving soon; I'm not looking for anything serious. So we're just having fun."

I rub a palm over my chest. Liam and I have skillfully avoided the looming deadline situation. My brother's wedding has bought us some more time, but eventually, that conversation will come, and I'm not sure I have an answer.

Since Liam told me he's in love with me, my insides have felt more like the Pont des Arts of yore sparkling in the sunlight. Cutting the shimmers out at the root to lighten the burden holds little appeal, even if it's inevitable.

"But Fionn's perfect for you," I whine. "Give it a go, shoot your shot. You never know. No holding back."

"Evie, do you really want to have this conversation right now?"

"Yes?"

"Okay, then have you two talked about what you're going to do?"

"No." I shrug, tempted to hip-check Eli for seeing right through me. "But there are other factors to consider."

"Mm-hmm." He smirks knowingly. "I love you, but honestly, you're the last person who should be telling me not to hold back. You haven't exactly been pursuing any of your dreams lately. And trust me. I get it. You have a lot going on. I'm just saying maybe you should get why I'm hesitant to go forward with this."

"You don't want to get hurt," I mumble. "Or hurt him."

"There you go."

"I still think it'd be worth it—what if it doesn't end poorly? What if it's the best thing that has ever happened to you?"

"Maybe you should be asking yourself the same thing. Seriously, woman? Pole." He nods my way.

I pull my eyes off the ornate facade of the Louvre and step aside, narrowly avoiding the brutal beam. They really need to do something about those damn things.

"It's just not that simple for me."

"What's not?"

An extra sharp pain stabs me in the side. I miss a step but hide that these are getting increasingly worse. Hopefully, sitting at the park will handle it. I'm sure I just need to rest, that's all.

"Dating with all of this." I gesture to my pelvic region. "It complicates a lot of things I feel like everyone talks about as cornerstones in relationships." I pull at my fingertips, remembering some asshat on a reality show who told the camera and the audience that a sexual appetite in his partner was one of his top priorities. That was probably a shitty thing to say, but that doesn't mean the earworm didn't stick.

His green eyes shine sympathetically, and it's far more comforting than I imagined it would be. "Like what?"

I blink at him. Is he really not getting this? "Sex hurts. A lot. No guy would want to have to deal with that."

"Liam would."

"Liam is the kind of guy who would stay out of obligation, which worries me."

Eli shakes his head. "I'm not going to pretend like I understand where your head is at or what you're going through, so I'll drop it, but promise me you won't let your endo take something it has no business taking." The sidewalk grows thick with tourists, kiosks, parked trucks, and other vehicles. Walking in tandem isn't an option, so I cut ahead, pausing in front of one of my favorite crêperies. Hazelnut, cocoa, and flour swirl around me. I inhale. *Come on, Nutella, give me strength.* The pain increases up the side of my leg, and my mask drops.

"I'm not saying no to relationships entirely. I'm just saying, past few weeks aside, I'm going to need time and to take everything at a glacial pace, so I'm certain he knows what reality with me looks like." I force another step. I'm okay. It's just pain. I can do this.

"A rocking good time with a kick-ass woman?" Eli snorts behind me.

A lightning-like streak shoots through the crook of my thigh, over the top of my vaginal area, and every step that follows is pure torture. I halt abruptly as my body plays the *let's crank this up to eleven* game, and Eli hits my back.

"Shit, you okay?"

A tear streaks down my cheek, my heartbeat escalates, and breath escapes my lungs. My brain scrambles with the blinding pain, and I get trapped in my mind, in my body, as the commotion of the city curls around me. I don't want to make a scene. I don't want to be a diva, but we're not close to a Métro station. A good half hour from the apartment, and I can't think. Can't speak. "Pain," I manage. "So much."

"Fuck—" He runs a hand through his hair. "Do we need to get you to the hospital?"

I shake my head. "Won't do anything. Home. I need home."

"Our apartment isn't too far—" He grabs the crook of my elbow and leads me along.

What should have been a ten-minute walk to Eli's apartment takes twenty. In that time, I manage a good forty versions of "I'm so sorry I sucked and ruined our day," to which Eli responds with his own variations of "It's fine, shut up," and "No seriously, stop apologizing. It's wicked annoying, and I don't care about the damn picnic."

Eli calls Liam at some point, who's home working on his thesis project. He meets us outside, and my racing heart halts. I've seen many versions of Liam in the past few weeks, Henley-clad, tailored suits, collared shirts, Gene Kelly, and shirtless gray sweatpants, but this—this is a blast from the past. Standing in front of me in his gray sweats, an old worn-out Patriots crewneck sweatshirt, and a backward baseball cap, is the man I had known for so many years, waiting to carry me into his apartment.

You love him cuts through every voice and cry of agony once more. It's equally terrifying and thrilling to feel this way because I don't know what's going to come next, and in the past, the unknown has been a terrible, desolate wasteland of broken dreams and crushed tomorrows. But today, even with the pain, I'm seeing life in technicolor, so I'll take the chance and see where this goes.

Liam and Eli's apartment building is thankfully fancy enough to house a tiny two-person elevator. It's a feature I haven't taken advantage of yet, but I am grateful to do so now. Eli follows us up, taking the stairs. I rest my head on Liam's shoulder and wrap my arms around him while we gradually rise from the ground. He rubs slow circles on my back. My legs weaken with the pain, but he stays firm and steady. He stays my rock.

"I'm so sorry I'm interrupting your work time," I whisper.

He lays a soft kiss on the top of my head as the elevator doors slide open. "Don't worry about it."

A mug of steaming hot tea already sits on the coffee table, waiting for me as Liam settles me onto the couch before walking to the kitchen and grabbing something from the microwave.

"You have your painkillers?" he asks, bringing over a lavender-scented pouch.

"I always have a few in my purse."

Eli, who's pacing, not used to my flares, grabs my purse, hollering, "I'll get them."

Liam hands me a pouch with a peach and lemon printed fabric cover-i g the outside. Lavender swirls around us in a force reserved for a heat pack's first use as if the pattern wasn't enough to suggest he purchased this specifically for me. "You got me a heat pack?"

Red tinges Liam's cheeks with gorgeous color. "I saw someone selling them at the market this morning and thought it'd be good to have here. Didn't expect to use it so soon." He stuffs a hand in his pocket and shrugs.

"Liam—I—" My gaze oscillates between the heat pack and him, amazed at how thoughtful he is. My toes curl with the threat of an "I love you." Sure, we've told each other we're in love, but we haven't just casually dropped an "I love you." And I don't know if that's a good idea with all the things I need to straighten in my head. Besides, there are a bunch of muscles curling inside, too, and I can't handle any of this properly.

"You can pretend I got it for an old shoulder injury if you need to." His lips tip up into a small smile, and he rotates his shoulder. "I just need to save some things on the computer, and then I'll come back and keep you company. You need anything else?"

I shake my head. "Please keep working." I place the heating pack where the significant pain is coming from, and it calms it a bit. "I didn't mean to bother you when you have things to do. I'm fine, honest."

"You aren't bothering me, Peaches," he hollers from the table. "Believe me, I'd rather spend time with you than this."

"A-ha!" Eli triumphantly plucks a pill bottle from my purse and hands it to me. Smiling, he dips close to my ear. "You hear that. You aren't a bother. He'd rather spend time with you."

I subtly swat at him. "I've been in this house for five minutes, and he's already rearranging his day, making me tea, and purchasing something for my ailment. He wouldn't have to do that with anyone else. How is that fair to him?"

"But he hasn't been in love with anyone else since he was five," Eli whispers back.

"What if I'm not interested in starting something uber serious when you're both going back to New England in a few days. You ever think of that?"

"Oh, come on, Evie. You're not starting anything. You're just ending the longest game of foreplay I've ever seen." He smirks, satisfied that I'm so taken aback that I have nothing to say for once, and then fakes a yawn. "That walk tuckered me out. I'm going to go nap if you think you got everything covered here." He glances at Liam. "She could use a nap too."

Liam furrows his brow at me crunched on the couch. "Maybe we should move you into the bedroom, Peaches."

I glare at Eli but nod.

Liam settles me into bed, pulling the sheets over my shoulder as the cold settles in. "You want company?" he whispers.

"No, I want you to get your work done so you aren't up late tonight." I faintly smile, wincing through another twist.

"What if I nap with you now?"

I chew on my bottom lip, my guilty conscience at war with the part of me that loves snuggling. "I guess I can't argue with that logic."

He climbs into bed and wraps an arm around me, pulling me tighter to him. His grounding touch anchors me, keeping me safe from the rocky waters threatening to capsize me.

Closing my eyes, I breathe through the pain. "I swear I'm fun sometimes and do other things than just lay in various beds and couches."

Recently? Not so much, but I remember doing other things once.

"I'd be okay if this was all we ever did." He presses a kiss on my forehead. "I just wish you weren't hurting when we did it." His fingers stroke my back, and I breathe through another stretch of intense pokes and prods. *All we ever did* has the air of permanency that a relationship with an impending deadline shouldn't, and it emboldens me to ask the question I've tried to ignore.

"Liam, what happens when I have to come back here without you after Caleb's wedding?"

The soft strokes on my back pause. "I honestly don't know, but if you want this to work, we'll figure it out. Trust me with that, okay?"

"Okay." I stretch out as another spasm grips my left ovary.

"Do you want me to distract you, or do you want quiet?" he whispers.

"Distraction, please."

"Let's see. Did I ever tell you about the day I met Nana?"

"No. But that sounds perfect." My head sinks peacefully against his chest, and I revel in his heart's slow, steady rhythm beneath my cheek.

"You're settled and comfy?"

I focus on the sandalwood curling around me and hope my surroundi g sensations will help me navigate through this flare until the medicine kicks in. "As good as I'm going to be."

Liam gently wraps his hand around mine. "Well, I guess I should ask you first, did you know my great-grandpa built both our houses?"

"No, actually, I didn't."

"That's why the backyards are connected. He built mine first, and then yours for my grandpa when he got married."

"So your dad grew up in my house?" I ask.

"For a short time, yeah. Once my great-grandpa passed away, his dad moved him into the main house and rented out yours until I came along."

"What happened then?"

"He moved into it, said because it was smaller it'd be easier to maintain and gave my parents the main house. He passed maybe a year before you moved in and left both the houses and the creamery to my parents. Now that I'm older, I can appreciate everything he did for us, but at the time, the street was full of older people who didn't like my mom or me much, and I was kind of lonely. The day you moved in, I was home alone. It wasn't supposed to be for long, but something happened that kept my mom out."

"You would have been five," I say quietly.

"I was a very mature five."

"No, you weren't." I snort.

"Anyway," he fake scolds, continuing the story in a low and steady cadence that calms my nerves with every word. "A huge commotion drew me to the window, and I saw the moving truck had just arrived. I crossed my fingers, peeking out. I had asked my mom if she thought whoever was moving into the new house had any kids I could play with, but she didn't know, so I sat by that window for a week waiting—and got way too excited that the time was finally here. I bolted out the front door, no socks or shoes, even though it was the middle of winter, and froze behind one of our shrubs, watching this tiny strawberry-haired fairy looking up at falling snowflakes like she had never seen them before."

"I hadn't." My breath catches in my throat. I remember that day, too. I remember watching my first snowflake drifting silently to the ground. Remember being amazed at the white blankets of soft rolling hills shining in the distance. But I don't remember Liam, not then. He came into the picture an hour later, sipping hot cocoa in the corner of our furniture-less living room, pillows serving as cushions on the floor. Nana put in *Take Me Out to the Ballgame* to keep Caleb and me entertained. I remember feeling like Liam's eyes were sliding toward me, but every time I peeked over, his attention was trained on the TV, enraptured by Gene's acrobatic dance moves and Jules Munshin's comedic relief.

"I must have stood there and stared for a good five minutes, watching snowflakes collect and glitter in your hair, not thinking about anything else, when a loud southern voice asked me where my shoes and coat were and if I wanted to catch 'p-neumonia.'

"Nana had her hands on her hips, staring at me. She followed my eyes, watching you skip into the house, and smiled. She told me that you were sweet as a peach, too, and if I went and got warmer clothes on, I could come over and she'd introduce us. I didn't say anything back. I don't think I talked much then, to be honest; I don't really remember talking before you. So I just nodded and walked back up the stairs with stinging feet while Nana watched me, but the door had locked behind me, and I didn't know what to do. I jiggled the handle again, trying not to cry. But my feet were burning, and I was worried I couldn't come over if I didn't get a jacket. She asked me if I was home alone, and I nodded.

"'Well, alright then,' she said, 'Your feet aren't going to get any warmer waiting out here. Let's find you some hot chocolate and a spot by the fire. Come on, hurry in.' I must have flown down those stairs to her." He laughs. "She asked if I had a name, and I told her it was Liam. She asked if I was left home alone a lot, and I shrugged with a *sometimes*. And then she asked if I had a nana around, and I shook my head. I had never met any of my grandmothers. They passed when I was still a baby, and my mom's dad was somewhere in Florida, but I'd always wanted something like the grandmas I'd seen on TV. 'Well, you got one now.' She said it so matter-of-factly, but it changed my world."

"She was the best." I sigh, the painkillers relaxing me a smidge. "Going home in a few days wouldn't be so bad if she were still there." I nuzzle further into Liam's shoulder, warmth from hearing Nana's story flooding me, mixing with a swell of emotions. "She always had a way of making everything better. But that house feels impossible without her there."

"She did." He strokes the back of my neck. "You know you can stay with me in my condo if you want."

"That's a very tempting offer. I don't think I've asked you where you live now."

"I moved up north to New Hampshire, actually. In Portsmouth. Have you ever been there?"

"No. But it sounds far, so I like it already."

"About an hour drive."

"How'd you end up there?"

"I'm getting my master's through a graduate program at the state university in Durham, so I got an apartment a few towns over for my first year there when my classes were in person, but I couldn't bring myself to move when I switched to online classes."

Liam's voice dips when he mentions his master's like it's not something he particularly cares for.

"Do you like what you're getting your master's in?"

His shoulders rise in a shrug. "It doesn't really matter. My dad's done more for me than I could ever ask. I owe him. He didn't want to work at the creamery. MIT was starting to talk to him when he dropped out. I thought in college maybe I could make it to the pros and pay them back, and he could retire early, but then I didn't recover right from the ACL injury."

My heart squeezes. Why did I ever think everything was easy for him, and he lived a charmed life? "You don't owe Harry anything for loving you. You know Nana's mantra about love."

He sighs. "It's freely given, or it was never love at all."

"Exactly. I'm so sorry your biological dad was an asshat who . . . asshatted . . ." Oh, my mental faculties are depleting exponentially now. "But that doesn't mean you have to live a life in service of someone else because they chose to love you. That was gifted to you. It wasn't a loan. And I know I've never gotten to know your dad well, but I think he'd want you to do what you want to do with your life. If this business stuff isn't what makes you happy, we're still young, there's still time to figure something else out." I yawn, drifting closer and closer to sleep.

"I'll think about it, Peaches. Get some rest." He kisses the top of my forehead, and I feel the nickname bloom in my chest, knowing he's connecting me to Nana somehow. He always has.

18

Sprinkle Kind of Life

"HOW MANY CUPS OF coffee do you think I can order before the barista thinks I have a problem?"

I lean into Liam's shoulder, dangerously close to using his hard chest as a pillow for a quick vertically inclined power nap in this quaint coffee shop. The curse of the last-minute flight sags heavily on my shoulders. Over the past twenty-four hours, I flew from Paris to London, to Iceland, to Toronto, then finally to Boston, where Liam was a saint and picked me up at five this morning, bringing me the rest of the way up to this seaport town in New Hampshire—Portsmouth. Which so far, is so cute want to pinch its cheeks.

Liam's been back in town for two whole days, most of which I was traveling for, but he stupidly took Caleb out for his bachelor party last night while still being terribly jetlagged because, apparently, he has zero chill when it comes to saying no to the O'Sheas and has heavy lids, harrowingly like mine.

"I don't know, but whatever that number is, I think we should double it," he whispers.

Shivers at his mouth's proximity to my skin shimmer down my spine, right on schedule, and I happily soak them all in. My body suffered through drastic withdrawals the past few days without him.

Inhaling, coffee and cocoa swirl around us. Brick adorns three of the four walls, with a big picture window open to the small street of restaurants and shops.

"We could always pretend that we're buying a bounty of cups for friends or something."

"Wouldn't work. They know I don't have friends." Liam points his chin at the blonde barista sporting space buns behind the counter.

My mother, in her haste to show off that despite my many deficiencies I've somehow managed to keep the attention of a man for longer than two weeks, has planned a party in our honor today, which means there will be no sleep, and a coffee scheme is needed.

"I find that hard to believe. You're so likable—who could ever have a problem with you?" My brows dance in jest. In the car ride when I said I missed him and kissed him senselessly, I realized something I had overlooked in our time at each other's throats. Liam Kelly is terrible at receiving a compliment. He turns red, sputters, deflects, squirms, whatever he can to not acknowledge it.

And because I am tired, and nettling Liam is my favorite pastime, especially when he's tired and grumpy, I'm now showering him with them.

He snorts, shaking his head. "I'll be right back." Liam's hand leaves the small of my back as the barista finishes the order before us and welcomes me with a broad, affectionate smile.

It's natural and kind. A smile I, in desperate need of coffee to resurrect me, cannot return.

"Hey there, what can I get you?" she asks, leaning over the maple countertop.

I blink at her. I've been navigating public interactions in a second language for so long that this reprieve is alarmingly comforting.

"Whatever your biggest cup of coffee is, can you fill that with espresso shots, please?"

"An extra large coffee with an espresso shot? Sure, coming right up."

I shake my head, beckoning her to draw closer. Same language or not, something was lost in translation. "No, I'm sorry, what I meant was, can you take that large cup over there"—I point to the stack of white paper cups behind the counter—"and fill it up with espresso."

"But that cup is twenty ounces. I can't—"

"Hey, Rebecca." Liam's hand presses on my shoulder as he leans over me. He flashes his big grin, and the worry I won't get the amount of coffee needed dissipates. I venture those dimples could get Liam just about anything, and I'm thankful to have them on my side for once. "She just got off the flight/layover combination from hell, I—uhm—overdid it at a bachelor party last night, and we have a family dinner neither of us are looking forward to, so whatever you feel comfortable doing, maybe a triple shot, if you could please do it and make it a double, we will be eternally grateful."

"I'll hook you two up." She nods with a wink.

A man in the New England uniform of choice, a Red Sox shirt and a flannel, cleaning the steamed milk handle further down the bar, picks his head up at the sound of Liam's voice and focuses his attention our way. "Hey, you're back!" he chimes. His eyes meet mine. "Oh, is this—"

"The friend Eli and I were meeting in Paris, yeah," Liam cuts him off with a quick shake of his head, like he's sending Paul some kind of non-verbal message.

I peek skeptically at Liam. *Friend?* How many friends does he dress up like Gene Kelly for?

"Not that she's my friend now—" He swallows.

"Have we discussed what we are, exactly?" I nudge his shoulder with mine, giggling at the flush creeping up his neck.

He exhales, mumbling, "I'm too tired for this shit today. Hey, Paul, this is Evie, the woman that Eli teased me about nonstop and whom I talked about periodically." He crosses his arms, staring at me. "Does that satisfy you, Peaches?"

"Yes, actually." I stick my tongue out at him, and his fake scowl surrenders to the tips of a smile.

"Ah, you mean the one you quit drinking beer and obsessively gave up carbs for. Well, it's nice to finally meet the famous Evie." Paul winks, wiping his hand on his towel before extending it to me for a shake. God bless that man for that ammunition. Liam groans next to me, probably having a similar thought. "Did you see we sold another lighthouse print while you were gone?"

My spine straightens with attention. "What print?"

Liam twists his panicked expression into one of indifference, and okay, now I really need to know what he's hiding. "It's nothing you'd be interested in," he says, studying his fingernails.

"Yeah, I'm not buying that performance." I snort.

"Go show her, dude. You're terrible." Paul hooks his thumb down a long brick wall lined with hanging Edison light bulbs. "I'll make sure Rebecca gets you enough coffee for the day."

Begrudgingly, Liam takes me by the hand, pulling me down past a row of tables to a wall of photos printed on canvas. Various landscapes grace the wall, gardens in bloom, a bridge stretched wide over a body of water, and brick buildings aglow in the rising sun.

"You took these?" I reach a hand out, running my fingers over a garden shot, the ocean in the back, sailboats floating by in the afternoon sun.

"Just a hobby I have. The one I took of a lighthouse at sunset keeps selling," he says bashfully, gesturing to an open space on the wall before crossing his arms and closing himself off. "I'll have to ask Paul if he wants another copy of that or try something from Paris."

"You took some in Paris? When?"

"I got up a few mornings and then did the bridges at sunset, too, like someone recommended." Leaning over, he nudges my shoulder with his.

"You do have an odd fascination with my bridge blog entry." I shake my head, eyes still scanning the gallery of pictures on the wall. In the chaos of the past month, if Liam was dragging himself up early for a hobby, then this is what he should be doing. I would only do that for the perfect laminated pastry—I would only do that for my passion.

He snakes an arm around my waist and tugs me tighter against him.

"Why do you keep hiding these amazing parts of yourself?" I whisper, resting my head on his shoulder. "See this—this is amazing." I point to a picture of a chain-link fence with locks hung along it glittering in the sun. A blue expanse of water runs behind it with a two-tower seafoam bridge looming in the distance. "This shouldn't be just a hobby."

Liam's fingers twitch on my side. "Our coffees should be ready," he deflects, cheeks red.

"You're lucky I didn't know compliments got you so flustered, or I would have started giving them long ago."

"You want to go for a walk and see that bridge? I think getting some of that sea breeze air would be good." He ignores me, pivoting toward the counter.

"Yes, and I can stare at your handsome face while it's happening." I pause, studying his photos one last time before following him back to the counter. A few steps behind him, I seize the opportunity to appreciate how Liam's dark-washed jeans highlight specific assets of his. "Or maybe I'll just keep two steps behind you."

"Why would you—thanks, Rebecca." He takes our cups and then twists, peering over his shoulder. His muscular shoulder blades bunch in his T-shirt as he peeks at me, absolutely busted. "I regret making you like me." He shakes his head, handing me my cup as I do a weird little dance because I'm running on the fumes of a twenty-hour flight and I don't know what to do with myself. "Go back to hating me. This is unsettling when I haven't slept."

"Oh no, I'm enjoying being the sunshine to your grump for once." I shimmy my shoulders. "Who knew our point of role reversal was lack of sleep?"

Liam glares at me over the lid of his cup. "I suddenly understand your annoyance with me. Seriously, what's with the dance?"

"If I stop moving, I'm going to die," I whisper in desperation.

"Let's get you walking then. See you, Paul. Thanks again, Rebecca."

"You two have fun," Paul says, head focused down on a few scratchers, his fingers deftly scraping off the coating with a quarter.

"If you have a heart attack from all that caffeine, it's your fault," Rebecca adds, her back to us. "I've washed my hands clean of the situation."

I inhale my life source, smiling and blinking in the light as we exit the café. Edison lightbulbs hang across the narrow alley between the Bean Pot and an adjacent brick building. A row of flowers dusts the edge of the sidewall with lavender and magenta hues, bordering a smattering of café chairs and tables.

The entire vibe is perfection.

Black Victorian streetlamps are evenly spaced on the main street among the red and gray brick sidewalk. A green awning hangs overhead, "coffee, paninis, pastries" in gold leaf lettering across it. We keep walking as my head whirls with so many new things to absorb. If Paris is the color of a café au lait, Portsmouth is a vintage pinot noir. Brick buildings rise and fall at random heights, so unlike the uniform row of buildings in Paris, and yet, I have the overwhelming feeling that they all belong. Signs noting the various restaurants, boutiques, art galleries, and cafés swing in the sea breeze, and I breathe in the fresh salt air, letting it cleanse my lungs.

A warm smile beams on my face. I'm deliriously tired, but I also have a sense of calm that hasn't found me in some time radiating from my chest, and I have a sneaking suspicion it has to do with the man next to me.

We come to an intersection, and my lingering gaze freezes on a church across the street. The church's base is brick, like everything else in this town seems to be. A white steeple points to the heavens, towering above the downtown area. Its ornate features and clock tower steal my breath away.

Liam follows my eyes. "That's North Church. It's my favorite too."

"It's beautiful. Do you know when it was built?" I ask, itching to uncover the past lives of the buildings around me.

"Some time in the 1800s. Most of the stuff around here was. The town itself was settled in the early 1600s. That's why there are so many older houses, but I think there were some fires or something, so a lot of the buildings here were built later."

"It's gorgeous." My eyes roam over the multiple narrow streets branching off the main stretch, honestly more like twigging considering their minimal girth. Liam sips his coffee, watching me intensely, and when I'm done studying the area in my spot, he takes me across the street until we turn left down another narrow road with the same aesthetic. More brick, more black lamps, more trees, and I'm absolutely living and vibing all of it.

A green expanse of land sits at the end of the street, abutting the wide mouth of a river Liam told me was called the Piscataqua as we drove along it earlier. The river connects Great Bay to the Atlantic Ocean, making Portsmouth an active seaport.

We walk through a black iron gate toward the patch of blue water along the back of the park.

The fence with the gold locks from Liam's photographs waits at the end. My heart dances along with the locks winking in the morning sun. I love love locks. The tradition of it all. To me, the permanence is in the moment, not the love. Because a lot of the time we measure success in forever, but with my disease, I've had to learn to have success in fleeting moments, or else what was the point of anything? Locks, to me, are a symbol that even if the relationship ends poorly—and it definitely ended poorly for Lainey and Brian if the massive c-word scrawled across their lock is any indication—two people were happy enough in the moment to put a lock on a gate, and in real life, sometimes, isn't that enough?

In the distance, a gorgeous iron, lattice-worked bridge looms over the river, connecting two land masses together.

"That's Maine across the way." Liam points over my shoulder before letting his hand fall to my hip and pulling me against him.

The breeze blows wisps of my hair free, but I don't bother smoothing them down. Something about the way the light dances off the water in a glittering haze calms my mind. Even though I'm balancing precariously between the realms of tired and dead inside, another part of me oddly feels like I have my toes in the sand, currently relaxing in paradise.

Liam rubs the small of my back.

Maybe this is paradise.

Maybe this is my fleeting perfect moment.

"Thank you for letting me stay with you. I don't know how I would have done this if I saw my family at security." I sigh, sipping my coffee. "We're definitely going to need a Dunks later too."

"Don't worry. I plan on having at least twelve coffees today." He smiles. "How are you feeling about later?"

"Better," I hum, leaning back into his hand. "I'm fairly certain it's still going to suck, but at least I have you on my side for once."

"You want me to distract you?" His fingers brush the hair off the nape of my neck before I feel his warm mouth press against the exposed skin there.

"At the party? How would you do that?"

"I could tell some jokes," he says against my skin.

"Eh, I'll be miserable enough already."

"There she is—the coffee must be kicking in."

"I mean, oh no, I don't think my cheeks could handle your complete and utter hilarity."

The foghorn of a distant boat wails hauntingly in the distance, disagreeing with me.

"You know, I could distract you another way."

"I have no clue what that could entail, but I give you free rein." I giggle. "Oh! Before I forget, I have a very important question to ask you!"

"Important questions from you scare me, but I'll allow it."

"Your fear is probably valid, and I'll try to work on that, but not today. So! When Paul said you gave up beer and carbs for me...?"

Liam groans behind me. "You couldn't wait to tease me until I'm not hungover?"

"Absolutely not. You knew what you were getting into with me."

Liam's breath pricks the nape of my neck as he dips his head and brings his lips to my ears. "It was worth it watching you gape at me."

"I did no such thing."

"You forgot basic sentence structures."

"You got a boner!" I shout far too loudly, causing an older lady power-walking through the park to move off the sidewalk to keep her distance. Fair. I blush, meeting that patented Gene Kelly stare fashioned on Liam's face, eye crinkles and all. "We should probably get home and shower before we have to see my family."

"I want to show you something first, but yeah, then we can go *home*." He takes a sip of his coffee, lips curled up behind the lid. I haven't even been here twenty-four hours, and I'm already claiming his apartment as my own.

Liam guides me past a fountain with a cherub and a fish over a brick sidewalk to a white-fenced area. My breath catches as we walk down a few tiny stairs and enter an area blanketed with a canopy of white blossoms. Twisted trees sit in barren beds dusted with fallen petals. A lace covering of blooms overwhelms their branches which bow under the encumbering weight, while three fountains with brick walls trickle throughout the petaled wonderland.

"Oh. Wow—this is—this is perfect," I whisper, worried my voice could break the delicate balance of the area.

A low-grown warmth sparks alive in my chest, like a fire softly crackling in its hearth. It's a comfort I haven't felt in years, not since Nana passed. I glance up at Liam staring back at me, dimples of doom severely popped, and the thought forms.

There are so many things to be anxious about right now.

I haven't seen my parents or brother in years.

In the next two weeks, I have to somehow drag my already exhausted body and mind through a family dinner, a dual baby/bridal shower, and a wedding. And I can't guarantee my body will be able to last through it all, even though it has to, which means pushing it past its limits.

I know all this. I spiraled over it during my flights from hell. And yet, standing here with Liam, I have this suspicious feeling that instead of the anxiety that should be consuming my chest, something akin to happiness has found residence there.

My tongue didn't slip. My heart has found its home.

I just never imagined home would be a person.

19

Donut Bring Me Down

"YOU DON'T THINK YOU'D rather have a salad, sweetheart?" My mother's lips press into a thin line, her eyes steady on me. The low glow of the garden lights accentuates her harsh frown lines that have deepened either with age or from my antics in the past few years.

A firepit crackles in the corner of the back patio of this Italian restaurant. We had to march through the main room to get back to this garden oasis, and with every person we saw that has formerly breathed the same air as Caroline, she stopped with a "Why hi there, have you seen? My Evie is back from *Paris* and oh, look whose arm she's on."

There were a few times at the delivery of this news that I jumped, feigning shock to find myself on Liam's arm, my need to nettle my mother at any given moment and make Liam laugh aligned for once.

All of this, of course, precipitated after she met me outside with a quick smooth down of my hair with her hands and an "I should have scheduled your hair appointment for today. Did you even try to cover up those bags under your eyes?" And my personal favorite: "That tunic does little to compliment your figure, sweetheart. You want to look curvy, not rotund."

A harshly cleared throat forces my attention back to the present. I blink myself out of the frozen state my mother's question created and shift in my seat, hemming and hawing some more.

Do I want a salad? No.

Do I want a few more minutes of peace? Yes.

Should I be letting my mother's reactions to things affect my choices? Also no.

But also.

Peace.

"She'll have the garden salad with the grilled chicken. Hold the garlic knot." Caroline slowly plucks my menu while the waiter looks on with unease.

"I can't believe she's already pulling this shit," Caleb mutters. He removes a pair of sunglasses that disguises none of his thoroughly wrecked hungover disposition and digs his palms into his eyes. Holly smiles sympathetically.

Liam gives my knee a tiny reassuring squeeze. "Get what you want."

I swallow, avoiding the swell of awkward silence the table has fallen into. Mr. and Mrs. Kelly pick at their dinner rolls while my dad's attention rests heavily on a TV in the back garden bar, playing highlights from the Bruins post-season run.

"The salad sounds fine, but I'd like the garlic knot, please." I don't want to start a scene in this restaurant. I'm too tired, and after the past two days and way too much airport food, greens probably wouldn't be a bad thing.

I pick up my knife, twiddling it in the pads of my fingers and avoiding my mother's stare.

Liam orders the ravioli, and my mouth waters. This area of Massachusetts used to be a heavy mill area where a lot of Italian immigrants ended up, so the Italian restaurants, like the one we're currently in, are top-notch.

And I got a salad.

Liam leans over to me, bringing his mouth to my ear. "Distraction time?" I shiver as his breath warms my neck, making my hairs stand on end. Too much into my reaction to him, all I can do is nod in response. "PG or MA?"

Blushing, I pick my gaze up from the table and raise a brow, curious as to what the MA distraction would entail.

My brother stands up, clearing his throat. "I know tonight is about Evie, but while we have everyone here—Holly and I have an announcement we'd like to make."

Oh dear god, now? Caleb, seriously?

"MA. MA," I hiss.

"I know some of you were a bit skeptical when Holly and I announced that we planned to pull off this wedding in three months, and we appreciate all of the help. Mom and Dad, thanks for letting us use the backyard. Mr. and Mrs. Kelly, thank you for being so cool about the mess of a road we're about to have with parking. And well, I just wanted to say, the speed will be worth it since Holly and I are going to be busy taking care of a baby in five months." If Caleb didn't look like he partied with death himself last night, I imagine his face would house a wide and cheerful grin right now instead of the grim line with a faint upward twitch he's wearing.

"Oh, that's so exciting." Mrs. Kelly claps her hands, feigning like this is a surprise.

"You don't say," Mr. Kelly adds, buttering his dinner roll.

My dad grunts. Whether it's at the announcement or his favorite hockey player getting thrown in the penalty box, I don't know.

And my mother . . . I wince, gearing up for whatever is about to hit the fan. Lips pursed, she brings her wine glass to her mouth and demurely sips on her cabernet. Not a stray hair, or emotion, out of place, all tucked safely away under a layer of hairspray and repression.

Caleb and I blink at her, waiting in anticipation. I reach for a dinner roll.

"Yes, well, I'm glad that after no more than six other people congratulated me on my first grandchild, my son finally had the decency to tell me." At least she's not throwing shade at me, I guess. "Lord knows they weren't talking about Evelina expecting." *Never mind.* "Sweetheart, don't pick at the rolls. Harry, would you like another? Here." She moves them toward the other end of the table.

"Speaking of marriages—" My mother turns her attention to me.

I don't meet her gaze, narrowing on the red and white checkered tablecloth draped across the wooden table. "We weren't actually—"

"Should we keep the tent up for another backyard wedding?" Her perfectly manicured hands reach across the table and fall on mine. "You know we're so happy you two finally put your differences aside and figured it out. This is exactly what Nana wanted for you."

My lips press into a thin, harsh line. Scowling whenever Nana is involved feels disrespectful, but I can't help it after my mother's petty invocation of her. "It's been less than a month."

"Oh hush, you two have been attached at the hip since you were five. Do you remember their little backyard wedding, Natale? Wasn't that the cutest?"

Mrs. Kelly nods, her hair piled high on her head dotted with specks of gray. "We still have the pictures from Liam's camera that day."

"Oh! Speaking of Liam's camera." I jolt up straight in my chair, enthusiastically taking the opening to change the direction of this conversation. My knees hit the top of the table, and water splashes beyond our well-filled glasses.

"Evelina—settle," my mom scolds under her breath.

"Sorry! I got a little excited. Okay, so earlier today . . ."

Liam shifts in his seat, a hint of tension raising his shoulders, and I pause my story, sliding my gaze to him. His mouth relaxes, curling into a devilish smirk.

Suddenly, Liam's hand glides up my thigh under the table, pricking the skin on the back of my neck.

"I'm sorry, what were you saying, Evie?" Mrs. Kelly asks.

My pulse quickens. His hand slowly climbs under the edge of my skirt.

"Oh. Uhm," I fumble.

A gleam of mischief hangs in his eyes, proud when he sees how tongue-tied the sensation is making me. His hand creeps further up.

"Yes, what were you going to say, Peaches?" the bastard asks, damn near smug.

A low unsatiated fire burns in the pit of my stomach as a nervous energy courses through my veins, and my cheeks heat.

What was I saying?

Oh. His pictures, right. No, he's not going to win this. I will not be distracted!

"Liam has a bunch of photographs hanging in a café in Portsmouth, and they're phenomenal, and that's the gist of my story, okay?"

Mr. Kelly pauses buttering his bread and glances at Liam. "You still like doing that artsy crap, huh?"

"Harry," Mrs. Kelly scolds in a whisper, "be nice."

"I'm just giving him a hard time, Nat. He knows that means I love him."

"It's just a hobby anyway." Liam clears his throat, retracting his hand. His knee bounces, and I gently caress the top of his thigh to help it settle.

"I'd love to see some of them," Holly interjects.

"Me too, love." Mrs. Kelly pats his hand. "You were always so talented. I'm happy to hear you've kept with it."

A spring peeper sings his agreement in the growing dusk around us.

"You think you'd be able to do that in Paris, though? The city looks pretty ugly." Harry glances at him. The hint of a smile curls his lips, brightening his otherwise ruddy exterior.

Liam's nervous energy shifts as he straightens in his chair. "You serious?" His dimples deepen as a wild, dangerous uncontained grin erupts across his face.

Harry nods, shoving another roll into his mouth. "If Evie doesn't think she'll get sick of you quickly, I worked the position out."

A record scratches on the turntable in my mind. It's been playing "Moses" on a loop since we sat down and I desperately needed the serotonin, but now, I fear I missed something. Paris? Liam? What?

"Liam, what is he talking about?" I whisper.

"It's just something I've been working on. I didn't want to say anything until it was official." His eyes flicker around the table. "I, uhm, kind of wanted to do this privately, no offense to anyone, but if you'll have me, I can stay in Paris and head the European office."

Liam in Paris. That's the ultimate dream, isn't it?

For me. But what about him? I can tell in how his shoulders hang or his voice dips when he's talking about his masters and working for his dad that it's not his passion. And I get it, I do. We all can't have our passion projects be our jobs, but there's a difference in how he's carried himself in Portsmouth versus how he navigated Paris. He stands a bit taller on this side of the Atlantic, even on a day when he's grumpy and exhausted.

"But you hate all this business stuff," I murmur.

Harry cocks his head to the side. "You do?"

"No—not really, it's not that big of a deal." He scrapes a hand through his hair. I catch the tremor and sigh. I wish Liam could understand where I'm coming from with Harry. There's no way this guy wants him to force a career he hates, not after everything he's done for Liam. But it's not my place. He has to get there himself. "We should talk about this later, anyway. It's not why we're here."

Mrs. Kelly clears her throat, glancing at Liam and me with a comforting, sympathetic smile. "Evie, Liam tells me you're looking at opening some kind of pastry shop? That sounds exciting."

"That's the dream." I chew my lip, avoiding my mother's subtle, heated glare. "I'm finishing up the details for funding, and then, I don't know—all the fun stuff is planned: the name, design, menu. I just have to wade through the logistical side a bit more."

"You're still going through with it?" My mom takes another measured sip of her wine.

I swallow, eyes flickering to Liam and back to my mother. "We'll see." I shrug.

"What about your family? Do you really think you can handle starting that and a new business simultaneously? You know it's not going to be easy, what with your—"

"I think our family and its size will stay a discussion between Evie and me, Mrs. O'Shea. No need to put undue pressure on anyone. We're still young, and this is still new. I know personally, I'm not ready for that responsibility." Liam's eyes laser in on my mother, and for the first time ever, she really looks five-two. I pick my mouth up off the table. Wonder Boy just snapped at *Caroline* to stick up for *me*? I never thought I'd see the day.

My mother smiles curtly, dabbing her lips with her napkin. "Of course, excuse me." She pushes up from the table in an odd rush. My brows furrow as I watch her walk to the bathroom, too hurried to be proper.

My dad miraculously notices it too, and he follows her lead back into the restaurant.

The waiter emerges from the same door, carrying two trays of food with a grace I never could possess. I beam warmly at Liam, mouthing "thank you," grateful to have him, photography incident aside, on my team tonight.

The waiter finishes grinding pepper on Caleb's chicken piccata and lays a bowl containing a feast suitable for rabbits in front of me, eliciting very little excitement on my part. But again, my body probably needs this anyway.

Next to me, tomatoes, garlic, and basil bathe Liam's ravioli in a rich, decadent aroma. My mouth waters in an instant.

Liam nudges me with his shoulder. "You mind splitting with me? Your salad looks good."

I blink. Liam doesn't eat carbs. It's a realization I'm having far too late because my mind literally can't comprehend it as reality. But it's true. He's only made a handful of exceptions to the rule in the past few weeks. "Are you eating carbs for real now?"

"Felt like trying something different." He shrugs, grabbing a bread plate and putting more than half of the ravioli on it for me.

"Seriously? I fucking love you." It slips out, but I don't fight to take it back. Liam's smirk grows into a wild, crushing smile as he leans, bringing his mouth to my ear.

"I fucking love you too, Peaches." He kisses my cheek, and my insides twinkle like the stars winking to life in the night sky. As beautiful as Paris is, I haven't seen stars in a good five years, not like this, and my heart yearns to look up into the cloudless expanse of sky overhead. I reach for my glass, still held captive by the celestial bodies above, and in my distracted state knock over my red wine, jumping as it spills all over my white tunic.

"Oh hell." I stand quickly. "Excuse me, I should wash this off."

I head toward the bathroom on the restaurant's bottom floor, passing a few high school acquaintances in the basement bar.

Logan Stanley, a high school teammate of Liam's, stumbles out of the long winding hallway that leads to the bathrooms. These old mill buildings are gorgeous but not laid out for easy navigation.

"Finally put him out of his misery, nice!" He lends out a fist to bump.

"Yup!" I nervously laugh, extending my fist to his. Hopefully he's outgrown the handwashing habit (or lack thereof) that earned him a place on Clare's never again list.

"Went out a few months ago for my bachelor party, and the guy still had it bad. Higgins told him it was probably for the best it never happened. There was no way reality could match what he had built up in his head."

"Oh." *Leave. Leave now.* "Excuse me, I need to take care of this." I gesture to my shirt, sidestepping Logan and attempting to leave before the anxiety earworm is laid, but it's too late.

I will spiral over this later, without a doubt. But first, I need to get through this family dinner.

"Hope for the bastard's sake it holds up."

"Me too. It was nice to see you. Bye." I hasten my steps, hurrying around the corner toward the bathrooms, but my mother's panicked pitch slows my efforts.

"If he goes there, then she'll never come home, Cal—I'll lose my baby girl for good."

Ice floods my veins. I've never heard myself being referred to by her affectionally, and it's unsettling.

It's sad it's unsettling. But here we are.

"She's already gone, Caroline," my dad says in a clipped tone. "And trying to control what she's eating here and questioning her life decisions isn't helping if you want to change that. I don't know how many times we have to have this discussion."

My father's argumentative tone takes me by surprise. While my mother and I had a tumultuous relationship growing up, the one with my father was nonexistent. His eyes were always glued to some sporting event on TV. He didn't enable my mother's antics as much as he ignored them and left me to fend for myself.

"I just wanted to make sure she had someone to take care of her so I wouldn't have to worry about her ending up like Aunt Norma. I didn't want him running off to Paris and keeping her there too." My mother's voice breaks as it carries through the hallway.

"If you'd just paused, you'd have seen she's doing fine, Caroline. On her own."

I step forward on my toes, inching closer to confrontation. My fists ball to my side, and my hand shakes with a tremor. *Not now.* I don't know who the hell Aunt Norma is or why my mother is using her existence as an excuse to control my life, but I know I promised Caleb peace, and I can't imagine busting in on this private conversation will give him that. So instead, I swing the door open to the restroom, wet a paper towel, and try desperately to eradicate a stain that doesn't seem inclined to budge.

At least the scrubbing takes the edge off my nervous energy.

The door swings open again and my mother freezes, blinking at me. In my childhood, I can only think of one occasion when my mother appeared disheveled. It was a stomach flu that turned her oddly human for twenty-four hours. She watched movies on the couch, hair a mess, and even split a grilled cheese with me when she felt a little better.

That moment has nothing on how she looks now in the harsh florescent lighting of this bathroom. Thick black mascara coats heavy bags under her eyes, her skin is red and blotchy, and her blonde hair hangs in a frizzy tousled mess.

"Oh, hi, sweetheart—" She smiles tight, wiping under her eyes and frowning at my wine stain.

"Clumsy me." I awkwardly laugh.

"I have one of those pens in my purse. Hold on." She rummages through, motioning for me to turn to her when she pulls it out. Sniffling, she dabs at my stain with extreme concentration.

"Can't take me anywhere—" Again, I offer a self-deprecating joke. I'm a fish out of water with the whole Caroline-has-emotions news bomb. Hell, she didn't even cry at Nana's funeral.

"Yes, well, I'd rather have you here and making stains than not at all."

I paste a smile on to match her own as we settle into an unnatural silence.

One of the hardest things I've had to learn as a supposed adult is how to adjust my ever-evolving lens to see the world more clearly, especially when something challenges the neat little boxes I have in my head. I can't just look at Caroline and think "evil," but I also can't give her shitty actions a pass.

"Mom, what's going on? Who's Aunt Norma?"

"Ah, you heard that, did you?"

"I mean, I didn't mean to—I was just . . . here." Creepily waiting outside the door and listening to every word of your conversation.

I really should stop doing that. Nothing good comes out of listening to this stuff.

"She was my great-aunt." My mom keeps dotting my tunic. "She had endometriosis, too, you know."

"She did?"

"At least I think she did. It was never confirmed."

Someone else in my family having the disease shouldn't be surprising; there's plenty of research to suggest that it's genetic in some capacity, and people with family members with it are more likely to have it. Still, I'm twenty-seven and this is the first I'm hearing about Aunt Norma or the fact that she probably had endometriosis.

"What makes you think she had it, then?"

"Just some things in her life. People in the family would tell stories about how Aunt Norma always seemed to have a pain that ailed her, said she was probably a hypochondriac. She was married at one point, too, but they divorced without having any kids. Her husband didn't leave her with much. He didn't have to because the court found her at fault, something about alienation of affection because she wasn't intimate." My mother lowers her voice and blushes at the last few words. "She had a hard time taking care of herself financially after that, lived with my grandmother and grandfather for most of her life. I didn't think anything of it until you were diagnosed, and I started digging a bit."

"Is that what you're worried will happen to me?"

"No, honey. I know Liam would love you no matter what. Don't worry about it. I'm just being my overdramatic self." She presses a kiss to my forehead, and a small tear leaks from her shut eyes.

Unless I don't live up to the fantasy in his head, sure.

I really fucking hate this restaurant.

"Why don't you head back to the table, and I'll be there shortly, okay?" She straightens her shirt.

"Yeah, okay." I nod. "Thanks for the help."

"Of course." She grabs my hands as I slake by her. "I'm going to try, Evelina. I really am. Please don't stay away forever."

I sigh. I'm so tired of all of this. Everything is hard, and the people who are supposed to be the founding members of my support system are making everything harder for me.

"Show me you can respect my life decisions, even if you don't like them, and then maybe we can talk. I'm not going to become Aunt Norma just because I might have the same disease as her. She was more than that, and so am I." The door swings shut on my mom. I text Liam asking him to pack up our food as I walk back to the table.

I've had enough of this damn place.

Oh, we should get a cannolo to go, too, though.

20

Sprinkle en Français

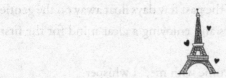

"Oh my word, I missed poutine and Rohr's waffles, but I think my huge-ass eyes might actually be bigger than my stomach." I groan, sitting on the edge of a rock wall jutting into the ocean. It's a breakwater, or at least that's what Liam told me it was called.

This morning, we went to Rohr's for a very New England-style breakfast and some great company. Clare and her husband Josh, Holly, Caleb, and a sullen, misses-a-certain-Fionn-O'Connor-and-is-living-in-denial Eli Blythe all met us there—each member of the party claiming victory for their matchmaking skills. A discussion ensued that ended with a stern warning to Caleb to never ever pull a surprise like that again, even if it did seem to work out for the best.

After breakfast, Liam brought me here to his spot—his Place Dauphine. An old abandoned military fort, guarding a million-dollar view.

A month ago, I would have been convinced that Liam had taken me to this decaying fort to finally be rid of me. But instead, he took my hand and led me around it. After navigating over rocks, branches, and other hazards, a clearing of seashells and pebbles opened up, giving way to water slowly lapping to shore in one spot and crashing wildly against the breakwater in another.

With a steady hand on my back, Liam guided me over a long row of uneven boulders that ended in this concrete platform that was once a lookout. The perfect seat to watch the sun glitter off the expanse of water before us.

Inhaling, I let the burdens of the past few days float away on the gentle sea breeze, rolling my shoulders and enjoying a clear mind for the first time in a while.

"I bet you'd miss this if you come with me," I whisper.

"I can find another one." He rubs his thumb across my knuckle. His professional camera sways against his neck.

A tugboat chugs slowly across the glittering sapphire waters in the distance. It's pulling along a large tanker, at least four times its size, headed toward a collection of hazy islands dancing along the horizon.

Liam said they're the "Isles of Shoals" and that he took a tour of the Appledore Island one summer a few years back. There's a massive garden there that belonged to a writer named Celia Laighton Thaxter, and he toured her garden and took pictures of sailboats floating in the distance behind it.

"Are you going to snap a picture of the tugboat?" I ask, briefly letting my eyes shutter closed and soak in the warmth of the rays on my face.

"I'm waiting for it to get closer to the lighthouse."

"Oh, good idea. That's why you're the professional."

"Definitely not."

I crack one eyelid open, peeking at him. "Definitely should be."

He shakes his head with a sigh and lifts his camera, angling it at the lighthouse off in the distance. "Photography won't pay my dad back."

"There's nothing to pay back. He loves you—that's it."

"It won't keep me with you either." His lips tip into a smile as he points the camera at me.

"Do you want to break your camera with my mug?" I tease, dipping into a Southern accent to sound like Nana.

"What do you think about me coming, though, Peaches? We haven't really had a second to talk about it."

Dragging the salt air through my lungs, I take a moment to collect the thoughts that have been swirling with the frenzying speed of a tornado in my mind since the suggestion was made at dinner last night. Logan Stanley's and Caroline's contributions haven't helped, either, and there's entirely too much noise up there.

As excited as I am at the idea of having Liam in Paris with me, there's a louder voice screaming that I'm not enough, and I'll never be okay with Liam making a move across continents *for me*. If I'm reading him wrong and he likes living in Paris and the job, and I happen to be there too, that's completely different.

"That depends, I guess. Would you still take the job if I wasn't in Paris, or we didn't have—whatever this is—going on?"

The nervous bob of his throat before he answers tells me everything I need to know.

I sigh. "Honestly, Liam, what I really want is for you to do what makes you happy, and if I'm in the picture, then I'd really love it, but I don't want to be why you make this big life decision. This is still too new to be making a leap like that."

"This isn't new for me–" He shakes his head, and his shoulders sag. I don't know if he was expecting me to jump up and down and be like "Yes! Yes! Yes!" even if a large part of me *wants* to do that.

The idea of me probably isn't new to Liam, but I'm anxious that with his far-off dreamy looks, there's an idolized version he made of me in his mind that I can't possibly hold a candle to. I will disappoint him with the reality of who I am; that's the only logical progression here.

I should just stop this now. Put us both out of our misery before we get too attached.

I peek over at him, snapping a photo. His corded forearms flex holding the camera up to his face. My eyes follow the curve of his arm to the bend of his elbow and over the shirt sleeve cutting tight against his bicep. I *should* stop this, but I don't because I still remain, above all else, an absolute masochist.

"You know—" I look over with him, a sly smile on my face, hoping to cut the tension. "Today's a pretty good day down there." I nod to my pelvis. "If there were things you wanted to do, in maybe the bedroom or whatever—I don't know. Maybe, you could show me some stuff."

Look at me, natural seductress.

Liam's head shoots up, a soul-crushing grin busting across his face. The dimples of doom pucker his cheeks as the gold flecks in his eyes twinkle in the warm rays of the sun. Excitement radiates off him, arcing between us. It jumbles the nervous energy bubbling inside me at the thought of what we're about to do, and the pressure builds like a champagne bottle ready to bust its cork. "Fuck yeah, let's go."

I'm not sure how I made it off the rock jetty. Or into the car. Or off the island. But I swear I blink, and we're back in Liam's condo. I kick my shoes off, and they land on his hardwood floor with a satisfying thud. Liam wraps his arms around me and places me on the stone counter. He cups my cheek, laying a soft kiss on my lips.

"Still feeling good?" he asks in between kisses.

"Still good." I unbutton his shirt. "Don't feel like you have to be gentle."

"Just taking my time," he says against my lips. "You don't have anything planned for the rest of the day, do you?"

"Just sleep."

"We should have a good five hours before we need to do that." Liam's kisses grow rougher. His fevered hands rush over my sides, grabbing the edge of my dress and sliding it up and off.

"Five hours! Are you trying to kill me?"

"Just close to death. Don't worry." He winks before lowering his shoulder and wrapping his arm around my torso. In one smooth motion, he hoists me over his shoulder like it's nothing and brings me into the bedroom.

He places me softly on the bed, and I prop up on my elbows, watching his own frantic undressing. He catches his eyes on me, his lips quirk, and then he slows, grabbing the collar on the back of his shirt, and lifting it over his head at an agonizing pace.

Light streams in from a picture window behind him, and I squint through a halo to admire the dips of his abdomen and the strength of his chest. "Hungry eyes." He tsks. "Looks like I didn't feed you enough this morning."

"What can I say? I'm craving something sweet," I say, shielding my eyes from the sun as his sure fingers undo the button on his denim, and he steps out of them.

"I hate to break it to you, but I think you came to the wrong place for that, Peaches." He crawls up on the bed, hovering over me and then dips down, devouring my lips with his own. I didn't know it was possible to be more attached to him, but I'm this close to considering being selfish and screaming *"Yes, of course, you can stay with me in Paris for good."*

He hooks a finger and slowly drags my underwear down. I reach for him to do the same, and he gently grabs my hands. "Let me take care of you, Peaches."

"Okay, but I feel like I should be doing something too. You're just...."

"Lavishing you." He smirks and climbs fully over me, settling on his side. "Worshipping you." His hand draws slow, adoring circles on my abdomen. "Loving you." He drags his finger along my pelvic bone and inner thigh crease. Butterflies follow wherever he goes.

"Torturing me," I breathe out.

"You're the one who accused me of being selfish in bed. I have to defend my honor, Peaches."

Oh. I may regret that.

He turns my head, brushing his mouth along my jaw. Slowly, he traces the edge of my entrance, my insides throbbing at his growing proximity.

A peal of nervous laughter escapes me before a tiny cramp punctuates the excitement. *Uh oh.* The pain should be a red flag to stop, but I'm not ready to admit defeat. It's confusing, feeling euphoria and agony simultaneously, but here I am.

He brings his lips to the edge of my breast, traveling inch by inch. With each inch, I yield more control to my body, surrendering to my primal instincts, to the truth that's been clawing its way to the surface for some time now. If I let him go further, if I go all in tonight, no one else will ever do. I'm seconds, inches, from being thoroughly his.

No, not his—but he'll be my only, and heck, in these moments, every inch of me wants to be his only too. He's the only one with the power to make me this completely undone. Like there's some cosmic energy that we share, and when it mixes together it creates something perfectly complete.

Logic loses. Sanity lost. He wins, and we've barely played.

The cramps heighten, and the agony starts to outweigh the euphoria. I tighten a fraction, anxious I'm a ticking time bomb with my pain, but I don't want to kill the mood by telling him to hurry up.

Liam draws circles around the edge of my pelvic bone, and then he hovers, and a finger enters. "Oh." My breath hitches. His thumb presses on my bundle of nerves. I'm a bundle of nerves. He rubs me in a slow circular motion. I huddle into him, breath becoming more erratic.

Another cramp. Another bit of pain. But it also feels good?

My hands tangle into his hair. My back arches. My feet try to grab hold of his legs. I pull him in tighter for a kiss. Maybe I don't have to say hurry up, maybe . . .

He doesn't budge—only the rubbing gets faster. A fire rips through my stomach. I bury my fingers harder into his back.

"Seriously, you're still this much of a tease?" I gasp.

He presses his body further into me, returning to my lips. "Tell me what you want, Peaches, and I'll gladly do it." He leans in, kissing the corner of my lips like a little cheat. "Is this what you want?"

My breathing quickens as his rubbing slows. "I want you to kiss me."

And also to hurry up before everything inside roars with pain and I can't hide it anymore.

"I am kissing you, Peaches," he murmurs against the skin along my collarbone and blows on the spot where my clavicle dips. "What do you really want?"

"I. Want. You," I get in through panting breaths. "Liam, please."

Liam pauses a hover above my lips, a cocky-ass smile cut across his face. "Good. Now you know how I've felt every second of every day since you first speared me with those big blue eyes of yours."

You're going to lose this soon. Something in the back of my mind reminds me. *Your muscles are getting angry.*

"I'm going to win you, Evie. That's the only thing between us I've ever cared about. If you let me, I want every ounce of you to call to me like I've always called to you."

Thorns and roots latch into the sidewall of my abdomen at a dizzying speed. He'll figure it out soon, he can read me too well, but we've already gone so far. It wouldn't be fair if I stopped now.

I pull him in as every inch of me throbs, more so with pain at this point than the good stuff. My fingers tangle into his hair. Legs curl around him. For a second, I swear we're both lost in each other. The pain takes a backseat, and my thoughts are consumed with a single thought, a single name. *Liam. Liam. Liam.*

And I tell him. I tell him with my frantic kisses and the little sounds I can't control. I tell him with my fingers clawing deep into his hair, into his hard-muscular shoulder blades. And he tells me with the urgency of his tongue, with the way his teeth graze my lip, with the way his hands claim every inch of me in our shared state of frenzy.

My eyes connect with his. I swallow, knowing all vulnerability and reality are washed on my face, and I can't hide it. I love him rather hopelessly.

"I need you." I grab for him. "Please."

He hesitates. "Are you sure? We can take our time. I want you to be ready."

Positive, because bad things will happen if we don't do this soon.

I nod, reaching for a wrapper from the nightstand drawer and handing it to him. He swallows, putting it on, a little less sure for someone who just had my back arched and me literally begging for him, and then he enters, slow and gentle. I hesitate, evening my breaths as his lips brush up against mine again, this time much softer. But the passion hasn't diminished.

I tense, anxious. I'm already in a fair amount of pain, and this isn't helping.

It's fine. It'll be fine. Get out of your head.

Something gets pressed. I don't know what *it* is. A button for hellfire and agony, perhaps. My lower stomach further ignites in cramps. I tighten too much, and now everything doesn't just hurt, it kills. With every thrust, it grows and grows. I fight back the yelp and panic, not wanting to ruin the mood for Liam. Just a few more minutes (hopefully). It'll be fine.

Subtly, I attempt to draw a calming breath, keeping my mask on to hide the pain. It doesn't work, and I wince.

Liam stops. Did he—did I miss it?

"What was that?" he asks, gently pulling out, doing a plank above me.

"What was what?"

"You winced."

"I didn't wince."

"Peaches, seriously, I'm not doing this again." Liam looks down at my stomach and then back up at me. "Evie, does that hurt for you?"

I bite my lip. I can't lie to him. "Only a little." Okay, so I can lie to him a little bit.

"Are you kidding me? Why would you push this if—"

"You can finish, it's fine."

"I'm not finishing anything," he huffs, falling on his back.

"I can help." I turn over, reaching out. I owe him that much after what he made me feel.

Liam stands up, pulling up his boxers and heading to the bathroom. "I'm fine."

I lay on my back, a headache surging through. Exactly what I need right now. Guilt gnaws away at me. That wasn't a fair exchange. No way is he going to want to do that again.

It was stupid, but I hoped Liam would be different. That I could just be with someone. Like everyone else on this damn Earth seems to be able to do.

Hope's fading that pain-free intimacy will ever be possible, that my lower half won't burst into painful, gut-wrenching flames every time something other than a finger enters. I wipe away a tear, but the flood follows. Liam pauses briefly in the doorframe before crawling into bed and folding me into him.

"I'm so sorry." I sob into his chest. "You have every right to be frustrated I couldn't finish."

"Hey—hey no, I'm sorry I got frustrated. But it wasn't because we didn't finish, Peaches. I need you to speak up when it hurts, okay?"

"It's not that simple. I *want* you. I *want* this. I'm sorry. I just—I don't know." A string of frustrated expletives escapes me. I want to be *normal* for one damn day down there—why is she so freakin' high maintenance? "I wouldn't blame you if you don't want to try again. A lot of guys would give up or don't care. It's just she gets to a point and it's game over. But you felt nice before that—and I know that doesn't make sense—but the kisses are good—really frickin' good—and—"

Liam's stare remains heavy on me. He cups my face and leans, leaving a soft, intentional kiss on my lips like he's imprinting. "I'm not going anywhere if you don't want me to. We'll get there."

He makes a pained grunt, shifting in bed.

"Can you please let me help with that? I feel awful—" I reach out, and he gently pulls my hand away.

"No offense, Peaches, but we're not doing anything in this bed because one of us feels guilty."

"But—"

"Let's just get some rest, okay? You have a busy week ahead of you."

He wraps me up, and I turn so my back is to him, like so many times in the past few weeks.

But for the first time, the sunshine doesn't chase away the dark clouds. He had a five-hour plan, and I lasted all of ten minutes before I ruined that. A relationship with an unstable foundation like this can't last—it has to crumble eventually.

21

Let's Talk about Donuts, Baby

"JOSH IS CARRYING THE next baby. I'm freaking five months along, and this baby is already half the size of me." Clare slowly lowers herself on the faded floral-patterned couch in my parents' living room, resting her swollen feet on the ottoman.

We escaped back in here after setting up for the shower outside for a quick breather before guests start arriving. It's an unseasonably warm May day, and the decision to have the baby/bridal shower in the same tent as the wedding made sense financially until now—people are going to be sweltering in there during a midday, peak sun event.

I hug my heating pad to my midsection, trying to give it a few minutes of rest. Liam and I kickstarted a flare with our attempt at being intimate, which is a neat trick I'm super happy to have discovered right before I had a million things to do. The usual welcomed heat itches in the accompanying humidity, but endo's going to endo, hot or not, so I fan away the beads of sweat on my face and accept my fate.

My mother's back upstairs fixing her hair because what should have been a demure loose curl is now thoroughly wrecked with the morning sweat. She encouraged me to try an updo, too, in the weirdest passive suggestion that's ever left her lips. I agreed in my own Evie way, piling my curls on the top of my head when she probably meant for me to style it in a chignon or something like that.

A lightning pain streaks through my thigh and calf, and I inhale sharply. Sciatica flare. Oh. Yay. I massage the back of my leg with my fist.

"You okay?" Clare nods at my knuckles digging into a knot.

"Just some sciatic pain. Not a big deal."

"Ugh. I know exactly how you feel. I had a bout of it during my second trimester, and it's just the worst."

I smile tight. I firmly believe I shouldn't judge another person's pain or pain tolerance because I don't want to diminish anyone's plight. It's all valid. But sometimes, I wish that in validating other people's pain, I didn't feel like I was diminishing my own. I understand sciatic pain is something that pregnant people experience. I understand it's incredibly painful. I even understand that my pain cannot eradicate theirs; they both exist. But when Clare says she knows *exactly* how I feel, I can't help but get the sense that it's misplaced empathy. People don't have to connect or commiserate to show kindness and compassion. Sometimes it's better if it's clear they can't relate.

Because Clare can't relate. Not entirely, anyway. And honestly, I love that for her. And her trying to connect means that my own reality is not being acknowledged. I'm in pain because I have lesions growing in my body wherever they damn well please. I'm in pain because when they shed themselves like they're having a period, I bleed internally and build up scar tissue that adheres my ligaments and organs to each other and to my sidewall over time. That's it. There's no nine-month countdown to relief. No baby-shaped reason behind it. My contractions don't come with a purpose either. It's all pointless pain.

A small hand falls to my forearm, waking me from my deep spiral. "I'm sorry, I wasn't thinking." Clare smiles bashfully at me.

"It's fine." I wave her off.

"Please, I can tell by how you bit the inside of your cheek that it wasn't. And that's fair because it was a stupid thing to say on a day that's probably already stressful for you." She grabs my arm, huddling into it. "But I love you, and I missed you, and I'm so happy you're here and snuggable when I fuck up because Josh says it's harder to stay mad at me this way."

"Absolutely. It'd be like being mad at a teddy bear." I kiss the top of her head, letting it rest on my shoulder, and breathe through a few more spasms and lightning streaks. "Why don't you try some of the treats I made? I plated those for you." I nod to the coffee table, where I set a plate of miniature pastries and petits fours. I spent the last day and a half perfecting them with a pretty hot sous chef, and I'm rather proud of how they turned out. The menu was my only contribution to the shower planning. Clare handled invites, decorations, games, etc. But hell, I nailed that menu.

"Oh my word, Evie, these are delicious." Clare moans, picking at the laminated flakes of my miniature pain au chocolats. "What did you use for the chocolate inside?"

"I panicked with my limited options and froze some truffle balls before putting them in there to see what would happen."

"Good. Freakin'. Call. I love your experiments." Clare takes another bite. Her head tilts up, and she closes her eyes, savoring it.

My heart flips as I watch her enjoy my food. Usually when I bake at home, it's just for me, myself, and I, and the occasional stoic "Oh yeah, this is nice" Maria, but it's a rush to see someone genuinely enjoy the moment the pastry melts away on their taste buds.

I did that. I made that moment.

A camera flashes to the left of us. I blink back the dots now spotting my vision, and Liam comes into focus with a tiny guilty smile.

"Seriously, bro, that couldn't have been flattering for either of us." Clare groans, eyes closed.

Liam glances innocently at his viewfinder. "You said to take pictures of the event."

"Yeah, like the tent, and the flowers, and the food, and people when they get here—not me with my eyes closed, swollen ankles out, stuffing my face."

"But you've got a cute chocolate soul patch going on." I giggle.

"Which I should go wash off." Clare swings her legs off the ottoman, pushing off the couch. She squares her shoulders, sizing up her five-two figure against Liam's six-four one. She may be a foot shorter, but at the rate he's shrinking into himself, that might not be the case for long. "There will be serious consequences if any pictures of me stuffing my face today surface. I haven't had an Evie pastry in years, and I will not feel guilty about how many miniature items I'm about to consume. Understood?"

He sticks his hands up in surrender, worry creasing his brows. "I swear, I won't take any pictures of you eating."

"Good." Clare nods, satisfied. "I have to check with Josh and see where he is with the balloons anyway. Go snuggle your Peach and get her to relax before the day from hell starts."

"You don't have to tell me twice," Liam says with a lopsided grin.

"Again, you're welcome," Clare hollers down the hallway.

Half joking, I shift to the left side of the couch. Liam and I have shared this couch hundreds of times, but there was always a dance to it. Especially on movie night, a tradition we both stubbornly kept even after Nana passed and Caleb left for college. The left cushion was mine. His the right. Snacks in the middle.

"Hey there, Peaches." He settles into his spot, leaving his arm lounging on the top of the sofa like he always did.

"Hi, I missed you," I murmur, breaking protocol and leaning in his direction. My head falls against his shoulder, and I rest a hand on the top of his thigh.

With a happy sigh, he pulls me in tighter against him. "Yup, this is much better."

"Than what?"

"Sharing this couch with you and having you buried into that corner, clinging to the armrest for dear life."

"I haven't a clue what you're talking about. I was always the perfect picture of calm on this thing."

He leans over me, inspecting my side. "Definitely see some claw marks." He smiles, righting his posture and paying the toll on my lips before straightening again. "Not that I'm complaining."

"I didn't want my hands to do something they shouldn't," I grumble. "What about you? You always took up half the damn couch with your arm stretched out lounging on the top, dive bombing for snacks whenever I reached for them and—*oh*."

Does a stronger word than *clueless* exist?

I glance at the gleam in Liam's eye, my heart leaping at his knowing smirk.

"You could have just said something, you know." I playfully nudge his shoulder.

"What would you have wanted me to do?" He gently rolls me so my back hits the offending armrest, bracing himself in a hover over me but careful to keep pressure off my abdomen. He dips into a push-up and kisses the corner of my lips, mine part in response, anxious for him. "What would have happened if I begged? Would you have put me out of my misery then?" he asks.

"I mean, it couldn't have hurt the situation."

He dips for another kiss. "What if I told you that after the first thirty minutes of whatever movie we watched, you'd forget I was there and relax into this face that's seared into my skull? One where your eyes would go wide and sparkle, and you'd push out this damn bottom lip." He nips at it. Still propped on one hand, he trails a finger slowly up the inside of my thigh, exposed under the flimsy shift dress of choice. I suck in a breath at the sensation, my eyes fluttering closed, and reach for him with a whimper. "Just like that, good girl."

Oh. My eyes pop open with a nervous chuckle at Liam calling me *a good girl.* "You're such a cheeky asshole." I push him off me, and he pulls me up.

"You relaxed, though?" His grin spreads wide across his disaster of a gorgeous face.

Partially relaxed. Partially other things. Life with Liam in a nutshell.

"Unfortunately. I can't wait to unpack that with someone someday." I shake my head.

"How are you feeling otherwise? You were on your feet all last night." He leans down and checks the remote on the heating pad, pressing a few buttons. Sometimes the timer turns off, and I forget to flick it back on and just sit there in pain and wonder why. It's weird I've had this disease for over ten years, but I still get surprised by silly things like that. Liam's been a guardian of the heating pad ever since he saw it happen, constantly monitoring it and ensuring I don't fall into my own trap.

"Tired, but good."

"Don't push it today. Clare has the details, and I'm good at picking stuff up and putting it down."

"I'll be fine," I say, resting my head back on his shoulder. A baby balloon floats across the picture window, heading to the backyard and the tent. It pricks a sadness in my chest I've become skilled at avoiding until I'm staring right at the culprit. Something that I don't talk about with anyone.

I know my body. I know my ovaries are riddled with scar tissue, and my fallopian tubes have been severely damaged. I know that even after I carry, the effects of endometriosis will still be there, and the prospect of taking care of another human life when I can barely take care of myself somedays is daunting.

And I don't know if any of that matters or if I even want children. But the thought that the choice might not be mine to make anyway? That's the one that's hard to cope with.

Holly and Caleb? They didn't have to think about this stuff. They just thought *Hey, having a cousin the same age as Clare's sounds like a good plan. Let's do it*, and that was it. But it's never going to be that simple with me. It's why it's so important to me that whatever happens next with Liam and me, we go slow. I can keep a lot of the endo experience to myself, but if he wants a life with me, that's a reality he'll have to shoulder too.

I wipe at a tear.

This was the wrong freakin' day in my cycle for a baby shower.

Clare and Holly may be secretly evil.

No. Scratch that. They definitely are.

"Evie. I'm thirsty," Holly hollers from her seat of honor.

I groan. "Seriously, how are you this thirsty?"

"Just do it!" Clare calls. "There are so many left, and we can't pour them back into the bottle."

"Fine." I reach for one of the flutes of champagne and toss it back to the whoops and hollers of the Bell sisters.

I'm not sure when they both decided to tag team to get me drunk, making me take shots of champagne for them (which, by the way, is a terrible idea). But apparently, because Holly's missing out on a wild bachelorette party, she has decided to live vicariously through me at this shower, and I can't argue with two pregnant women. They scare me.

The bubbles tickle the back of my throat after a pronounced swallow. My head spins. I don't think I've ever had this much to drink. But after a whole day of

"Don't stick your stomach out like that, sweetheart, you don't want people thinking you're the pregnant one," and *"Oh, I'm sure you'll be next,"* and a few *"You're not expecting too, are you?"* I'm ready to not think for a while.

Maybe Clare and Holly aren't evil as much as they know me and that I need something to keep me from breathing *"I'm not pregnant. I just have a disease that makes it look like I am, and maybe as a society, we should stop commenting on stuff like that"* fire on everyone who nears my dragon heart.

I make a plate of the cherry blossom macarons I repurposed for this reception and let the flour and sugar melt away on my taste buds, hoping it soaks up some of the alcohol.

A hand falls on the small of my back, then plucks one of my creations off my plate. "I hope you don't think I'm going to make a habit of sharing my food with you." I pivot to face Liam and wobble a smidge. His hand stabilizes me, landing on my hip.

"Not sharing if I steal it from you." He grins, cheeks full of my macaron.

"Evie," Holly shouts, inspecting a fluffy pink onesie with bear ears we all cooed over moments ago. "I'm still thirsty—"

"I just finished a flute," I whine as Clare collects some hastily tossed wrapping paper. With the wall of presents Holly had to open, we sent the guests homes with happy stomachs, bouts of laughter, and smiles on their faces instead of having them endure hours of Holly opening toasters, wooden spoons, baby bottles, and a million different onesies. But now, Holly's fingers are itchy, tearing through all the presents with wide eyes and a huge grin.

"You're like halfway to where I was for Clare's bachelorette," she calls over, innocently flipping through a children's book with a boy and the moon on the cover.

Clare flops back down on a chair and swipes a bead of sweat off her forehead. "Yeah, and I mean, I'm not holding it against you, but you *did* miss like the whole bachelorette and wedding so—"

"And I thought you held a grudge." Liam snorts.

"Hearing still works great, bud," Clare hollers.

My mother's heels clop over the hardwood dance floor, warning me her stint of ushering people to their cars with gratitude and a large toothy smile is over. "Evelina, if you have a second, your father and I would love to talk to you before you leave," she says, smoothing out her skirt.

My eyes widen. Not today. Not before the wedding.

After everything I've trudged through this week, one last thing could break me, and I don't want to risk it when I'm so close to the finish line.

I grab another flute of champagne sitting on the table of pre-poured glasses. "I'm sorry, I'm making up for lost time with Clare and Holly. Maybe tomorrow?"

"I thought you might say something like that." My mother sighs. "So here." She hands me a card, my name scrawled across in her perfect cursive. "I'll be here when you want to talk about everything."

I tuck the note in my purse. Whatever it is, I'll read it when I'm back in Paris.

"Evie!" Holly says, grinning at the tiniest pair of sparkling ballet flats. "We need more alcohol."

"Okay, seriously, how drunk did you get at Clare's bachelorette?"

"I don't know. I can't remember."

Oh, good!

"More, more, more." Fists pound on the table, and consequently in my head, in O'Reilly's, the town pub.

"Maybe I should take this one." Holly's friend Kylie snakes the shot glass out of my hand and downs it. My head spins, already two shots too far gone. In my current inebriated state, I'm having a hard time deciphering who exactly Kylie is. I've never heard Holly or Clare mention her, and the look of terror that cut across Holly's face when she came and awkwardly hovered over the table before Clare invited her to sit wasn't encouraging. But she's taking bullets for me right now, so Kylie's a benevolent queen as far as I'm concerned.

I bury my head in my hands, trying to steady *something, anything*. "I have to tap out. No more, you menaces."

"I'll go order you some poutine. You were a good sport." Clare giggles, pushing off the table.

"I'll come with you," Holly says, her chair scraping against the dusty hardwood floor.

Clare awkwardly glances between Kylie and me. Warily, she leans into Holly. "Do you think that's a good idea?"

I don't know why she's so concerned. I'm not that far gone that I can't be left alone. Besides, I have Kylie, beautiful, shot-taking, auburn-haired Kylie.

"I really have to pee." Holly grimaces.

Reluctantly, Clare nods, and they leave Kylie and me behind.

In their absence, my hazy vision swirls around the back of the bar. O'Reilly's is a time capsule to Boston's heyday, the mid-to-late '00s, with Patriots Super Bowl, World Series, Stanley Cup, and Celtics championship banners and pictures hanging from every inch of wall around us. Over Kylie's shoulder, a signed photo of Adam Vinatieri kicking a field goal in the snow sits below a framed picture of Tom Brady with his hands on his head in disbelief. The red and blue confetti falling around him blurs in my current state. Uh oh.

I pull out my phone, sending Liam an SOS to come get me. I never should have let Holly shoo him away and leave me to fend for myself. I manage to clack out the message before the phone falls from my hand in a clatter on the table.

"They did you dirty." Kylie laughs, downing the last shot on the table.

"They're five-foot-two terrors." I sip on my water. A dangerous undertaking considering I'm not entirely confident I have a mouth or a head to supply water to, since I can't feel either. "Why would you willingly be friends with them?"

"Nah, they're good eggs," Kylie says with a small smile. She looks deeply into the empty shot glass, swirling it around on the table.

My brow furrows. Kylie's view on the situation doesn't seem to match the heightened tension in Holly's shoulders when Kylie approached the table, and I don't know what to make of that. "Do you know Holly from work?" I ask since Holly works for a large software company. A coworker might explain it.

"Oh, uhm, no. Actually, it's kind of a funny story how we met."

"I like funny stories." I fumble with my tongue, trying to find my straw again.

"I had this massive crush on one of her friends, and I was working on a project for our MBA together. It was obvious that he was emotionally unavailable, but because I apparently hate myself, I tried to push a whole friends-with-benefits thing with him and pretended like I was totally fine with it because the sex was *good*." She blushes, looking at me. "Who could say no to earth-shattering sex, you know?"

"Not me." I laugh nervously, shifting in my seat. How many of Holly's friends are getting their MBAs? Please tell me it's a fad, and everyone is doing it.

"Anyway, one night I got tanked and told him I wanted more. He tried to let me down gently, but I made this huge scene in one of the local bars, and Holly came to my rescue. And, well, now we're best friends, and dude switched to online classes, so good riddance."

I take a long pull of my water and smile tight. Keeping my mouth occupied so I don't say anything regretful is the best path forward.

"Oh!" Kylie perks up, angling energetically in my direction. "You might know him since he was such good friends with your brother."

"Know who?" Clare mercifully rejoins us. She lays a plate and fork in front of me with a wary grin.

"Liam." Kylie's shoulders slump as she runs her hands over the tops of her arms. "I was just telling Evie how Holly and I met."

"Oh." Clare's voice dips. "We try to forget that start."

"What are we trying to forget?" Holly slides back into her seat.

"Liam." Kylie pouts, resting her chin in her hands.

"Ah." Holly's gaze darts up to me and back at Kylie.

"And how stupid I was." Kylie's eyes gloss over.

"Oop, and now the spiral's started," Holly whispers. "Sorry."

"And the earth-shattering sex—"

"Okay. Whew, I need some air." I exhale, standing from the table.

Everything inside burns in a hot angry buzz, but I'm not jealous. At least, I don't think I am. Liam's free to have his own history, and I can't blame Kylie for being interested.

You're jealous because you'll never have that. The Chaos Gremlin bursts onto the scene inside my brain.

Dammit, Chaos Gremlin. You're the worst.

"You need company?" Clare awkwardly laughs.

"Nah, I'm fine." I smile tightly. "I need to catch a friend before they get here anyway."

"Ah. Yeah, probably a good idea this many in." Holly frowns.

Outside, I inhale the fresh Tallow air, wobbling along a lilac-dusted downtown street. If this week could stop coming for my knees when I already have so much to process, that would be great.

I place my hands on my head, marching toward the florist shop at the corner. Hopefully I'll be able to collect myself by then.

My airways tighten, killing any buzz I had, a wave of dizzy nausea washing over me instead.

This is why I don't drink much, because after a certain point, all I feel is ill, and I already feel like that most of the time.

One or two glasses would have been fine.

I try to drag another breath through my lungs, but the shallow breaths I manage never seem to reach deep enough.

Oh hell. I know what this is.

My heart races, and my blood pounds against my ear.

I walk into the alley to find some solitude, leaning against the brick wall.

Sweat beads my forehead. I inhale, but again minimal air finds its way to my lungs. I slide down the length of the wall, pulling my knees tight against my chest.

A broad figure strolls across the alley, and I manage a fragile, "here" with the last of my reserves.

Liam peeks his head around the building. "Evie?" he whispers.

I don't say anything.

"Why am I always finding you in alleys?" He laughs, but his face falls when my stare meets his. "Hey, hey, what's going on?"

I can't respond. My brain's frozen in the grip of a pair of talons. They rip through every damning thought I've ever had, leaving only carnage in their wake.

I can't have sex without it hurting. Who knows about babies. And there's always a fucking pain.

He crouches down on the balls of his feet, a harsh worried line forming between his brows. "Peaches?" Anguish is washed in his gaze, and great, I can add causing Liam distress to the *Reasons I'm Crap* list.

"Fine," I manage after what feels like a few minutes. "Panic attack."

Uttering those words takes everything out of me, and I keep trying to breathe through the moment using the grounding technique. Liam's hand falls to my knee. It's warm and firm, and the grip is strong. There's a Red Sox game on not too far away at an outside bar, and the groan at the hard thwack that just happened probably means the visiting team hit a home run.

I take another breath. This time it's a bit easier to draw up air. That's a good sign I'm on the backside.

Liam comes to a full sitting position on the ground, wrapping his legs around me and pulling me into his chest. "These sometimes happen at this time of the month. It's okay." I finally manage a whole sentence. My head is swollen with fatigue, my limbs lifeless like I burnt through all my energy reserves.

"It doesn't have to be okay. That looked like it sucked."

"I just didn't want to freak you out."

"Stop worrying about me when stuff like that happens." He trails a finger down my arm. "Did anything happen to set this off?"

I could tell him that I talked to Kylie and got jealous because she could do something with him I never could. And there's a huge part of me screaming he'd be happier with someone like her, where the earth-shattering things get to stay that way. Someone where everything is uncomplicated and less messy.

But I don't. Because I'm tired, and we're also in a dirty alley, it's hot, and I just want to go home.

"No particular reason, but can you take me home?"

"I love that you keep calling it that. Sure, let's go home, Peaches."

22

Donut Go Breaking My Heart

SILVERWARE CLINKS AGAINST FINE china as Caleb and Holly lean in for the thousandth kiss of the night. I've been stealthily watching them from the not-so-dark corner of the wedding party table. They separate, and I bide my time until they're as far apart as possible. Bringing my knife to the flute, I rap the glass again, the clink echoing in the cool twilight air filling the tent.

Caleb's shoulders sag as he looks around for the culprit. His eyes narrow in on me, and I mouth, "Payback's a bitch."

He shakes his head, taking a pull of his beer and yelling, "Wife, where are you? My sister's being a pain in the ass."

Could Caleb ignore this tradition of kissing your bride every time someone clinks their glass?

Absolutely.

Will he?

No. Because he's very superstitious, and there's no way he's going to risk the future well-being of his marriage because he didn't want to kiss his wife.

And after Caleb's sneak attack and Holly's hangover from hell, I can promise him this—these two will kiss their lips off tonight.

Caleb separates after a round of cheers, heading toward the table with food, and I ready the torture weapon a second time. My knife raps once, Caleb deflates, and then a warm hand curls around mine and gently pulls the metal battalion out of my hand.

"Let me have this." I go to pick up my silverware, and Liam moves it out of my reach.

My brother's head shoots in my direction as he mouths "thank you" to Liam.

"I'm about to give you the plastic silverware from the kids' table if you don't let the poor bastard eat."

"Boo, I thought Tyler Higgins was supposed to be President Party Pooper. I knew I should have tried to talk him out of doing his laundry."

"Please, you'd have Tyler hiding in the bathroom by now. I was made specifically to balance you out."

"Well, that's a terrible life purpose."

"It's been a miserable existence thus far." He threads a hand through his hair, narrowing his gaze on me. Clad in a well-fitted tuxedo, Liam may have a license to kill me tonight. My eyes stay transfixed on the way his coat falls along his broad shoulders, the lapels accentuating his already tapered waist. Unabashedly, my teeth graze along my lower lip.

An amused clearing of a throat forces my attention to the hulking figure's face again. Liam's lips tick up in a knowing smile. "How long do you plan on ogling me for?"

"I haven't decided. Would you mind giving me a twirl?" I perch my chin on my hands, fluttering my eyelids in a way that I hope says, "pretty please."

He doesn't, unfortunately, twirl for me and instead extends his hand out as the fast-paced club song slows to an acoustic ballad. "Why don't I twirl you on the dance floor instead?"

I accept, standing far too close to him. His presence steals the air from my lungs right on schedule. His lips twitch like he knows he still has that effect on me, and he's rather proud of it.

We glide together on the dance floor. He pulls me against his chest, swaying me cheek to cheek. A warm smile spreads across my face, and I melt into him.

"Thank you for being such a perfect date." I sigh.

He brings his lips to my temple, pressing a kiss there. "You change your tune pretty quick."

"I'm a sucker for a slow dance. Oh! Remind me to text Maria about Caleb and Holly's first dance later. She has a playlist of potential songs for clients, and I think that cover of 'Every Little Thing She Does Is Magic' was super cute."

Holly and Caleb's first dance, unrehearsed and full of blissed-out giggles, was the sweetest thing I've ever seen. I have a residual toothache just thinking about it.

"Did you add our first wedding song to that list?"

"Sadly no, I don't think B*Witched's 'Rollercoaster' really lends itself to a cute acoustic cover."

"Oh, come on." He tightens his grip on my back, pulling me closer to him. His lips hit my ear, and he sings a low, slow version of 'Rollercoaster's' chorus.

My head tilts back, as a euphoric laugh passes over my lips. It draws the attention of one of my mom's first cousins, Polly, I think. She turns, beaming at us. "Oh, looks like you two aren't too far behind! Congratulations!" My mirth falls away, meeting her eyes and following their line of sight right to my stomach.

Fumbling, I hurry to correct her, but her husband twirls away, and I relent, chasing her around the dance floor just to yell, "*Actually, I'm not expecting,*" isn't worth the energy today.

"I'm sorry." A crease forms between Liam's brows when he catches the look cut across my face. "What exactly did she just congratulate us on?"

"She thinks I'm pregnant," I say with a sigh, glancing down at my stomach, which is protruding somewhat significantly right now. Thanks for nothing, chiffon. "I should probably give the endo belly a rest, or everything will spasm out of control soon."

"I think they're doing the speeches soon, too, so sitting sounds good." He walks me back to my chair, and sure enough, the DJ calls for the maid of honor and best man to meet him at the front.

Liam is slated to give his speech first. He clears his throat with a nervous bob, pulling the sheet from his pocket with a trembling hand.

"As some of you know, my name is Liam Kelly. I technically lived in that house back there." He hooks his thumb behind him. "But I'd say I grew up in the O'Shea's. I don't know if Caleb had much of a choice in being my friend. I think I followed him like a shadow the first year we met, but I wore him down eventually."

"How could I say no to those dimples and that gorgeous face?" Caleb heckles. "Weak. I'm weak."

"No offense, but I would have preferred them to wear a different O'Shea down first. But we got there." He peeks at me, his lips tipping into a little smile.

A swooning "aww" undulates over the crowd. I reach for a piece of bread and my knife to butter the roll because attention like this makes me uncomfy, and when I'm uncomfy, I eat things.

"But in all seriousness, the O'Sheas have always been great about welcoming people into their family, and Holly, I'm sure you're already feeling that too. Caleb, I can't think of anything better than starting a family with the person you love. I know I can't wait to do the same, and I'm so freakin' happy for you, man."

The knife slips out of my hand, clattering to my plate. It's luckily quiet enough not to draw attention. My fingers tremble with Liam's words. I can't think of anything better than starting a family with someone you love.

Whatever Liam continues to say, my mind is a sieve, and I miss it.

My lungs tighten in my chest. My hands shake, and I'm worried another panic attack is imminent. They always happen more at this time of the month. I glance around. Everyone's attention is on the podium. No one would care if I slipped out right now.

I slide out of the tent and tiptoe to the Kelly's side of the yard, brushing past the lilac bushes separating the two properties. A chair creaks on the back deck, and I slow my steps. I thought the Kellys were in the tent with the rest of the crew.

A toast to the bride and groom. The applause drowns out the spring peepers singing in the wooded marsh at the edge of the Kelly property line. I lean against the side of their house, collecting my breaths.

"You know, I think this is the first time an O'Shea is sneaking over to this side. I feel like I was usually trying to find my son somewhere in your yard." Mr. Kelly's voice carries over the residual clamor in the tent.

"Just needed a second, sorry if I'm bothering you—"

"Never were."

Before our dinner a few days ago, I could have counted the times on one hand that I had had a conversation with Mr. Kelly, a quick congratulations at our high school graduation, and that one time I was out shoveling our front path when Caleb was in college where he said "Leave that, Liam could use the workout."

Of course, this inspired me to not leave it, pushing through on a day I probably shouldn't have.

Our pathway was always shoveled first after that, Liam getting up at the ass crack of dawn to beat me to it.

"I have some leftovers from your baking spread here if you want some."

I don't really want to talk to anyone right now if I'm being honest, but it'd be rude to say no.

I turn the corner, climbing the stairs and plucking one of the mini pain au chocolats off the plate.

"You have quite the gift, you know." He motions for me to sit on the glider across the way, and I settle, relishing the cushioned seat that relieves the pressure on my pelvic area those terrible chairs in the tent did not.

"Thank you." I blush, apparently just as bad at receiving compliments as Liam.

"Liam sent me some of the paperwork for his project to look over, and I was just sitting here thinking how someone with your skillset would do very well with a shop on this side of the Atlantic. You'd be a rarity here."

I pick at my lamination. It's certainly a thought.

"And maybe your shop could have gallery walls for someone to hang their pictures."

I raise my eyes to meet his; he has a proud smile fashioned on his face.

"Just a thought." He shrugs.

"I'll think on it." I smile tight and lie. After this week, what I need is to go back to my apartment in Paris and sleep, breathe, and think about all these things much later. Because this past month has been an absolute whirlwind, and after approximately five years of living stagnantly, I'm more than overwhelmed with all the sudden twists and turns of everything. I don't do pivoting well. Never have.

"Wouldn't complain if it meant we had grandkids running around over here instead. Nat's been wanting a little one for a while."

Oh, for the love of children, why does everyone keep mentioning them?

Also, I don't know . . . Maybe it's because everyone has weddings on their mind, but Liam and I have been feeling out a relationship for less than a month. So everyone needs to chill. I've had periods that lasted longer than that. Were they healthy? No. But still. And I love Liam, I always have—but who's to say that's enough for life, for all the hits and setbacks? We've never tested our relationship, like at all, because it's still so damn new.

Is he undeniably sweet and the man of my dreams?

Yup.

Does he make my toes curl and is one hell of a kisser?

Also yup.

But a life? Together? When I barely know how my body will behave the next day? I've been so content staring at the immediate present for so long because when I looked ahead and tried to make goals, I usually ended up disappointed and unfulfilled. What makes me think life will grant me a freebie, and this one thing will work out?

I shift in my seat, going to stand. I don't know where else to hide. Maybe my old bedroom, but clearly, this wasn't the right spot. "Excuse me—I should—"

"You know, when Nat told me she was pregnant, it felt like I had been punched in the gut. I had been so jealous of Will from a very early age. He could do a lot of things I couldn't—I developed hypogonadism in my pre-teens that made me scrawny, and he was tall and made Nat blush. But he was also a scumbag who didn't deserve to breathe the same air as her, and I knew it—"

I settle back in the glider, unsure where Mr. Kelly is going with this. But the man is usually very stoic and silent, and here he is telling me an incredibly personal story.

"I assume you've picked up I'm not Liam's biological father—"

"He told me." I nodded.

"But that doesn't mean he isn't mine. Life found a way." He chuckles to himself. "I didn't know then for sure, but one of the complications of this condition is that it can make you sterile. So hell, I saw an opening to have a family with my dream girl, and I took it—best thing that ever happened to me. Can't imagine life unfolding any other way, you know?

Even if I had to make some quick irrational decisions at a young age. And I'm not going to lie to you, it gnawed on me that I couldn't give him a sibling; it did—but then he found you and Caleb, and maybe he wouldn't have turned out the same, been the same solid guy I'm wicked proud of." Mr. Kelly shrugs, looking out over the horizon of pine trees looming in the distance. "All I'm saying is I wouldn't stress the unknown. Once you know it, it usually turns out it was pretty good, and there were things you wouldn't change about it for all the world."

"Thank you for sharing." I rub my hands on my dress. They've collected with sweat in the time I've sat out here, shaking. "Truthfully, it's not my regrets I'm worried about."

"Kellys move the world for the ones they love. He'll be fine."

"But who's going to move the world for him?" I sigh. "Mr. Kelly, honestly, I respect you for your choices. Clearly Liam's selfless streak comes from you, but I don't know if I have it in me to let him make these sacrifices for me this early in our relationship. It's not about regrets; I want to protect him too."

"What would I need protecting from?" Liam's baritone voice jumpstarts my heart. I pick up my gaze to meet his crooked smile, hands stuffed in his pockets.

Mr. Kelly shoves another pastry in his mouth and wipes his hands. "That's my cue. The introvert has recharged. He can go back to being the life of the party."

He raises a hand, patting Liam's shoulder as he walks by. "You never did have a figure for a tux. You look like shit," he says, beginning his trek to the tent.

"Your voice carried down the field, by the way—" Liam hollers over his shoulder. "Secret's out that you're proud of me."

"Don't let it get to your head," his dad calls back. "'Course I'm proud of you. Love you, too, you complete pain in my ass."

Liam snorts, turning his gaze to me. "Evie O'Shea on my porch. You are a sight." He whistles, climbing the stairs. "Whatchu doing out here?"

"I just needed a second to breathe."

"In the middle of our speeches?" He sits beside me on the glider and nudges me with his knee. "Come on, I know you better than that. Don't close up on me now."

I look at him, a nervous energy settling on me, and I swallow. I don't know what the next few months will bring between my visa and Maria, but I know I don't want Liam to make a life-altering decision based on me. No matter what Mr. Kelly just said. I'm not together enough for that. And he should take more time to think about everything he's going to take on. "I don't think you should take the job in Paris. At least not right now."

"Oh." His shoulders curl in on themselves, and his left knee bounces. "Well, I can't really take it later. My dad needs someone to fill it now."

Shit, well, that complicates things.

"I don't want you making a decision you'll regret in a few months on my account."

"You still don't trust me," he murmurs, shaking his head.

"Of course I trust you. I'm just trying to protect you, and I don't think we're being rational about this."

"If you trusted me, you'd let me make my own decisions." He stands, raking a hand through his hair. "Answer me this—do you want me there?"

I shift in my seat. Well obviously. "I mean, I do—"

"Then I don't see the problem here. I've been out-of-my-mind, wild in love with you since I first saw you, Peaches. That's not going to change in a few months."

"I'm just worried you love an idea of me. There's no way you could understand the kind of mess you're getting into, and I don't want you making a decision like this until you understand everything."

My pulse skitters, thudding wildly in my ear. I want to trust this. I want to be the person who makes irrational decisions because of love. But there's no way that Liam sees the situation's reality. He can't. Not with how his eyes settle on me like I'm holding him spellbound.

He groans, scrubbing a hand over his face. "How many times do I have to tell you you're not a mess before you believe it, Evie?"

I shift on the bench. "If I say the limit doesn't exist?" I let out a self-deprecating laugh. But it's the truth, especially with the weight of the past few days crashing over me. Tidal wave after tidal wave, threatens to destroy me. Our only attempt at intimacy was a failure, something Kylie didn't seem to have a problem with. Maybe she would make him happier in the end, she clearly wasn't over him anyway. My reserve weakens. Liam wants to start a family, and there's no guarantee I won't ruin that. Another wave, another crash, more destruction. And what about Aunt Norma? Didn't her husband divorce her for these very reasons?

Another wave. Another crash. And this time, it obliterates me.

"You're going to hate me," I whisper. A tear slowly rolls down my cheek, and my body starts to shake. "For real. Not this little game we've played all these years. You're going to give up all these things, and then one day when you're sick of me, you'll question why you made so many sacrifices and why sex with me isn't like sex with Kylie, and you'll resent me, and the family we can't have."

"Evie—" Liam reaches for me, and I turn my body away. "First off, if this is all because of the speech, Peaches, I meant you and me hopefully, someday could make a family. Two people, that's all. Whatever happens after that, we'll figure it out together. Okay?"

I nod with a sniffle, but the anxiety still crashes over me, wave after unyielding wave.

"Good. Now I have to ask, what the hell is this about Kylie?"

"It's nothing. I'm just—" I groan, burying my head in my hands. Liam's shoe scrapes across the wood as he paces, and I don't pick up my gaze. He's anxious, and I can't handle seeing him like that. "I'm way too overwhelmed, and this trip's brought up a lot of issues that I was clearly just ignoring and need to work through. I'm so sorry. I can't do this right now."

The sharp cut of his foot halting slices through the air. "Do, what, exactly?"

I drag a collecting breath through my lungs because I don't want to say this, but there's no way I can handle the pressure of a relationship—a new one, where someone moves to be with me. Not right now, not with where my head's at. "I think it's better to cut this off before it gets too serious. That way, no one gets hurt." I wipe at my eyes, rubbing my arm.

"You know it's too fucking late for that, Evie. Come on." He kneels down, gently grabbing my hand and lifting my chin to meet his imploring gaze. "Seriously, please don't punish me for something I haven't done. I've given you no reason to think I'd do any of that to you."

And I want to believe him, I do. But another wave of self-doubt crashes over me, and I'm too tired to fight against the tide as it pulls me out, abandoning me in the middle of a depthless ocean. I'm in pain. It never stops. I'll make plans difficult. I'm dramatic. Selfish. I hold grudges. I'm impulsive in the worst ways and timid when I should be bold. There's no way he won't see this eventually. Whatever spell he's under will break, he'll have given up so much, and he'll hate me.

I don't know, I'm probably not thinking anything through right now, but I know enough to know I need time on my own to figure some things out.

I wrap my hand around his neck, threading my fingers through his hair, and press my forehead against his. "I'm not saying this is final. But I need time. Please. I don't expect you to understand everything I'm going through now, but please give me that. I don't get why you'd want it, but we'll never work if I don't figure some stuff out on my own for a while."

He pulls away, pinning a stare on me. "Whatever you need, I can't stop you. But Evie, I need you to understand something since you're talking like you're somehow a fucking burden. All I've ever seen you as is my other half. I wasn't thinking irrationally about this move. I know you, Peaches. And I love you. All of you. I think there's a chance we could have something great, that maybe we could have that once-in-a-lifetime shit I never wanted to believe in, and I'm willing to take a risk for that, but I can't force you to see that."

"I thought you'd be okay with the perfect moment." I sniff. "*Roman Holiday*, right?"

"No, Evie, you were right. That's never going to be enough with you. I want all of you, Peaches. I want the chance for this to be something great."

"But what if it's not? What if it crashes and burns?"

"Then at least we'd know where this spark goes."

"I need time," I whisper. "Please. I can't do this. Not right now. Not like this." Another tear rolls down my cheek, and he brushes it with his thumb.

"I could never say no to you, you know that." He stands and scrubs a hand over his face, muffling a "fuck." "You should be the one to go back into the tent. It'll mean more to your brother if you're there, anyway."

"You aren't going back?"

He shakes his head. "No, I don't think it's a good idea for us to both be there right now."

"Did you want to talk again later?" I ask.

"I can't, Evie. You're asking me to give you some time, and that's fine. But I'm going to need some too. I can't stand here knowing we both love each other, and that somehow still wasn't enough for you."

"It was. It is. Please don't think that's the problem."

"Right, we can disagree on that too, I guess," he mutters, his stare pinned on the woods folding into the fallen night sky. "We can figure out yo grabbing your stuff later, but I'm going to—" He hooks his thumbs towards the slider doors that lead into his parents' house.

I nod, watching Liam's sullen figure bow under the doorframe, and for the second time in my life, I wish the woman in the scene would find the courage to chase after the love she wants. But instead, I stay on the glider for a few more minutes, an unsettling feeling sinking into the pit of my stomach. I was so worried this was moving way too fast, worried we were making a mistake. But as I sit on the glider with the damage already done, it feels like I made a huge one anyway.

23

Bittersweet Symphony

"TODAY IS A GOOD day to let the light in, dear," Maria says, opening the curtain on day fifteen of a total wallowing session. It's a rainy day in Paris, so the impact is thankfully minimal. "At least metaphorically," she says with a sigh.

I pause *Roman Holiday*, playing for the fifth time in the past two weeks. I've tried desperately to let myself connect with the ending, to be okay with the perfect memory of running around a city with someone and letting that be that. But I can't shake the feeling that as much as I beg for a happily ever after in movies, maybe I want one in my life just as badly. Even if just a month ago I had written off such a possibility.

Maria bends down, tidying around me frenetically, and I groan, curling further into my heating pad. I expected the stress of the past month to kick-start a flare, but it really has gone above and beyond here. I haven't left the couch much as a result, though I did manage to post a sunshine and rainbows post that's elicited a constant stream of "yas queen" and "your life is so amazing, super jealous" comments.

Amazing life. Hah, right. Social media's such bullshit sometimes.

Okay, I'm bullshit. I fed the beast, but it's what people want to hear, right? They don't want to hear about the uterus from hell or that my life is a hot mess. Or that I'm running dangerously low on ice cream and cheap wine and feel like everything is over.

A loud knock on the door bounces off the tiny walls of our apartment. My heart stutters. Declan would never bother knocking . . .

"Oh, he got here fast," Maria mutters to herself.

"Who?" My head jerks up.

"Eli."

"Eli's in the States." I let my head fall back on the pillow, my heart returning to its natural melancholic pattern.

"No, he's not," a grumpy voice on the other side of the door yells. "And you'd know that"—Maria swings the door open—"if you answered your damn phone," he says, marching into the room.

I shoot up, sitting straight and immediately regretting it as dots spot my vision. After a few seconds, I bring my attention to my curly blond-haired best friend holding coffee and a bag of donuts. My brow furrows. He should be in Massachusetts. We said our goodbyes. Twice. "What are you doing here?"

Is Liam here too? Or is this a solo visit?

He sits next to me, tossing the bag of donuts at me. "I got an SOS call." He motions to Maria.

"I'll be in my bedroom," she hollers, blushing.

"You came to Paris for *this*?"

"Nah." He laughs. "I was already here. Had something else I needed to do, and then Maria asked me to come pick the 'little shit' up."

"No way she called me a little shit."

"It was implied." Eli shrugs.

I glare at him. I prefer Maria's coddling.

"The other thing you had to do wouldn't have had anything to do with a certain Fionn O'Connor, would it?" I smirk, nudging his knee.

He sips his coffee with a nod, a cheese-busting grin peeking out behind the lid. "Seems a month away was all I could handle, and Harry needed somebody here since . . ."

"I fucked up."

"You said it. I didn't. But yeah. It'll be a lot more work for me than the normal wining and dining I do, but I said what the hell, Fionn's worth the risk, you know?"

I swallow. Because I do know. Kind of. Except when it was my turn, I wasn't brave enough. I'd been burned too many times and I didn't want to get hurt again, so I shut down instead.

Eli lightly taps my shoulder with his. "Do you remember when you promised me you wouldn't let your shit take something it had no right taking?"

I drag my teeth over my bottom lip. "Yeah, but I suck, so did we really think I'd keep it?"

"Evie." Eli presses his lips into a thin line, pinning his emerald eyes on me in a dead-serious fashion.

"Eli." I try to conjure a similar intense glare his way, but tiny giggles bust out of me.

"No more of this 'I suck', shit. Liam told me what you said to him. And you know me, I stick up for my friends, and right now, you're being an asshole to one of my favorites."

"I didn't mean to hurt him," I mumble.

"I'm not talking about him, even though he is a fucking wreck, by the way. I'm talking about you. Evie, if you can't see how amazing we all think you are, you're never going to figure this out with Liam or anyone else who wants to have a relationship with you. Think about the friends you've made here. Why do you think you only have a few?"

"Because I can't offer much, so why bother trying?"

"And why do you think that?"

"I mean—you know what happened with Harmony. We were solid, and then shit got worse, and so did we."

"Yeah, because Evie . . . Harmony sucks. She's the shitty friend, not you. Not the person who drove across multiple state lines in the middle of the night in college to watch a stupid movie with me when my heart was breaking for the millionth time. Or never complains about my drunk FaceTimes at three in the morning because Drunk Eli can't do time zones. Don't let someone who never appreciated you dictate your self-worth."

"I mean, it's not *just* her." I fiddle with my hand on my lap. "You've met Caroline. She hasn't exactly kept my deficiencies a secret. I guess I just figure people will see them eventually and get sick of me."

"And you believe her?"

I shrug.

"Look, I could try to convince you that you're so much more than what Caroline's tried to sell you or what a few shitty friends made you think. But if you couldn't trust Liam or those who've stayed by you for years before now, me saying this today won't make a difference. You have to figure this out for yourself—otherwise, you're going to run into this again, needing love and affirmations from someone else while living in the fear that they'll 'see reality' and run."

My mouth drops. Eli. Eli Blythe is saying this? The guy that asked me if there was a Bob Ross in the Louvre only a little over a month ago? Where the hell did this come from? "When the hell did you get this smart?" I ask, my voice dripping in disbelief.

He shrugs. "Therapy. There's a reason I used to act like a desperate lovesick puppy when I met someone who showed a passing interest. Now, why don't you close that mouth back up because it's mildly insulting, and we go get a crêpe," he says, standing and offering out his hand.

His terrible Boston accent butchers what I hope is his attempt at saying *crêpe*, anyway. Otherwise Eli just asked me to go get a crap with him, and hard pass. "You want to try that one more time?" I smile. "It's a crêpe."

"That's what I said—crap."

"Not even remotely close." I stand. "But thank you for restoring the balance. I was scared I was turning into the clueless one."

"Definitely are." He wraps me up in a huge hug and lays a kiss on my cheek. "Your turn to be on the receiving end of break-up protocol fucker."

I sigh, walking into the bedroom. After years of driving the ten hours up to Notre Dame to rescue Eli from whatever break-up destroyed him and endless FaceTimes full of movie nights and wine where I'd tell him he was so much better than the latest prick who broke his heart, I'm not exactly looking forward to this role reversal.

"So what's this bridge called again?"

"Pont de l'Archevêché. It technically translates as Bridge of the Archbishopric or Archbishop's Bridge." I lift my chin, raising my face to the sun peeking out in the late July sky, leaning against a wall of glittering locks on this nineteenth-century bridge.

"Yeah, I don't even know what the hell that means in English." Eli snorts. His shoulder bumps against mine, and he grasps the rail along with me.

I wouldn't say Eli's thoroughly acclimated to the city yet, but he's learned to appreciate the days when the sun peeks beyond the ever-present clouds and to soak in the vitamin D.

"You want to keep trekking?" He nods toward the stairs leading down to the quay along the Seine, and it gives me pause. "Or we could head back to the apartment if you aren't feeling up to it."

"Oh, no. I'm okay, it's just . . ." My eyes stay trained on the spot where Liam danced with me along the Seine, and I swear I can see the ghost of us there, even now. *It's okay if a good memory makes you feel sorrow. Don't feel guilty about it, just feel.* My therapist's words coach me through the moment. I've only had a few sessions with her, but I can already tell how necessary it was. How everything was knotted and whirled in my mind, and now we're slowly untangling it. I can feel my bundle of anxiety and doubt steadily unraveling with each tug on another thread. I take a deep breath, steadying my nerves. "This is where Liam took me on my birthday, that's all. But I think we should try to walk it."

"You sure?" Eli raises a brow.

"Positive." I nod, feeling nowhere near confident inside, but it's okay if this hurts. It just means there was a moment in my life so absolutely gorgeous that I'm missing it, even now. I don't know if the ache will ever genuinely dull.

We walk down the cobblestone path, passing picnics and sunbathers as the water laps to the shore. The weight of Liam's hand presses into my back, and my chest awakens with the sensation of his body against mine. Gooseflesh prickles the nape of my neck as I remember him singing soft and low against my ear. *He loved me.* I've tried to process the thought so many times in the past few months. Tried to get my brain to comprehend his words the day we parted. But I haven't been able to get there, not yet, anyway. Eli was right: I let the words and actions of other people strip away my love for myself until it had all but vanished, and I need to find that self-love again, or no relationship I have will ever build itself on solid footing.

My therapist has been helping me see this, helping me see that beyond the familial issues, I had somehow wrapped my disease around my identity, and because I've always been at war with it, I could never see any of the good past it. It made sense when she explained how easy it is to

TORIE JEAN

confuse the two. Because I can't see my disease, it manifests itself in the pain I feel in my body. But it's not me.

It's a part of my lived experience, yes.

But that's different.

Give yourself the grace you give others. That's another lesson I've been trying to learn, but it helps because if Liam had something like this, I would recognize his reality, but it wouldn't alter my love for him. It wouldn't limit how much I want him to be a part of my life. Even now. Even if I blew it. So I shouldn't let it change how I expect others to see me.

Standing here, watching the sun glitter off the blue expanse of the river, I get it now. *He loved me.* The man who bought me a heat pack. The man who always made sure my heating pad was on. The man who brushed up on puns for me. Who sent me postcards for years with zero intention of getting any credit for it. The man who dressed up as Gene Kelly and encouraged me to fight for my dreams. He saw me and he still loved me. *And those were the wild, intimate moments that mattered.*

I've been trying to detach myself from the societal pressure that sexual intimacy is the be-all-to-end-all in a relationship. Because a relationship is a sum of its parts, not this one defining feature. Do I wish it was easy and amazing for me to have sex? Absolutely. Is that reality? Unfortunately, no. But that doesn't mean I'm not worthy of being in a loving relationship.

Eli leans in, nudging my shoulder with his. "Evie. Call him."

"I don't even know what I'd say. It's not like he can take the job now."

Eli purses his lips. "No, I guess not, and have I said thanks, by the way?"

"Watching you two be insufferably adorable and not fearing I'll have to pick up the pieces is enough." I wave him off.

Eli stuffs his hands in his pockets, his tattoos peeking beneath a white-collared shirt with the sleeves rolled up. "I've heard a pastry shop would do really well in a town like Portsmouth once or twice, and it would save you the embarrassment of submitting your lackluster visa application."

The thought has crossed my mind a good hundred times since I boarded the plane after Caleb's wedding, I'm not going to lie. And it is awfully tempting. But for all the journaling, reading and community boards I've looked through the past two months, I am still an incredible weenie at heart. I groan. "I know, but that's such a huge, life-altering decision. And why is adulting so hard?" I spiral. "In the movies, they get a damn sign or something, and they just know what they're supposed to do. But out here, it's not that simple. There are seven million options, and you just have to hope you don't mess up, pick the wrong one, and live with a lifetime of regrets. Seriously! Paris, do you still love me? Should I stay here and move on, or am I making a huge mistake?" I turn my attention to the sky, arms out. "Can I just have a sign? Is that too much to ask?"

A well-dressed child turns up a flock of pigeons at that moment, and they fly around Eli and me in a frenzy. I blink as a pigeon slaps me in the face with its wing, then take a step on my heel and land right in the path of a falling sludge of bird poop. It drips slowly down my forehead, and I wipe at it with disgust.

Very funny universe.

Eli's face waffles between horror and amusement. "Well, little shit." He laughs. "I think you have your answer."

I'm not going to pretend being bitch-slapped by a bird knocked any kind of sense into me. It was probably the mail I received a few days later that had the bigger impact. Either way, I've spent more time in the past five days looking at shops in New Hampshire and figuring out places to apply for grants and loans than I had in the past year.

A shiny cardstock sears into the top of my thigh where it's perched. I haven't let it go since it came in. The front has a picture of a lobster sitting in a cage on a boat, *"'tis the sea-son for the Maine attraction,"* written across it.

Tallow News Report,

The Rausch's apple orchard and farm opened up today. They're selling cinnamon rolls on Saturdays. Clare and Holly get so excited. It's kind of a-dough-rable.

I've seen nicer buns, though.

The town beach and camping ground were closed because of an E.coli outbreak. Apparently, you aren't supposed to feed the geese, further proving that no good deed goose unpunished. If anyone asks, Caleb and I had nothing to do with it. We just went to the lake for a gander.

Not entirely sure how to sign this now,
But I guess "Liam" is a good start.
So …

Yours Affectionately,
-Liam Kelly

This morning, I finally had the courage to text him and thank him for the postcard. I haven't heard back yet, and I don't expect to for at least a few hours, if at all, what with the time difference and everything. But it's the first text message I've sent him since I left after Caleb's wedding, and it feels good. It feels like a solid start.

My phone dings as if on command, and I steady my racing heart and check it.

Caroline.

Someone else I haven't talked to since Caleb's wedding.

I haven't wanted to let her shovel heaps of guilt on my head over the breaking up with Liam situation when I'm already buried under a mountain of my own making. I open the text so I can read through it quickly and delete it like I have all her others. I'm sure it's just a petition to call her.

CAROLINE: Evie, please read your card soon. It's important.

How does she know I haven't read it already? That's bold of her to assume.

I tap my pencil against my notebook, staring at my screen, and then back at the drawer where Caroline's letter has sat since I came home. Screw it. I fling off the bed, opening the drawer.

My Paris checklist flutters out with a bunch of other papers. I glance at it, curious to see if any of my pros would alter the course I've set myself on. *Think of the architecture; think of the history; you love the love locks* is scrawled under a myriad of things in the pro column, right above the one that sticks out: *Liam isn't here.* I chew on my lip, bringing the paper to my bed, crossing out the line with my pencil, and scribbling the same sentence under the "con" column.

A smile settles on my face as I sit back on the bed and open my mother's envelope, pulling out the white card with a simple illustrated lily on the front.

Evelina,

Your father and I are so incredibly proud of you. It probably came to my attention far too late that your dream may not be the same as mine was at your age, but I hope this gesture will show you how much we love and support you.

We've been saving for your wedding since you were younger. It would have been an extravagant event that you probably would have hated anyway, to be honest, but I believe the money in the account is enough to help you get started on your business if that's genuinely what you want. We want you to have it.

I blink, staring at the letter. I was still with Liam when Caroline wrote this, and she was just ready to give up on my wedding and try to support my actual dreams? Obviously, this doesn't fix everything, but it's one big-ass gesture in the right direction and helps quiet one of my final nettling hesitations. I don't know if there's hope for a healthy relationship with Caroline yet, but maybe I don't need an ocean of separation anymore.

My gaze oscillates to the sheet where "Liam isn't here" is scribbled in the "con" column, the postcard resting on my bed, and I look up at the sky with a smile. Good. Freakin'. Sign.

A familiar brick building with an alley café sits on the top of a real estate page of Portsmouth listings Mr. Kelly emailed to me.

Hope Paul is okay.

Last week, I reached out to Mr. Kelly and asked for help navigating the business side of this, and things escalated pretty quickly from there.

By "escalated" I mean he wants to fund half the shop and give it to Liam.

But he doesn't want to tell him.

"Think of his face if he walked into the building and saw you. It'll be like one of those big gestures in the movies."

I'm not a fan of surprise attacking people, but I also don't want to second-guess my new employer. He scares me.

Confident that no other building will do when I can have the Bean Pot's old digs, I email Mr. Kelly back *The one on Market Street. It's perfect.*

My phone dings, and I smile, reaching for it, imagining all the endless possibilities that spot holds.

Liam's name highlights on the screen, and my heart skips. We've texted back and forth since the postcard came two weeks ago, but it's been mainly surface-level awkward tiptoeing and a lot of gushing about how cute Eli and Fionn are together.

LIAM: Coffee shop Paul won a million on some scratchers.

I exhale. As excited as I am about the shop, I was a little worried something had happened to Paul, so this is fantastic news.

ME: Damn, he hit the javapot!

The dots dance, and my foot shakes with anticipation.

LIAM: It's going to be hard to keep him grounded now.

ME: How long have you had that brewing?

LIAM: Not long, puns are the only way I know how to espresso myself.

ME: I missed this a latte. Thank you.

Again, the dots dance for some time.

LIAM: I miss this too, Peaches. Talk soon?

I glance at the pile of boxes I have ready to pack up my things. Maria and my lease ends at the beginning of September, along with my expiring visa, and we both decided even though it'll be crazy chaotic for me and a heck of a lot of changes all at once, the best thing to do is really just go for it.

ME: Things are kind of busy right now, but I should have some time in a few weeks.

24

Sprinkly the Best

"I'm NOT SURE WHY you want me to go there, sir. This really isn't my role," Liam Kelly grumps through the phone to his dad. My heart races hearing his voice on the other line. It echoes against the stainless-steel appliances in the back kitchen of our soon-to-be café and reverberates in my heart. I haven't heard his low, steady cadence in months, and I miss it terribly. I busy myself with a bag of frosting, attempting to pipe a cinnamon and caramel-flavored buttercream inside a pumpkin-spice-inspired macaron I hope to include in the menu where we're set to open at the end of September. My hands shake, and the buttercream bursts out of the bag. Apparently, I didn't secure the piping nozzle correctly.

r. Kelly jumps back, narrowly avoiding getting the sugary explosion all over his shoes. "I'm asking you to go because the shop is a block from your apartment, and I don't want to drive there. What, do you have something better to do?"

"Kind of. I'm supposed to talk to Evie."

"I'm sure she'd be fine if you moved your call for an hour later." Mr. Kelly winks at me.

I rest my hand on the counter, breathing through a spasm. I accidentally knock over one of the baking trays, cursing as it falls to a clatter on the floor.

"Shit. Shit. Shit," I mutter, gathering a hoard of wildly flung macarons off the floor. Seriously, what was I thinking trying to bake on a day when Liam could walk through that door at any minute and decide that none of this was a good idea?

"What was that?" Liam asks.

"What was what?" In a panic, Mr. Kelly coughs into his hand, drowning out my hushed "sorry."

"There was a clang and a voice? Is Alice with you?"

"Yes. Alice. Alice is here. Are you sure the clang wasn't on your side, though? I thought I heard it through the line."

"No?"

"Just go check up on the shop, kid. I want to make sure that we start this investment off on the right foot. It's an important one."

"Do I need to suit up? Otherwise, I can head there now. I'm actually a street over finishing my run."

"Nah, doesn't need to be formal. Who knows, she might appreciate those tight-ass shirts you run in."

I cover my mouth with my hand to muffle a laugh at the eyebrow wag Mr. Kelly supplies with this. I wish I hung out with him more growing up because he's freaking hilarious and a total softie.

"Right, well, this has been the weirdest phone call from you. Congratulations on that. I'll let you know how it goes. I'm hanging up now."

Mr. Kelly chuckles to himself, shoving the phone in his pocket. "He really has no clue what's about to happen."

My phone pings a second later, and I wipe my hand on my towel and reach for it. "I don't know if that's a good thing," I say with tremoring hands.

LIAM: Hey, I have a quick work thing to deal with. Do you mind if we move our call back an hour?

ME: Oh yeah. Totally fine. Talk to you then!

LIAM: Looking forward to it.

I wince, shoving my phone back in my apron. I'm still very anti-surprise, especially with a big gesture that is so involved. But I also don't want to kill Mr. Kelly's joy. So I'm trusting the man and taking the biggest damn risk of my life.

"How much longer do you think until he gets here?" I ask, peeking fruitlessly through the tiny circle window in the kitchen door, but brown construction paper covers the shop windows, obscuring any view of the outside.

Anxiously, I grab a towel and dip it in a sudsy bucket, wiping down the almond flour-covered counter in front of me.

"Evie, it's going to be fine." Mr. Kelly reaches up and gently places a hand on my shoulder. "I know my son. I know how he feels about you. I know this setup will better suit him occupationally, too, and the wall of his photos will only enhance that. Relax, kid. It's all going to work out."

The front door opens and shuts, and my heart skips.

"Hello, ma'am? Sir?" the deep baritone voice I've desperately missed calls from the other room.

My arms flail; apparently my immunity to him has already waned significantly, and I knock the bowl of water over on the floor. It lands on my foot, suds spilling everywhere, and I peek bashfully at Mr. Kelly. "I swear I won't be this accident-prone every day." I smile tight.

"I don't buy that for a second," Mr. Kelly whispers, eyes shining bright at my bumbling demeanor.

"Are you okay?" Liam asks in the other room.

"I'll clean it up. Go." Mr. Kelly motions to the swinging door leading out to the front portion of the café.

I nod, take a collecting breath, and push the door open. My shoes squeak against the hardwood floor.

Liam's striding at a hurried pace toward the back. Toward. Me. His eyes catch mine as his feet continue propelling him forward.

"Evie?" he rasps.

At the same time, I say, "Hey, *Liam*. Liam! Pole."

But it's too late, his head collides with one of the metal support beams in the middle of the café and it takes him the fuck out.

"Oh shit." I rush over, leaving a dust cloud of flour in my wake, and kneel down next to him.

His eyes slowly flutter open. "Evie?" he manages again.

"Are you okay?" My hands tremble, and I reach out to his temple, feeling for any bumps or bruises.

He props himself up on his elbows and slowly brings himself to a sitting position. "I'm fine." He blinks. "My body took most of the hit—but—"

"Oh, what am I supposed to do? Follow my finger, right?" I raise a shaky finger in front of his face.

He gently grabs it, bringing it down and threading his fingers through mine. "Peaches, I'm fine, seriously. But what the hell is going on?"

"I would like to preface this entire story by saying I was very anti-surprise." I glance down at our hands. Liam's thumb rubs soft circles into my palm like it's second nature to him. The gesture calms me, and I stand, offering my hand and pulling him up into a standing position. Sparks and jolts shoot up my arm right on schedule, and it takes everything in me not to pull him closer and press a kiss on his lips right now. "So this"—I gesture around us—"someday soon, is actually going to be a cheese and pastry café with a dessert wine bar. Obviously, there's still a lot of work to do, but I was thinking, okay, so we keep the counter here, right? And then we'll have some cute café stools—"

"Evie—"

"Or maybe fancy stools, I don't know. I haven't decided if I want to go with a more rustic café look or just go all in on the Marie Antoinette's bedroom vibes. Oh. Maybe you have an opinion on that." I pause, raising on my toes, and Liam blinks back at me.

"Marie?"

"Honestly, kind of felt like the only option, but I'm glad you agree." I nod. "So if I did that, I thought that here, we could plaster roses and macarons and donuts, etc., and then spray-paint them gold to make it look like that ornate trim that's all over her room. Oh, and here. I thought on this wall we could fill it with a bunch of photos you've taken, maybe comb through the Paris ones, and then mix in some of Portsmouth, too, whatever you want. But we can hang them to look like one of those gallery walls in Versailles."

"Evie," Liam says a bit more sternly, rubbing his temple. "What's going on here, and why do you keep saying 'we'?"

"Because half of this is yours," Mr. Kelly proclaims, swinging the kitchen door wide open in a grand entrance of his own.

"I'm sorry. You helped with this?" Liam's brow furrows, his gaze oscillating between his dad and me.

I bite my lip, bouncing on my toes. "So. Do you like it?"

Liam rubs his head with his forefinger, and my hands itch wanting to reach up and make sure he's okay. "I'm still trying to understand what this is?"

Mr. Kelly crosses his arms, staring up at Liam. "It may have come to my attention in the past few months that you think you owe me something, so you've been lying about your interest in the creamery."

"I just wanted you to retire early." Liam's shoulders curl in.

"Kiddo, I'm forty-three. If I retired now, I'd be bored out of my mind and drive your mother to tears. I appreciate that you care about me enough to want to sacrifice part of your life for me, but that stops now. My dad passed the creamery to me when he died, and since I don't have any intention of dying anytime soon, I thought I could give you the next best thing because that's the way this dynamic is supposed to work, not the other way around, not until I'm like eighty or something. Sound good?" His lips twitch, satisfied at the look of sheer stupor washed over Liam's face. "But I'm going to let your partner finish cluing you in because I've got places to be." He heads for the door. "Oh, but watch her in the kitchen. She seems a bit accident prone," he says with a wave and an exit.

Liam scratches at the scruff on his cheek, jaw slack, eyes wide in disbelief as his dad leaves.

"So." My eyes struggle to find a place to settle. The athletic shirt Liam's sporting is clinging to every ridge and ripple, stretching wide across his broad chest and biceps. Mr. Kelly wasn't wrong, that shirt is definitely—

"You about done ogling me there, Peaches?"

I pick my eyes up, heat staining my cheeks, and meet a mischievous smirk.

"Mm-hmm," I squeak. It's not even worth trying to deny it.

"Great. Because I'm still a little confused here."

"Oh, right. So I'm Evie." I extend out my hand.

"Yes. I got that part." He shakes his head, placing his hands on his hips and staring at me.

"I'm a decent baker, but as my investor said, I'm a bit accident-prone. I'm also terrible at accounting, so we both agreed it might be a good idea to have a business partner and buddy baker. Provided, of course, said buddy agrees not to dump copious amounts of sugar over my head."

"Still contend I didn't have anything to do with that."

"Still contend it was your aura." My lips twitch.

He takes a step toward me. "That aura seemed to grow on you for a bit."

"Like a fungus." I nod, letting my back fall against the pole and tilting my chin to meet his stare.

"And how about now? Are you just looking for a business partner?" He takes another small step. Up this close, I can see his eyes that shone with mischief just a few minutes ago have grown darker, a flicker of a wild flame burning inside.

I swallow. The shitty thoughts I've been learning to tell myself are just thoughts, not reality, nettle my conscience again. I'll make things complicated. He's going to have to deal with my endo too. A lot of life blessings people often take for granted become frustrated, complicated hell fires with me. I shake my head. I'm done letting this thing take more of me than it already has. I'm done sacrificing my dreams. And I'm done not trusting that Liam means what he says. If he still wants this, he knows what he's getting into.

And I know that if the roles were reversed, it wouldn't matter to me. I'd still want him, every second of every day, mess and all. Because he'd be more than a complication. And so am I.

"I'm working on this, I swear." I laugh, breathing through the spiral.

He reaches for me. "Banish whatever shitty thing you're trying to tell yourself right now, Peaches." He wraps his hand around my waist and pulls me tight against him. "And tell me what you want."

"I want you," I whisper as he pushes my hair off my forehead and lays a soft kiss on top. My eyes flutter closed when his lips meet my skin, and my whole body explodes with a rush of shimmers. "I want everything with you. If that's something you're still interested in."

"Does it look like something I'd still be interested in?" he murmurs against my skin. "Or do you need me to be more explicit?"

"I just didn't want you to feel obligated because—I don't know, the business partner thing or—"

Liam stops his exploration, holding my head in his hands. "No. Stop that. Nothing I ever fucking do with you is an obligation. If I do it, it's because I love you, and I want to do it. That's it. Understood?"

I nod.

"Good. Now one more question."

I drag my teeth across my lower lip. "I'll allow it."

"Why are you here, Peaches? What happened to Paris?"

"What do you mean?"

"It was your home. I would have come."

"Oh. Well. You see. It's funny. One of the things I learned in the past few months is that home isn't exactly a place for me. It's a person. It always has been. Nana filled that role for so long. That's why I felt so untethered when she passed. That's why nothing ever fit, not here, not Paris. But with you, I finally feel like I'm home again. That warm comfort I've craved since I was twelve, that's here." I point to his chest. "You're my home. And maybe, knowing that, I thought about my brother, and about how being an aunt and spoiling his kids sounds pretty fantastic, and maybe I thought about this town a lot while I was away, and want to explore it with you, or wherever you want to go. I don't care as long as it's with you."

The tips of Liam's ears turn red, and his throat bobs.

"Too much?" I smirk. "Because I really think I should tell you that I'm in love with you, with how sweet, and thoughtful, and patient you are—"

Liam grabs my face and presses a hungry kiss on my lips, silencing me instantly. His hand falls to my back and pulls me hard against his chest.

J'ai eu un coup de foudre. I have had a lightning strike. That's what it's like when Liam kisses me. That love-at-first-sight, lightning strike moment, over and over and over.

If he won't let me tell him with my words how much I love him, then I'll have to do it with my lips.

I don't want anyone else but you.

My right hand reaches up, and I thread my fingers through the hair on the back of his head.

You're my forever.

My other hand falls to the side of his face, shamelessly running over his flawless stubble.

You are everything.

You are enough.

Liam wraps his arms around my waist and slowly picks me up, pressing my body firmly into his. Electricity floods my veins as he sweeps over my mouth with his tongue, reminding me of what I am to him.

He releases from our kiss and rests his forehead on mine, his breath heavy and erratic. "I didn't know if I'd ever get to do that again."

I smile, whispering back, "You don't have to worry about that now, I'm here, and I'm sorry." I lean back in, kissing him slow and deliberate.

I'm going to love you forever.

Liam lowers me to the ground, holding my stare with a twinkling gaze that's shining brighter than the sun itself. "Where are you staying?" he asks hoarsely.

"I'm in a hotel up the street while I try to find an apartment."

"Hmm. I might know of a place pretty close with decent accommodations if that's not too fast for you."

"You sure you wouldn't get sick of me? That's a lot of Evie time."

"Good thing, I can't get enough of you, baby." He winks.

"So cheesy." I shake my head.

"I don't know. I thought it was pretty gouda." He shrugs, wrapping me up and pressing a kiss to the side of my lips. "Let me take you home and show you how much I swissed you, Peaches."

"Oh, you know actually I left a load of laundry in the washer, and I have to change it. So I think I'll have to raincheck."

"Yeah, bullshit." He laughs.

"I'm serious. I'm sorry if that hurts your ego but I need to keep my priorities straight."

"I think you showed your hand coming here, Evie. You've got it bad."

"Yeah, but so do you. And who could blame you? I'm a freakin' catch."
I flutter my lashes as Liam sparks my insides back to life with his lips. "But
maybe we should go back to my room first. I have this thing that helps
with penetration in my suitcase. I've been doing exercises, but still—"

"I could just take care of you, and we don't push it today." He traces
the curve of my jawline with his mouth.

I pull away with a shake of my head. "No. If we're serious about this,
we take care of each other. That has to be my condition."

"You can take care of me by letting me take care of you," he murmurs
against my skin.

"I'm serious," I scold, pressing my fingers to his lips to stop them from
crashing into mine. "I know this is your love language. I get it. I love it.
And I appreciate it. But I'm not okay with a one-sided dynamic. I want
to work you into a stupor too."

He pauses, searching my eyes and conceding with a nod.

"So maybe you can take me back, and we can use it? Pack up my stuff
while we're there . . . bring it home." The final three words curl my lips
into a cheese-busting grin.

I've got a home.

A dream.

Here.

With Liam.

And really, who could ask for anything more than that?

25

Happily Endo After

I CAN'T REMEMBER HIS name. Dan? Maybe? My brain lists every stereo-typical New Englander guy's name, and none seem right. No matter. If I make his order now, I can slide it over without having to call his name out, saving us a whole bunch of awkward. I contort my body, bending down under a shelf in the glass case. Of course he wanted the last damn confetti donut. I pluck it with the tongs. Victory! Thank you, yoga.

I pull my body out of the case, and my head raps on flesh.

Not just flesh. A hand. A hand that is saving me from whacking my head on the glass.

"My hero." I flutter my eyelashes at the man hovering over me with an a itated scowl.

"If you could watch your head, so I don't have a heart attack before I'm thirty, I'd appreciate it."

"Glass case came out of nowhere."

"Glass case has been where it's always been, baby." Liam's lips twitch.

The man lumbering over the counter waiting for his confetti donut clears his throat. Right! A customer! Whose name I have definitely for-gotten.

"Sorry. Here you go." I smile, handing him his order.

He nods, which is the silent thank you in New Englander, before walking away and settling into one of our overly foofy Marie Antoinette-inspired chairs, giving the glass of rosé he ordered to a pretty blonde across the table. Our café has become a prime date spot, and I am here for the people-watching.

Except I can't right this second because I have a serious conundrum that needs to be solved. Namely, how to get my leprechaun donuts to wear the cute hats I made for them. "I just want you to wear your damn hat. I don't understand why you have to be so difficult!" I scold one as his fondant hat falls in a rebellious, rather droopy plop.

"Does the donut really need a hat?" Liam asks, being absurd as his hand falls on the small of my back. He tightens the strings of my hot water bottle wrapped around my waist. One of the lovely things about owning my own business is the uniform can be anything, and here—the uniform includes a hot water bottle wrap most of the time.

"Of course it does. It's a goddamn leprechaun. Stop being ridiculous."

"Yeah. I'm the ridiculous one." Liam rolls his eyes as I shove the donut into my mouth. "Don't—we need to sell those, you know."

"If it won't wear its hat, it's dead to me," I say, voice muffled through my mouthful of donut.

"I can't believe I get to marry you," he says in a flat, humorless tone.

"You love me. Shut up." I almost choke on a laugh, cheeks still full of donut.

Liam studies the donut. "Did you try piping cream through the hole and then squishing it?"

I snort.

"Really?" Liam smirks.

"Cream, hole, and squish were all mentioned in the same sentence. Don't judge me." But he's right. I pipe some more cream into the donut and stick the hat on top. It stays. I study it approvingly and then put it on the display tray.

"Seriously? That's all you had to do?" Liam side-eyes me. "And you ate—"

"I will not apologize for eating those four donuts. I had to make sure they were delicious." I brush a crumb off my cheek. "I am happy to report they were. I can now sell them with confidence."

Liam shakes his head, stalking away.

The bell perched above the door rings and Clare Williams runs into the café, a little one-and-a-half-year-old in her arms, followed by a stroller and Holly O'Shea. "Look who I have!" she shouts.

My head shoots up, and I beam. Clare and Holly went to pick up Eli, Maria, Declan, and Fionn at the airport. We have hotel rooms in Portsmouth for them; the wedding is set for a week from now, March 24. *Our lucky day.*

It's an obscure nod to *Singin' in the Rain* that only Liam and I will get, but that's the beauty of it, isn't it?

We've seen the crew once since I moved back home. Liam lied and said he needed to help Eli out with something, and honestly, maybe he did, but I blacked out everything after he dropped down on one knee in front of the sparkling Eiffel Tower and asked me to marry him, so I can't be sure it wasn't a ruse.

I brush off my hands, giving Maria the biggest freakin' hug. Not having Maria in my life every day is different. We FaceTime weekly and text daily. But still. Judging by the massive bear hug Liam has Eli in right now, he feels the same way.

"You're crushing me," Eli manages.

Liam's arms tighten.

"Not. Helping."

Liam releases him, and the two cough and adjust their shirts, looking around. "So uh, the Bruins, am I right?" Liam says in a deeper-than-necessary voice.

"Could see them making a run for the cup."

I shake my head, coming over and giving Eli a big hug, and Liam works his way through the rest of the crew.

A black and white tattoo on Eli's wrist catches my eye.

"Oh, what's this?" I grab his wrist, studying it. It's a Claddagh. The heart in the middle has "Fionn" written in cursive on the outside edge. Fionn has a similar one that reads "Eli."

"Are they new?"

Eli nods, cheeks pink.

"We're getting married." Fionn smiles.

"Is that why you were getting squeezed to death?" I squeal.

"Yeah." Eli laughs. "It was."

"Well, prepare to get squeezed again!" I wrap my arms around him as tight as I can.

But I should have known better than to challenge the master, and Eli returns the hug, threatening to rupture my chest. Too tight, going to die.

"You win, you win," I choke out.

Eli releases, kissing my cheek. "This week is about you guys, though. Our little secret, okay?"

I nod. "Deal."

I rush around the counter as the Paris crew looks over the shop for the first time. Their eyes move over the floral wallpaper, gold-rose trim, glass backsplash, and giant chandeliers. We went all in on the Versailles aesthetic, and I regret nothing. Jaws drop. Mouths water. Smiles deepen. That's what this place does to people. I load up a plate with a little bit of everything, cheese and pastries alike, and pour everyone a glass of rosé from our tap system. "Come on, sit. Sit." I motion to the countertop.

All my friends gather around the counter. Liam snuggles me from behind, wrapping me up and rocking me side to side. He gets just as geeked up about people trying my pastries as I do. They pluck over all the goodies, moaning, smiling, and telling me about everything. Liam's hands move up and down my arms. Goosebumps, shivers, butterflies. Almost two years later, still there. I smile. I will never be more content than I am in this moment. This is it, I found my wild, gorgeous dream. I found my Gene Kelly.

Everyone I love, all here, family and found family alike. My last decade manifested in human connections.

I look up at Liam, and a cramp passes through. It's getting close to the time another excision surgery will be needed, and I'll admit, I'm kind of looking forward to getting thoroughly spoiled in recovery. Whatever happens next, he's enough; he's all the family I need. This is all the family I need.

"I love you," I whisper to him.

He smiles, kissing the top of my head and pulling me closer.

"I love you too, Peaches."

Yeah. Paris was definitely a good idea.

Acknowledgements

Finding Gene Kelly was a passion project that spanned over five years and found itself supported by so many people. I'm going to forget someone here, I know, but please know if you made it this far, I appreciate you, love you—thank you, thank you for being here.

Thank you to the Instagram and Twitter Writing and Bookstagram communities for supporting me and believing in me along this journey. I wouldn't have gotten to this point without your unbridled enthusiasm. Thank you to everyone who has screamed about this book, shared it in their stories, and passed its existence along to friends. I cannot tell you how many DMs I've gotten from people with endo who found this book because a friend was excited and shared it with them. I appreciate it all.

Thank you, thank you, to my husband. Thank you for sitting down with me so many years ago, when I was losing the dream career I had fought so hard for, and saying something along the lines of "you have a chance to do whatever you want, what's a crazy dream you've had? Whatever it is, let's do it." Thank you for believing me before doctors did. Thank you for believing in me when I don't. Thank you for being there through every bad doctors appointment, every rough surgery recovery, and every flare. You are my absolute rock and I am so very appreciative of you. I'm sorry I made you blush, but you're just awesome, okay?

My sisters and family, thank you for being so supportive of my dream.

Thank you to my dear Maria, for sending me your book and writing "your turn" in the card. The very first words of this story were penned the next day, and quite frankly saved my life. I've heard this makes a good door stop too, I can't wait to send you yours. Jag gillar dig.

Sonja and Kayla, my forever CPs, who have read more versions and changed more commas than I care to admit. Thank you for never giving up or tiring of Evie, Liam, and me. Thank you for being the cornerstones of my writing family, always. I love and appreciate you both tremendously, and I will forever be thankful the Twitterverse gave you to me.

Jo, what can I even say to thank you? Thank you for withholding your complete and utter shock when I would scream at you that much to my surprise someone actually liked the book. That's the only logical explanation since your taste is immaculate. Thank you for reading a million drafts and talking me off my dumpster fire ledge and just being the best friend I could ask for. I am so thankful you busted into my DMs with a dissertation on enormous panties. You've had my heart in a death grip since "now, let's talk about poop."

Rae, thank you for your constant support. For teaching me not to settle about certain things. And for always being the best literary intimacy coach.

Zoe, thank you for letting me be the milk to your cookies. For always being around to listen and for yelling at me (with affection) during my imposter syndrome.

Cassie, thank you for your incredible patience, which is the only logical explanation to how you've stuck around for twenty-five years of friendship. Thank you for the motivation GIFs, and the thoughtful writing themed gifts throughout the years. I love you. You know. And I appreciate you to boot.

Rebecca, thank you for being the best working and walking buddy. Thank you for being a great example in my life about what a good friend to someone with a chronic illness looks like. I am so incredibly thankful for your friendship.

Morgan and TL, thank you thank you for being the best friends an introverted girl like me could ask for. Thank you for our craft breaks. For believing in me against all odds or explanations. For being supportive, and wonderful, and just complete lights in my life. I appreciate you both tremendously. (Morgan, thank you for not yelling at me too much when I say this sucks.)

Allison Ashley, thank you for the "shit, this is good," email and for helping me grow as a writer of kisses. I feel so incredibly blessed to have had this much support from the queen.

Jax, thank you for always giving me honest feedback and helping me grow. I'm a better writer because of you.

Courtney Kae and Jenny Howe, thank you for tossing some of your sparkles and kindness my way. I'm so thankful to be debuting with you both. Thank you for welcoming along for the ride.

Laurie, merci beaucoup for all the drafts you read, and your constant love and support.

Jonny, thank you for being my 2021 anchor. I'll never have the words to thank you for being on the other end during some hard phone calls. Thank you for always supporting me and for your gorgeous friendship.

Emma, Becky, and Rachel, I am so thankful Bookstagram connected us. Thank you for you screaming. I rode on the wings of your screams to the finish line.

I'm sorry I unalived you.

Megan, Lindsey, Starla, and Sonia—thank you for being my indie publishing pals, this journey was a lot less lonely because of you.

Kayleigh, thank you for making me turtle with your kind words.

Antwan, thank you for all of your gorgeous support, I'm so appreciative of your friendship.

Joey T, I'm laughing at myself thinking that you'll ever see this, but thank you for asking "What's my motivation?" when I needed help drafting, and letting me bounce ideas off you, and thank you for asking if there was a Bob Ross in the MFA, no I'm apparently never letting it go.

Lauren B, thank you for being my Paris best friend and keeping me around after all these years.

Sinehan, thank you for the years of being the best friend a girl could ask for and being my French pastry date for life. I will happily always be your little croissant, even though I am neither little or flaky. I might be buttery though, haven't checked.

JAC, MV, RMM, BT, BK, EB, TO – Thank you for reading FGK when it was still developing, you helped keep me going and taught me a lot along the way. This story wouldn't be where it ended without you.

Heather and Susan, thank you for your kind words and believing in my voice.

Cathy and Blue Willow Bookshop, thank you for your support with my preorder campaign.

PK, thank you for the gift you gave me, it will forever be appreciated.

Dr. V, Dr. C, and Dr. G, thank you for being the first medical professionals to believe me, and for changing my life.

2021 me, thank you for not giving up and for realizing you needed a win more than anything, and taking it. I've cursed your decision many many times in the past few months, but all hollow grumbling aside, if I could tell you anything, it's that we did it. We found our Gene Kelly.

And a special, final page thank you to the people who gave me the best thirtieth birthday gift. I don't know what I did to deserve this gorgeous group of friends, but I am so appreciative of each and every one of you.

They know what they did, but I want to make sure they know how much that gesture meant and still means to me, so I will close this out with their names.

A very big, I'm-tearing-up-just-typing-this-up-and-no-body-makes-me-feel-my-own-feels, thank you to:

Terri Lynn, Neelam, Chris, Caitlin, Morgan, Jo, Reese, Sam, Jane, David, Nadya, Alex, Shilpa, Rebecca, Kayleigh, Anne Rain, Hunter, Henry, Shrina, Jay, Mike, and Dan.

There are certain people who make the world a better place just by being it, and I have a lot of those in my life. Thank you.

Torie Jean's favorite memory growing up is the way her Memere's fingers flew over the keys of her two-tier electric organ, playing songs like "Singin' in the Rain", "I've Got Rhythm", and "What a Wonderful World". Her undying love and affection for the magic and charm of Gene Kelly and Audrey Hepburn followed her from childhood, to a seventh grade book report on a Gene Kelly biography, to studying abroad in Paris and finding the den of thinking men. Torie is married to her high school sweetheart and is blessed with the best gaggle of nieces and nephews she could ask for. She has had endometriosis for over half of her life now, and hopes to raise more awareness of the disease with her writing while providing the happily ever afters people with endo deserve.

CPSIA information can be obtained
at www.ICGtesting.com
Printed in the USA
LVHW091242310822
727215LV00013B/526